I0637500

ISBN-13: 9798992133387

Library of Congress Control Number: 2018675309
Printed in the United States of America

# Contents

# Chapter 1

Alex sat in her tiny studio apartment as the glow of her laptop screen illuminated her tired face. It was almost noon, and she had been working on the same client project for hours. The uninspired brief was a series of bland graphics for a local car dealership's social media campaign. She had tried everything to breathe life into the designs: bold typography, minimalist layouts, and even playful animations. None of it mattered. The client's feedback was always the same: *"Can we make it pop more?"*

She took a sip of her now-cold coffee and grimaced at the bitter taste. *"Make it pop more."* Those words were vague and meaningless yet somehow wielded the power to erase hours of work with a single email. She looked at her inbox. Another message from the client had just arrived. With a deep breath, she clicked it open.

*"Hi Alex, these are close, but could we make them more exciting? Maybe add some sparkle? Something that really grabs attention!"*

She exhaled sharply as she leaned back in her chair. *Sparkle? What did that even mean?* Although tempted by a dozen neon gradients, she knew she couldn't use them. She cared too much, even if the job didn't deserve it. She was determined to find the kind of work that made her feel something. Unlike this. But rent was due.

She got back to work. Her fingers hovered over the keyboard. She hesitated before hitting "export" on her latest revision. The lifeless and dull mock-up stared back at her. Much like a mirror of how she felt inside. With a frustrated sigh, she leaned back in her chair and rubbed her eyes. This wasn't what she had imagined for herself.

At twenty-six, she had dreamed of being a graphic designer for innovative brands or magazines and creating art that made people feel something. Instead, she spent her days churning out forgettable content for clients who cared more about engagement metrics than creativity. Her phone buzzed on the cluttered desk beside her, catching her attention. It was a text from her boyfriend, Ryan.

*Running late again. Work's a nightmare. Don't wait up.*

She stared at the message. This was the third time this week he had bailed on her. She set the phone down without replying and debated whether to respond *"It's fine."* That's what she always did, and that's what he expected. But it wasn't fine. Not really. Instead, she locked her phone and set it aside. If he would not try, maybe it was time she stopped, too.

She looked around her small apartment. It was functional but lacked personality, much like her life these days. A small couch with worn cushions sat in one corner while a tiny kitchen nook held a single mug that read *"Design Is Life."* The walls were mostly bare except for a corkboard above her desk. It was littered with faded Polaroids from college, old ticket stubs, and postcards from places she'd always dreamed of visiting.

Her gaze landed on a postcard of the Amalfi Coast. The vibrant blues and greens were a stark contrast to the gray monotony of her current reality. Beneath the glossy image, she had scrawled in black marker years ago: *"One day."* She sighed, feeling the weight of that promise. *One day,* she thought bitterly. But when?

She dragged herself to the kitchen to make a fresh pot of coffee. As the coffee brewed, she scrolled through some more emails and was already dreading the rest of the day. Her phone buzzed with a new message from her best friend, Sarah.

*Brunch tomorrow. No excuses. You need a break. Love ya!*

She smiled faintly. Sarah always knew when to check in with her. It was like she had a sixth sense for when Alex wasn't feeling her normal self. They had been friends since high school, and she had been the one constant in Alex's life. Someone who she could depend on when everything else felt chaotic.

*Wouldn't miss it. Love ya too.*

As she sipped her coffee, her mind wandered to her career. She wasn't bad at her job. If anything, she was great at it. Her professors in college had raved about her talent and she had graduated at the top of her class with a portfolio full of bold, creative designs. But somewhere along the way, the passion she once had for design had faded. Her current job at a small marketing agency was stable, but it was far from fulfilling. The projects were uninspiring, the deadlines relentless, and her boss seemed more concerned with keeping clients happy than nurturing creativity.

"Alex, can you just tweak the font?" her boss would have said. "It's too... artsy."

She hated that word. *Artsy.* As if it was a bad thing to infuse art into her work. Returning to her desk, she opened her laptop. She stared at the overwhelming to-do list, a testament to the many things she had to accomplish. By the end of the week, she had four projects due, all of which were tedious, uninspired, and frankly, quite a bore. She put her cup down as she worked. By mid-afternoon, the monotony of the day was wearing on her.

She pushed her chair back and stood and walked around the small apartment. Her reflection caught her eye in the full-length mirror by the door. She looked tired. Her usually vibrant auburn hair was pulled into a messy bun, and dark circles shadowed her hazel eyes. *Is this it?* She wondered. *Is this my life now?* She felt stuck in her career, in her relationship, in herself.

That evening, she tried to unwind by sketching in her notebook. She hadn't opened it in months, and the blank pages seemed to taunt her. She flipped through old, vivid, imaginative pieces that reminded her of the person she used to be. Her pencil hovered over a blank page, but no ideas came. The creative spark that had once been her lifeline felt like a distant memory. Frustrated, she threw the notebook onto the coffee table and grabbed her phone. She scrolled mindlessly through social media, comparing her mundane life to the carefully curated highlight reels of others.

A photo caught her eye of a friend on vacation in Bali who was standing on a swing that overlooked the jungle. The caption read: *"Living the dream."* She stared at the photo with a pang of longing that hit her hard. In her heart, she yearned for that specific type of unrestrained freedom, coupled with an interesting sense of exciting adventure. She wanted to feel alive again. Instead, she was here, in her apartment, working on projects she didn't care about and waiting for a boyfriend who barely made time for her.

Her phone buzzed with a new notification: *"Design Trends for 2025: How to Stay Relevant in a Competitive Market."* She dismissed it without reading. The last thing she needed was more advice on how to keep up in a field that was already draining her soul.

She looked back at the Amalfi Coast postcard that seemed to call to her. It was a reminder of the dreams she had once chased so fiercely.

*"One day,"* she whispered to herself.

But as she stared at the postcard, something shifted inside her. Maybe she couldn't change everything overnight, but she could start somewhere. As she continued to stare at it, she was thinking, *"What was stopping her? Excuses? Fear? The comfortable weight of routine?*

A deep breath steadied her resolve. She grabbed a pen and a notepad and jotted down the first step. It was just one small thing that she could do to move closer to the life she wanted. The thought sent a spark of energy through her. Maybe today wasn't the day she stood on a sun-drenched Italian balcony, but it could be the day she stopped waiting for life to happen to her.

# Chapter 2

Alex stood in front of the bathroom mirror brushing her hair, when Ryan called out from the bedroom.

"I'm heading out soon. I'm grabbing dinner with some coworkers."

She stepped into the doorway. "Oh, nice! Should I wear the black dress or the green one?" She smiled, hoping for a straightforward answer.

Ryan, who was already pulling on his jacket, paused mid-button. "Uh… Alex, it's just me. Like a work thing. You're not invited."

The words landed like a slap. "Oh." Her smile drooped . "Right. Of course."

He didn't seem to notice her deflation. Instead, he checked his watch, grabbed his keys, and kissed her on the cheek. "Don't wait up," he said before he left.

She stood frozen for a moment, completely stunned. Not knowing what to do, she called her best friend.

"He did *what*?" Sarah's voice shot through the speaker.

"He told me I wasn't invited," she repeated as she sat on the couch. "Like I'm not even part of his life anymore."

"Then you *go* anyway."

"What?"

"Go. Put on that green dress, do your hair, and show up. Remind him you exist."

Alex stared at the closed door.

"Unless," she added, "you're okay with fading into the background."

"I'm not okay with that at all. I'm going to get dressed and surprise him right now."

"Do you want me to come pick you up or meet you there?"

Alex looked at the clock. If she hesitated any longer, she'd lose her nerve. "No. I'll go by myself. I need to do this anyway," she said, heading toward her closet. "But if things go south, I'll call you."

"Fine. But don't hesitate. If you need me, I'm there."

"Thanks, bestie. You're always there when I need you."

She hung up and stared at the green dress again. It was bold, confident, and everything she wanted to be in that moment. But as she slipped it off the hanger, doubt crept in. *What if showing up uninvited made her look desperate? What if Ryan got angry?* After a moment, she put the dress back and pulled on a soft sweater and her best pair of jeans instead. Understated. Casual. Less of a statement.

She took one last look in the mirror. The outfit felt safe, but there was still a knot of unease in her stomach. *Was this a mistake? Was she really about to show up uninvited just to remind her own boyfriend that she existed?* Shaking off the doubt, she grabbed her keys and stepped out into the night.

She tugged her jacket tighter as she walked. She glanced at her phone to check the time. Ryan hadn't responded to her last text, but that wasn't surprising. Every time she texted him about her concerns, he'd either brush them off or say he 'needed space.' Still, she was trying. That's what relationships were about, right? Putting in the effort, even when things got hard.

She put her phone back in her pocket. The restaurant was only a few blocks away now. She could already see its warm glow visible in the distance. With each step closer, her nerves twisted tighter. *She wondered if he would be annoyed. Embarrassed? Would he act like she didn't belong there?* She shook off the thought and focused on the steady rhythm of her footsteps. She *did* belong there. At least she should. They were supposed to be a team, weren't they?

The elevator ride to the top floor was nerve-wracking.

She felt out of place in her jeans and sweater as she imagined Ryan surrounded by his impeccably dressed colleagues. The doors opened, and she stepped into the lounge. She scanned the crowd, but it didn't take long to find him.

Ryan was at a corner booth, sitting very close to a blonde woman in a sleek black dress. Her hand was on his thigh as they laughed together, completely absorbed in each other. The way he smiled at her made Alex see things for how they really were. He wasn't just entertaining a coworker. It wasn't just a casual dinner he was out for. He was *with* her. She wondered if she was imagining things, but the casual way he draped his arm over the woman's shoulders left no room for doubt.

"No," she whispered under her breath. Her vision blurred for a moment before she blinked the sting away. No. She would not cry. Not here. Not over *him*. Summoning every ounce of courage, she marched across the room with the sound of her boots clicking against the polished floor. She felt people's eyes on her, but she didn't care.

"Ryan," she said sharply. His laughter died instantly. His head snapped up and his eyes widened as he took in the sight of her standing at the edge of the booth. The blonde woman beside him gently pulled her hand from his thigh.

"Alex?" Ryan's voice wavered slightly, as if he weren't sure she was real.

"What the hell is this?" she demanded.

The woman beside him looked startled.

Ryan shifted uncomfortably. "It's not what it looks like."

"Oh, really? Because from where I'm standing, it looks exactly like *this* is why you didn't want me here tonight."

The woman frowned. "You said you were single."

"He what?" She turned to him. "Is that true? Are you telling people you're single now?"

Ryan stammered. "I didn't mean for this to happen."

"Didn't mean for *what* to happen? You didn't mean to cheat on me? You didn't mean to lie to my face for weeks?"

"Alex, calm down," he hissed. He was worried that she

would make a scene.

"Don't you dare tell me to calm down!" she snapped. "I've been trying to fix this relationship while you've been sneaking around behind my back. How long? How long has this been going on?"

The blonde woman stood looking clearly uncomfortable. "I think I should go."

"Good idea," Alex shot back.

The woman left without another word.

"Look," he began in a defensive tone. "I didn't mean for you to find out like this. Things between us haven't been good for a while—"

"Don't," she interrupted. "Don't you dare put this on me! I've been here. I've been trying. You're the one who checked out."

"I just… I didn't know how to tell you. I didn't want to hurt you."

Alex let out a bitter laugh. "Hurt me? Do you think *this* doesn't hurt? Watching you with her and hearing her say you told her you were single. That doesn't hurt?"

"I'm sorry, okay? I didn't mean for it to get this far. I didn't want to break your heart."

"You didn't want to break my heart?" she repeated. "You didn't even have the decency to be honest with me. You let me think this was all my fault, that I wasn't enough while you were out here… doing this."

Ryan stood and raised his hands in a placated gesture. "I made a mistake. I'm sorry. Hurting you was never my intention."

Tears formed in her eyes, but she refused to let them fall. She took a step back and shook her head. "No. You didn't make a mistake. A mistake is forgetting to take out the trash or missing an anniversary. What you did was a choice. You betrayed me."

"Alex, please," he said. "Can we just talk about this?"

"There's nothing left to talk about. We're done."

He looked stunned. "Come on. Don't be like this."

"Like what? Like someone who knows her worth?" She squared her shoulders and met his gaze with unwavering determination. "I deserve better than this. Better than you."

Without another word, she turned and walked away. She didn't look back, even as she heard him call her name.

The night air hit her like a slap as she stepped outside. Her vision blurred with tears, but she kept walking, not caring where she was going. She ended up at the park near her apartment and collapsed onto a bench under the glow of a streetlamp. The enormity of what had just happened crashed over her, and the tears she'd been holding back finally spilled free.

For years, she had built her life around Ryan. She convinced herself that their love was worth fighting for. She had ignored the red flags, the growing distance, and the gnawing feeling in her gut that something wasn't right. And for what?

She wiped the tears from her cheeks. She felt angry, humiliated, and heartbroken all at once. But beneath the pain, there was something else. Something quieter but stronger. Relief.

It was over. She didn't have to keep fighting for someone who wasn't fighting for her. She didn't have to keep pretending that their relationship was something it wasn't. But the thought brought a strange sense of clarity. For the first time in years, she felt like she could finally breathe.

Her phone buzzed in her pocket. She pulled it out and saw a message from Sarah:

*"Hey, you forgot to check-in. Just letting you know that whatever happens, I'm here for you!"*

She stared at the message for a moment, a small smile tugging at her lips. She typed back:

*"I'll talk to you tomorrow. I have a lot to tell you."*

As she slipped her phone back into her pocket, Alex looked up at the stars twinkling above. The night felt colder now, but also brighter. She didn't know what came next, but she felt ready to find out.

# Chapter 3

The next day, they met at their favorite brunch spot. The scent of fresh pastries and coffee filled the air, but Alex barely noticed. Her eyes were glued to her plate, where a half-eaten stack of pancakes sat untouched.

Sarah leaned back in her chair and studied her friend with a look of concern. "Okay, spill," she said. "What happened last night?"

Alex poked at her pancakes with her fork. "I caught Ryan cheating," she said quietly.

"What? Are you serious?"

"I went to that rooftop bar he said he'd be at, and there he was with another woman. His arm around her, leaning in close. She even told me he said he was single."

"That *asshole*! Oh, Alex, I'm so sorry. Are you okay?"

"I don't know. That is to say, I ended it right there. I walked out and didn't look back. But now I just... I feel numb."

Sarah reached across the table and squeezed her hand. "You did the right thing. He didn't deserve you. And you deserve so much more than some lying jerk who doesn't even respect you enough, to be honest."

"I know," Alex said, her voice cracking. "I know I deserve better. But it still hurts. I spent three years of my life with him. Three years, and this is how it ends."

Sarah's grip on her hand tightened. "Of course, it hurts. You loved him. You built a life with him. And now, you're grieving that. Even though he turned out to be complete garbage, it doesn't erase what you felt."

She stared at the untouched coffee in front of her. "I just keep thinking... was I blind? Were there signs, and I ignored them?"

"Maybe. Maybe not. But you know what? It doesn't matter. Because the moment you *knew*, you walked away. You didn't stay and make excuses. You chose *you*. And that's what matters."

Alex blinks back the sting in her eyes. "So, what now?"

"Now? Now you heal. You let yourself be sad, angry, whatever you need to be. And then, when you're ready, you start saying yes to things that make *you* happy."

"Easier said than done. It just feels like there's this... emptiness now. Like I should be relieved it's over, but instead, I just feel lost."

"That makes sense. You spent time building something with him. Even if it turned out to be built on lies, it doesn't just disappear overnight."

She laughed bitterly. "Funny how he seems just fine, though. Out there laughing, moving on like I was nothing."

"Because people like him always do. But that doesn't mean he wins. You do because you get to move forward without someone who was dragging you down."

"I just hate that it still hurts. I don't want to care, but I do."

"I get it. It's going to hurt for a while. But this is also your chance to start fresh, you know? No more dead weight holding you back."

"Start fresh? I don't even know where to start. My job is soul-sucking, my relationship was a lie, and I can't remember the last time I felt excited about anything."

Sarah raised an eyebrow. "Okay, first, you're being way too hard on yourself. You're incredibly talented, you know that. You're just stuck in a rut right now. But that doesn't mean you can't get out of it."

"It's not that easy. I feel like I've been stuck for so long, I don't even know what it's like to be... unstuck."

"Then let's figure it out. Let's get you unstuck. What's one thing you've always wanted to do but never had the chance?"

Her mind immediately flashed to the corkboard in her apartment. The postcard of the Amalfi Coast stood out, vivid and clear. "Travel," she admitted after a moment. "I've always wanted to travel. I want to see the world, experience new cultures, and take in all the beauty out there. But I've never had the time or money or... courage."

"Now we're getting somewhere. Why don't you start there?"

"Because it's not that simple. I have bills to pay, a job that's barely keeping me afloat, and no idea where to even begin. It's a nice dream, but that's all it is. A dream."

"No. It's not just a dream. It's a goal. And goals can be planned for and worked toward. What if you started small? Save up some money, pick one place to visit, and just... go."

"It's not that I don't want to. It's just... what if I fail? What if it's a waste of time and money?"

Sarah laughed, a sound that made Alex look up in surprise. "Fail? You? You've been playing it safe for so long, you've forgotten how to take risks. Traveling isn't about succeeding or failing. It's about living. Experiencing. Growing. And if there's anyone who could use a little living right now, it's you."

"You make it sound so easy."

"It's not easy," Sarah admitted. "But it's worth it. Look, I've known you forever. And I've never seen you as defeated as you've been lately. You need this. You need something to shake you out of this funk."

Alex stirred her coffee thoughtfully as her best friend's words echoed in her mind. *Could she really do it? Could she leave behind the safety of her routine and take a leap into the unknown?*

"And don't think I'm going to let you talk yourself out of this," she added firmly. "You're too smart and too talented to waste your life on things that don't make you happy."

"What if I don't even know what makes me happy anymore?"

"Then it's time to find out."

Their conversation shifted to lighter topics for a while, updates on Sarah's job, funny stories from her new coworkers, but Alex's mind kept drifting back to the idea of traveling. She could picture herself standing on the edge of a cliff with the ocean stretching out endlessly before her. The thought sent a shiver of both fear and excitement through her. As they finished their meal, Sarah leaned back in her chair and studied Alex. "So? What's the plan?"

Alex blinked. "Plan?"

"For getting out of this rut," Sarah clarified. "We've identified the problem. Now it's time for action. What's your first step?"

"I don't know. I guess… maybe I could start by saving up. And researching places to go."

"Good start. But don't overthink it, okay? Sometimes you just have to take the plunge and figure things out as you go."

"I'll try."

Sarah reached across the table and took her hand. "You've got this. I believe in you."

It was something about those words that gave Alex a spark of hope. She didn't know if it was just hearing them aloud, but it was the boost she needed. She didn't know what her future held, but sitting there with Sarah's unwavering support, she felt she had the strength to find out.

# Chapter 4

The steady hum of chatter, the hiss of an espresso machine, and the clinking of mugs filled the small cafe as Alex pushed open the door. She rubbed her gloved hands together as she stepped inside. The warmth hit her immediately, along with the comforting aroma of freshly brewed coffee and baked goods.

She wasn't sure why she'd chosen this place today. It wasn't her usual spot. It could have been the handwritten sign in the window advertising "the best caramel lattes in town" or the inviting glow of the Edison bulbs strung across the ceiling that attracted her. Either way, the location felt perfect for a peaceful afternoon.

She joined the short line as she studied the menu. When her turn came, she ordered her caramel latte and stepped to the side to wait, clutching the receipt between her fingers. Her eyes wandered the room to search for an empty seat. The cafe was busier than she'd expected, most of the tables occupied by solo patrons with laptops or small groups deep in conversation.

"Order for Alex!" the barista called out as she placed a steaming cup on the counter.

She stepped forward to reach for the cup just as another hand grazed hers. She blinked in surprise and pulled back instinctively.

"Sorry about that," said the man standing next to her. "Looks like we've got the same taste in coffee or the same name."

She looked at the stranger. He was tall and tan, with dark, curly hair appearing windswept. His hazel eyes sparkled with amusement, and a camera hung casually around his neck.

He wore a leather jacket that looked well-worn but somehow still stylish, paired with a scarf that hinted at his practicality in the cold.

"Oh, no, I'm Alex," she blurted. She noticed her cheeks flushing.

The man raised an eyebrow while a playful grin tugged at his lips. "Funny, so am I. Small world, huh?"

Alex blinked, surprised by his teasing tone until she realized he was joking. "Right," she said, laughed softly despite herself. "That would be a little too coincidental."

He stepped back slightly to give her room to grab her cup. "Jamie," he offered his hand.

"Alex," she replied with a quick shake. "I forgot I just told you that."

"Nice to meet you," he said. "Looks like I'll have to wait for my coffee. Yours beat me to the punch."

"Better luck next time," she said as she grabbed her cup and sat down.

"Do you mind if I sit with you?" He asked as he pointed to a table.

She hesitated, then looked around. It wasn't like she had much choice. It was the only empty table with two chairs. "Sure," she said as she took her own seat across from him. He put his camera gently on the table before sitting down, and she couldn't help but look. It looked professional, with a wide lens that gleamed even in the dim cafe light.

"Nice camera. Are you a photographer?"

He leaned back in his chair with a wide grin. "Guilty as charged. I'm a travel photographer. Mostly landscapes and street photography. What about you?"

"Graphic designer," she answered as she stirred her latte absentmindedly. "But I've always loved photography. I used to take a lot of pictures when I was younger."

"Used to? What happened?"

"Life, I guess. Work got in the way, and I kind of... forgot about it."

"That happens. However, a fresh start is always an option.

She smiled faintly. "It's possible. You appear to have found a solution. Traveling and taking photos must be amazing."

"It has its moments," he admitted. "However, appearances can be deceiving. Long flights, heavy gear, unpredictable weather. That isn't for everyone. Still, I wouldn't trade it for anything."

Alex found herself drawn to his passion and the way his eyes lit up when he talked about his work. "Where's the most incredible place you've been?" she asked.

"Hmm." He tapped his fingers against his coffee cup. "That's a tough one. But if I had to pick, I'd say Iceland. Its scenery is unreal; waterfalls, glaciers, and volcanic beaches are present. It's like stepping into another world."

"Wow," she tried to imagine the scenes he described. "That sounds incredible."

"What about you?" he asked. "Your ideal destination: anywhere on Earth, where?"

"Italy," she said. "The Amalfi Coast. I've always dreamed of experiencing that firsthand.

His face lit up. "Great choice. I was there a few years ago. It's everything you imagine and more. The cliffs, the water, the food …well, everything is unforgettable."

She smiled. "I hope to experience that someday."

He raised an eyebrow. "Someday, huh? That's the simplest method to avoid going.

"That's what my best friend says. She's always telling me I need to stop playing it safe and take more risks."

"She sounds like a smart friend," he said with a grin. Seriously, prioritize what matters. Life's brief. Visit the Amalfi Coast; it's worth it. There's no perfect moment; seize the opportunity.

His words struck a chord in her. "You're making that sound easy." She teased.

"It's not simple," he admitted. "But the payoff is worthwhile. Taking that leap is scary, sure. But it's the only way to grow."

They lapsed into a comfortable silence, sipping their coffees as the cafe buzzed around them. Alex glanced at his camera again as her curiosity bubbled to the surface.

"Do you have a favorite photo you've taken?" she asked.

His face softened, and he pulled his phone from his pocket. "Actually, yes. Let me show you."

He swiped through his photo gallery before turning the screen toward her. The image was breathtaking: a lone figure standing on a cliff, silhouetted against a golden sunset. Below them, the ocean stretched out endlessly, waves crashing against the rocks.

"That's incredible," Alex said, her voice filled with awe. "Where was this?"

"Big Sur. It was one of those moments where everything lined up perfectly. The light, the location. It seemed like magic.

She stared at the photo a moment longer before handing the phone back. "You have an amazing eye."

"What about you?" he asked in a gentler tone. "What's your story? What makes you tick?"

She was unsure of how to answer. "I'm still trying to figure that out," she said finally. "I used to love art. Drawing, painting, anything creative. But at some point, it lost its significance."

"What changed?"

"Life, I guess. I got caught up in being practical. Bills to pay, responsibilities to juggle. I thought if I followed the 'right' path, everything else would fall into place. But it hasn't."

"That's tough. But there's still time. To figure it out, I mean."

She gave him a small smile. "I wouldn't have a clue how to begin."

"Well," he grinned, "what if you started by doing something that scares you?"

"Like what?"

"Anything. Book a trip. Take a class. Quit your job."

She laughed, though the idea sent a thrill of fear through her. "Quitting my job seems a bit extreme."

"It's possible. It could be just what you need. The point is, you've got to shake things up. Do something that makes you feel alive."

"Alive?" she said with disbelief. "I don't even remember what that feels like."

"Life is too short for doubts and fears. You're allowed to want more," he said gently.

"Want more? I can barely make it through the week without falling apart."

"Exactly," he said. "Which is why something has to change. It doesn't have to be big. Just... different. Even one choice, one risk. Say yes to something that scares you a little."

"Saying yes would scare me a lot. I probably wouldn't know who I was if I did that."

"Believe me when I say that it will be worth it. The hardest part is taking the first step. After that, it gets easier."

She marveled at his confidence and clarity. She doubted if she would ever be so sure about anything else in her life. Eager to change the focus, she asked, "So, what's next for you?"

"I'm heading to Morocco next month. There's a festival in the desert I've always wanted to photograph, and I figured it was time to make it happen."

"That sounds incredible," she said. "Do you plan everything out in advance?"

"Not really," he admitted. "I like to leave room for surprises. Some of the best moments happen when you're not looking for them."

She couldn't remember the last time she'd let herself be surprised. They fell into a simple rhythm after that, trading stories and sipping their coffees as the afternoon slipped by.

He told her about wandering the streets of Tokyo, climbing sand dunes in Namibia, and camping under the stars in Patagonia. Each story painted a vivid picture, sparking something deep within her. A sense of longing and of possibility. By the time they finished their drinks, she had the impression she'd been on a journey herself, even though she hadn't left the cafe.

"Thanks for letting me monopolize the conversation," he said as he stood to leave.

"I didn't mind," she smiled at him. "It was nice to hear about all the places you've been. Inspiring, even."

"Well, perhaps one day you'll have some stories of your own to share."

Possibly.

He reached into his jacket pocket, pulled out a small business card, and handed it to her. "If you ever decide to take that leap, get in touch. I'd love to hear about it."

She took the card, brushing her fingers against his briefly. She glanced down at it: *"Jamie Rivers–Travel Photographer"* along with an email address and Instagram handle.

"Thanks," she said as she pulled her card out of her wallet. "And if you want to share more stories of your travels, here's my card."

He grabbed her card, then departed with a "See you later."

She watched him walk out of the cafe, the jingle of the bell signaling his departure. She sat there lost in thought for a moment. Something stirred within her for reasons unknown. It faintly glimmered, yet it existed.

*Don't wait for the perfect time,* she thought. *Maybe it's already here.*

Later that evening, she sat on her couch, twirling his business card between her fingers as she listened to the phone ring.

Sarah answered on the second ring. "Hey! Anything good happened today? I remember you saying you tried that new place today. Were they crowded?"

"It was... unexpected. In a good way."

"Oh?" Sarah's voice perked up with interest. "Do tell."

"I met someone today while waiting for my drink. His name is Jamie. He's a travel photographer. He's super laid-back, like the kind of person who just goes wherever life takes him. We talked for hours, and," she glanced at the card again. "He gave me his info. Said if I ever wanted to take a leap, I should tell him.

There was a brief pause before Sarah spoke. "Wait. Are you saying he invited you to, like, *go somewhere* with him?"

"Not exactly," she clarified, though the idea sent a tiny thrill through her. "But he kind of planted the idea. Like... I should possibly stop waiting for life to happen and just go."

Sarah let out a dramatic gasp. "Are you telling me that my best friend is considering being spontaneous? Who are you, and what have you done with Alex?"

"I don't know. But when he talked about all these amazing places, I sensed something. It seemed I was waking from a very long nap.

"So... are you gonna do it?"

She traced the edge of the card. "I'm not sure," she admitted. "Yet after a long time, I feel the urge to."

# Chapter 5

Alex sat at her desk, staring blankly at the open design file on her computer screen. Her thoughts weren't on the client's latest demands or the impending deadline. Instead, her mind kept drifting back to Jamie with his amiable smile and magnetic energy. It had been two weeks since their chance encounter at the coffee shop, and his words still echoed in her mind.

*"Life's too short to put off the things that matter."*

A soft chime from her phone pulled her out of her thoughts. She picked it up and saw a notification: an email from an address that looked familiar. Opening it, she saw the subject line: **"An Invitation–Jamie Rivers."**

She instantly smiled as she read the message:

*Hey Alex,*

*It was great chatting with you at the cafe. I've got an exhibit opening this Friday night. Thought you might be interested. It's at The Loft on Main, 7 PM.*

*Hope to see you there.*
*Jamie*

She stared at the screen. Part of her felt excited, but another part hesitated. Did he really mean to invite her? Would it be weird if she showed up?

"Do something that scares you," she murmured. With a deep breath, she typed out a response:

*Hi Jamie,*

*Thanks for the invite! It sounds amazing. I'll be there.*

*Alex*

The Loft on Main was a chic; industrial gallery space nestled in the heart of downtown Lakehaven. Its large windows spilled warm light onto the sidewalk, and a small crowd had already gathered outside. Alex smoothed down the front of her navy dress and adjusted the strap of her bag. She tried to calm the nervous flutter in her stomach.

Inside, the space buzzed with conversation and the faint strains of jazz music. Photographs lined the exposed brick walls. Soft, focused lighting illuminated each photograph. She scanned the room, and the stunning images immediately caught her eye: a lone tree in the middle of a golden desert, a bustling market in Marrakesh, and a tranquil sunrise over misty mountains.

*"Alex!"*

She turned at the sound of her name and spotted Jamie weaving through the crowd toward her. He wore a simple but stylish dark button-down shirt and jeans; his signature camera slung over his shoulder.

"You made it," he said with a wide smile.

"Of course. Thanks for inviting me. This place is amazing."

He glanced around. "Yeah, it came together better than I expected. What do you think of the photos?"

"They're incredible. Each one seems to tell a story. It's like I can sense the air, hear the sounds, and even smell the food in some of them."

"That's exactly what I was going for," he said, as his eyes lit up. "I wanted people to believe they were there with me, experiencing it all."

"Well, mission accomplished."

He gestured toward one of the walls. "Come on, I'll show you some of my favorites."

As they walked, he explained the stories behind the

photos. He pointed to an image of a weathered fisherman casting his net in Sri Lanka as the golden sunlight glinted off the water.

"This guy was incredible," he said. "He'd been fishing that way since he was a teenager. I spent the entire morning with him, only watching and learning."

"And he didn't mind you taking his picture?" she asked.

"Not at all. He seemed proud that someone wanted to capture what he did."

They moved on to another image. This one was of a young girl holding a bouquet of wildflowers in a remote village in Nepal. Her smile was radiant, and her eyes were full of wonder.

"I met her while hiking through the mountains. She ran up to me and handed me one of the flowers. I asked if I could take her picture, and she nodded like it was the most natural thing in the world."

"You're very skilled at capturing people's essence. It's like you see them. More than their faces, but their identities."

He looked at her. "That's the goal. Photography is more than the visual; it's about connection. If I can move someone emotionally when they see one of my pictures, I've succeeded."

They continued walking, stopping occasionally so he could greet other guests or answer questions about his work. Alex found herself captivated not only by the images but also by his passion and the way he animated each story. At one point, they stopped in front of a black-and-white photograph of a winding cobblestone street that was lit by the soft glow of lanterns.

"This one's from Kyoto," Jamie said. "I took it late at night when the streets were empty. It was so quiet, almost like stepping back in time."

"It's beautiful," she said. "There's something so peaceful about it."

He turned to her. "What about you? Have you thought any more about what we talked about at the cafe?"

"A little," she admitted. "But I still don't know where to start."

"That's okay. You don't have to figure it all out at once. Take one step. Do something that excites you, even if it scares you a little."

She looked up at him. "What if I fail?"

He gave a soft, reassured smile that sent a wave of calm through her. "You learn from it and try again. Failure's not the end. That's part of the process."

For a moment, they stood in silence. The sounds of the gallery faded into the background. A strange mix of vulnerability and possibility came over her, as if the door to a new chapter of her life was creaking open.

"Thank you," she said finally. "For inviting me, for sharing your work, and for reminding me it's okay to take risks."

"Anytime. And hey, if you ever need a push, you know where to find me."

Alex smiled as she looked at him. There was something about him, his ease, his quiet confidence, that gave her a sense she could be a little braver.

She glanced around the gallery, taking in the vibrant strokes and intricate details of his paintings. Each piece told a story, unafraid and unapologetic. She wanted to feel that way about her own life.

"You thinking about something?"

"Just… that I don't want to keep waiting around for life to happen to me."

"In that case, don't."

The simplicity of his words settled deep inside her. No overthinking, no hesitation. Do it.

"Come on, let's get out of here. I know a place with the best coffee in town."

Alex raised an eyebrow. "Oh yeah? You're sure that they're opened this late?"

He grinned. "If not, I'm sure we can find a place to sit and have a drink."

She laughed, shaking her head but grabbing her bag anyway. "Alright, I'll be the judge of that."

# Chapter 6

Alex pushed open the door to the diner where she and Sarah often met for their biweekly catch ups. The warm aroma of coffee and freshly baked pastries enveloped her as she stepped inside. She spotted Sarah immediately, seated at their usual booth by the window, sipping from a large mug and scrolling through her phone.

"Hey!" Alex slid into the seat across from her.

Sarah looked up and smiled. "There you are. You're late."

"Sorry," she said, shrugging off her coat and draping it over the back of the booth. "I got caught up thinking about last night."

Sarah raised an eyebrow and set her phone down. "Last night? Don't tell me you had a date and didn't text me about it.

She laughed. "No, not a date. I attended a photography exhibit.

Sarah's expression shifted from playful curiosity to genuine interest. "Photography exhibit? That's... new. What brought that on?"

She launched into the story. "Do you remember Jamie? The guy I met at the coffee shop?"

"The travel photographer?"

"Yeah, him," she said. "He emailed me out of the blue and invited me to his exhibit. It was at this gorgeous gallery downtown, and Sarah, his photos were incredible. Like, jaw-dropping, make-you-want-to-book-a-plane-ticket incredible."

Sarah leaned forward and rested her chin on her hand. "Okay, tell me everything. What was it like?"

She took a sip of the coffee Sarah had ordered for her before diving in. "The space was beautiful, industrial, and lots of exposed brick. His photos were everywhere, lit perfectly. There was this one of a fisherman in Sri Lanka, and another of a little girl in Nepal. Every picture had a story, and Jamie told them so well. It was like being transported to all these incredible places without ever leaving the room."

"You're glowing. I don't think I've seen you this excited in a while."

The comment surprised her. "Really?"

"Really," Sarah said firmly. "So, did you two talk?"

"Oh, yeah," she said. "He walked me through the exhibit and explained the stories behind some photos. He asked about my well-being since we last spoke. And, of course, he reminded me that I need to take a leap."

Sarah smirked. "Sounds like he's not just a photographer, but also a motivational speaker."

"Pretty much. But he's not wrong. His work made me think. About how much I've been holding myself back. About how I haven't really done anything bold in years."

"Did he give you any advice?"

"He said I don't have to figure it all out at once. Just take one step. Do something that excites me, even if it scares me."

"That's solid advice. So, are you going to take it?"

"I want to. I'm unsure how to begin. It's like there's this wall between me and the life I want, and I don't even know how to climb it."

Sarah reached across the table and placed a hand on Alex's. "Hey, you've already started. You visited the exhibit, didn't you? You've been considering what brings you joy. That's more than you were doing a month ago."

She relaxed a little. "Thanks. I needed to hear that."

"That's what I'm here for. And if you need help figuring out your next step, you are aware I'm always down for brainstorming sessions."

Alex laughed. "I might take you up on that."

"Good," Sarah said, leaning back in her seat. "It seems to me this Jamie guy might be onto something. And if his work is as amazing as you say, I wouldn't mind tagging along next time."

"Who knows?" Alex said, her smile widened. "There could be a next time."

"You're actually going to do it?"

"Yeah. I've been considering it and after everything with Ryan... I don't know. It just made me realize how much I've been holding myself back. I don't love my work anymore, and I don't want to waste more time being in this position.

Sarah let out an excited squeal, drawing a few glances from the nearby tables. "This is *huge*! Do you have an idea of what you're going to do next?"

"Not exactly. But I want to concentrate on projects which genuinely thrill me. Consider freelancing temporarily, or perhaps a different career path altogether. I just... I need to take the leap."

"Hell yes, you do. And you know what? I'm proud of you. This is brave."

A warmth spread through Alex. Brave. It wasn't a word she had used to describe herself before, but it was possibly beginning to fit.

As they finished their coffee and planned the rest of their day, she felt a small but growing sense of hope. The spark Jamie had ignited at the exhibit was still burning and made her sense that she was progressing toward something instead of going in circles.

She decided that when she got home, the first thing she would do to take the first step was to leave her job. She had to admit that she wasn't happy there and that she would never get the chance to really show what she can do. Now the next decision was to resign or quit on the spot.

Alex sat on her couch with her laptop balanced precariously on her knees. She had spent the past hour staring at the same blank email draft addressed to her boss. The subject line read: **"Resignation Letter."**

She ran her hands through her hair and let out a groan

of frustration. *"What am I even doing?"* she said to herself. Her phone rang on the cushion beside her. She picked it up and saw Sarah's name flashing on the screen.

"Hey."

"Hey, yourself," Sarah replied, sounding bright and full of energy. "What's going on? You sound weird."

Alex sighed. "I'm trying to write my resignation letter, but I can't even get past the first sentence. I have no idea what is troubling me.

"You're overthinking," she said immediately. "Just say what you need to say and hit send. It's not like you're writing a novel."

"Easy for you to say," she grumbled. "You've always been decisive. I, on the other hand, can't even decide what to eat for dinner half the time."

"True, but this isn't about dinner. It's about you finally doing what you've been wanting to do for months. You hate that job, remember?"

"Ugh, I hate it, but could I be wrong? What if I quit and don't find anything better? What if I can't make it doing freelance?"

"Whoa, whoa," Sarah said, her tone softening. "Slow down. First, you will not fail. Second, even if things don't go perfectly at first, that doesn't mean it was the wrong decision. You're allowed to figure things out."

She stared at the blinking cursor on her laptop screen. "It's just... dreadful. Giving up the security, even if it sucks."

"Change is always scary," Sarah said gently. "But staying in the same place when you know it's not right for you? That's even scarier."

"I know you're right, but it's hard to dismiss this intuition. Like, who am I to believe I can do better? What if I'm just not meant to have a fulfilling career or—"

"Stop right there. I'm not letting you talk like that. You are *more* than capable. You're talented, you're smart, and you're a hell of a lot braver than you give yourself credit for."

"Thanks," she murmured, her voice barely audible.

"You're welcome," Sarah said, her tone softening again. "Now, do you want me to come over and help you write this thing? Or at least distract you with some wine while you figure it out?"

"Tempting, but I need to do this on my own. If I can't even write a resignation letter by myself, how am I supposed to handle everything else?"

"Fair point. But remember, you're not alone in this. I'm here. Jamie's been a great motivator, and honestly, you've got an entire army of people rooting for you, whether or not you realize it."

"Thanks, Sarah. I mean it. You know how to put it in perspective for me."

"Anytime. Now, go write that letter and free yourself from that soul-sucking job. You've got this."

When the call ended, she set her phone down and took a deep breath. Sarah's words echoed in her mind and bolstered her confidence. She clicked back into the email draft and began typing. She read the email one last time before she hit send.

**Subject:** *Resignation Letter*

**Dear Martin,**

*I am formally submitting my resignation from my position at BrightEdge Designs, effective in two weeks. While I've appreciated the opportunities I've had during my time here, I've come to realize that it's time for me to pursue a new direction in my career. Thank you for your support and understanding. Please let me know how I can help with the transition.*

*Sincerely,*

*Alexandra Greer*

"Come on, Alex," she whispered to herself. "Just do it."

Reminders of endless revisions for uninspired projects, and the suffocating monotony of her job flooded her mind. Then, another image surfaced: Jamie's photos. The vibrant colors, the untold stories, the sheer sense of *freedom* they represented. She thought about all the missed opportunities and before she could overthink it again, it was sent.

The email disappeared from her outbox, and for a moment, the weight of her decision felt unbearable. Then, as the seconds ticked by, a sense of liberation crept in.

"I did it," she said in disbelief. Later that night, she called Sarah again.

"Well?" She asked the moment she picked up.

"I sent it," she answered.

"Yes! I'm so proud of you. How do you feel?"

"Terrified," she admitted. "But also… lighter. Like I've just peeled off a layer of something I didn't need anymore."

"That's because you have. You just took the first step toward something better. I always believed in you."

"Thanks for believing in me. It means more than you realize."

"Always. Now, how are we celebrating? Because this calls for champagne, at the very least."

"Let's save the champagne for when I figure out what the hell I'm doing next."

"Fine," she said teasing. "But don't wait too long, okay? Life's too short for that."

"I won't," she promised.

As the call ended and she got into bed, a blend of fear and excitement surged within her. She snuggled under the covers and stared at the ceiling. So much had changed in such a short time. Ryan was in the past now meaning a painful chapter had closed. And Jamie… well, that was something new, something uncertain. But ever since she met him, uncertainty didn't feel so scary.

She turned onto her side, clutching her pillow as a small smile played on her lips. Sarah was right. This was her chance to start fresh, to stop waiting and start *living*. With that thought, she let out a slow breath, closed her eyes, and allowed herself to dream. Not about what she had lost, but about everything that still lay ahead.

# Chapter 7

The morning sunlight poured into Alex's window as she stood in front of her mirror. She adjusted the strap of her backpack and stared at her reflection. *"You got this,"* she thought to herself. *"Change is a part of life. Everyone goes through it."* She wore a simple outfit; a pair of well-worn jeans, a soft cream sweater, and her favorite sneakers. But she felt different today. Today she will take her first trip out of town. She was low key excited and a little nervous.

Her two-week notice had ended, and now she stood at the edge of something she couldn't define. The decision to leave her job was behind her, but the uncertainty of what came next loomed ahead. She turned around and looked at the envelope on the counter by her keys. Inside was a round-way ticket to New York City. Jamie had mentioned he'd be giving a brief lecture at a photography workshop there, and she had taken him up on his invitation to come along. Her phone buzzed on the kitchen table.

*You good? Or do I need to come over*
*and shove you out the door?*

She laughed and typed a reply.

*I'm leaving now. Promise.*
*Good. Remember, worst-case scenario, you call*
*me, and we laugh about it over margaritas.*

She smiled. Sarah always knew how to ground her. She put the phone in her pocket, grabbed the envelope, slung her backpack over her shoulder, and stepped out the door. The air was crisp as she walked down the busy street. Her heart pounded with a mix of nerves and exhilaration surged through her with every step.

She had rehearsed this moment in her head countless times. She'd imagined the conversations and the weight lifting from her shoulders as she took control of her future. But now that it was real, her fingers trembled. When she got to the train station, she paused at the entrance and took a deep breath. *This is it.* No more excuses, no more second-guessing. She was ready.

With one last glance at Sarah's message, she straightened her shoulders and pushed through the doors. Inside was just as busy with the hum of voices blending with the announcements crackling over the loudspeaker. She clutched her ticket in her hand as she navigated the crowded platform. Both excitement and nerves consumed her.

"Alex!"

She turned at the sound of her name and saw Jamie standing a few feet away. He dressed in a denim jacket and dark jeans, his camera slung around his neck. His calm smile was a balm to her jittery nerves.

"Hey," she said as she approached him. "I wasn't sure if you'd already boarded."

"I wanted to make sure you made it. Figured you might need a familiar face."

She laughed. "You're not wrong."

They boarded the train together and found seats near a window. She stared out as the city landscape shifted from urban sprawl to open fields.

"So," Jamie said, "how does it feel?"

"How does what feel?" she asked, turning to look at him.

"Taking the leap."

She considered his question. "Honestly? Terrifying. But also... kind of exhilarating. Like I'm stepping into this giant unknown, and I do not know what's waiting on the other side."

"It's difficult," he admitted. "I've had plenty of moments where I questioned everything, like whether I was good enough or whether I was making the right choices. But every time I took a chance, it brought me closer to the life I wanted."

"I just don't want to mess it up."

"You won't," he said.

"How can you be so sure?"

"Because you're doing something most people are too scared to do. You're betting on yourself. That takes guts. And even if things don't go as planned, you'll find your way."

His words gave her a small flicker of confidence. When they arrived in New York, the city greeted them with honking taxis, throngs of people, and towering skyscrapers. Alex clutched her backpack as she followed him through the crowded streets. She was overwhelmed but exhilarated.

They arrived at the photography studio. Photographs lined the walls, telling a story more vivid than the last. Jamie led her to a small seating area near the back. "You can hang out here while I set up. Feel free to look around. I'll come grab you before we start."

She watched as he disappeared into the crowd of photographers and attendees. She wandered the space admiring the images on the walls. One photograph caught her attention. It was a black-and-white shot of the Big Sur photo.

"It's beautiful, isn't it?"

Turning, she saw an older woman standing next to her. She pulled her gray hair back into a sleek bun. In: One hand held a notebook as she wore a tailored blazer and jeans.

"It is," Alex said. "There's something so... raw about it."

The woman smiled. "That's the mark of a brilliant photographer. They know how to capture a moment that feels universal and personal at the same time."

Her mind drifted to Jamie and the stories he had shared about his travels.

"Are you a photographer?" the woman asked.

"Oh, no," she blurted. "I'm... figuring things out right now."

The woman studied her for a moment, then said, "Well,

whatever you're figuring out, don't rush it. Sometimes the journey is just as important as the destination."

"Thank you. I needed to hear that."

The woman nodded and moved on, leaving Alex alone with her thoughts.

Jamie's lecture was captivating. He spoke about the art of storytelling through photography. He also spoke about finding beauty in the mundane and meaning in the insignificant. As he showed slides of his work, Alex sensed something stir within her. It was a desire to create, to explore, and to see the world in a way she had never had before. When the lecture ended, he found her near the refreshments table.

"What did you think?" he asked.

"It was amazing. Learning about your process and seeing your work is inspiring."

"I'm glad you came. So, what's next for you?"

"I don't know yet," she admitted. "But I think... I'm ready to find out."

"That's all you need to start."

As they left the studio and stepped back into the bustling streets, a strange sense of peace washed over her. She glanced at Jamie, who was pointing out a nearby food truck with enthusiastic gestures.

"Best tacos in the city," he declared with absolute confidence. "And I won't take no for an answer."

She laughed. "Well, I *was* going to say I wasn't hungry, but now I feel like I don't have a choice."

"Exactly. No overthinking, just saying yes to new things, remember?"

She exhaled and let the words settle. He was right. She had spent too long hesitating, doubting, and waiting for the right time. But the right time was *now*.

"Alright," she said, stepping toward the truck. "Let's do it."

As they ordered and took their first bites, she savored more than just the food. The city lights, the laughter, and the excitement of the unknown all seemed different now. Not overwhelming, not intimidating. Just… full of possibilities.

# Chapter 8

Alex put her suitcase by the door and sighed in relief at the familiar sight of her apartment. Somehow, it felt smaller now, as if she had unknowingly outgrown it. The trip had changed her. Travel experiences with new people and places helped her realize life shouldn't be a constant state of exhaustion and discontent. She had spent too long being afraid of stepping into the unknown. Not anymore.

She set her backpack down, pulled out her laptop, and flipped it open at the kitchen counter. The blank screen stared back at her. *Alright,* she thought, rolling her shoulders back. *Time to build something of my own.*

She opened a new document and typed:

**Freelance Goals—Step One: Get started.**

A slow smile spread across her face. No more waiting. No more doubting. She was ready to bet on herself. A couple of hours later, she covered every surface with papers and open notebooks. Her laptop had tabs open to everything from freelance platforms to destination guides. Her phone buzzed, and she grabbed it without looking at the screen.

"Hello?"

"Now that's not how you greet me," Sarah joked. "Anyway, how's the chaos going?"

"That obvious, huh?"

"I can almost hear the caffeine in your voice. What's the plan, boss?"

"I'm creating a list of potential clients and projects. There are a ton of freelance opportunities out there, but it's overwhelming trying to figure out where to start."

"Take your time. You don't need to solve it all at once. Just pick one thing and go from there."

"I know. But it's tough to escape the impression that everything needs to happen right away. I gotta keep moving or I'll lose my momentum."

"You're already moving forward. Just deciding to take this step is huge. Give yourself some credit, okay?"

"Thanks, bestie. I needed to hear that."

"Anytime. Now, tell me, what's the next move?"

The next step was creating a professional presence online. Alex spent the afternoon updating her portfolio, carefully showing her best work, and writing descriptions that highlighted her skills. When she hit the "publish" button, her heart fluttered. It was a small step, but it felt monumental. She refreshed the page and studied her work as a mix of pride and nerves bubbled inside her. It felt official now.

Next, she tackled social media by setting up profiles dedicated to her freelance work. She drafted her first post, hesitating for only a second before publishing:

*"Exciting news!!! I'm officially stepping into the freelance world! If you need bold, creative design work, let's connect. Here's to new beginnings!"*

She stared at the screen, half expecting nothing to happen. Suddenly, a notification appeared. Then another. A like, a comment, a message from an old colleague asking about her availability. She was excited. *This is happening.* She grabbed her phone and texted Sarah.

*Just shared a post about freelancing. Excited and terrified at the same time!*

*You mean equal parts unstoppable and badass? Because that's what I'm hearing.*

A laugh lightened Alex's mood. She no longer feared the future. She wanted to create a new one. Later that evening, she sat at her desk composing an email to pitch a rebranding project to a local boutique owner she'd met at a community event months prior.

"Okay," she said to herself. "Short and professional, but not too stiff."

Her fingers hovered over the keyboard as she tried to find the perfect opening line.

*"Hi, I'm Alex Greer, a graphic designer..."*

"No, too generic," she said and deleted the line.

She started again. This time, she tried to focus on the boutique's unique vibe and how her design style could enhance it. Half an hour later, she had a polished email ready to send. She read it over twice. Finally, she hit "send" and let out a shaky breath.

"One down, a million to go," she said with a small smile.

The following day, she met Jamie for lunch. He'd been out of town, and she was eager to update him on her progress.

"Look at you," he said as she slid into the booth across from him. "You've got that determined glow."

"It's either determination or sleep deprivation."

"Either way, it suits you," he said smiling.

They ordered their food, and she launched into a recap of everything she'd been working on; the portfolio updates, the pitch emails, and her tentative plans to travel once she secured a steady stream of work.

"I'm impressed," he said when she finished. In just one week, you've accomplished what others take months to achieve.

"It doesn't feel like enough," she admitted. "I keep think I should do more."

"Trust me, you're doing fine. Building something new takes time. The important thing is that you're moving forward."

"It's just hard not to doubt myself, you know? What if

this doesn't work for me?"

"Let me tell you something I've learned from years of chasing my dreams. Doubt is always going to be there. That's just how it goes. But you don't have to let it control you. The fact that you're even trying puts you ahead of most people."

She smiled, "You're superb at this motivational speaking stuff."

"Comes with the territory. No, really, you got this. I believe in you."

By the end of the week, her efforts paid off. The boutique owner she'd pitched emailed back to express interest in her rebranding ideas. They scheduled a meeting for the following week, and Alex spent hours preparing mock ups and researching ways to align the new branding with the boutique's aesthetic.

She also received her first inquiry through her online portfolio. A small startup looking for a logo design. It wasn't a huge project, but it was a start. On Friday evening, she called Sarah to share the news.

"I got two potential clients!" she said as soon as she picked up.

"That's amazing! Tell me everything."

Her excitement spilled out in a rush of words.

"Wow, this is actually happening!" she said when she finished. "I mean, it's still small, but it's a start."

"And that's all you need. One step at a time, remember?"

"Right. Thanks for always being in my corner."

"Always. Now let's go celebrate. You've earned it."

An hour later, Alex slid into a booth across from Sarah at their favorite bar. Sarah raised her margarita with a grin.

"To new beginnings," she declared.

Alex clinked her glass against hers. "To taking risks," she added.

They both took a sip, and she let out a deep breath as she felt doubt slipping further away.

Sarah asked, "So…What's next on the master plan for *Alex Greer, Freelancer Extraordinaire*?"

"Honestly? I want to keep this momentum going. Get more clients, refine my niche, even design a brand for myself."

"I love it. And you *know* I'll be your first customer when I finally get around to starting my own business."

Alex raised an eyebrow. "Oh? Is this you officially declaring your *own* new beginning?"

"One thing at a time, bestie. Tonight is about *you*."

Alex couldn't stop smiling. She reflected on her situation weeks prior. She was lost, uninspired, and trapped in a life that was alien to her. Now she felt like she was heading in the right direction, and she was ready to see where the journey would take her.

# Chapter 9

While enjoying a warm mug of chai at the coffee shop, Alex felt the familiar buzz of an incoming notification on her phone. As she briefly looked at the screen, her eyes fell upon the name Jamie.

*Got a question for you. Call me when you have a sec.*

Curious, she took a sip of her drink and hit the call button.

"Hey, what's up?" she asked as soon as he answered.

"Hey, I was wondering... how do you feel about Italy?"

She blinked. "Uh, I mean, I feel *good* about it? Pasta, art, history, what's not to love?"

He chuckled. "I mean, how do you feel about actually *going* to Italy?"

She gasped. "Wait. What? Are you serious?"

"Very. Someone invited me to do a photography project in Venice. It's a mix of travel photography and a personal series I've been wanting to do for a while. And... I want you to come with me."

She couldn't believe what she was hearing. It had to be a dream. "You want *me* to go to Italy with you?"

"Yes," he said simply. "You've been working nonstop for a couple of months now. I know you love what you do, but I also know you've never really traveled before. You should experience this. And honestly? I just *want* you there."

She set her mug down, suddenly afraid her shaking hands would spill it. "You do remember that I've never even been on a plane before."

"I remember," he said. "And I get that it's scary. But you

took a risk starting your freelance career, right? This is just another adventure."

The idea of flying terrified her. But the thought of turning down an opportunity like this, of *not* seeing Venice, of *not* waking up in a new country with fresh possibilities, terrified her more.

"Okay."

"Okay?" Jamie echoed, as if he couldn't believe she agreed.

She let out a shaky laugh. "Yeah. Okay. I'll go."

"Alex, that's amazing!" His excitement was infectious. "You'll love this, promise! I'll help with everything. I'll book the flights and plan the trip. You don't have to worry about anything. All you need to do is say yes."

"I already did," she said, smiling. "I'm saying yes."

In the weeks that followed, Alex's life became a chaotic and busy whirlwind of preparations for the upcoming event. She got her passport, booked her first-ever flight, and spent hours researching Italy, making lists of things she wanted to see and do. Sarah, of course, had a field day with the news.

"You. Are. Going. To. Italy," she had squealed when Alex first told her. "This is the most exciting thing to happen since you quit your job. No *since ever*."

Sarah had taken it upon herself to help Alex shop for luggage, travel essentials, and, of course, the perfect outfits.

"Just imagine it," she had said as they browsed through dresses. "You, standing in front of the Basilica, looking effortlessly chic. Or sipping espresso at a tiny cafe in Naples while Jamie gazes at you like you're his next great masterpiece."

"It's not like that."

"Uh-huh. Keep telling yourself that."

But as the days ticked down and the reality of the trip set in, Alex couldn't deny the thrill that came with it. This was *happening*. She was going to Italy.

The sky was still painted with the faint hues of dawn

as she wheeled her suitcase through the crowded airport terminal. Her heart pounded in sync with the rhythm of hurried footsteps and boarding announcements. She glanced at Jamie, who walked beside her, effortlessly confident and carrying a camera bag slung over one shoulder.

"You look calm," she said.

Jamie glanced at her and smirked. "This isn't my first rodeo."

"Right, world traveler. Meanwhile, I'm just trying not to faint."

"You're going to be fine," Jamie reassured her. "Flying is way easier than it seems. Besides, you've got me as your personal in-flight guide."

"Lucky me."

At the security checkpoint, Alex fumbled with her belongings. She juggled her laptop, shoes, and jacket as she tried to keep up with the unspoken efficiency of seasoned travelers.

"You're doing great," Jamie teased as he handed over his own items with practiced ease.

"Don't mock me," she said as she struggled to get her laptop back into her bag.

"I'm not mocking," he raised his hands defensively. "I'm admiring your determination."

She gave him a look but couldn't help smiling. Once they reached the gate, the trip finally hit her. They were heading to Italy. She, Alex Greer, who had never been on a plane before, was about to fly across the Atlantic Ocean.

"This is really happening," she said excitedly as she stared at the massive plane parked outside the window.

Jamie nudged her gently. "Yep, and it's going to be amazing. Nervous?"

"Terrified," she admitted.

"You'll be fine. Just think about everything waiting for us on the other side. Gelato, stunning architecture, sunsets over the Tuscan countryside..."

"Okay, that does sound worth it."

As they boarded the plane, her nerves kicked up a notch. The narrow aisle seemed endless as they made their way to their seats. Jamie, ever the optimist, insisted she take the window seat.

"You'll thank me later," he said, settling into the seat beside her.

Alex stared out at the wing as her hands gripped the armrests. "So, what should I expect during takeoff?"

"It's like being on a roller coaster. But smoother. Mostly."

"Mostly?" she repeated, her eyes narrowing.

"Relax," he laughed. "It's totally safe. I promise."

The engines roared to life, and she felt her stomach tighten as the plane taxied down the runway. He noticed her tense posture and gently tapped her arm.

"Hey," he said softly. "Breathe. Deep breath in, deep breath out."

She followed his lead, inhaling and exhaling slowly.

"There you go," he said soothingly. "You've got this."

The plane sped up and pressed her back against the seat. She squeezed her eyes shut as the wheels lifted off the ground.

"We're flying," he nudged her arm again.

She cautiously opened one eye, then the other. Outside the window, the world below shrunk and Lakehaven turned into a patchwork quilt of buildings and streets.

"Wow," she whispered. She forgot about being scared for a sec when she saw the view.

"See? Not so bad," he grinned.

Once the plane leveled off, she relaxed. The hum of the engines became an almost comforting background noise. Jamie pulled out his camera and started fiddling with the settings.

"What are you doing?" she asked.

"Capturing the moment," he said and lifted the camera.

"Don't you dare take a picture of me right now," she laughed nervously.

"Why not? You look great. You look like someone on the brink of a life-changing adventure."

"More like someone on the brink of a nervous breakdown."

Jamie snapped the photo anyway. A flight attendant came by with drinks, and he ordered coffee while Alex stuck with water.

"To new beginnings," he raised his cup.

"To new beginnings."

"So, what's the first thing you want to do when we get to Italy?"

Alex thought for a moment. "I don't know. Everything? I feel like I should have a plan, but honestly, I just want to soak it all in."

"That's the best plan. Traveling isn't about checking off boxes. It's about experiencing the moment and creating lasting memories."

The longer it went on, the more at ease she became. She even managed a little nap before Jamie woke her up gently.

"Hey, wake up. You're missing it."

"What?" she blinked groggily.

"Look outside," he gestured toward the window.

She leaned over and gasped. The plane was gliding above a sea of clouds, their tops glowing in the soft light of the setting sun.

"It's beautiful," she said, her voice filled with wonder.

He smiled as he watched her reaction. "I knew you'd like it."

When the captain announced their descent, her nerves returned, though excitement tempered them.

"Landing's easy," Jamie said. "Just a little bumpy."

He wasn't wrong. The plane touched down with a slight jolt, and she let out a breath she hadn't realized she was holding.

"You survived." He grinned at her.

"Barely," she said, but her smile was genuine.

As they stepped out of the airport into the warm Italian air, she felt a rush of emotions, relief, excitement, anticipation. The world around her was alive with the sound of foreign voices, the scent of blooming flowers, and the hum of car engines.

"This is it," Jamie said and spread his arms. "Welcome to Italy."

Alex looked around, her heart swelling. She'd done it. She'd taken the leap.

"What now?" she turned to him.

"Now," he said, grinning, "we find gelato."

She laughed, her nerves melting away. "Lead the way."

With her suitcase in tow and Jamie by her side, she stepped into the adventure she'd always dreamed of, ready to embrace whatever came next.

# Chapter 10

As the train rolled into Venice, Alex pressed her face to the window, her breath fogging the glass. The view outside was like something out of a dream: canals glistening in the morning sun, ancient buildings with peeling paint that only added to their charm, and narrow streets alive with the chatter of locals and the distant hum of gondoliers singing.

She gasped, "Wow," an audible whisper escaping her lips.

Jamie, sitting beside her, smiled. "Told you it would be worth it."

"I mean, I've seen pictures, but... this is something else."

"It's one of those places you can't understand until you're here." He slung his camera bag over his shoulder as the train slowed to a stop.

As she left the station, the Grand Canal greeted her. Gondolas and vaporettos filled the shimmering water. Salt, sea, and ancient stones perfumed the air. For a moment, she remained perfectly still, allowing the scene to fully register in her mind and heart. The facades of centuries-old palazzos loomed over the canal with their weathered stone and intricate balconies whispering stories of the past. The air carried a mix of salt, espresso, and fresh pastries from a nearby cafe.

Jamie nudged her. "Not bad, huh?"

She turned to him. "Not bad at all. It's even better than I imagined."

They wheeled their suitcases toward the water taxi stand, where a line of sleek boats bobbed against the docks. The operator, a gruff-looking man with salt-and-pepper hair, asked them for their destination.

"San Marco," Jamie replied and handed over a few euros.

Alex climbed in, noticing the boat shift beneath her feet. She settled onto the wooden bench beside Jamie, her grip tightening on the railing as the taxi pulled away from the dock and wove into the canal's traffic. The ride was exhilarating. The cool spray of water against her skin, and the low hum of engines mixed with the occasional melodic call of a gondolier.

"This city is unreal," she murmured.

Jamie, camera in hand, snapped a few photos before turning to her. "Just wait until you see it at sunset."

A few minutes later, they arrived at a small dock near Piazza San Marco. As Alex stepped onto solid ground, she found herself in the heart of Venice's magic. The vast and majestic square opened before her. The towering beauty of St. Mark's Basilica and the soaring Campanile framed it. Pigeons fluttered about, tourists milled around with cameras, and the sound of a violin drifted through the air from a nearby cafe.

Jamie walked up behind her. "So, what do you think so far?"

"Okay, you win. I've never seen a more beautiful place.

"Wait until you try the gelato."

"Jamie," she groaned, nudging him.

He led the way toward a small gelateria tucked into the corner of a narrow alley. "Come on. First things first. Proper Venetian gelato."

With every step, Alex sensed the weight of her past life slowly disappearing into the distance, leaving her with a sense of lightness she hadn't experienced in years. She wasn't just visiting Venice. She was living it, breathing it, embracing every moment. She felt completely free.

"Unreal," she whispered, slowly turning to absorb her surroundings.

"Seeing it for the first time is always like this. Overwhelming, right?"

"Absolutely," she confessed.

"After you try this , we'll drop our bags at the hotel so we can really explore."

The hotel was a charming, centuries-old building tucked into a quiet corner of the city. Their room had a small balcony overlooking a canal, and Alex couldn't resist stepping out to admire the view. The water below shimmered in the afternoon light, gondolas drifting past as their gondoliers called out in melodic Italian. The faint sound of laughter and clinking glasses echoed from a nearby cafe. She gripped the wrought-iron railing, taking a deep breath. It smelled of briny water, aged stone, and something faintly floral.

Jamie dropped his bag on the bed and stretched. "Not a terrible place to stay, huh?"

"Not bad at all," she murmured, still mesmerized by the view.

He joined her on the balcony, leaning on the railing. "Alright, what's the game plan? Should we explore backstreets, enjoy cicchetti, or visit St. Mark's Square before it gets too crowded?"

She turned to him, excitement bubbling in her chest. "Let's just wander for a bit. I'll experience it completely, without a plan.

"Now you're thinking like a traveler."

After freshening up, they set off, winding through Venice's labyrinth of narrow streets and hidden passageways. As they walked, the stone paths, twisting and turning in unpredictable ways, led them past an array of tiny shops, some displaying handcrafted masks, others displaying delicate Murano glass, while still others overflowed with stacks of old books piled high in their store windows. Between the buildings, laundry moved gently in the breeze, while the captivating scent of garlic and fresh basil drifted on the air from a trattoria located close by. Every turn revealed something new. A hidden courtyard, a quiet canal, or a picturesque bridge.

They stopped at a small bacaro, where locals sipped wine

from tiny glasses. Jamie's order showcased the best of Venetian cuisine with a selection of cicchetti, small, flavorful tapas, comprising plates featuring the freshest marinated seafood, a decadent creamy baccalà, and perfectly crisp-fried polenta, creating a tantalizing spread.

Alex took a bite and sighed. "Okay, this is amazing."

He raised his glass in a toast. "To spontaneous adventures."

The dreamlike, floating city fostered a sense of limitless possibility.

He took a slow sip of his wine as he watched the way her eyes lit up as she savored the moment. "You're getting it," he said with a knowing smile.

She set her glass down and leaned back against the worn wooden bar. "Get what?"

"The magic of letting go. Focus on being present here rather than worrying about the future."

She stared at the canal's glittering reflection. He was right. Back home, she'd been so caught up in planning and fearing the unknown. The winding streets and the echoing laughter spilling from nearby alleyways created an atmosphere of unparalleled freedom for her. It was a feeling she had never known before.

They paid their tab and started strolling. The streets, now slightly less crowded, revealed the subtle sounds of the city: the quiet rhythm of water against stone, the distant, melancholic strains of an accordion carried on the breeze from a gondola gliding past, and the soft, indistinct chatter of residents enjoying their evening meals.

"Do you ever get lost here?" She asked as they crossed yet another narrow bridge.

"All the time," he said, grinning. "But that's part of the fun. The authentic way to experience Venice is to lose yourself in its captivating streets and canals. You have to allow yourself to wander without a set plan."

She let the idea sink in as they continued walking.

As they slowly made their way through the alleyways, passing numerous shuttered storefronts and quiet canals, they eventually arrived at their hotel.

Back in the quiet confines of their room, Alex was compelled to return to the balcony. She was drawn by the mesmerizing sight of the water below. It felt like a dream come true to be in the city she had always dreamed of visiting. The truth was it surpassed even her wildest imaginations.

Jamie leaned against the doorway, watching her. "Ready for more tomorrow?"

She turned to him with a serene look. "Absolutely."

The next morning, the city was alive with fresh energy. The distant toll of church bells echoed through the air as the smell of fresh bread and coffee drifted up from the streets below. They stopped for a breakfast of flaky cornetti and strong espresso to fuel themselves for another round of sightseeing.

They came across hidden courtyards with walls adorned with climbing ivy, and found themselves in small piazzas where locals were chatting among themselves while sipping their morning cappuccinos. They stopped so she could look at the artisan shops that were filled with delicate lace and hand-blown Murano glass. Then they continued on to another bridge. This one was to a bustling Rialto market, where vendors called out daily specials of fresh seafood, ripe produce, and fragrant spices.

Awestruck, Alex murmured, "Incredible!"

From one of the market stalls, Jamie selected a piece of fruit warmed by the sun and gave it to her. "Told you. There is always something new to discover in Venice around every corner.

As they continued walking, she seemed lighter than she had in years. No deadlines and no expectations. Street-by-street global exploration yields thrilling, fulfilling discoveries. As she walked, she suddenly stopped when a quaint and charming art shop immediately caught her eye. The window displayed hand-painted Venetian masks, each one a masterpiece of color and detail.

"Can we go in?" she asked, already stepping toward the door.

"Of course."

Inside, the shop was a treasure trove of creativity. Gently, Alex traced the delicate features of each mask, her fingers lightly gliding over the smooth surfaces. She was lost in wonder at the exquisite artistry and skill clear in their creation.

"These are incredible."

"They are," he agreed, as he snapped a quick photo of a particularly elaborate mask.

As they continued their walk, Jamie paused at a quiet spot by a canal. "Alright," he pulled out his camera. "Time for your first lesson."

"Lesson?" she raised an eyebrow.

"I'm going to show you how to see Venice through my lens," he handed her his camera.

"What if I break it?"

"You won't. Come on, trust me."

Although hesitant and unsure, she reluctantly lifted the camera to her eye, peering through the viewfinder with a mixture of apprehension and curiosity. He offered his help, guiding her hands and making a slight adjustment to the angle of her posture.

"See that gondola coming under the bridge?"

"Yeah."

Time your shot; press the shutter when it's perfectly framed in the arch.

As the gondola gracefully glided into the precise position, she held her breath, her heart pounding in her chest with a mixture of excitement and nervous anticipation. The camera softly clicked as she pressed the button, signaling that she had successfully taken the picture.

"Got it," she said, a hint of pride in her voice.

Jamie took the camera back and checked the photo. "Not bad for a first shot. You've got a good eye."

"Is that so?"

A genuine smile touched his lips as he uttered the word, "Really. You might have a hidden talent."

A blush crept up Alex's neck. "Thanks. It's kind of fun."

They spent the rest of the day wandering the city, with Jamie teaching her the basics of photography along the way. She learned about lighting, composition, and how to find beauty in unexpected places.

"It's not just about capturing images," he mentioned while taking a break. "It's about how you feel when you see it. That's what makes a picture special."

She nodded, taking in his words. Until this moment, she had never grasped the depth of his intense dedication to his work, but now, she understood the reasons behind it.

As the day turned to evening, they found themselves in St. Mark's Square. The golden light of the setting sun bathed the basilica, and a soft melody drifted from a nearby quartet playing for tourists.

"This is incredible," Alex said, her voice full of awe.

Jamie raised his camera. "I'll take your picture."

"Do I have a choice?" she teased.

"Not really," he grinned.

She posed awkwardly, and he laughed. "Relax. Just be yourself."

She let out a breath. He snapped the photo and then lowered the camera to show her.

"See? Perfect," he said.

Alex was surprised by how natural and happy she looked. "Venice might bring out my better side," she joked.

"You might view yourself through the world's eyes," he suggested.

Those words from him made her heart race.

As they returned to their hotel, a deep sense of contentment washed over her. Stepping outside her comfort zone proved to be a transformative experience, revealing a world of unparalleled beauty and vibrancy that surpassed all her expectations and dreams.

"Thank you," she blurted.

He looked at her. "For what?"

With a sweep of her hand towards the city, she said, "For this. For showing me what's out there. For helping me see things differently."

A warm smile spread across Jamie's face. "You're the one who took the leap. I just gave you a little nudge."

"I would say that it was more than a little nudge," she winked. "But it was you who did the rest. I'm proud of you."

As they crossed one last bridge, she looked at him with gratitude and something else she wasn't ready to name just yet. Lightness filled her heart; she was perfectly content to let Venice's charm and the thrill of new opportunities direct her path.

# Chapter 11

Alex awoke to the quiet hum of a motorboat passing their hotel as the sun rose. A momentary lapse in her awareness caused her to forget where she was, but the constant splashing of water against the canal walls served as a potent reminder that she was, indeed, enjoying the beauty of Italy. The whirlwind of emotions she had experienced in the past few days, combined with the effects of jet lag, meant her body was still struggling to adjust.

"Morning, sleepyhead," Jamie called from the small balcony.

She covered her head with the blanket. "What time is it?"

"Time to get moving," he replied. "We've got a lot to see today."

She peered from under the covers. "Define 'a lot.'"

He entered with a pair of espressos. "Spontaneity, Alex. That's the theme for today. No plans, no schedules, just going where the city takes us."

Sitting up, she rubbed her eyes. "You know, some people like itineraries. Structure. A heads-up about where they're going."

"And some people learn to let go."

She stretched, then swung her legs over the side of the bed. "I don't suppose you're going to tell me where we're headed?"

He shot her a playful grin. "Where's the fun in that?"

She sighed, but there was no real annoyance behind it. Despite herself, she was enjoying his spontaneous way of doing things. She got dressed quickly, and met him by the door.

"At least tell me if I need to wear walking shoes or if we're hopping on a gondola," she tried.

"Walking shoes. But trust me, it'll be worth it."

An hour later, they were weaving through Venice's labyrinthine streets. She was trailing behind him  as he navigated with an ease that frustrated her. He insisted she borrow one of his spare cameras so she could take her own pictures. She held onto it like it was precious metal and tried not to trip over the uneven cobblestones.

"So, where are we going first?" she asked as she struggled to keep pace.

"Wherever we end up."

"That's not an answer."

"It's the only answer that matters."

She tightened her grip on the camera strap. This was her first real foray into the unknown, and it was already testing her patience. As they continued their journey, their next stop was a little bakery. It was tucked away down a hidden alleyway that Jamie had unexpectedly stumbled upon and she was certain that it wasn't marked on any map. The smell of freshly baked pastries wafted through the air, and her stomach growled.

"This is what I mean by letting go," he pointed to a display case filled with flaky croissants and golden-brown biscotti. "You don't find places like this in guidebooks."

She skeptically eyed the pastries. "How do we know they're good?"

He paid for two croissants and handed one to her. "There's only one way to find out."

She hesitated before taking a bite. The buttery, flaky pastry practically melted in her mouth, and she couldn't help but moan softly.

"Good, right?"

"Okay, fine," she admitted and took another bite. "You win this round."

While they wandered, he paused repeatedly to capture

images she would have missed. The sun's rays illuminating a building, the fine carvings on a worn door, and the gentle waves created in the canal by a passing gondola.

"What are you looking for when you take pictures?" She asked as she watched him adjust the focus on his lens.

"Stories."

"Stories?"

"Yeah," he said and turned to her. "Every place, every person, every moment has a story. The key is to learn simply how to perceive it, and with practice, you will see it."

"I don't see any stories. Just tourists and buildings."

"Then you're not looking closely enough," he handed her the camera. "Try it."

She raised the camera, unsure of where to start. After a moment, she focused on a small flowerpot sitting on a windowsill. The vibrant red blooms stood out against the dull, peeling paint of the wall behind it. She snapped the photo and showed it to him.

"Not bad," he said. "What's the story?"

Alex blinked. "It's just a flowerpot."

"Is it, though?" he pressed. "Who put it there? Why? Maybe it's their way of brightening up a gloomy corner. Or it's a reminder of someone they lost. The point is, there's always more to see if you're willing to look deeper."

This time, she studied the image again with fresh eyes. "I never really thought about it like that," she admitted.

"That's the beauty of storytelling. Whether it's through words, photos, or anything else. It's not just about what's in front of you. It's about what it means."

She turned back to the street. She wanted to look for something else that might have a hidden story. A gondolier adjusted his hat as he waited for passengers. An elderly woman tossed breadcrumbs to a gathering of pigeons. A little boy tugged impatiently at his mother's hand as he pointed excitedly at a gelato stand. Lifting the camera again, she snapped another shot. This time it was of the boy's outstretched hand and how his face was filled  with anticipation.

Jamie peeked over her shoulder. "Now that tells a story."

She felt a spark inside her that she hadn't expected. Maybe there was more to photography than just taking pictures. Maybe it was another way to see the world and to capture the moments that made life feel alive.

She turned to Jamie with a newfound excitement in her eyes. "I think I want to keep doing this."

"Good," he said with a grin. "Because we've got an entire city left to capture."

"Okay. I'll admit, this whole 'go with the flow' thing isn't as terrible as I thought."

"High praise coming from you."

"I mean it. I've spent so much of my life planning every little detail, trying to control everything. This... this is different."

"It's freeing, isn't it?"

"Yeah," she said with a small smile. "It is."

That evening, they found themselves in a quiet piazza far from the bustling tourist spots. From a nearby cafe drifted the delicious scent of freshly baked pizza, complementing the hauntingly beautiful melody a street musician was producing on his violin; the two combined to create an enchanting and memorable atmosphere. With her camera resting gently in her lap, she settled onto the edge of the fountain, patiently waiting. "Do you ever get scared?" she asked suddenly.

"Scared of what?"

"Of not knowing what's next. Of things not going according to plan."

He thought about her question for a moment. "Not really. I mean, sure, uncertainty can be scary. But it's also where the magic happens. By releasing your desire to control every minute detail, you open the door to unexpected and amazing possibilities and incredible things you never could have imagined will unfold. Things that might just change your

FINDING MY WAY TO YOU

life."

"I'm not sure I'm built for that kind of life," she admitted.

"You'd be surprised," he said and smiled at her. "You're already doing it."

Later, as they made their way back to the hotel, she couldn't help but feel a shift within herself. The day was full of wrong turns and unexpected discoveries. Despite everything, it unexpectedly became one of the most rewarding and meaningful days that she had ever experienced. It was a day filled with profound personal satisfaction. As they crossed one last bridge, he stopped and pointed to the reflection of the city lights on the water below. "See that?"

She nodded.

"That's what letting go looks like," he said. "Beautiful, unpredictable, and completely worth it."

Alex shook her head with a small laugh, still catching her breath from their whirlwind day. The sky had deepened into a velvety twilight, showing how the city glows with a golden light that reflects off the canals

"So," she nudged his arm, "what's the plan for tomorrow? Or am I supposed to just keep embracing the unknown?"

Jamie smirked. "A little of both. But I'll give you this much. We're heading for Tuscany."

Her eyes widened. "Tuscany? As in rolling hills, vineyards, and those picture-perfect villages?"

"That's the one."

She let out a slow breath as excitement bubbled in her chest. "That's an idea I can certainly agree with and support."

"Good. Because we leave first thing in the morning."

Her mind raced ahead, already envisioning the thrilling and unexpected new adventure that awaited them. "Then I guess I better pack."

# Chapter 12

Stretching out before them in a seemingly endless expanse, the rolling hills of Tuscany revealed a captivating patchwork of fields. The golden hues contrasting beautifully with the vivid green of the vineyards that snaked through the landscape. They passed by rustic farmhouses, which added to the idyllic charm of the scenery. As they drove the rental car, Alex was taking in all the sights and sounds surrounding them. A gentle breeze wafted the sweet fragrance of wildflowers, mingled with the rich, earthy smell of sun baked soil that made her smile.

"This feels like a painting."

Jamie glanced at her with a grin. "Told you Tuscany was special. Wait until you taste the wine."

With a self-conscious tuck of a strand of hair behind her ear, she confessed her uncertainty about her enjoyment of wine, admitting, "I don't even know if I like wine."

"Trust me," he steered the car onto a dirt road leading to a vineyard. "By the end of today, you'll be a believer."

The car came to a stop in front of a charming villa surrounded by rows of grapevines. An elderly man in a straw hat warmly waved to them from a nearby table with several neatly arranged bottles of wine.

He cut the engine and grinned as he looked at Alex. "Ready for your crash course in Italian wine?"

Alex took in the picturesque view. "I guess there are worse places to learn."

They stepped out of the car, and she took a deep breath as the scent of earth and ripe grapes filled the air. The older gentleman approached them with a welcoming smile. Alex admired the way the sun and laughter had etched themselves into his face, leaving a roadmap of time and joy.

"Benvenuti! Welcome!" he said in his thick accent. "I am Marco. You are here to taste the best wine in Tuscany, si?"

Jamie clapped a hand on her shoulder. "She's a total beginner. We're relying on you to convert her."

He chuckled. "Ah, a challenge! Good, good. Come, sit. We start slow."

He led them to a rustic wooden table under the shade of an old olive tree. A few glasses and a platter of bread, cheese, and olives were already waiting for them. Marco poured a deep red wine into her glass. She lifted it uncertainly and sniffed it like the way she'd seen people do in movies.

"Don't think too much," he advised. "Just taste."

She took a small sip, letting the flavors settle on her tongue. It was rich, a little bold, but not nearly as harsh as she expected. She glanced at Jamie, who was watching her reaction closely.

"Well?" he prompted.

Alex set down her glass, a slow smile spreading across her lips. "I think I might actually like this."

Marco beamed. "Ah! I knew it. By the end of today, you will love it."

Jamie smirked. "Told you."

As the afternoon wore on, they continued their wine tasting, each sip revealing a unique narrative and previously unknown nuances. By the time the sun dipped low over the vineyard, she felt lighter. She was unsure if the overwhelming emotion she was feeling stemmed from the effects of the wine she had consumed or from the sheer beauty and significance of the moment itself.

She leaned back in her chair and watched as Jamie laughed with Marco over some joke in Italian she couldn't quite follow.

Marco walked over, poured another splash of deep ruby wine into her glass, and gestured for her to try it. "This one is special," he said with a knowing smile. "From my family's oldest vines. You taste history in this."

She lifted the glass and swirled the liquid slowly. "No pressure, huh?" she teased before taking a sip.

The taste was smoother. The rich and velvety flavors unfolded slowly and left a lingering warmth. She closed her eyes for a moment, letting it settle, and when she opened them, Jamie was watching her expectantly.

"Well?" he asked with a smirk.

She shook her head in amusement. "Okay. I might be a wine person after all."

Jamie raised his glass. "To discovering new things."

Alex clinked her glass against his. "To stepping out of comfort zones."

The meal Marco had prepared had been nothing short of incredible. It was homemade pasta, fresh bread, and local cheeses. A feeling of fullness washed over her. It wasn't just the delicious food and fine wine, but the profoundly moving experience itself that left her feeling so completely satisfied.

"You were right about everything," she admitted as she carefully placed her glass on the table.

Jamie grinned. "I like the sound of that. You should say it more often."

She rolled her eyes but couldn't hide her smile. "Don't push your luck."

Marco returned to the table with a small plate of biscotti. With the words "You absolutely must try a little vin santo," he poured each of them a glass of the sweet dessert wine.

Selecting a piece of crunchy biscuit, Alex carefully dipped it into the glistening amber liquid before taking a sizable bite. The dessert was perfectly balanced and elicited a small, contented sigh from her.

"It's been a long time since I felt this happy," she admitted.

Jamie looked at her. "If you had told me a few hours ago that you weren't sure if you liked wine, I never would have believed you'd be enjoying it so much now."

"I know! Turns out, I just hadn't been drinking the good stuff."

With the meal ending, the sun set painted the vineyard with a warm, golden light as the day transitioned into dusk. Jamie stood up, stretched out his limbs, and then looked over at her. "Come on, let's walk."

Moving at a leisurely pace, they strolled through the rows of vines, their footsteps barely disturbing the quiet of the vineyard. As she trailed her fingers along the leaves, she delighted in the sensation of their rough texture against her skin.

"Are you always on the go?" she asked.

"Not really. There's too much to see and too many stories out there waiting to be told."

"I don't think I've ever been like that. I've always been... cautious. Afraid of making the wrong choice, I guess."

Jamie stopped walking and turned to her. "What's the worst that could happen?"

She laughed bitterly. "Failure. Disappointment. Losing everything."

"And what's the best that could happen?"

As her eyes met his, she began to respond, but was unable to say a word. She had spent so much time focusing on the worst-case scenarios: *what if she failed, what if she regretted it, what if she wasn't good enough?* that she didn't even allow herself to think about the best. She hadn't let herself dream that far. He didn't push her for a response. Instead, he simply smiled and started walking again.

While they continued their walk, she couldn't help but steal glances at him. His journey through life was marked by remarkable ease and a striking lack of fear in the face of uncertainty and the unknown. She envied that quality in him; however, as time went on, a slow dawning realization allowed her to understand its true significance and meaning. With the sun dipping below the horizon, she mustered the courage to open to him as they relaxed together on the blanket Marco had generously lent them for their sunset viewing.

"When I was in college," she began, "I thought I had everything figured out. I had dreams of a future career as a big-time graphic designer in a top agency in a dynamic city such as New York or Los Angeles."

He gave a small nod of encouragement, silently urged her to go on with whatever she was talking about.

"But then life happened. Because my dad unexpectedly fell ill and needed to be hospitalized, I made the tough decision to move back home to provide support and care. After he got discharged, I just... stayed. While I could find a job that paid my bills, it wasn't fulfilling and didn't reflect my ideal career path. And then I met Ryan."

His jaw tightened at the mention of her ex, but he said nothing.

"For a while, I thought maybe he was my purpose," she admitted. "But looking back, I think I was scared. Scared to go after what I really wanted, scared to take risks. It was easier to settle."

Jamie reached out and covered her hand with his. "You're not settling anymore."

She looked up at him. "I'm trying not to feel that way. But it's hard to shake the fear."

He spoke gently. "Fear's always going to be there. The trick is not letting it control you."

The night sky mirrored the conflicting emotions stirring within her. The feeling of profound vulnerability mingled with an equally potent sense of strength, created a unique and powerful inner experience. Sharing her story with him felt like shedding a heavy coat she'd been wearing for years.

She quietly said, "Thank you."

"Why?" he asked.

"For listening. Thank you for just being yourself.

"Anytime. And for the record, I think you're a lot braver

than you give yourself credit for."

Alex looked at him. She felt a delightful aching in her heart; his eyes held such warmth that it was almost painful, but in the most wonderful way.

# Chapter 13

As the next morning began, there was a sense of exciting promise and potential in the air. The sun's golden light illuminated the Tuscan landscape as it majestically rose above the hills, creating a stunning display of color across the vineyards below. With a steaming cup of coffee in hand, Alex stood on the balcony of their charming little villa, observing the gradual awakening of the world around them as the sun rose. The tranquil setting felt almost too perfect. Almost like a dream she was afraid to wake from. Jamie had gone out early to scout locations for his next photoshoot, leaving her with a note on the counter: *Be ready by 10. We're heading to a market I think you'll love.*

She smiled at the thought. He had a knack for finding hidden gems, and she was excited to see what he had planned for the day. When he finally came back, though, a sense of disquiet settled upon her, making her realize that something wasn't quite right. He entered the room with an expression that wasn't there earlier. To her, it was a clear sign that something was wrong. He set his camera bag down a little too carefully, as if his mind were elsewhere. "Everything okay?" she asked.

Jamie hesitated for a second too long. "Yeah. Just... ran into something unexpected."

"Something or someone?"

A subtle, almost imperceptible smile played on his lips, but it failed to extend to his eyes, which remained serious and unsmiling, hinting at a hidden emotion. "Someone. An old friend, I guess you could say."

"Guess?"

"It's nothing to worry about. Just someone I didn't expect to see here." He glanced at the clock and forced a grin. "But forget about that. You ready for the market?"

She felt a powerful urge to press him for answers, to find out not only who had caused him such grief, but also precisely what had so deeply upset him. How he shied away from her eyes, told her: he was not yet ready to engage in a conversation about it. So instead, she nodded slowly. "Yeah. Let's go."

As they stepped outside, the streets of Tuscany felt a little different, still beautiful, still full of life, but now carrying an unspoken tension between them.

"Yeah, just a lot on my mind," Jamie said in a clipped tone. He started fiddling with his camera and adjusting the settings without looking up.

"Are you sure? You seem… off."

"It's nothing. Let's just get going."

They drove to the market in silence. His focus on the road prevented her from reading his expression, despite her best efforts. As they parked near the bustling market square, she hesitated before stepping out of the car. She wasn't used to this closed off and distant version of Jamie. It unsettled her.

When they arrived, the market was bustling with life. Stalls overflowed with fresh produce, handmade crafts, and colorful flowers. Baked bread and roasted chestnuts filled the air with their aroma. Normally, Jamie would point things out, crack jokes, or convince her to try something new. But now, he barely spoke.

As she was walking, she paused at a stall where many scarves were being sold, each one woven with an intricate and beautiful design. From the many items she held one up, that were noticeably different and more striking than the rest. A vibrant pattern of blue and gold immediately caught her eye, and the way the colors danced and shimmered as the sunlight played upon them mesmerized her.

"Look at this."

He barely glanced at it. "Nice."

She dropped the scarf back onto the pile. "Okay, what's going on? Did I do something?"

He looked clearly frustrated. "It's not you, Alex. I just... I'm dealing with something, and I don't know how to talk about it."

"Then try. Because whatever it is, it's throwing your mood off."

Jamie scanned the busy market as if looking for an escape. Finally, he said, "This trip, it's supposed to be about finding stories and capturing moments. But I feel like I've lost focus. Like I'm just... drifting."

"You? Lost focus? That doesn't sound like you at all."

"I know. It's stupid but seeing you... seeing how much this is all new to you, it's making me question if I've been doing this for the right reasons. Have I been chasing experiences, or running away from something?"

"That's not stupid. Everyone questions their path at some point. It's human."

"Yeah, but what if I don't like the answer?"

Alex studied him for a moment. She watched the way his fingers twitched at his side and the way his usual calm confidence seemed to waver. It was strange to see him uncertain and vulnerable.

"Then maybe it just means you're ready for something different."

"And what about you? Do you ever wonder if you're on the right path?"

"Every day. But I think that's the point, isn't it? To keep figuring it out as you go."

"You're a lot braver than you give yourself credit for."

"I learned from the best," she teased and nudged him playfully.

His fingers tightened around her hand, a subtle gesture that quickly vanished as he released her. "Come on," he motioned toward a vendor selling fresh figs and honey. "Let's get something sweet. We could both use it."

As they wandered deeper into the market, the tension between them eased, but Alex knew the conversation wasn't over. Something had shifted. Whether it was in Jamie, in herself, or in whatever they were to each other. She wasn't sure yet, but she had a feeling they were both about to find out.

When they reached a quiet corner of the market, she couldn't hold it in any longer. "If you're second-guessing everything, where does that leave me? Am I just... part of the mess?"

He stopped in his tracks. "No. You're not a mess. You're... the opposite. You're grounding me in a way I didn't expect."

"Then why does it feel like you're pushing me away?" she asked.

"Because I don't want to hold you back," he admitted. "You're just figuring out what you want, and I'm scared that if you stay too close to me, you'll get stuck."

She felt a mix of hurt and anger rising within her. "You don't get to decide what's best for me. That's my choice."

"I know. But I've seen it happen before. People lose themselves trying to follow someone else's path. I don't want that for you."

The rest of the day passed in a haze. They walked through the market in near silence. By the time they returned to the villa, she felt emotionally drained.

As she sat on the balcony that evening, he joined her with two glasses of wine in hand.

"I'm sorry," he set one glass in front of her. "Please know that I would never intentionally make you feel like an outsider. That's the last thing I want."

She looked at him. "I just want to understand. Let me know if you're struggling. Don't shut me out."

"I've always been a loner. It's easier that way. Less risk, less chance of hurting someone. But you... you make me want to try. And that terrifies me."

Her heart softened at his vulnerability. "You don't have to do this alone. Whatever you're feeling, we can figure it out together. But you must let me in."

He was lost in thought, before offering a response. He then extended his hand, his fingers closing around hers, a tender gesture connecting them. "Okay. I'll try."

While sitting together and observing the sun's last rays gently fading from view, a sense of relief washed over her as she felt the atmosphere between them become more relaxed.

# Chapter 14

Alex awoke to the soft melody of morning life stirring beyond the villa's sun-warmed stone walls. Dappled light danced across the terra-cotta floor, while birds sang from the olive trees just outside. The gentle hum of the countryside was broken only by the rich, earthy aroma of freshly brewed espresso drifting in from the kitchen.

Jamie was already gone. He'd mentioned something the night before about catching the golden light along the Tuscan hills. Probably halfway up a vineyard path by now, camera slung over his shoulder, chasing that one perfect shot. She sipped her coffee and glanced out toward the open balcony doors.

Today seemed different. The air felt lighter, as if some unseen weight had been lifted. Not entirely gone, but softened at the edges. There was a stillness to the morning, but not the kind that ached. This one hummed with quiet possibility. Her thoughts drifted back to the night before.

The way his voice had softened when he spoke about his fears. The pause before she let her own walls down. How their confessions had come not with dramatics, but in small, unguarded moments. His fingers tracing circles along her arm as he listened and her head resting against his chest as she spoke. It wasn't something she remembered from her last relationship.

No matter how deeply she dug, she couldn't recall that kind of safety or that emotional ease. Back then, vulnerability had felt like a risk she had to beg for, a door that only opened when it was convenient. But last night? Last night had been different.

There was something in the way they had looked at each other. Not as people trying to fix or impress or protect, but as two souls simply choosing to see. And in that quiet honesty, she had felt more herself than she had in a long time. She smiled to herself. Not wide or showy, but the kind that came from somewhere deep, somewhere rediscovered.

His words about following stories and capturing moments lingered in her mind. He didn't just photograph what he saw, he *felt* it. Lived it. And in doing so, he made it impossible not to feel it, too. That kind of passion was magnetic. It stirred something in her she hadn't felt in a very long time. A restlessness that curled in her chest, asking *Why not you?*

Fresh from the shower, she wandered to the kitchenette, devoured a croissant and a few slices of blood orange, and was halfway through pouring another cup of coffee when she saw it: her sketchbook lying untouched on the corner of the desk.

She blinked at it. The cover was slightly warped from travel, the edges dog-eared from years of use. She'd brought it out of habit, the same way someone might bring an old favorite sweater on a trip, even if they knew the weather wouldn't call for it. But the pages inside, every single one, were blank. She stared at it for a moment, biting her lip, caught in the quiet war between doubt and desire. Then she reached for it.

By the time she stepped out onto the sun-drenched balcony, the late-morning light had softened into something golden and forgiving. The breeze carried the scent of lavender and rosemary, the distant hum of cicadas blending with the occasional clatter of voices from the village below.

She set the sketchbook down on the small iron table and placed her charcoal pencils beside it. The view before her was a masterpiece in itself. Rolling hills quilted with vineyards, rows of cypress trees stretching toward a cerulean sky, and terracotta rooftops glowing in the sun's embrace. And yet, the page remained blank. She sat, fingers grazing the paper, pausing just before they committed to the page.

This wasn't about drawing the hills. It wasn't even about proving something to herself. It was about answering the quiet voice inside her that whispered, *Create. Begin again. Let something move through you.*

"Just start," she whispered to herself.

It was harder than she thought. The stark whiteness of the paper felt like a challenge. It dared her to create something meaningful. Suddenly, a torrent of memories from her early days as a graphic designer overwhelmed her, bringing the past alive. The excitement of seeing concepts become tangible creations and the overwhelming pride that followed upon the completion of her work were intensely satisfying emotions. But over time, that excitement had faded under the weight of deadlines, uninspired projects, and a boss who dismissed her creativity. She took a deep breath and closed her eyes.

As soon as she opened them, her eyes fell upon her sketchbook and she sketched, her mind already filled with images. At first, her strokes were simple lines to outline the villa's balcony railing. But as she continued to work, her confidence grew. The hills rolled into view on the page and the sunlit vineyard came to life in shades of shadow and light. Time seemed to fly by as the hours slipped away unnoticed in a flurry of activity. As she moved her pencil, she became consumed in the creative process, the rhythmic motion of her hand creating something beautiful from an initially empty space. When Jamie returned, she didn't notice at first.

"Hey," he murmured, his body relaxed as he leaned casually against the balcony door.

The sudden noise completely startled her. Her cheeks flushed. A nervous smile touched her lips as she looked up at him. "Oh, I didn't hear you come in."

Jamie looked at her sketch. "Wow. That's... incredible."

She looked down at the half-finished drawing. "It's nothing, really. Just a sketch."

"Don't do that," he crouched beside her. "Don't downplay

it. This is amazing."

Their eyes met. She was surprised by his gaze. "You really think so?"

"I don't just think so. I know so." He pointed at the page. "Look at how you captured the light on the hills. It's so alive."

"Thanks. I guess it's been a while since I've drawn anything just for me."

They moved inside as the afternoon heat intensified. She brought her sketchbook with her and flipped through the blank pages as they sat at the kitchen table.

Having poured glasses of water for them, Jamie then leaned back in his chair, taking a moment to rest. "So, what made you pick it up again?"

She hesitated. "Honestly? You."

"Me?" He raised an eyebrow.

"Yeah." Alex tapped the edge of the sketchbook with her pencil. "Watching you work, seeing how passionate you are about what you do. It reminded me of how much I used to love this."

"That's the thing about passion. Once you find it, it's hard to let it go, even if it gets buried for a while."

"I think I let myself get stuck for so long because I feared failing. It was easier to settle for something safe."

"But you're not settling anymore. You're here. You're doing it. And for what it's worth, I think you're insanely talented."

"Thank you," she said, blushing.

They devoted the rest of the afternoon to a kind of quiet magic. A shared exploration that asked for nothing more than presence. The villa itself, with its weathered stone archways and ivy-cloaked corners, seemed to breathe history, while the gardens beyond unfurled in wild bursts of rosemary, lavender, and poppies.

She moved with her sketchbook pressed to her chest, pausing often to crouch by a fountain or lean against a sun-warmed wall. Jamie trailed beside her, sometimes ahead, camera in hand, his expression focused and thoughtful. He knelt to capture the curve of an iron gate overgrown with jasmine, or the way the light caught in the petals of a climbing rose. They didn't speak often. They didn't need to. Their art was the language, and the silence between them was full of meaning.

At one point, they wandered beyond the trimmed paths and into the wilder edges of the estate, where the gardens gave way to groves of olive trees that had stood for centuries. They stopped beneath a wide, ancient olive tree. She settled on a low stone wall nearby, sketchbook open across her lap. Jamie sank into the grass beside her, stretching his legs and tilting his face to the sky, camera resting on his chest like it had grown heavy from the day.

"Let me see," he said.

For a moment, she paused, a flicker of uncertainty in her eyes, before she showed it to him. It was a rough sketch of the landscape in front of them. A scene of idyllic beauty presented itself: gently rolling hills softened the landscape, a vineyard sat quietly in the distance, and a dirt path, twisting and turning, meandered back towards the inviting villa. But there, in an inconspicuous corner, almost invisible to the casual observer, someone sat beneath the branches of an olive tree, camera in hand, waiting for the perfect moment.

"Is that me?"

"Maybe."

He studied it for a moment longer before nodding. "You've got a good eye."

She smirked. "Coming from you, that's high praise."

"You ever think about doing this full-time?" he gestured to her sketchbook.

She traced the edge of the page with her thumb. "I might. The thought of freelancing used to terrify me, but now... I don't know. It seems increasingly likely."

"You should go for it. You've got something special."

The certainty surprised her in his voice. "You really

think so?"

"I know so. And hey, worst-case scenario, you become a traveling artist, sketching in cafes, and trading drawings for food."

She laughed. "That's your backup plan, not mine."

"Fair enough," he said with a grin. Then, before she could stop him, he lifted his camera and clicked the shutter, capturing her mid-laugh, eyes lit with something she hadn't felt in ages; freedom.

"Hey!" she reached over and nudged him, trying to snatch the camera.

He pulled it just out of reach, laughing. "Just capturing the moment. You'll thank me later."

She rolled her eyes, but her smile betrayed her. "You're impossible."

"And yet, here you are," he teased.

Later, as the sky melted into gold and violet, they returned to the villa. A quiet comfort wrapped around them like a blanket. It was the easy closeness of two people who had shared something unnamed but real. As the sun set, she sat by the window, finishing the sketch she'd started that morning. Jamie was beside her, scrolling through the photos he'd taken.

"This feels good," she said after a while.

Jamie looked up. "What does?"

"This." she pointed to her sketchbook and the photos on his camera. "Creating something just because I want to. No deadlines, no pressure. Just... passion."

"Yeah. It's easy to forget why we started when we got caught up in everything else."

Alex glanced at him. "Is that what happened to you?"

"Maybe. Somewhere along the way, it became about the next big trip or the next project. I was always chasing something, but I don't know if I ever stopped to ask myself why."

She studied him for a moment, then turned her sketchbook around so he could see. The drawing had evolved throughout the day. What started as a simple landscape was now filled with details she hadn't initially planned. The texture of the olive tree's bark, the folds of his shirt as he leaned back against it, and the way the sunlight filtered through the leaves.

"That's beautiful."

She shrugged. "It just… happened. I didn't overthink it."

He tapped the edge of the page. "That's exactly it. That is the type of work which has a significant and lasting impact. It is the kind of work that makes a difference in the world. The kind that just happens."

"Then maybe that's what I need to focus on. Not what's safe or expected, but what just feels right."

Jamie grinned. "Sounds like a plan to me."

# Chapter 15

In the villa's kitchen, the overhead lights cast a soft, golden glow, bathing the space in a warm and welcoming hush. While Jamie moved about quietly brewing a pot of tea, Alex sat at the small wooden table, immersed in the quiet rhythm of her sketching. Outside, the gentle chorus of crickets drifted in through the open window, layering the evening with a soothing soundtrack.

Jamie placed a steaming mug beside her sketchbook with a careful touch, then slid into the chair across from her.

"Still sketching that same view?" he asked, a smile tugging at his lips.

"It's hard not to. There's something about this place that has a timeless quality.

"That's what makes Tuscany, Tuscany. You are really getting back into the swing of things, is that right?"

She set her pencil down and wrapped her hands around the mug. "Yeah. I forgot how much I missed it. In a way, you've been the driving force behind this."

"Me?"

"Yeah. Watching how passionate you are about photography, how much you put into every shot, it's inspiring."

"Funny you say that. I wasn't always this way about photography."

"What do you mean?"

He paused. "It's a bit of a story."

"I've got time."

"I guess it started when I was a kid. My dad was an incredible photojournalist. He traveled all over the world, covering stories that mattered. Wars, natural disasters, moments of joy and resilience... he captured it all."

"Wow," she said. "That sounds amazing."

"It was. But it also meant he was gone a lot. I didn't understand then. I just knew he'd leave for weeks, sometimes months, and come back with these incredible photos. He'd show me the world through his lens, and for a while, it felt like I was there with him."

Alex could see the mix of admiration and sadness in his expression. "That must have been hard, though. Having him away so much."

"It was. But the thing is, when he was home, he'd tell me the stories behind the pictures. Not just what was in the frame, but everything outside of it. The people he met, the challenges he faced, and the moments that didn't make it into film. Those stories... they stuck with me."

He traced his fingers around the edge of his mug. "My dad covered a Middle East conflict when I was seventeen. It was supposed to be a quick assignment, but... he didn't come back."

"Oh, Jamie. I'm so sorry."

"Thanks. It was hard losing him. But after he passed, I found his old camera gear. I knew little about photography then, but holding his camera... it felt like I was holding a piece of him."

"Is that when you started taking photos?"

"Yeah. At first, it was just a way to connect to him and a way to keep his memory alive. I'd take the camera out and shoot whatever caught my eye: trees, birds, the kids playing soccer at the park. I didn't really know what I was doing, but it felt good. Like I was seeing the world the way he did."

The hard lines of his face softened,p and his voice dropped into something more intimate. "But over time, it became more than that. I started noticing things I hadn't before. The way light changes everything, the mood in a shadow, the way people's faces tell stories when they're not looking. I realized photography isn't just about freezing a moment. It's about feeling it. It's about connection."

He looked at her then with an earnest expression. "My dad used his camera to show the world what mattered to him. I guess I wanted to do the same."

She was quiet for a moment. "That's beautiful. It sounds like you're carrying on his legacy, continuing his work and honoring his memory."

"Maybe," he said with a hint of sadness in his eyes. "But it's not just about him anymore. Somewhere along the way, photography became my way of making sense of the world. It's how I process things and how I connect with people. Each time I take a picture, I'm pouring a little piece of my heart, my energy, and my essence into it."

"I've always seen you as this free-spirited adventurer, chasing beauty and excitement. But hearing this... it makes what you do so much more meaningful."

"It's not always easy, though. Sometimes I wonder if I'm doing enough if my work really matters. But then I remember why I started, and it keeps me going."

"It matters. It really does. You have this incredible gift of seeing the world in a way most people don't. And that you share this, this generosity. It's something unique and heartwarming."

"Thanks. That means a lot."

A heavy silence settled between them, thick with the unspoken emotions of Jamie's story, as they sat for a while. Finally, Alex broke the silence.

"You know," she said, her eyes sparkling with playful curiosity, "I think you should teach me how to use a camera. I've been wanting to try photography."

"You? A photographer? I thought you were a sketchbook kind of girl."

"Who says I can't be both?" she shot back, grinning.

He shook his head, still chuckling. "Alright, deal. But only if you promise to teach me how to draw."

"You? Drawing? This I've got to see."

"Hey, don't underestimate me," he said, feigning offense.

"Alright, deal," she held out her hand for him to shake.

Jamie took her hand. "Deal."

As the night continued , their conversation unfolded with an easy, quiet intimacy. They shared their passions, dreams, and the winding paths that had led them here, to this villa tucked in the Tuscan hills, and to each other.

For Alex, it felt as though something inside her had shifted. As he spoke, she began to see him in a new light. Not just the confident photographer with a quick smile and a curious eye, but a man shaped by loss, driven by love, and deeply attuned to the beauty in small things.

And in turn, she felt herself opening too. The walls she hadn't even realized she'd built began to soften. It was as if a door had quietly creaked open within her, revealing not just more of Jamie, but more of herself. Who she had been. Who she was becoming. The space between those two selves no longer felt like a chasm, but a bridge. A path forward.

A warmth bloomed in her chest that was steady and full of promise.

"You've been doing this for years," she said. "Traveling, documenting, always moving. Do you ever consider stopping?"

"Sometimes. But then I wonder. If I stop, would I still be me?" He looked at her with a small smile. "What about you? Do you think you'll settle somewhere?"

"I once believed I needed stability to be happy. A steady job and a predictable future. But now? I don't know. Perhaps happiness is… movement. Change."

"Spoken like a true traveler."

She nudged his arm playfully. "Don't get ahead of yourself. I still have a lot to learn."

"Then it's a good thing we're going to Rome next," Jamie said.

Alex's eyes lit up. "Rome? Seriously?"

"Yes. And you'll get to meet my mentor."

"Your mentor? The one who got you into photography?"

Jamie nodded. "Yeah. Marco introduced us years ago, but he's the one who really pushed me to take this seriously. He's in Rome for a few weeks, so I figured it'd be a good chance for you to meet him."

Alex grinned. "That sounds amazing. And after that?"

"After that, we're playing full-on tourists. The Colosseum, the Trevi Fountain, and perhaps the Vatican if we have the energy.

Alex laughed. "I can't believe I'm actually going to see all of that."

"Well, believe it. Tomorrow, we take on Rome."

A thrill fluttered in Alex's chest as she pictured the upcoming adventure. For so long, the fear of change had been a heavy cloak, stifling her spirit. But now she was saying yes. And it was amazing. Eventually, exhaustion tugged Alex's eyelids, but the anticipation of the next day kept her buzzing with energy.

"Alright," Jamie said, standing and stretching. "We should probably get some sleep. Big day tomorrow."

Alex nodded, standing as well. "Yeah. Rome waits for no one."

Jamie grinned. "Exactly."

As they parted for the night, Alex couldn't help but smile. A sense of boundless possibility filled her as she prepared to meet whatever the world held.

# Chapter 16

As the train to Rome glided smoothly along the tracks, the Italian countryside unfurled outside the window in a blur of golden morning light. Fields of sunflowers danced in the breeze, their bright faces turned toward the sun, while distant mountains loomed like hazy purple silhouettes on the horizon.

Alex leaned her forehead against the cool glass, watching as vineyards and gentle hills slowly gave way to the hazy sprawl of the city. The fresh, earthy scent of grapes was gradually replaced by the faint tang of exhaust as they neared the outskirts. Across from her, Jamie sat with his camera in hand, snapping candid shots of their journey: blurred landscapes, quiet moments, the way the light caught in her hair.

"You're going to love it," he said, lowering the camera with a smile. "Rome has this... energy. It's chaotic and beautiful all at once."

She smiled, her heart already quickening with anticipation.

"I still can't believe I'm here."

The moment they stepped into Roma Termini, the world seemed to erupt around them; rushing footsteps, the hum of rolling suitcases, the joyful clamor of a street musician playing a lively tune on his accordion. The air was thick with the aroma of strong espresso and buttery pastries, creating a heady blend that tugged at the senses and stirred the soul.

Outside, the city greeted them in all its chaotic splendor. Warm sunlight spilled across the uneven cobblestones as they made their way through the crowd. Their footsteps echoed faintly against the ancient stone, grounding them in the rhythm of the city's heartbeat.

Jamie came to a sudden stop and reached instinctively for his camera. His eyes lit up as he framed the scene ahead.

"Alright," he grinned, raising the lens toward the towering silhouette in the distance. "First shot of the day."

The Colosseum stood proud and timeless against the Roman sky. The weathered arches glowed in the late-morning light. Alex watched as Jamie snapped the photo. He had a look of awe across his face.

She smiled as well. Rome had barely begun to reveal itself, and it was working its magic. She pulled out her own phone. "I'm taking one too. You're not the only one who gets to capture this moment."

The city thrummed with life as they wandered. The energy was electric, chaotic, and endlessly captivating. The scent of sizzling street food mingled with the sharp tang of exhaust, creating a blend that was uniquely, unmistakably Rome.

Their fingers stayed busy, snapping photo after photo as they wove through narrow alleys and sprawling piazzas. Each frame told a different story: sun-drenched courtyards where children's laughter rang out like music; walls adorned with vibrant street art, bold and alive with movement; towering ancient columns, their stone worn smooth by centuries, standing like silent witnesses to history.

At one point, they paused beneath the shadow of an old cathedral as the light spilled through cracks in the buildings like liquid gold. Jamie lowered his camera and looked at her with mischief.

"Here," he said, holding it out to her. "Your turn."

Alex blinked, surprised. "Me?"

"You've got an artist's eye," he said, slipping the strap over her neck. "I've seen your sketches. Now show me how you see the world through this."

She hesitated, fingers curling around the camera's body, feeling the weight of it. Then she looked up, scanned the square around them, and raised it to her eye. She focused on an old man scattering seeds in gentle arcs to a gathering flock of pigeons near the base of the majestic Pantheon. The birds fluttered and cooed around him. The soft rustle of their wings blended with the murmur of nearby tourists and the occasional ringing of a distant bicycle bell.

It was an easily missed moment in the rush of the city, but something about it struck her deeply. The patience in his gesture. The stillness among the noise. The way he seemed to belong there, as if he'd been part of the square for centuries. She held her breath and clicked the shutter, capturing it just as a few pigeons took flight, their wings framing the old man like brushstrokes on a canvas.

Jamie glanced over, watching her lower the camera with a subtle smile on her lips.

"That," he said softly, "was perfect."

She didn't look at him right away. Her eyes lingered on the scene she'd just preserved.

"It felt like it," she whispered, surprised by the warmth rushing through her."It's not just about the shot. It's about the moment."

He nudged her playfully. "You get it. Now you're sounding like me."

As they continued through the streets of Rome, she felt lighter than she had in months. She immersed herself in the rhythm of discovery. At a street vendor's cart, he bought them both gelato and handed her a cone piled high with pistachio and stracciatella. "Fuel for more exploring," he said with a wink.

They wandered through Piazza Navona. The square buzzed with street performers playing soft melodies on violins, children chasing bubbles that shimmered like glass, and the rich scent of espresso mingling with fresh paint.

Dozens of artists lined the edges of the piazza with their easels depicting different styles.. Cityscapes in bold hues, caricatures drawn in minutes, and quiet, soulful portraits of tourists and locals alike. Each work captured not just the likeness of the place, but its energy.

Alex paused in front of one artist in particular, drawn in by the fluidity of his brush. He was painting a young couple seated on a nearby bench. Their bodies were close but not touching. With practiced ease, the artist's strokes traced the lines of their posture, the soft angle of her head rested near his shoulder, and the way their fingers nearly brushed.

She stood in quiet fascination as she watched the intimacy unfold on canvas. There was something raw and beautiful about how quickly the moment was captured. No filters, no hesitation, just instinct and emotion. Her hand moved almost unconsciously to the strap of her bag, where her sketchbook lay tucked inside.

Jamie snapped a quick picture of her as she observed. "Caught you in your element."

A grin spread across her face, though her eyes rolled in mock exasperation. "Maybe I should start charging you for all these photos of me."

"I'd go broke," he said with a laugh.

As they turned onto the quieter street, the city's clamor faded and was replaced by the sweet melody of a violin. He slowed down and nodded toward a  cafe with a few tables outside.

"This is it," he said. "Mark's favorite spot."

Inside, the café wrapped around them like a comforting embrace. The faint aroma of roasted coffee beans weaved through the air. The low hum of conversation mingled with the occasional hiss of the espresso machine, created a cozy rhythm that made the world outside feel miles away.

Jamie led her toward a small table tucked in the corner, where an older man with a neatly trimmed gray beard and kind eyes sat cradling a steaming mug.

"Mark!" Jamie called out.

The man looked up with a bright expression. "Jamie, you troublemaker!" he stood to embrace him.

They exchanged a hearty hug before he turned to Alex. "Mark, this is Alex. Alex, meet Mark, my mentor and one of the wisest people I know."

Mark extended a hand. "It's a pleasure to meet you. He's told me quite a bit about you."

"All good things, I hope."

"Of course," he said with a chuckle. "Though he mentioned you're on a bit of a journey right now. Finding your footing in the world?"

She felt, a little exposed yet curious about what else Jamie told him. She was curious about what Mark might say, wondering if his words would be kind or critical.

"Come, sit," he gestured to the chairs. "Let's talk."

They settled into their seats and made their orders. Once their drinks arrived, Mark turned to her.

"So, Alex," he began. "Tell me about yourself. What's brought you to this crossroads?"

She was unsure of how much to tell about the whirlwind of emotions and decisions that had led her here. "For years, I've been doing what I thought I was supposed to do: college, a steady job, a long-term relationship. But none of it made me happy. It all seemed... empty."

"That's not uncommon. Society has a way of setting expectations for us, but those expectations don't always align with who we are. And when we try to fit ourselves into a mold that doesn't suit us, the pressure can seem like a vise around our chests.

"That's exactly it," Alex exclaimed with newfound understanding. "I've always loved drawing and painting, but I put it aside because it didn't seem practical. And now, I'm trying to find my way back to it, but I'm scared I've waited too long, or that I'm not good enough."

"Do you know why you're afraid?" he asked.

"Because... I might fail. Because people might not like what I create?"

"Those are surface fears. Dig deeper. What are you really

afraid of?"

She stared at him. "I think… I'm afraid of putting myself out there. Of being vulnerable. If I fail at something I care about so deeply, it'll seem like I've failed as a person."

"Ah, vulnerability. It's one of the greatest challenges we face as creators. But here's the thing: vulnerability is also your greatest strength. When you create from a place of authenticity, when you allow yourself to be seen, that's when your work resonates the most."

Jamie chimed in. "That's what I've always admired about Mark's work. He doesn't just take pictures. He captures emotions and connections. And that's what makes it special."

Mark smiled. "He's right. Technical skills matter, sure, but it's the heart you put into your work that makes it memorable. People aren't just looking for pretty pictures or well-executed drawings. They're looking for pieces of you, your perspective, your truth."

"But what if my truth isn't… enough?" she asked quietly.

"It is enough. The simple fact that it belongs to you gives it immeasurable worth. No one else can see the world the way you do, and that uniqueness is your gift. The key is to trust it."

"That's easier said than done."

"Is it, though? You've already done it. You've stepped out of your comfort zone by traveling, taking pictures, and sketching. Every time you create something, you're trusting yourself a little more."

"What if I take that leap of faith, only to discover that it leads to the same emptiness that I feel now?"

"Then you keep searching. You keep creating. But you don't stop just because the answer isn't immediate."

"I spent years failing to meet expectations. The perfect student, always prepared and top of her class; the reliable employee, never missing a deadline; the steady girlfriend, always supportive and understanding. I kept thinking that if I just stuck it out a little longer, things would click into place. But they never did."

"So, what changed?"

"I did. Or at least, I started to. The first trip to New York made me realize how small my world had been. I don't want to go back to that. I don't want to spend my life waiting for happiness to find me."

"That's a hell of a realization. And now?"

"I want to discover my passions. I want to create, to take risks, to stop second-guessing every step I take."

"Then you're already on the right path."

They continued talking for another hour. Their conversations danced between practical tips about lighting and shutter speed to the occasional philosophical question. It was a blend of the mundane and the profound. Mark also shared stories from his early days behind the camera.

He spoke of the sting of a critique that almost ended it all. A gallery owner who told him his work was technically fine but soulless. "Cut deep," Mark admitted, his voice low and steady. "I nearly walked away from it that night."

Alex listened, caught between admiration and recognition. Jamie watched, too, eyes never straying far from Mark's weathered face, as if each word carried weight he didn't want to miss.

He continued, describing the slow, grueling climb back from that low point. The nights spent questioning every frame. The doubt that clung like fog. The quiet moments when he'd nearly given up until he stopped trying to impress and started trying to express.

"That's when everything changed," he said. "When I stopped trying to be a great photographer and started trying to be an honest one. That's when my work finally had something to say."

Alex felt something stir inside her, a flicker of recognition in Mark's story. How closely it mirrored the hesitation she'd carried, the doubt that had kept her sketchbook closed for too long.

Jamie broke the silence. "I think that's what a lot of us are chasing, whether we admit it or not."

Mark nodded slowly. "You're not chasing the perfect shot. You're chasing the moment that means something. That hits you in the gut. That's the one you keep."

Alex glanced down at her coffee, now gone lukewarm, and felt the truth of those words settle deep in her chest.

"Every setback taught me something," he said. "Every failure added to my understanding of who I was and what I wanted to say. And in the end, it wasn't the applause or the recognition that mattered most. It was the fulfillment of knowing I was living my truth."

Jamie nodded. "That's why I wanted you to meet him. He has this way of putting things into perspective."

"You definitely have a gift for that," she admitted.

With a thoughtful expression, Mark offered one last piece of advice as they prepared to leave. "Alex, remember this: The journey of self-discovery isn't a straight path; it's a winding road with unexpected turns and detours. There will be soaring highs and crushing lows, moments of brilliant clarity, and moments of agonizing self-doubt. But every step is valuable. Even the ones that seem like detours. Trust yourself and trust the process."

Alex turned to Jamie outside the cafe as they strolled toward their hotel. "Thank you for introducing me to him," she said. "I feel like I understand things a little better now."

Jamie smiled. "Mark has that effect on people. And he's right. You've got everything you need. You just have to trust yourself."

She thought about her sketchbook and the new drawings that were coming together. They were still rough, still uncertain, but they were hers. Each mark held something real: a captured feeling, a memory, a flicker of light that had moved her enough to try.

What had once felt like an overwhelming fear, the blank page, the pressure to get it right, had begun to shift. The fear was still there but it had softened. It no longer screamed. Now, it whispered. In its place came something quieter but steadier: a subtle sense of potential. Like a thread tugging her gently forward.

She wasn't sure where it would lead, but the thought of continuing no longer paralyzed her. It stirred something hopeful instead.

"I think I'm starting to," she said softly.

# Chapter 17

A faint hum from the air conditioner and distant city sounds barely broke the silence in the hotel room. With her sketchbook open and resting on her lap, Alex sat comfortably on the bed. She found she couldn't stop thinking about the conversation that she'd had with Mark. She replayed it in her mind, like a favorite song stuck on repeat, each detail vivid and clear.

Jamie sat at the table editing photos on his laptop. Every so often, he'd steal a glance at her. His eyes would linger long enough to check in; not with words, but with presence. A silent reassurance. A way of saying I see you. He didn't interrupt. He didn't need to.

It was enough just to watch her settle into herself with growing confidence. And though she didn't always look up, she felt that quiet, steady attention that asked for nothing but gave so much.

"What are you working on?" he asked.

"I'm not sure yet," she admitted. "I feel like I need to get something out, but I don't know what it is."

"That's part of the process, though, isn't it? Sitting with the uncertainty until something clicks."

"You make it sound so effortless, like a simple stroll in the park."

"It's not," Jamie said. "But it's worth it."

She tapped the end of her pencil against the page. "I guess I'm just afraid whatever I put down won't be good enough."

He shut his laptop and turned his chair to face her. "Good enough for who?"

Alex opened her mouth, then closed it. She wasn't sure. *Was it for herself? For some invisible audience? Or was it for the version of her who was still figuring things out?*

"It's alright if you don't nail it on the first try; the process of trying is important, too."

"I guess you're right."

"I like the sound of you saying that" he joked.

"Don't get used to this. I don't want your head getting any bigger than it is."

After staring at the page for a moment longer, she gathered her thoughts before finally taking a breath and letting her pencil move across the page. At first, it was just lines, uncertain and aimless. Initially, there was nothing to see, but then, gradually, shapes emerged, and even what appeared to be the faint outline of a cityscape in the distance. Rome.

He watched quietly. "There you go."

Alex glanced at him. "It's messy."

"So is life," he said with a shrug. "Doesn't mean it's not worth creating."

Despite a soft laugh, she continued her task. She didn't overthink it. She just let it be. The pencil glided effortlessly across the page, leaving behind a trail of graphite as the rough sketch of Rome's skyline, with its iconic dome and ancient ruins, took shape. It wasn't perfect, but something about it felt honest and unfiltered.

Jamie continued to watch her work. "See? That's the sweet spot. When you stop thinking so hard and just let it happen."

She didn't look up. "Are you always this wise, or is this just the wine talking?"

"A little of both."

She continued drawing as her pencil moved in slow, deliberate strokes across the page. The world around her had quieted. The only sound was a faint, almost imperceptible strumming from a street musician playing somewhere below.

It wasn't a song she recognized, but the melody carried something familiar.

She pictured the musician tucked into a shadowed corner of the street. The music and voices intertwined, weaving a gentle soundtrack to her thoughts. Outside, the city kept moving, unaware of the quiet moment blooming inside the room. But here, in this space, it felt like everything had slowed enough for her to breathe, to create, to feel.

"Do you ever get stuck? Like… creatively?"

"All the time. There are days when I question everything. Whether my work matters, whether I'm good enough, whether I'm just fooling myself. But I've learned to push through it. Sometimes that means stepping away, taking a walk, or just letting myself feel whatever I'm feeling. Other times, it means forcing myself to create, even if what I make isn't great. The important thing is to keep going."

"I think that's what scares me the most," she said. "The idea of putting in all this effort and still not being good enough."

"You are good enough. I wish you could see the version of you that everyone else sees. You're amazing, you're brave, and you're incredibly talented. Why can't you see that in yourself?"

"Why do you always seem to say the right things?"

"Because it's true."

No words came to her lips. Despite her doubts, a small part of her felt he was telling the truth. And she could hear the sincerity in his voice that resonated deep within her.

He got up from his chair and walked over. "Alex, can I tell you something I've learned?"

She tilted her head up, her eyes meeting his.

"It's not about being 'good enough.' Art isn't a competition. It's not about meeting some arbitrary standard. It's about expression, connection, and growth. The only person you need to be better than is the version of yourself from yesterday."

"That's... a different way of looking at it," she said.

"It's the only way to look at it. If you're always chasing perfection, you'll never catch it. But if you focus on growth and honesty in your work, you'll find something even better."

She thought about what he said. Perhaps she had spent too much time measuring her self-worth against others.

"That makes sense."

"I have my moments."

"Don't get used to me admitting that."

"So, what are you going to do about it?"

Alex glanced at her sketchbook. Slowly, she flipped through the pages. She came across some filled with half-finished ideas, and others abandoned before they even had a chance. She ran her fingers over one of the rougher sketches. It was one she had started in Venice but never finished.

"I think I'm going to stop holding myself back. I'll finish this one. Not because it must be perfect, but because I want to."

"That's the spirit."

"I think I'm starting to understand what Mark meant. About the journey not being linear."

"Exactly. And you're already on it. Whether or not you realize it, every step you've taken, each one leaving its mark on the path, has brought you closer to your destiny."

She started on the sketch, feeling more confident than before.

Jamie watched her as a small smile played on his lips. "That's it," he whispered. "Trust yourself."

She didn't respond. Her brow furrowed in concentration. She was oblivious to everything but the page. She wasn't worrying about its quality or reception. It gave her a sense of freedom. She was letting the moment guide her brushstrokes and inspire her next move. And as the pencil moved across the page, she felt something shift inside her. It was a small but significant step forward on a journey she was finally ready to embrace.

He watched her for a moment before speaking.

"Tomorrow," he said, "we're heading to Sperlonga."

She looked up with curiosity in her eyes. "Sperlonga?"

He grinned. "It's a coastal town, about halfway between here and Naples. Whitewashed buildings, stunning beaches, and just the right amount of hidden corners to explore. I think you'll love it."

"Sounds like another adventure."

"That's the idea."

# Chapter 18

The train ride to Sperlonga lulled Alex into a quiet, contented stillness. She sat with her forehead resting lightly against the window, eyes half-lidded as the sun-drenched Italian countryside slipped by in a blur of gold and green. The scent of wildflowers and pine drifted in through a cracked window, soft and earthy, stirring something gentle inside her.

Outside, the landscape slowly shifted from rolling hills blanketed in olive groves and terracotta-roofed villages to glimpses of the coast. Then, all at once, the land opened, and there it was: the Tyrrhenian Sea, stretching wide and endless beneath the midday sun.

The water shimmered like glass, deep blue with flashes of silver where the light danced along its surface. Whitewashed buildings clung to the cliffs in the distance, and fishing boats bobbed in tiny harbors looking like brushstrokes on a canvas. Awe bloomed in her chest.

She could almost feel the sun on her skin and hear the faint, far-off cry of gulls circling above the waves. The scene was so vivid, so breathtaking. It felt like stepping into a dream she didn't know she'd been waiting for. And for the first time in a long while, Alex felt not like a visitor, but like someone arriving.

Jamie sat beside her snapping the occasional shot through the window. "This place is special," he said. "You'll see."

"You always say that."

"And have I been wrong yet?"

The smirk on her face spoke volumes, though she offered no protest. Instead, she closed her eyes and let the gentle rocking of the train soothe her. The rhythmic motion and soft hum of the tracks lulling her deeper into the moment. When the train finally slowed and pulled into the small coastal station, the air shifted. A cool, salty breeze swept through the open doors, laced with the scent of ripe peaches and citrus from a nearby fruit stand. The sounds of gulls overhead and distant laughter wove together with the aroma, creating a vibrant, sunlit welcome.

As they stepped onto the bustling platform, the hum of the train and the distant buzz of the last city they'd left behind faded into the background. Here, everything felt brighter. Simpler. Full of possibility. Jamie turned to her, his bag slung over one shoulder, eyes lit with that familiar spark.

"Ready?" he asked, grinning.

Alex took in the sight of the sea just beyond the rooftops, the glint of sunlight dancing off the waves, and the charm of the winding streets ahead. The pastel buildings, stacked like a painter's dream along the hillside, shimmered under the midday sun. She turned to Jamie and met his gaze with a smile that was soft but certain.

"More than ever."

They began walking, weaving their way down the cobbled path that led into the heart of Sperlonga. The village opened up around them like a secret kept well by time; whitewashed walls splashed with flowering vines, narrow staircases winding between quiet homes, and the faint hum of the sea never far from earshot.

At a corner café, they paused to share a pair of espresso shots that left their lips tingling and their laughter louder. Jamie tried ordering in Italian, much to the delight, and amusement, of the elderly barista, who corrected his pronunciation with an exaggerated flourish and a wink.

She snapped a picture of the moment: Jamie half-laughing, half-embarrassed, holding up two tiny cups like a toast to spontaneity. From there, they wandered aimlessly without agenda or direction. They ducked into artisan shops tucked beneath archways, sampled fig jam from a street vendor, and stood in quiet awe before a centuries-old chapel where the sound of a single bell echoed through the stone.

At one point, they stumbled upon a bookstore tucked beneath a blooming bougainvillea. Alex drifted through the aisles of worn paperbacks and dusty hardcovers, while he captured her in a candid frame as the sunlight filtered through the window behind her. She didn't notice until he showed her the photo later..

As late afternoon approached, they climbed toward the cliffs, following a narrow trail lined with wild thyme and wind-worn rock. At the top, the town gave way to the vast open sea.. They sat side by side on the edge with their legs dangling.

Now, the only sound was the steady rhythm of waves pounding the rocks below. It was a comforting silence. Alex let out a quiet sigh as she settled back onto the stone with her sketchbook resting across her knees. The pages fluttered slightly in the breeze which were inviting her to begin. Beside her, Jamie adjusted the dials on his camera  His eyes were trained on the horizon, where the sky melted into the sea in layers of dusky gold and silver-blue. Neither of them spoke, yet everything felt understood.

She dipped her pencil to the page and began to sketch with ease. The shapes came slowly at first: the curve of the cliff, the soft sweep of waves, the faint suggestion of Jamie's silhouette against the backdrop of sea and sky.

He glanced at her and lowered his camera.

"You're quiet."

She looked at him, startled. "Just thinking."

"About what?"

"I'm speechless. This place is incredibly beautiful; just listen to the gentle sounds of nature."

"It is. But something tells me that's not all you're thinking about."

The sound of rushing water drew her back, and she quickly turned her gaze to its source. "You always do that."

"Do what?"

"See right through me."

"It's not a superpower, you know. I just pay attention."

Alex smiled despite herself, the corners of her mouth lifting before she could stop them. He always noticed the little things. The way she tucked her hair behind her ear when she was deep in thought, or how she bit her lip just before sketching a new line. She wanted to brush it off with a laugh, to keep things light, but the truth tugged at her just beneath the surface.

She couldn't tell him what she was really thinking. She couldn't admit that being near him made her feel alive in a way she hadn't felt in years. That his laughter had become her new favorite sound. That his quiet encouragement made her brave, even when doubt clung to her like a second skin.

The intensity of it was terrifying and she didn't know what to do with. It wasn't supposed to happen like this. They were friends. Travel companions. Sharing a few incredible weeks under the Italian sun. She shook her head gently, trying to chase the thoughts away before they rooted too deeply. This was Jamie.

Jamie, who made her laugh when the day felt heavy. Jamie, who handed her his camera without hesitation. Jamie, who listened, really listened, when she spoke. The last thing she wanted was to ruin what they had. What if this feeling that was growing broke the quiet, perfect rhythm they'd found?

"You're doing it again," he said, breaking into her thoughts.

"Doing what?"

"Overthinking," he said with a grin. "I can practically see the gears turning in your head."

"You're imagining things."

"Am I?" Jamie asked, raising an eyebrow.

"Yes," she said firmly. She flipped open her sketchbook and pretended to focus on the half-finished drawing inside.

He didn't press further and went back to setting up

his camera. But she couldn't concentrate. Her mind was a whirlwind of conflicting emotions. She thought back to all the moments they'd shared over the past few weeks. The late-night conversations, the inside jokes, the way he always seemed to know exactly what she needed, even when she didn't. It was more than friendship; she knew that now.

But what did it mean for him? Did he feel the same way? Or was she reading too much into their connection? The thought of risking their friendship by misinterpreting his intentions made her chest tighten.

"You know," he said suddenly, his voice thoughtful, "one of the things I love about photography is how it forces you to see the world differently, to notice the details, the light and shadow, the textures and colors you might normally miss."

She turned to him. "What do you mean?"

He picked up his camera and held it out to her. "Here," he said. "Look through the lens."

She carefully lifted the camera to her eye, its smooth surface cool against her skin, and composed the shot. Peering through the viewfinder, she composed the shot, adjusting the focus to capture every detail. The waves thunderously crashed against the shore, the sky was brilliantly blue, and a distant sailboat silhouetted against the setting sun.

"Now move it around," Jamie instructed. "I want you to discover something small, something hidden, something you would typically ignore."

Alex adjusted the lens and focused on a cluster of wildflowers growing between the rocks. Their vibrant colors stood out against the gray stone, delicate but resilient.

"Beautiful, isn't it?"

She nodded, lowering the camera. "I never would've noticed them without the lens."

Jamie smiled. "Exactly. Sometimes, we miss the most incredible things because we're not looking. Photography taught me to slow down and to pay attention to the details. And it's made me realize that the best things in life are often the ones you almost overlook."

His words struck a chord, and Alex felt her heart ache. Was she overlooking something now? Or was she trying to see something that wasn't there?

She handed the camera back to Jamie. "That's... a good lesson," she said, her voice quieter than she intended.

He studied her for a moment. "Alex," he said softly, "are you okay?"

"Yeah, I'm fine."

But she wasn't fine. She had something to tell him, and she didn't know how he was going to take it. She was falling for him hard, and it terrified her. Because Jamie wasn't just some passing infatuation. He had become a part of her journey, someone who saw her in a way she wasn't sure anyone ever had. And the more time they spent together, the harder it became to ignore the way her pulse quickened when he smiled at her, or how safe she felt when he was near.

Taking a breath, she forced a small smile and looked up at him. "Really. I'm fine."

"Okay. But if you ever feel like not being 'fine' around me, that's allowed too." She nodded, but she wasn't sure how much longer she could keep pretending. That evening, back at the hotel, she sat curled up on the balcony with her knees drawn to her chest. The lamps along the winding streets glowed like fireflies, while the sea beyond whispered quietly into the night. Jamie had gone to bed early, claiming exhaustion, but she suspected he knew she needed time alone.

Now, wrapped in the hush of twilight, her thoughts ran unchecked. She replayed their conversation on the cliff. The way he spoke about photography as if it were a language of the soul. The way he noticed things no one else did. The way he looked at her when he thought she wasn't watching, like she was something rare and worth understanding. And suddenly, there was no use denying it anymore. She was in love with Jamie.

The truth settled over her slowly at first, like morning

fog creeping over the hills. Then, all at once, it struck her. It was in the way her heart leapt when he laughed. The comfort of his presence. The fact that he saw her. Not just the version she presented to the world, but the one she usually kept hidden. It was exhilarating. And utterly terrifying.

She wanted to tell him. Every part of her ached to. To say it aloud. To let him know that something real and bright had taken root in her heart. But then came the fear. The what ifs.

What if he didn't feel the same?

What if it changed everything; the laughter, the ease, the gentle rhythm of their days? What if she lost not just a moment, but him?

And so she sat there, in the hush of a Roman night, heart full and aching, words trapped behind her lips, watching the lights flicker below and wondering what tomorrow might bring.

She grabbed her sketchbook and tried to focus on her sketches, but the lines wouldn't come. Her hand hovered over the page hesitantly, but her heart was too full and her thoughts were too tangled to translate into art. Even the beauty of the scenery couldn't stop her restlessness.

With a quiet sigh, she closed the sketchbook and set it aside, folding her arms over her knees. Then she closed her eyes. She didn't have all the answers. Yes, she was scared. But for the first time, she was beginning to understand something deeper. Her journey through Italy had started as an escape, a way to reconnect with herself. But somewhere between the sunlit piazzas, the candid laughter, and the quiet moments shared with Jamie, it had become more than that.

This wasn't just about finding herself anymore.

It was about finding the courage to embrace the unknown; especially the parts that came wrapped in risk, in vulnerability and in love. Even if it meant risking her heart. She sat there a while longer. Then, just as she began to think she might finally go to bed, she heard the soft creak of the door behind her. Her heart jumped. She'd thought he was asleep.

When she turned she saw him standing in the doorway. Barefoot, hair a little tousled, and eyes still heavy with sleep , but unmistakably focused on her.

"Couldn't sleep either?"

As he leaned into the door frame, she saw he was barefoot and rumpled from lying in bed. He had thrown on a plain gray T-shirt, and his hair stuck up slightly in the back. Even in the dim light, he seemed so effortlessly himself, and it tugged at something deep inside her.

"Just...thinking," she pointed to the empty chair beside her. "Want to join?"

He nodded and settled into the chair with a soft sigh. For a few moments, they sat in silence and listened to the distant crash of waves.

"Beautiful night," Jamie said.

A nervous habit took hold, and she twisted the soft cotton of her sleeve between her fingers. "It is."

Jamie glanced at her. "You've been quiet since we got back. What's on your mind?"

She couldn't tell him the whole truth, not yet. But maybe she could give him a piece. "Do you ever...second-guess yourself?"

"All the time. Why?"

"It's just that this trip, everything we've done, it's been amazing. But sometimes I feel like I'm holding myself back. Like I'm scared to fully dive in."

"What are you scared of?"

"Failing. Disappointing myself. Wasting this chance."

"You're one of the bravest people I know. Do you realize that?"

"Me? Brave? You've got to be kidding."

"I'm not," Jamie said firmly. "You left behind everything comfortable and familiar to come on this journey. That takes guts. And from what I've seen, you're doing more than just traveling. You're growing, pushing yourself, facing things most people would avoid. That's bravery."

"I don't always feel brave," she admitted. "Most of the time, I feel...lost."

Jamie's lips quirked into a small smile. "That's part of it. Being brave doesn't mean you're never scared. It means you keep going, even when you are."

She stood and walked over to the railing. Her heart pounded, a steady rhythm she could feel in her throat, her fingertips, everywhere.

How was he always so calm? So steady and sure of himself, even in moments like this?

She envied that about him. The way he carried himself, and the ease with which he spoke, as though he always knew where he stood in the world. But as she watched him now, framed in the soft glow spilling from the room behind him, something shifted in her perspective. Maybe he wasn't as sure as he seemed.

Maybe the confidence was just a layer, like hers had once been. Maybe he had doubts, too. Fears he hadn't named. Feelings he didn't know how to express. The thought softened something in her. And she didn't feel so alone in her uncertainty.

"Jamie," she turned to face him fully. "Can I ask you something?"

"Of course."

"Why did you invite me on this trip?"

"Because I saw something in you," he said after a moment. "When we met, you seemed...stuck, but not in a bad way. More like you were searching for something. And I guess I wanted to give you a little push and see where that search would take you."

"You believed in me before I even believed in myself."

"I still do. And I'm not the only one. I've seen the way you've come alive on this trip. You're more capable than you think."

Her chest tightened, and she felt the overwhelming urge to tell him everything. To lay it all out in the open. But fear held her back. Instead, she asked, "Do you ever regret choosing this life? Traveling all the time, not having a home base?"

"No regrets. It's not always easy, and yeah, it can be lonely sometimes. But it's who I am. I don't think I could be happy any other way."

Her heart sank a little. His words were a reminder of how different their lives were. He was a wanderer, always chasing the next adventure, while she was still figuring out who she wanted to be.

"But you don't have to live the way I do. Your path doesn't have to look like mine. It just has to be yours."

They fell into silence again, the air between them charged with unspoken emotions. Alex's mind raced with everything she wanted to say but couldn't. Finally, Jamie stood, stretching his arms over his head.

"We should get some rest," he said, his voice soft. "Big day tomorrow."

Alex watched as Jamie disappeared back inside, the soft click of the door leaving her alone once more with the quiet hum of the night. Crickets chirped somewhere in the distance, and the sea whispered below like a secret just out of reach.

She wrapped her arms around herself as she exhaled slowly. The breeze tugged at the hem of her shirt, and for a long moment, she simply stood there. Everything felt uncertain, yes. The lines between friendship and something more were beginning to blur. The future loomed vast and unknown. But for once, she wasn't afraid of it. Because the uncertainty wasn't hollow anymore. It was alive. Full of color and motion and possibility.

This journey had started as a way to reconnect with her art, to rediscover something lost. But it had grown into something deeper. It wasn't just about sketchbooks or breathtaking landscapes. It was about choosing a life she wanted to live. One where she wasn't simply observing, but participating. One where she allowed herself to feel, to risk, to leap.

And Jamie...

He was becoming a part of that in ways she hadn't expected. In ways she hadn't dared imagine when they first boarded that train together. But it was happening and pretending otherwise would no longer protect her. It would only keep her from something real.

She shook her head, more in wonder than doubt, and finally let go of the railing. The air inside was warmer, softer somehow, as she made her way back into the room.

Tomorrow was another day. And no matter what it brought, she had promised herself one thing. She wouldn't run from it. Not anymore. The next time the moment came, she was going to tell him.

# Chapter 19

A sudden, violent storm lashed against the small cabin, the relentless rain pounding the windows like a battering ram. The rhythmic drumming of droplets racing down the glass held Alex's attention. Despite the crack of distant thunder, the steady rhythm of rain was oddly soothing; each drop a soft percussion on the windowpane.

They had everything planned for a hike that afternoon, but a storm had arrived suddenly and forced them to retreat to the little cabin they'd rented for the night. It wasn't much. Just one room with creaking floorboards, a mismatched rug, and a kitchen too small for more than one person to stand in at a time. But it was warm. And quiet. And somehow perfect.

Jamie moved around the kitchen, making tea by feel more than focus. He glanced over his shoulder at her, offering a crooked smile.

"Well," he said, "so much for our hike."

Alex returned his smile. "I don't mind. There's something kind of... beautiful about being stuck here."

He poured two mugs and handed one to her before settling onto the couch beside her. "Yeah," he murmured. "There is."

They sat in silence listening to the rain's steady drumbeat and the occasional groan of wind through the trees. The crackle of the fire offered a soft contrast, a grounding comfort in the heart of the storm.

She stole a glance at him—how the firelight danced across his features, catching in the gold of his eyes, softening the sharp angles of his jaw. He looked more like himself here, in this quiet, space. Not the easygoing traveler making people laugh in crowded piazzas or the focused photographer chasing the perfect shot, but something quieter. Realer.

"Do you ever think about what comes next?" she asked suddenly.

Jamie didn't answer right away. He sipped his tea, then rested the mug on his knee, turning it slowly in his hands. "Sometimes," he said finally. "But I try not to get too far ahead of myself. I've spent so long chasing moments. I don't always know what to do with the ones I'm in."

She understood all too well. She looked down at the swirl of tea in her cup, then back at him. "I used to plan everything. Every step. Every outcome. But lately..." Her voice trailed off.

"You've changed," Jamie said gently.

She glanced at him, surprised.

"In a good way," he added quickly. "You're not just watching life from the outside anymore. You're in it. Creating it."

Alex felt something catch in her chest at his words, like he'd reached in and found something she hadn't yet been brave enough to admit aloud.

The rain intensified and a fresh wave of wind rattling the windows. Jamie stood and stretched slightly before crouching near the fire. He added a few small logs with care, coaxing the flames to life again. The scent of wood-smoke filled the air as he sat on the floor near the fire, their orange light flickering on his face. Rainwater still clung to his damp hair, and a thoughtful frown had replaced his usually cheerful grin.

A slight shiver ran through Alex as she pulled the worn blanket tighter around her shoulders. She got up and sat down next to him.

"Did you get caught in storms like this a lot when you were traveling?"

"More times than I can count. In Vietnam, I once found myself stranded in a tiny village for three days. The power was out, and I barely had any cell service. But it ended up being one of the best experiences of my trip. I got to know the locals and learned how to make pho from scratch. Sometimes getting stuck isn't the worst thing."

"Maybe we need moments like this," she mused. "Forcing us to pause. To just… be."

"Yeah," he said quietly. "Exactly."

She stretched her legs out. "I think I kind of like being stuck here with you."

"Good," he said, his voice carrying something deeper. "Because I don't mind being stuck with you, either."

A whirlwind of emotions surged to the surface. Curiosity, longing, fear, hope were all tangled together, crashing like waves against her chest. It left her breathless, and unsure where one feeling ended and the next began. She tried to steady herself, but everything about the moment was overwhelming. The quiet intimacy of the space. The gentle crackling of the fire. The scent of wood smoke blending with the warm trace of his cologne. His nearness, not quite touching, yet close enough that she could feel the heat radiating from his body.

It was too much and not enough, all at once. She curled her fingers tighter around her mug as she tried to make sense of the storm inside her.

Jamie turned back to the fire, but his expression had changed. As if he was feeling it too. This pull. This shift. This quiet, undeniable something blooming in the silence between them.

"What's on your mind?"

"Nothing," she lied.

"Come on. I've been around you for a while now. I know better than that. Spill it."

"It's just…everything," she admitted. "This trip, my life back home, where I'm going. Sometimes it feels like too much to figure out."

"You don't have to figure it all out at once, you know," he said. "Nobody has it all together, no matter how it looks on the outside."

"I used to think I'd have it all figured out by now. A career, a relationship, a sense of purpose. But I feel like I'm starting over from scratch."

"Starting over isn't a terrible thing. It means you're brave enough to admit when something isn't working and make a change. Most people are too scared to do that."

"I don't feel brave. Most of the time, I feel like I'm just winging it."

"Welcome to the club. That's what life is, isn't it? Figuring it out as you go."

She felt a wave of gratitude for his presence. His ability to make her feel seen and understood.

"Can I ask you something?"

"Anything."

"Why photography? Why not something more...stable?"

"Because photography saved me," he said simply.

"What do you mean?"

He was quiet for a moment, as if deciding how much to share. "A few years ago, I was in a really dark place," he said finally. "I was stuck in a job I hated, in a city I didn't love, surrounded by people who didn't know me. I felt...trapped."

"What happened?"

"One day, I finally reached my breaking point. I quit my job, sold most of my stuff, and bought a one-way ticket to Southeast Asia. I didn't have a plan. I just knew I needed to get out."

He paused. "I brought this camera with me, just for fun. But somewhere along the way, it became more than that. It became my way of seeing the world, of connecting with people. It gave me purpose."

"That's...amazing. I wish I had that kind of courage."

"You do. You just don't see it yet."

Their eyes locked, and in that still moment, everything else fell away. The storm outside, the soft crackle of the fire, even the pulse of time itself. She wanted to tell him. How he made her believe again. In herself, in passion, in moments that mattered. How his way of looking at the world made her want to pick up her pencil and draw again, not out of habit, but out of hope. How his laughter had become a sound she looked for.How she cared for him more than she ever expected or could understand. But the words felt too big. Too vulnerable. Too real.

So instead, she offered him a faint smile. Jamie didn't press her. He didn't have to. Because in that gaze she saw something that made her believe he already knew.

"Do you ever miss it? Having a home, a routine?"

"Sometimes. But then I remind myself that home isn't a place. It's a feeling. And I've found that feeling in so many unexpected places."

His words hung in the air, and Alex felt a pang of longing. She wondered if Jamie could ever feel that sense of home with her.

"What about you?" he asked. "What do you want? It's not about what you think you should want, but what you truly desire."

"I don't know," she admitted. "I want to feel like my life has meaning. I want to wake up excited about what I'm doing. And…I want to stop being afraid of failing."

"You're already doing it. You're chasing what matters to you, even if it's scary. Most people don't do that much.

Early morning sunlight filtered through the cabin's slightly fogged windows. The scent of damp earth and pine wafted in from the slightly open window was mixed with the smell of freshly brewed coffee.

Alex stirred beneath her blanket on the couch. Her eyes watered slightly from the sudden brightness as she blinked. She rubbed her eyes and looked around the room. She saw Jamie pouring coffee into two mugs. He looked more relaxed than usual.

"Morning," she said, as she stretched and sat up.

"Morning. Coffee?"

"Please," she pulled the blanket tighter around her as she shuffled to the small dining table.

He joined her a moment later. He set a steaming mug in front of her before taking the seat across the table. "How'd you sleep?"

Alex took a cautious sip of the coffee. "Surprisingly well, considering how much was on my mind. The storm was kind of soothing."

"Yeah, there's something about storms. They force you to slow down and take stock of things."

Alex studied him over the rim of her mug. "You mean like last night?"

"Maybe. Did it help?"

"Yeah. It's strange, but I feel...lighter. Like I don't have to have all the answers right now."

"Good. Because nobody has all the answers,. And if they say they do, they're lying."

The sight of his calm demeanor melted away her tension. "You always know what to say, don't you?"

"Not always," Jamie admitted, a playful glint in his eyes. "But I do my best."

She glanced out the window as her thoughts drifted back to the night before. She couldn't stop replaying his words and the way he had looked at her with such sincerity.

"Jamie," she said suddenly.

He looked up, his expression curious. "Yeah?"

"I've been thinking about what you said last night," she began, her fingers tracing the edge of her mug. "About bravery and not needing to have it all figured out."

He waited for her to continue.

"I think you're right," she admitted. "But it's still hard. Letting go of all the expectations I've put on myself is scary."

"Of course it's scary. Change always is. But you're stronger than you think. I've seen it."

"Thanks," she said softly. "I really appreciate that."

"Anytime. And for what it's worth, I think you're exactly

where you need to be right now."

"I hope so," she said.

"You are," Jamie said firmly. "And you're not alone in this. I'm here, okay?"

"Okay."

"So, what's the plan for today? Are we going to let this sunshine go to waste?"

Alex laughed. "Definitely not. What do you have in mind?"

"Well," he began, "There's a trail nearby that leads to an amazing overlook. I was thinking we could pack some snacks and make a day of it."

Her eyes lit up at the suggestion. "That sounds perfect."

"Good. Because I already packed the snacks."

Alex laughed. "Of course you did."

Laughter and the rustling of backpacks filled the morning as they prepared for their hike, the time slipping away in a pleasant haze. By the time they set out, the sun beat down on them, and the world sparkled with the heat and the vibrant colors of the day.

The winding trail stretched ahead and cut through golden fields of wildflowers. She adjusted the strap of her small canvas backpack, where Jamie had stashed their snacks, and glanced over at him. He was walking a few paces ahead, the sunlight catching in his hair, making it look like strands of bronze.

"You sure you know where you're going?" she teased.

Jamie glanced over his shoulder with an exaggerated look of offense. "You wound me. I've only been here twice before. I practically *am* the trail."

She laughed as she stepped carefully over a cluster of uneven rocks. "Oh, is that right? Well, Trail Master, I'm trusting you not to get us lost."

He slowed slightly. "Trust me," he said, a glint in his eye, "if we get lost, it'll be entirely intentional. I mean, what's the point of exploring if you always know exactly where you're going?"

She shot him a mock glare. "You're one of those people."

"Guilty."

Alex let her gaze drift across the landscape. The cliff side dropped off sharply to their right, offering a breathtaking view of the sea far below. The water was rich, endless blue, glittering beneath the sun. She could hear the distant roar of waves crashing against the rocks.

After a while, Jamie pointed ahead. "We're almost there. Just one more stretch."

As they rounded a bend, the path narrowed, with wild lavender and clusters of white and yellow flowers surrounding it. The faint fragrance filled the air, and Alex savored the fresh, earthy scent.

"You were right," she murmured. "This is already perfect."

"You know I'm keeping a mental record of each time you say that."

"You would, but just so you know, it doesn't count."

They reached the overlook a few minutes later, and Alex stopped in her tracks. The view was stunning. The sea stretched endlessly before them, with white-crested waves rolling against the jagged coastline below. She took a slow step forward, as though afraid moving too quickly might break the spell. "Wow..." she said breathlessly.

He came up beside her. "Yeah. It gets me every time."

# Chapter 20

They sat on the cliff edge enjoying the cool breeze whispering through the grass. The hike had been challenging, but the panoramic view from their hard-earned vantage point was worth every step. As the evening air cooled, a quiet contentment settled over them as they watched the sunset paint the sky.

She had spent the entire hike considering the words she wanted to say and even rehearsing them in her mind. But now, with him sitting so close, she couldn't say them.

"You're quiet again," he said. He turned to look at her. "What's going on in that head of yours?"

She forced a small smile. "Just...thinking."

"Dangerous," he teased. "Care to share?"

This was it. This was her moment. If she didn't say something now, she might never work up the courage again. With a shaky breath and a catch in her throat, she finally managed, "Jamie, can I ask you something?"

"Of course." He sat up straighter and gave her his full attention.

"What if...what if you make the leap and it doesn't work out?"

"Is this about you? Or something else?"

"A little of both, I guess."

"If it's about you, I'd say you've already made the leap. You quit your job, left your comfort zone, and took a chance by coming on this trip. That shows bravery."

"That doesn't feel brave at all. It feels...terrifying."

"It's okay to be scared," he said. "Courage isn't about not being scared. It's about doing it anyway."

"Hey," she began.

"Yeah?"

She turned to face him. "I've been trying to figure out how to say this, and honestly, I'm still not sure I'm going to get it right. But I...I need to tell you something."

"Okay."

She took a deep breath. "This has been on my mind for the past few days. I've been trying to get this out and I believe now is the perfect time. I think I'm falling for you," she blurted.

A look of surprise crossed his face as his eyes widened slightly at the unexpected sight. "Alex..."

She quickly held up a hand. "You don't have to say anything. I just...I needed to get it off my chest. Pretending I didn't feel this way was driving me crazy."

He gently placed a hand over hers. The warmth of his touch sent a shiver up her spine, and she forced herself to meet his gaze.

"I'm glad you told me," he whispered. "Because believe it or not, I've been feeling the same way."

"You have?"

"Yeah. I didn't want to say anything because I didn't want to mess this up. But you're...you're incredible. And the more time I spend with you, the harder it is to ignore how I feel."

Relief and disbelief washed over Alex in equal measure. "I thought I was imagining it," she admitted.

"You weren't. I've just been trying to play it cool, but clearly, I'm terrible at it."

"So...what do we do now?"

His smile softened, crinkling the corners of his eyes, as he said, "We take it one day at a time. No pressure, no expectations, just us."

"I think I can handle that."

"Good," Jamie teased. "Because I'm pretty sure we're stuck with each other for the rest of this trip. Especially our next stop."

"I'm just glad we get some more time together."

"So, you don't want to know where we're going next? I'm surprised."

"I know eventually you'll tell me."

As the sun dipped below the horizon, she felt a sense of peace she hadn't known was possible. Jamie's presence beside her soothed her anxieties, and a quiet joy bloomed in her chest. She realized that sometimes taking a risk was the only way to truly live. After their heartfelt conversation, he suggested taking a walk to stretch their legs and let the cool evening air clear their heads.

"You know. I think this might be one of my favorite parts of traveling is walking somewhere quiet like this, with nothing but the stars for company."

She glanced up at the sky. "I can see why. It's peaceful. Gives you time to think."

"Exactly," he said with a smile. "But tonight feels different."

"How so?" Alex asked.

"Because I'm not alone this time. Sharing moments like this with someone... it makes them more special."

"I get that. I never thought I'd be the type to enjoy something like this, but...it's nice."

"You're full of surprises, Alex Greer."

She nudged him with her elbow. "Oh, am I?"

"Absolutely. Every time I think I've got you figured out, you surprise me with an unexpected word or action that throws me off completely.

"Well, I'll take that as a compliment. Maybe I'm good at keeping you on your toes."

"Mission accomplished."

She couldn't help but steal glances at Jamie, her heart fluttering with each stolen look. Every time their eyes met, her heart leaped, and a flutter of excitement and nervousness filled her chest.

"So, what happens after this trip?"

"What do you mean?"

"I mean…with us. Do we go back to our lives and pretend this never happened? Or…"

"Or we figure it out."

She was surprised by his straightforwardness.

"I like you, Alex. A lot. And I'm willing to do what it takes to make this work if that's what you want too."

Her heart swelled at his words, the vulnerability in his voice making her feel braver than she ever thought possible. "I want that," she admitted.

"Good. Because I'm not ready to say goodbye to you, not now and not anytime soon."

They resumed their walk. Alex felt lighter, her earlier fears and doubts fading into the background. As they reached the clearing, a breathtaking panorama of the valley unfolded before them, causing him to stop and take out his camera.

"Stay right there," he motioned for her to stand by the edge.

"What are you doing?" she laughed as she complied.

"Capturing the moment. You'll thank me later."

Alex stood still as he adjusted the camera settings. She couldn't help but smile, the weight of the day's events settling in her chest like a comforting warmth.

"Got it," Jamie lowered the camera and joined her.

"Can I see?"

He carefully showed her the photo, his eyes lingering on the image before handing it over. It perfectly captured the serene beauty of the landscape and her.

"It's beautiful."

"You're beautiful," Jamie said, his tone so genuine that it took her breath away.

She tilted her head up to look at him, noticing the way his hair fell across his forehead. The sincerity in his eyes was undeniable, and his smile spoke of a promise yet to be spoken.

"Thank you," she said, her voice barely above a whisper.

As the night deepened and the stars grew brighter, Alex

realized that taking a risk with Jamie wasn't just about love. It was about finding a part of herself she'd been missing all along. A wave of warmth washed over her as their fingers met. His touch was warm, steady, and reassuring, a familiar comfort like a steady heartbeat. With a slow exhale, she felt the comforting weight of his hand on her arm and the quiet strength of his presence beside her.

Jamie gently squeezed her hand, his soft touch and reassuring. "You okay?"

A soft smile tugged at her lips. "Yeah. More than okay."

The stillness of the night wrapped around them like a warm blanket; they stood there, reluctant to end the moment.

# Chapter 21

The train ride from Sperlonga to Positano was nothing short of enchanting. Lush green hills gradually gave way to jagged, rocky edges where clusters of pastel-colored villages clung precariously to the rugged slopes.

Alex sat by the window, mesmerized by the breathtaking view. The train curved along the coastline, revealing glimpses of secluded coves and rocky outcrops where the waves crashed in an enchanting display of white foam.

"I don't think I've ever seen anything this beautiful."

Jamie grinned from his seat across from her. "Just wait until we're standing on the cliffs. Pictures don't do it justice."

She turned to him, her expression wistful. "There's a postcard of the coast in my apartment," she admitted softly, the image of crashing waves and golden sand vivid in her mind. "I remember buying it years ago. My lifelong wish to visit this place came true. To stand by the windswept cliffs, feel the ocean spray on my face, and witness it myself was my desire."

Jamie's smile softened as he watched her trace a faint line on the window with her fingertip.

"And now here you are," he said quietly.

Her eyes flickered back to him, and a blush crept onto her cheeks as she felt the warmth of his gaze. For a moment, neither of them spoke, the silence thick with unspoken emotion. A shared, unspoken understanding, the sweet taste of a long-held dream finally realized, hung between them.

"Ready to see Positano?" he asked.

"Definitely."

The warm, humid coastal air, thick with the smell of brine and fish, hit them the moment they stepped onto the platform. A  short taxi ride to the hotel revealed more breathtaking views. Their hotel was a charming boutique spot with bougainvillea spilling over its balconies. The concierge greeted them warmly, handed over their keys, and pointed out the best places for dinner.

As soon as they entered their room, Alex dropped her bag by the door and walked straight to the balcony. The view was stunning. The cliffs, sea, and the twinkling lights of Amalfi below. Jamie came up beside her. "Worth the trip?"

"More than worth it."

"What do you say we take it easy tonight? Get some rest and start fresh tomorrow?"

"That sounds perfect."

"Great." he tossed his bag onto the bed. "Because a hunch tells me tomorrow will be filled with excitement and unforgettable moments."

Stepping from their hotel, the morning sun painted the Amalfi Coast in golden hues. Positano's streets were stirring to life. Bathed in sunlight, the colorful buildings clinging to the cliffs appeared impossibly vibrant, like a postcard sprung to life, defying the laws of reality.

"So," Jamie stretched his arms over his head, "where to first? Let's choose: explore the streets, or go straight to the water?"

She looked at him. "You've been here before. What do you recommend?"

"Getting lost is kind of the whole point of a place like this."

They set off through the labyrinthine streets, winding their way past sun-drenched courtyards and flower-covered balconies. Every turn revealed something new. A tiny artisan shop selling hand-painted ceramics, a gelateria offering scoops of lemon and fig, an elderly woman tending to a window box overflowing with lavender. The vibrant colors, the rich textures, the sound of waves echoing between the buildings. It was overwhelming in the best way possible.

"Why do I feel like I can't capture this in a sketch?" she mused as they walked.

"Because it's more than just what meets the eye; you can smell the essence of its soul. It's the movement, the smells, the way the sunlight plays on the walls. Sometimes a place pulses with such vibrant life, the sounds, smells, and sights, that it's impossible to capture it all on a page."

"That's frustrating."

"Maybe it just means you need to try a different approach."

They wandered downhill, following the pull of the sea. The closer they got to the marina, the more intense the aroma of salt and citrus became. She stopped at the edge of the dock. "I don't think I've ever seen water this blue."

"You should see it from above."

Minutes later, they were climbing the narrow stone path leading toward the cliffs. The incline was steep and winded through terraced gardens overflowing with lemon trees. Every so often, Alex paused, gasping for air, to admire the breathtaking panorama before her. The town of Positano spread out below. The pastel-colored buildings cascading down the cliffs like a mosaic.

"Almost there," he said as he led her toward a small overlook shaded by olive trees. "This is one of my favorite spots."

The moment Alex stepped onto the terrace, she understood why. The entire coastline stretched before them, showing the sea sparkling under the midday sun. Tiny boats left white trails in the water, and far in the distance, she could see other towns clinging to the cliffs, their rooftops blending into the landscape.

"It's like something out of a dream," she murmured.

He pulled out his camera and began adjusting the settings. "A dream you should capture." He handed her the camera.

When she took it, she let her fingers brush against his. She'd never considered herself a photographer. The feel of a pencil in her hand or the scratch of graphite on paper was where she felt most at home. The endless sea ahead made her creative itch returned.

"Just look for something that resonates with you," he said, a knowing glint in his eyes. "Something that makes you feel something."

She lifted the camera and scanned the view. It was all so breathtaking. How could she possibly narrow it down? Then, out of the corner of her eye, she spotted an old wooden boat tied to a dock far below. The old boat, worn and faded from years of sun and rain, still glided gracefully on the water. There was something deeply poetic about its endurance.

She focused the lens, adjusted the frame, and clicked the shutter.

Jamie leaned over her shoulder. "What'd you get?"

She showed him the screen, a mix of nerves and excitement fluttering in her chest.

He studied the image, a proud smile tugging at his lips as he felt a surge of satisfaction. "That's a damn good shot," his voice filled with pride.

"Seriously?"

"Really. It's got heart. You saw something beyond the obvious, and that's what makes a great photo."

Alex looked at the camera again, then of the view. Careful framing and keen attention to detail. Perhaps photography and sketching aren't so different. They are just another way of telling a story.

He nudged her gently. "So... think you might want to take more?" he asked, his eyes twinkling mischievously.

She lifted the camera once more. "Yeah. I think I do."

Lost in the moment, they lingered, each taking turns to capture the beauty of their surroundings. Jamie showed her different techniques, and Alex found details he hadn't noticed.

As the afternoon continued, she realized this trip was more than just sightseeing. It was about seeing herself differently, too and recognizing her own strength and resilience.

# Chapter 22

The deep blue waves hypnotized Alex as she leaned against the railing. The early morning sun reflected off the water in a dazzling, golden shimmer.

"I still can't believe places like this actually exist," she said, tightening her grip as the boat gently rocked.

Jamie chuckled beside her. "Just wait until we get there. Capri is even more surreal up close."

Under an hour, the ferry ride from Positano zipped by; however, the salty air, the cries of gulls, and the breathtaking views made every moment feel surreal. Approaching the island, the boat passed the majestic Faraglioni rock formations rising dramatically from the sea. The town of Marina Grande came into view, the sounds of distant church bells and bustling activity reaching her ears, and her heart raced with anticipation.

"Okay," she said. "You were right. This already feels magical."

Jamie grinned. "Told you. Now, let's go find our spot."

The sound of waves lapping against the shore filled the air as she sat on a blanket spread out on the pebbled beach. It was mid-morning, and the cove was nearly empty, except for a few other visitors and a couple of boats anchored nearby. In the distance, the Faraglioni rocks stood tall against the horizon, partially shrouded in a delicate mist. A gentle breeze carried the fresh scent of the sea and the faint aroma of lemon trees from the cliffs above.

Alex ran her fingers over the smooth stones beneath her. "This might be the most peaceful morning I've ever had," she murmured.

Jamie laid back on the blanket with his hands behind his head. "And we haven't even explored yet. Just wait until we hike up to Villa Jovis or take a boat to the Blue Grotto."

She smiled. "Let's just stay here a little longer first."

"I'm not complaining."

And so they sat in comfortable silence taking in the beauty of Capri. As the sun rose higher, she stretched her legs and dusted off the pebbles that had stuck to her. "Alright," she looked over at Jamie. "Time to see more?"

"Thought you'd never ask." He rolled up the blanket and tucked it into his backpack before slinging it over his shoulder. They made their way back up the winding stone path from the beach, stopping now and then to admire the view. As they reached the main road, he pulled out his phone to check the route.

"Villa Jovis is up that way." he nodded toward a steep incline lined with whitewashed buildings and terraces overflowing with flowers. "It's a bit of a hike, but trust me, the view is worth it."

Alex groaned playfully. "You and your hikes. Alright, lead the way, tour guide."

They walked past small cafes with baskets of fresh lemons stacked outside and boutique shops selling handmade sandals. Locals zipped by on scooters, expertly navigating the narrow pathways.

As they reached the outskirts of town, the road turned into a rugged trail lined with ancient stone walls. The higher they climbed, the more breathtaking the scenery became. Below them, the island stretched out in every direction. Cliffs plunged into the sea, lush greenery clung to the rocky landscape, and the buildings' rooftops glowed in the afternoon light.

Alex paused to catch her breath. "You weren't kidding about the climb."

Jamie grinned, barely winded. "Told you it'd be worth it."

When they finally arrived at Villa Jovis, the ruins of

Emperor Tiberius' palace sprawled before them. Massive stone walls stood against the brilliant blue sky. The site was nearly empty, giving the place a quiet, almost eerie atmosphere.

"It's hard to believe this was once a palace," she said as she ran her fingers over the rough surface of the walls.

He stood beside her with his camera hanging loosely from his neck. "Tiberius ruled the Roman Empire from right here. Imagine standing in this exact spot two thousand years ago, looking out at the same view."

She followed his gaze toward the sea. The island of Ischia and the distant coastline of Naples shimmered on the horizon. "I don't think I'd ever get tired of this," she admitted.

Jamie lifted his camera and snapped a picture of her as she stood there, lost in thought. "Neither would I."

She glanced at him, catching the soft expression on his face. Her heart skipped a beat.

"Alright," he cleared his throat and grinning. "Before you get sentimental, let's explore the rest of the ruins."

She laughed and nudged him playfully. "Fine. But only if we get gelato afterward."

"Deal."

Hand in hand, they wandered deeper into the ruins. The echoes of history surrounded them as Capri stretched out endlessly below. The sun was beginning to set as they made their way down the rugged path. Before they got to the end, she stole one last glance at the ancient estate perched high on the cliffs.

"Hard to believe Tiberius once ruled from up here." She adjusted her bag over her shoulder.

"Hard to believe he wanted to. It's beautiful, but can you imagine making this climb every day?"

"Guess that's why he had people carry him."

They reached the dock at Marina Grande just in time to catch their boat transfer. As they sped across the sapphire waters, Alex let her fingers skim the waves, soaking in the moment. She was still adjusting to this life, constantly moving, never quite knowing what was next, but there was something exhilarating about it, especially with Jamie beside her.

The sweet scent of lemon blossoms and the gentle buzz of bees filled the air around the villa, nestled among the groves on the outskirts of Anacapri. Its white stucco walls gleamed under the soft evening light, and vines of bougainvillea spilled over the terrace. A friendly woman greeted them at the entrance and handed them a pair of old-fashioned keys.

"Benvenuti. You'll find everything you need inside. We serve breakfast on the terrace in the mornings," she said with a warm smile.

Jamie opened the door to reveal a space bathed in soft amber light. The air smelled of citrus and fresh linen. Floor-to-ceiling windows framed the sea in the distance, its surface glistening under the last traces of daylight.

Alex let out a breath. "Okay... this might be my favorite stay yet."

He dropped their bags and wrapped an arm around her waist. "Glad to hear it. Now, how about we celebrate with a glass of limoncello?"

She leaned into him. "Only if you promise we'll watch the sunset from that balcony."

"Deal."

# Chapter 23

It was early morning, and Alex held her sketchpad in her lap. She had been meaning to capture the serenity of this moment, but her mind was elsewhere. Her thoughts kept drifting back to the person she used to be, to the life she had left behind. She sighed and closed the sketchpad. Instead, she stared at the water. Jamie appeared behind her with two steaming cups of coffee. He handed one to her and sat down beside her on the blanket.

"Morning."

"Morning."

"Not drawing today?"

"I was going to, but…I don't know. I guess I got a little lost in my head."

He studied her for a moment. "Want to talk about it?"

"I've just been thinking about…everything. My life before this trip. Who I was. Who I'm becoming."

"Sounds like some heavy stuff. What brought it on?"

"I don't know," she said quietly, her voice thoughtful. "I guess it just hit me all at once. Being here. Doing this. It's so far from the life I had before." She turned back to him. "It feels like I've been walking around in a fog for the last few years, just… going through the motions. Work. Sleep. Repeat." She shook her head faintly. "And now? It's like a veil has been lifted from my eyes, and I can finally see clearly again. Like I'm waking up."

"That sounds like a good thing," he said gently.

She gave him a faint smile, but there was a flicker of uncertainty in her eyes. She absently ran her thumb over the edge of the sketchbook.

"It is," she admitted. "But it's also terrifying. What if I

can't hold on to this version of me once we go back? What if I slip into the old routine and forget what this feels like?" She looked at him again, vulnerability flickering in her expression. "What if all of this," she gestured toward the horizon and the beauty of the moment surrounding them, "just becomes some faraway memory I can't reach anymore?"

His brow furrowed slightly, and for a moment, he didn't say anything. Instead, he let the weight of her words settle between them. Then, slowly, he shifted closer, closing the small space between them. He reached over and gently brushed a strand of hair away from her face, tucking it behind her ear.

"Hey," he murmured. There was a trace of a smile on his lips, but his eyes, God, his eyes, were steady and sure. "You won't forget."

His thumb lingered grazing her cheekbone in a soft, deliberate touch that sent her heart skittering.

"It's impossible."

She stared at him. "How do you know?"

"Because this isn't just some escape or some fleeting adventure for you. I've seen it. The way you come alive out here. The way you light up when you're sketching or when you're standing in front of something that takes your breath away. That's real. That's you."

A gasp escaped her as she stared at him.

"And when we go back," he added softly, "you'll carry it with you. Even when life gets busy or messy. You'll still have this in you. You'll still be you."

Tears welled in her eyes as she spoke. "What if I forget how to be brave?"

Slowly, he reached down and squeezed her hand gently. "Then I'll remind you," he said simply. "Every single time."

Her eyes softened, a slow breath escaping her lips as the tension in her chest eased, a wave of calm washing over her. She squeezed his hand back, clinging to the quiet reassurance in his touch.

They sat in comfortable silence for a while, the waves providing a soothing backdrop. Alex broke the quiet, her voice thoughtful. "Do you ever think about your past relationships?"

"Sometimes. There's one that taught me a lot. We were together for a few years, but in the end, we realized we wanted different things. It was hard, but I don't regret it. It shaped who I am."

"I guess that's what I'm realizing, too. As painful as my breakup was, it pushed me to reevaluate my life. To figure out what I really want."

"And what do you want?"

"I want to live a life that feels meaningful. To create art that inspires people. And...I want to be with someone who sees me. Who values me for who I am."

"You deserve all of that. And more."

Her cheeks warmed under his gaze, and she looked away. "Thanks. That means a lot."

As the sun rose higher in the sky, Alex felt a quiet sense of peace settle over her. She had spent so long clinging to the past, to the ache of what could have been, to the doubts that had once held her back. But now, sitting beside Jamie as the waves kissed the shore and the world stretched wide before her, she felt something shift. Something let go.

And in its place came lightness. Not the absence of weight, but the freedom of being fully present. Jamie reached for his camera, adjusting the lens with the practiced ease of someone who saw the world not just for what it was, but for what it meant. He gave her a glance and a soft grin before raising the viewfinder to his eye, ready to capture the moment. Alex smiled back, then picked up her sketchpad from her lap.

Her lines were rough, her shading uneven. But for once, that didn't matter. It was hers. A tangible piece of her journey. A reflection of where she'd been and how far she'd come. Every smudge and imperfection spoke of discovery. Not just of the world around her, but of herself. She was learning to see beauty in the flaws. In the unfinished lines and the missed proportions. In the process. And that beauty was everywhere. In the curve of a shoreline, in the laughter they shared, in the moments of silence they didn't rush to fill.

Later that afternoon, she found herself seated at the small table outside the cabin, her sketchpad open and pencils scattered like petals across the sun-drenched surface. The shoreline she had started earlier came to life beneath her hand. The winding contours, the gentle slope of the dunes, and the delicate play of light on water. She worked slowly shading the finer details with a quiet focus that had become sacred.

He emerged from inside. "Still working on that masterpiece?" he slid into the seat across from her.

"If by masterpiece, you mean another page of me figuring out how to draw waves, then yes."

He rested his elbows on the table as he peered at her sketchpad. "You're underselling yourself. That looks incredible."

"Coming from the guy who can make a bowl of fruit look like fine art, I'll take that as a compliment."

"It is. You've got a good eye for detail. It's not just technical skill. It's the way you see things."

"I think that's what I've always loved about art. It forces you to look closer, to notice things you might otherwise miss."

"That's exactly why I got into photography. It's not just about taking pictures. It's about capturing the essence of a moment. The way the sunlight felt on your skin, the way the air smelled after the rain. The little things that tell a bigger story."

Like what?" she asked softly.

A faint smile touched Jamie's lips as he delicately turned his camera over and scrolled through the shots he'd taken that day. After a moment, he turned the screen toward her.

"Like this," he tapped the image.

She looked at the photo. It wasn't of the sweeping coastline or the postcard-perfect architecture. It was of *her*. Natural. Candid. She was sitting on a low stone wall with her sketchbook in her lap. The wind had caught her hair, lifting it just enough to send a few stray strands across her face. Her fingers, smudged with charcoal, were stained dark gray, and a faint crease of concentration etched between her brows. She stared at the image, a lump forming in her throat as the details sunk in.

"I didn't even know you were taking this," she whispered.

His lips tugged into a small, crooked smile.

"That's the point. You were in your own world. Lost in it. That's what I wanted to capture. When you're creating something, you get into this zone, and the world fades away. There's a quiet intensity. Completely unguarded. Completely you."

Her eyes flicked back to the photo, studying the way he had framed it. The soft blur of the background made her figure stand out. She saw herself the way he saw her, and it made her chest ache. A faint static clung to her fingertips as they brushed lightly across the camera screen. She traced the edges of her image as though trying to hold the moment in her hands. Finally, she glanced up at him, her voice low.

"I still don't get it," she murmured. "Why me? Why not the dramatic cliffs, their edges sharp against the bright blue sky, or the breathtaking panoramic view? Why not the picture-perfect postcard shots, with their vibrant colors and idyllic scenes?"

A slight shake of his head accompanied Jamie's softening expression.

"Because you were the view."

A gasp escaped her lips as she stared, then quickly looked away, focusing on the rhythmic crash of waves against the shore. She could feel his eyes on her, unwavering and sincere.

Eventually, she let out a slow breath, her voice barely audible. "I've been thinking a lot about what you said this morning. About how far I've come. But sometimes, it feels like I'm still figuring out who I am. What I want."

"That's not a bad thing, you know. Life's not about having all the answers. It's about asking the right questions."

"What if I'm asking the wrong ones?."

"You're not. Trust me. I see it in the way you've been throwing yourself into this trip, into your art. You're chasing something real. That's more than most people can say."

Alex felt a warmth spread through her chest. "I don't think I've ever had someone believe in me the way you do. Wait … don't tell Sarah I said that."

"Oh, don't worry. Your secret's safe with me," he teased. "Though I might have to use that information as leverage if Sarah ever blackmails me. You know how she can be."

"Oh, so now you're threatening me with blackmail?" she teased in mock suspicion. "I knew you were trouble the second I saw you at that cafe."

"So, what's next on your creative agenda? More waves? Or are you branching out?"

"I don't know. Maybe I'll try sketching you."

"Oh, really? Think you can capture all this?" He gestured dramatically at himself, earning a laugh from Alex.

"I'll do my best," she teased, flipping to a new page in her sketchpad. "Now sit still and try not to ruin my inspiration."

Jamie struck an exaggerated pose; one arm draped over the back of his chair. "Like this?"

"Okay, maybe something a little less…statuesque."

"How about this?"

"Perfect," Alex said, her pencil already moving across the page.

As she sketched, he watched her with quiet admiration in his eyes. It was a moment of stillness, of connection, and as she worked, she felt the weight of her old wounds lifting a little more. Here, under the warmth of the sun and the steady rhythm of the waves, she realized she wasn't just revisiting old wounds. She was healing them.

# Chapter 24

Alex sat on a low stone wall near the fountain, barefoot and entirely immersed in her sketchpad. Her hair had slipped loose from its tie, a few strands brushing across her cheek as she leaned forward. Her pencil moved with quiet intensity, tracing each curve and petal of a flower she'd seen earlier on their walk through the hills. Her brows knit in concentration and her lips parted slightly in thought.

She was a portrait of focus.

Jamie stood a few feet away in the doorway of the open patio. His camera hung loosely around his neck. But his gaze wasn't scanning for distant vistas or dramatic skylines this time. He was watching her.

There was something about the way she moved now, so different from when they first arrived. Her shoulders, once always pulled tight, as if bracing for something unseen, now rested naturally. Her body seemed to flow with a new ease. Even the way she laughed, fuller, brighter, as if she was finally giving herself permission to feel joy without apology. She was changing, and he could see it in every detail.

The way her eyes lit up, not just when she was sketching, but when she was looking. At the world. At him. And though he had captured sunsets in Santorini, the first snow in Iceland, and rain-soaked alleys in Kyoto, he had never wanted to photograph anything more than this quiet, transforming moment. Not because she looked perfect, but because she was.

He lifted his camera slowly, carefully. Not to interrupt. Not to pose her. But to keep a piece of this moment forever. Because this, *her,* was the story he wanted to tell.

Silently, he lifted his camera and adjusted the lens. Through the viewfinder, her eyes, sharp and clear, came into focus. The peaceful yet determined look on her face, etched with the quiet wisdom of self-discovery, told a story of transformation of someone who was finally recognizing herself for who she was.

A soft *click* echoed in the stillness as the camera captured the moment.

She was startled by the sound. "Jamie?"

He froze for a moment. He was caught in the act. Then, a sheepish grin spread across his face as he lowered the camera. "Sorry. I couldn't help but stare. Your gaze was magnetic, captivating me in its intensity.

"You were taking pictures of me?"

"Guilty," he held up the camera as if to prove his point. "You looked so focused. I wanted to capture it."

She closed her sketchpad and set it aside. "Can I see?"

He walked over; the gravel crunching under his feet and crouched beside her. With a flick of his thumb, he scrolled through the photos, stopping when he found the one he'd just snapped; the vibrant colors of the scene popping on the camera's screen.

The photo was stunning. Soft and natural, with the sunlight highlighting the curve of her face and the delicate movement of her hair. She hardly recognized herself.

"Wow," she whispered. "Is that really me?"

"Of course it is. That's how I see you. Kind, compassionate, and full of light.

"I don't think anyone's ever looked at me like that before."

"Then they weren't paying attention."

She shifted slightly, breaking the intensity of the moment with a nervous laugh. "Well, now I'm self-conscious. Are you always sneaking photos of people when they're not looking?"

"Only when they're interesting."

"Interesting, huh? That's a new one."

"Trust me, it's a compliment," he said, slinging the camera back around his neck. "Come on. Let's take a walk. I'll show you what I mean."

They strolled through the villa's gardens, where bright hibiscus flowers and lush greenery framed winding stone pathways. He kept his camera at the ready, snapping photos here and there and of her as well.

At first, she felt awkward, aware of his lens whenever it turned in her direction. "Do you really need these many pictures of me? You're going to run out of space on your memory card."

"I have plenty of space," He assured her. "Besides, it's not just about taking pictures. It's about capturing moments like how the light hits your face, the way you laugh when you think no one's watching. It's all part of the story."

"You're ridiculous, you know that?"

"Maybe. But you're the one who keeps giving me such great material."

Her worries seemed to melt away as she breathed in the fresh air, the sun warm on her skin, the gentle rustling of leaves in the breeze whispering calm through her. The birdsong that floated above them was light and melodic, as if the world itself were humming a lullaby.

And then there was *him*.

Jamie made her feel seen in a way that bypassed performance, expectation, or insecurity. It was the opposite of the self-conscious dread she'd known in the past. The one that made her shrink from attention and from praise she didn't believe she deserved. This was different. With him, there was no mask to wear.

Just a quiet, steady affirmation that wrapped around her like sunlight and settled in her heart. She wasn't just someone he traveled with. She wasn't a muse or a fleeting inspiration. To him, she was a story worth telling.

They slowed near a small fountain tucked into a corner

of the garden path, half-covered in ivy and worn smooth by time. A flock of birds fluttered down, wings beating softly as they landed at the basin's edge, dipping their beaks into the cool water. Alex paused, mesmerized. She crouched slightly, watching the birds with a quiet fascination. A peaceful smile touched her lips.

Jamie didn't say a word. He didn't need to. He raised his camera and captured the moment. The soft curve of her posture, the reflection of birds in the rippling water, the sunlight catching the gold in her hair. But what he really captured was something deeper. The stillness. The beauty in the quiet. The unfolding of someone finally beginning to believe in herself.

"Okay, now I want to see this one," she said.

He handed her the camera, and she scrolled through the images. The shot of her by the fountain was breathtaking. She looked serene, almost otherworldly, with her hair falling around her shoulders and the sunlight reflecting off the water behind her.

"These are...incredible. I don't even know what to say."

"Say thank you," he said lightly. "And perhaps stop doubting how amazing you are."

"I don't know how you do it," she said. "You see things in a way that no one else does."

"It's not about my perspective. It's about showing you what's already there."

The words settled over her like a warm blanket, filling a space she hadn't even realized was empty. As the sun began to set, he took one last photo of her. She was looking out over the horizon with a thoughtful expression.

This, he thought, was the Alex he wanted the world to see. A woman who was no longer defined by her past, but by the strength and beauty she carried into her future. And as she turned to him, her smile soft and genuine, he couldn't help but feel like he was the one who had been truly captured.

That evening, the villa was cloaked in a gentle hush.

Alex sat curled up on the couch in the cozy living area with her sketchpad balanced on her lap. A single lamp cast a warm golden pool of light over her, and the faint scent of citrus and wood smoke still lingered in the air.

She was adding the final touches to a drawing of the fountain from earlier that day. Each line brought the moment back; the fluttering birds, the rippling water, the feeling of being still and completely present. But what had stayed with her most wasn't just the fountain or the garden. It was the way Jamie had looked at her.

She hadn't stopped thinking about his photographs. The candid shots he'd shown her just before dinner. There was one of her crouched near the fountain, utterly focused, sunlight filtering through the trees above her. It wasn't posed, and yet something about it felt almost intimate. Like he'd captured a part of her she hadn't even known was there. He saw her. Not the curated version, not the one who second-guessed her every move, but her, unfiltered and whole.

A soft creak of the wooden floor pulled her from her thoughts. She looked up to see him walking into the room barefoot and a towel slung over his shoulder. His hair was still damp and tousled from his shower. He wore a worn T-shirt and joggers, as if the evening itself had wrapped him in softness. In his hands, he carried two steaming mugs of tea.

"Thought you might want something warm," he said with a quiet smile, crossing the room and handing her one.

Their fingers brushed briefly, and the touch sent a shiver down her spine.

"Thank you," she murmured.

Jamie settled into the armchair across from her, watching her for a moment. His eyes drifted to her sketchpad, and a smile played at his lips.

"Is that the fountain?"

She nodded, glancing down at it. "I couldn't stop thinking about it." Then, after a beat: "About today. About... everything."

Jamie tilted his head, waiting. Inviting.

"And your photos. Especially the ones of me. It's like you captured something I didn't know I was becoming."

His gaze softened. "Maybe that's because you're finally seeing it, too."

They sat in silence for a moment. She set her mug down and glanced at him.

"Why do you care so much about showing people their stories? Through your photos, I mean."

"Because I've been where you are. Feeling lost, doubting myself, wondering if I had anything worthwhile to offer the world. Photography saved me. It gave me a way to connect, to make sense of everything."

"You're incredible, you know that?"

"I'm just a guy with a camera."

"No," she said firmly. "You're so much more than that. You have this way of seeing the world that makes it feel…alive. Like it's full of possibilities."

"You're part of that world, too. And I think you're starting to see how much you belong in it."

Alex felt her breath catch, the air in her lungs suddenly too fragile to hold. Her chest tightened with something far more disarming. It pulsed with vulnerability, with longing, with the undeniable weight of being seen. She wanted to look away. To soften the moment with a laugh or a self-deprecating joke. To retreat into the safety of sarcasm or distance. But she couldn't. She didn't want to.

Everything else, the firelight, the room, the soft tick of the clock on the wall, blurred into the background. The only thing she could truly feel was him. The warmth in his eyes. The steadiness in the way he looked at her, like she wasn't just someone passing through his life, but someone who mattered. His presence wrapped around her like gravity. Unshakable. Quiet. Certain.

And her heart was slamming against her ribs, loud and relentless, like it had been waiting for this moment far longer than she realized. She was sure he could hear it, by the way it echoed in her ears. Her fingers tightened slightly around the mug, still warm in her hands, and her voice escaped before she could stop it.

"Jamie…"

He didn't flinch. Didn't speak. He just stepped closer. His gaze dropped to her lips for the briefest heartbeat before finding her eyes again. The world tilted gently. And in that stillness between one breath and the next, she knew: if she wanted to step forward, all she had to do was let go.

His gaze went to her lips and she noticed the small, almost imperceptible clench of his jaw as if he were fighting some internal battle. The space between them shrank without either of them moving, as if their connection was a gravity of its own. For one lingering second, Alex thought he might close the gap. That his lips might find hers and the unspoken tension would finally break.

But instead, he let out a breath and let his hand fall from her cheek.

"You don't give yourself enough credit," he said. "You make the world feel alive, too."

His words hung in the air between them as if neither of them wanted to speak too loudly and risk shattering the fragile truth of the moment. The heat of his touch lingered on her skin and yet he didn't move closer. He just looked at her with an expression so tender it made her breath catch all over again. That restraint, that care, only made it worse. Because it wasn't hesitation. It was intention. It was him holding her heart gently, without rushing, without demand. And it made her heart twist in the most impossible, aching way.

She pulled in a shaky breath, let it fill her lungs, and released it slowly. She trying to steady herself against the storm of emotion building quietly beneath the surface. She didn't say a word. But in that silence, so much passed between them. Wanting, wondering, waiting. And somehow, without a single touch more, she felt everything.

"You make it easy," she admitted quietly. "Being around you...it makes everything feel possible."

His lips parted slightly, as if he were about to say something, but he just smiled. It was a smile that reached his eyes. He glanced down briefly, then let out a breath that sounded almost like a laugh.

"You're gonna kill me, you know that?" he teased softly.

"Why's that?"

He lifted his eyes to hers again, and this time there was no teasing in his expression. Only warmth. Only honesty. "Because every time I think I've figured you out," he murmured, "you go and prove me wrong."

She fought the urge to reach for him. But neither of them moved.

# Chapter 25

Alex walked barefoot along the warm, sun-drenched sand. The grains shifted beneath her feet like silk, warm from the day's heat but already beginning to cool. Her sandals swung lazily from her fingertips. The salty breeze lifted loose strands of hair from her face, and she closed her eyes for a moment, letting the air kiss her skin and the hush of the ocean wrap around her like a familiar song.

Behind her, just a few steps back, Jamie moved with the quiet focus that always settled over him when he had his camera in hand. The soft clicks of the shutter captured the sky melting into the sea. Since they'd left the villa, he hadn't said much. But it wasn't distance. It was something else. A peaceful kind of silence.

Alex stole a look over her shoulder and caught him mid-frame, his silhouette outlined by the fading sun, camera raised, gaze intent. There was something peaceful about watching him work. How he gave himself fully to the moment, how it calmed her even without words.

She turned back toward the water, the breeze tugging gently at her dress, and walked a little farther until the tide kissed her toes. She tilted her head back, closed her eyes, and breathed in. "It's almost too perfect," she whispered.

He came up beside her and lowered his camera. "It doesn't seem real, does it?" he asked.

She opened her eyes slowly and looked at him. "It's like stepping into one of your photographs."

"I'd trade all the photographs in the world to keep moments like this."

She blushed and turned back to the horizon. "It's

uncanny, how you always say exactly what I needed to hear at precisely the right moment."

"It's not about saying the right thing," he replied. "I'm saying what I mean."

Her gaze fell on him once more, lingering on his kind eyes. This time, her heart thudded a little harder in her chest. There was something about the way he was staring, as though he were memorizing every detail of her face. With a delicate throat clearing, she tried to lighten the mood. "So, what's the most stunning sunset you've ever seen? I bet this one's not even in your top five."

"I've witnessed sunsets in the Sahara Desert, over the Alps, and even on the cliffs of Santorini. But this one..." he paused and looked at her. "This one's different."

Her cheeks grew warm under his gaze. "Because of the ocean?" she teased.

"No," he said. "Because of you."

Not knowing what to say, she stared at the horizon.

"Alex," he whispered.

She turned to him, still clutching her sandals tightly. "Yes..."

He stepped closer, leaving only a few feet between them. "You don't have to say anything. I need you to know. Being here with you, it's changed something for me. It's no longer solely about the places anymore. It's about who I'm with."

"Jamie, I—" She stopped and shook her head as a nervous laugh escaped her lips. "I don't know how to do this."

A small, reassuring smile played on his lips. "Do what?"

"This," she gestured vaguely between them. "To let someone in again. It's terrifying."

"I get it. I'm not exactly fearless, either. But sometimes the scary things are worth it."

A wave of tenderness washed over his face as his eyes softened, and with a slow, deliberate movement, he reached out to her. He wanted to give her space, so he made sure to keep his distance in case she wanted to pull away. But she didn't.

She felt the warmth of his hand in hers. His warm touch sent shivers of pleasant surprise through her. A lump formed in her throat as she struggled to suppress the intense feelings welling up inside..

"You make it sound so easy," she whispered.

With a gentle pressure, his thumb traced circles over her hand. "It's not," he admitted softly. "But it's easier with you."

Mesmerized, her lips parted slightly, and her eyes were locked on his. The same eyes she had stared into so many times felt different now. Less of a mystery. Less of a window into the unknown and more like something familiar. Something safe. She held his gaze, the pounding of her heart echoing in her ears, a deafening rhythm against the silence.

"You scare me," she confessed softly.

Jamie's brows tugged together faintly. He was concerned about her confession. "Alex—"

"Not in a bad way," she clarified. "It's just... I'm scared because this feels real. And I didn't think I'd ever have that again. Not after everything. Not after..."

Her voice caught, and she closed her eyes. For a fleeting moment, the old ache she thought she'd left behind resurfaced. The betrayal. The heartbreak. The fear of letting someone else in, only to have them leave.

But he squeezed her hand gently. "Hey," he murmured softly. "I'm not him.

"I know," she whispered.

He cupped her face carefully. His thumbs brushed away a tear she hadn't realized had fallen, leaving a cool trace.

"I'm not him," he repeated quietly. "And I'm not going anywhere."

Her chest tightened, and she exhaled sharply, a shaky sound that was somewhere between a breath and a sob. They stood there. And then, slowly, she reached up, her fingers tracing the lines of his wrists as they lay against her face, a silent connection forming. She held onto him.

"Jamie," she whispered.

His eyes, soft and amber like warm honey in the fading light, searched hers with a depth that made her breath hitch. There was no pressure in his gaze—only patience, only her. He was waiting, not out of uncertainty, but because he knew.

He was letting her choose. The tenderness in that choice undid her. A quiet tremor ran through her as her fingers slid up, tightening around his wrists. Her heart beat a wild, disbelieving rhythm, but her feet were steady as she rose slowly onto her toes.

The moment their mouths met, time seemed to stop, and all that remained was the intense pressure of their lips together and the sensation of each other's breath. The swirl of doubts, fears, and uncertainties, a suffocating cloud of anxiety, fell away, leaving only his comforting presence. He pulled her close, his arms powerful yet tender around her as he kissed her. There was no urgency; it felt calm and peaceful, a quiet, unhurried process. It was patient. Steady. Like he was willing to hold her if she needed, his arms a steady, warm embrace until she felt safe enough to let go. And she did.

She melted into him, her arms winding around his neck, experiencing the warmth of his skin against hers. His hands caressed her back, anchoring her against him as their kiss deepened, a slow, unhurried exploration filled with a powerful, almost electric current. Something raw. When they finally pulled apart, her forehead rested against his; the lingering touch sent shivers down her spine, and both were breathless.

"Terrifying, huh?" he murmured.

"Completely."

His lips curved into a faint smile. "Still worth it?"

She let out a soft breath.

"Yeah," she whispered. "So worth it."

"No matter where you go, what you do, or how many times you question yourself, just know that you are enough."

Her chest ached with the weight of his words that come from hearing something she didn't know she needed. "You're good at this whole 'emotional wisdom' thing, you know that?"

"It's one of my many talents."

She laughed. "Well, since we're being honest... I think you're right."

"About what?"

"Loosening my grip. Taking it one step at a time." She exhaled and looked back at the endless horizon. "I'm learning that I don't have to have everything figured out right now. And it's okay to just be here."

"Now you're getting it."

"I don't think I'll ever get used to this."

"Used to what?"

"Feeling like this. Like I'm exactly where I'm supposed to be."

He smiled and kissed the top of her head. "That's the magic of it, isn't it? You don't have to get used to it. Allow yourself to have it."

She closed her eyes to let the moment sink into her bones. She had spent so long chasing after certainty and after security. But here, wrapped in his warm embrace, she felt a sense of peace wash over her.

She looked up again. "Promise me something?"

"Anything."

"No matter where we go next, no matter what happens..." She said. "We won't forget this."

"Not a chance."

After their sunset confession, they wandered along the beach until they stumbled upon a secluded stretch of sand with a clear view of the stars. Jamie carried a blanket he had grabbed from the villa, shaking it out and spreading it on the ground. "Perfect spot," he said, looking up at the sky.

With a sigh, she settled onto the worn wool blanket. "It's been a long time since I just...looked at the stars."

He settled next to her, lying back with his arms tucked behind his head. "They make you feel small, don't they? But not in a bad way. It's humbling."

"It's beautiful. Peaceful." She turned her head slightly to look at him.

"So, what's your next move, muralist?"

"I haven't made up my mind yet. But maybe I'll start with something small. A sketch, a painting. Just to see where it goes."

"Sounds like a plan. And if you ever need inspiration, I'll be here."

"I'll hold you to that."

He smiled, a tender smile that reached his eyes, and without another word, he pulled her close for another kiss. Slower this time, but just as sure. Like he had all the time in the world.

# Chapter 26

They walked back to the villa holding hands and still feeling the kiss from earlier. Reaching the porch, he gave her fingers a gentle squeeze, as if silently asking her if she was still okay. She squeezed back.

*I'm okay,* she wanted to say. *I'm more than okay.*

His lips parted slightly, as if he were about to say something, but then he didn't. Instead, he looked at the villa door.

"Do you... want to sit out here for a while?" he asked quietly. His voice sounded almost uncertain, as though he was giving her the option to slip away if she needed to.

She paused for only a moment. She should have been tired. The long day of exploring should have left her drained, but she felt wide awake. "Yeah... I'd like that."

A relieved smile tugged at his mouth. Without letting go of her hand, he guided her to the small bench on the porch. They sat side by side. His arm rested along the back of the bench, sending the occasional spark along her skin. For a while, they just watched the moonlight dance on the water. The waves caught the silvery glow, creating shifting patterns of light and shadow. It was hypnotizing, but not nearly as mesmerizing as the warmth of his presence beside her.

Alex turned her head slightly to sneak a glance at him. His hair was still slightly tousled from the breeze, giving him an easy, unguarded look. *God, he's beautiful,* she thought. He must have felt her eyes on him because he turned to meet her gaze. A crooked smile tugged at his lips.

"What?" he asked softly.

She smiled. "Nothing."

"Liar."

She shook her head. But before she could say anything else, he brushed his fingertips lightly along her jaw.

"Tell me what you're thinking," he whispered.

Her breath caught slightly at his touch, her skin suddenly tingling beneath his fingertips.

"I'm thinking..." she started softly, "that I don't want this night to end."

His gaze softened, and he slowly leaned closer. His forehead brushed against hers, and she could feel his breath feathering against her lips.

"Me neither," he whispered.

For a moment, they just stayed in that same position. And then his lips found hers again.

"I could kiss you forever."

"You might eventually have to let me eat or sleep, you know."

He grinned and pressed a playful kiss to the corner of her mouth. "Details."

Her heart fluttered at the tenderness in his eyes. They stayed there for a long time, exchanging lazy kisses and whispering words. Occasionally, he would brush his lips against her temple or the curve of her shoulder, and each time, she leaned into him just a little more.

Eventually, the night grew cooler, and the faint sound of the tide rolling in became softer and more distant. Jamie pulled the light throw blanket from the back of the bench and draped it around her shoulders. She sank into his side and laid her head on his chest. Neither of them spoke. They didn't need to.

"I think it's time we go inside now," she said finally.

He stood up and held the door open for her. She stepped inside, the familiar warmth of the villa wrapping around her like a blanket. The cozy living room felt more welcoming than ever.

Jamie moved to the small kitchenette and filled a kettle with water. "Chamomile okay?" he asked over his shoulder.

"Perfect," Alex answered and settled onto the couch. She noticed a stack of photographs spread across the coffee table.

She picked one up. It was a black-and-white shot of a bustling marketplace, the motion of the crowd beautifully blurred. "These are yours?"

"Yeah. I was sorting through some older stuff earlier, trying to decide what to keep for a portfolio update."

"They're incredible," she said.

He crossed the room and sat down beside her. "Thanks. That one's from Marrakesh. The markets there are chaotic, loud, and full of life."

Her curiosity was piqued. "Do you have a favorite place you've visited?"

Jamie thought for a moment. "It's hard to pick just one. But I think it's less about the place and more about the moments."

"What do you mean?"

He looked at the photograph in her hands. "I mean, there's no single 'best place' for me. It's about the little things like the way the light hits a street at sunset, the sound of waves against a rocky shore, or the conversations with strangers who feel like old friends. Those moments stick with me more than just a location on a map."

Alex studied the photo again. This time she was seeing it in a new light. "That's a really beautiful way to look at it."

"What about you? You've been on this trip for a while now, any favorite moments?"

She thought back to the nights spent wandering unfamiliar streets, the sunrise over the Amalfi Coast, the feel of warm sand beneath her toes in Capri, and the way he looked at her just before he kissed her. "I think... I'm starting to understand what you mean. The places are incredible, but it's the moments that make them special."

He nudged her playfully. "See? You're getting it."

She laughed. "I guess I am."

The high-pitched shriek of the kettle sliced through the

quiet moment. Jamie walked to the kitchenette and poured the tea. She smiled to herself as she watched his graceful movements. He returned and handed her a mug of something fragrant and warm.

"Thanks," she said.

He settled back on the couch with his own mug cradled in his hands. "So," he began in a playful tone, "are you going to keep avoiding talking about what happened back there?"

"I wasn't avoiding it," she protested.

"Sure, you weren't."

She sighed. "Okay, fine. I was avoiding it a little. It's just...a lot to process."

"I get that. And I don't want to rush you into anything you're not ready for."

She set her mug down and turned to face him fully. "It's not that I'm not ready," she said carefully. "I think I've just spent so much time being afraid of feeling anything too deeply. It's like I forgot how to let myself...fall."

He rested his hand lightly on hers. "You don't have to have all the answers right now. We can take this at whatever pace you're comfortable with."

"Thank you for being so patient with me."

"Patience isn't exactly my strong suit, but for you, I don't mind waiting."

A blush crept onto her cheeks, but she didn't look away. There was something about his presence that made her want to stay in the moment. The sincerity in his gaze, the quiet strength in his words, and the way he saw her filled her with a warmth she hadn't let herself feel in years.

The clock on the wall chimed twelve gentle notes softly into the stillness of the night. Midnight. And yet, everything felt settled. A wave of contentment washed over her. It was more than just peace. It was belonging. To the moment, to herself, and to him. Jamie stood and gathered their mugs. When he turned back to her, his smile was softer now, touched with something that made her heart flutter.

"You should get some rest. Big day tomorrow, right?"

She stretched her arms over her head and let out a contented sigh. "Yeah. Santorini."

The name alone sent a thrill through her. Another place she had only ever dreamed of visiting, now just hours away.

Jamie stood and offered her a hand. "Come on, let's at least try to get some sleep before the adventure continues."

She let him pull her to her feet. As they made their way toward their rooms, she hesitated at her door. "Hey, Jamie?"

"Yeah?"

"Thank you. For everything. For bringing me here, for being patient with me, for just... being you."

His lips curved into a small smile. "You don't have to thank me. I want to be here with you."

Warmth bloomed in her chest, and for a brief second, she considered said more, but she just smiled and said, "Goodnight."

"Goodnight."

# Chapter 27

From their Santorini villa's balcony, they enjoyed a tranquil soundtrack of gentle waves lapping against the shore. With the early morning breeze whipping through her loose hair, Alex leaned against the railing. Jamie stood behind her taking pictures.

"You know, I didn't think a place like this could exist outside of postcards."

"It's one of those places that feels too perfect, isn't it? Almost like a movie set."

"You've seen so many places. Does it ever stop feeling magical?"

"Some places, yes. But it's not about the location. It's about who you're with. When you're sharing it with someone who sees it the way you do, it makes all the difference."

Their eyes met, and she felt a warmth bloom in her chest. She looked back out at the horizon, trying to hide the blush creeping across her cheeks.

After breakfast, they ventured into Oia, where whitewashed buildings with blue-domed roofs stood in stark contrast to the cerulean sky. The streets were alive with the smell of fresh-baked pastries, the chatter of shopkeepers, and the distant hum of tourists marveling at the view. She carried a small sketchbook folded in her bag, which he had encouraged her to bring along.

"Here." He stopped at a quiet corner overlooking the sea. "This spot is perfect. Sit here."

She raised an eyebrow. "Are you just scouting good angles for your photos?"

"Always," he flashed her a grin. "But really, it's a good

place to sketch. The light is perfect and the views are inspiring. Trust me."

She sat on the cool wooden bench and pulled out her stuff. He sat close enough to make her skin tingle. He was more captivated by her than the surrounding landscape.

"Stop staring," she said without looking up.

"I can't help it. You're a better subject than the sea."

Alex rolled her eyes but felt her heart race at the compliment. She focused on the scene in front of her and let her pencil glide across the paper. After a while, she turned the sketchbook around to show Jamie.

"What do you think?"

He studied it carefully. "It's beautiful. You have such a way of capturing the essence of a place. It's like you're telling a story with every line."

"Thanks. That means a lot, coming from you."

He set his camera down. "You know, you're more talented than you give yourself credit for. You could do this professionally if you wanted to."

"I don't know about that. Sketching is just…something I do for me. It's personal."

"Exactly. And that's what makes it so special. It's authentic."

As the day wore on, they wandered through the town, stopping to browse local shops and sample treats from street vendors. At one stall, she found a small pendant with a delicate wave design carved into it.

"It's beautiful," she held it up to the light.

"It suits you."

She ran her thumb over the smooth surface of the pendant. "I don't know…"

Before she could decide, he reached into his pocket and handed a few euros to the vendor. "Consider it a gift," he said with a wink.

"Jamie," she protested. "You didn't have to do that."

"I wanted to," he said simply. "Call it a souvenir for this

chapter of your life."

Later that evening, they returned to the villa, where he suggested they watch the sunset from a secluded spot he'd scouted earlier. They hiked up a narrow trail to a small cliff side clearing, carrying a blanket. As the sun dipped lower in the sky, she felt a deep sense of peace.

"Do you ever think about what comes next?"

"Sometimes. But I try not to plan too much. Life's unpredictable, and that's what makes it exciting."

"I guess I'm still learning to let go like that."

"You don't have to have it all figured out. Just take it one step at a time. You've already come so far."

"I couldn't have done it without you."

She smiled as she brushed a strand of hair away from her face. "You've had it in you all along."

As the sun disappeared below the horizon, leaving behind a sky full of stars, Alex said wistfully, "Jamie. I don't know where this is going, but I know I want to see it through."

"Me too."

Jamie held a flashlight and guided their steps along the uneven path, while she clutched the blanket they'd brought to watch the sunset. She was still buzzing with the warmth of the evening.

"Careful here," he said as he shined the light on a rocky patch. He offered his free hand, and she took it without hesitation.

"You know," she teased as she stepped carefully over the rocks, "for someone who loves adventure, you're surprisingly good at this whole 'making sure I don't fall on my face' thing."

"What can I say? I've learned that the best adventures are even better when your partner's in one piece."

It amazed her how natural this felt walking with him, teasing him, sharing these moments. She hadn't realized how much she'd craved this kind of connection. When they reached the villa, she slipped off her sneakers and sighed with relief. "I don't know how I walked so much in those. I swear my feet are plotting revenge."

Jamie grinned as he set the flashlight down on the kitchen counter. "You're adapting to the travel life. Blisters and sore feet are all part of the package."

"Well," Alex said, dropping the blanket onto a chair and heading for the fridge, "if I'm going to survive this 'package,' I need fuel. Want something to drink?"

Jamie leaned against the counter, watching her with a curious expression. "Sure. What are you thinking?"

"Maybe tea? Or wine if we're feeling indulgent," she said, pulling out a bottle they hadn't yet opened.

"Wine," he decided with a smile. "We've earned it after today."

They went to the terrace. The view of the sea was mesmerizing, and the cool night air carried a faint scent of salt and wildflowers. He swirled the wine in his glass thoughtfully. "You know, today was one of those days that reminds me why I fell in love with travel. It's not just the places, it's the stories you find in them. The people."

Alex watched him as he spoke. He wasn't just talking about the hike they'd taken that afternoon or the cafe they'd stumbled upon in the village. He was talking about something deeper. Something that stirred in him every time they wandered into the unknown.

"The people?"

He lowered his glass and turned his gaze toward her.

"Yeah. Like the woman who sold us the pastries. She could've just made the sale and sent us on our way. Instead, she shared stories of her childhood. Her eyes sparkled as she described the sights and sounds that filled her young life here. She made it personal."

She loved the way his smile crinkled the corners of his eyes and his infectious laugh. The way he noticed the details most people overlooked, like the subtle shift in light or the almost imperceptible change in a bird's song. To him, travel wasn't simply about picturesque locations. It was about the immersive experiences from the touch of ancient stones to the taste of local delicacies.

"You make it sound magical," she murmured, a hint of wonder in her tone.

"Yes, it is. Or at least, it can be. When you slow down enough to see it."

The way he said made her realize that this wasn't about a trip anymore. He was talking about life, as if sharing a secret. The key was to fully immerse oneself in the moment. Truly taking the time to observe it.

"Being with you makes even ordinary moments feel enchanting, like a fairy tale."

The unexpected tenderness in his voice made her heart flutter and her breath catch.

"Being around you makes me feel...alive."

Jamie turned to her. "What do you mean?"

A thoughtful pause settled over her as she searched for the right words. "Back home, everything felt so gray. Wake up, go to work, come home, repeat. Even the things I used to love, art, music, friends, felt dull. But ever since I met you..." She gestured vaguely to the world around them. "each new place we go to makes me feel it's like I'm waking up. And it's terrifying, but it's also incredible."

"You deserve to feel that way. You deserve to live a life that excites you."

Her breath hitched at the sincerity in his voice, and she looked down at their hands. She felt enveloped in comforting warmth from his gentle touch.

"That will not happen. Because the person you're becoming isn't someone you'll lose. She's already a part of you. She always has been. You're just giving her space to grow."

# Chapter 28

As they walked along the dramatic cliffs of Santorini, the warm air resonated with the distant tolling of church bells and the gentle touch of a sea breeze. Gazing out at the Aegean Sea, they felt a sense of awe as its vastness enveloped them. The sun was setting, painting the sky in a myriad of colors—an awe-inspiring view that took their breath away.

She took her sketchbook from her bag. "I don't think I'll ever get tired of this," she murmured.

He was watching her more than the horizon. "Me neither," he said softly.

She glanced at him and grinned. "You're not even looking at the sunset."

"That's because I've got something better to look at."

Alex rolled her eyes but felt her cheeks warm. She couldn't believe how easy he can make her heart melt with just a look.

"Smooth," she teased.

"Just stating the truth."

She shook her head but couldn't hide her smile. Turning back to the view, she flipped open her sketchbook to trace over the lines she had drawn earlier.

He peered at the pages. "Can I see?"

She angled it toward him.

"These are incredible. Your art captures the very soul of a moment. That is something that a camera simply cannot."

"Says the photographer."

"Hey, I love photography, but your sketches. There's something more personal about them. More... alive."

"Thanks. It's funny, I used to be so afraid of showing

people my art. It felt too personal, like they were seeing a piece of me I wasn't ready to share."

"And now?"

"Now... I want to share more."

"Good. Because I want to see every single one."

Alex laughed as she flipped to a blank page. "Then hold still. I need to add another sketch to the collection."

"Make sure you capture my best side."

"Oh, don't worry," she teased, already dragging her charcoal across the page. "I always do."

Jamie smirked but held his pose. He watched her with a mix of curiosity and admiration as she worked. The scratch of charcoal against paper was the only sound between them for a moment, aside from the gentle rustling of the evening breeze.

Occasionally, her eyes would drift upwards, taking in the peaceful posture of his shoulders and the way the dying light of day touched his hair with golden strands. The sight filled her with quiet joy. She loved moments like this. The way she could lose herself in the lines and shadows of the world around her. After a few minutes, she turned the sketchbook toward him. "Well? What do you think?"

"You make me look... deeper. Like I'm thinking about something profound."

"Maybe you were. Or maybe that's just how I see you."

He reached for her hand, smudged with charcoal, and brushed his thumb over her knuckles. "Come on," he said lightly. "Let's keep walking before we lose all the light."

She tucked her sketchbook into her bag and followed him along the narrow pathway that clung to the cliff side. They walked until he gently led her to a secluded spot where the white stone of the cliffs met the deep blue sea. Before them unfolded a cozy, intimate scene: a soft wool blanket spread over the dewy grass beside a bucket chilling a bottle of crisp white wine, with two crystal glasses waiting patiently.

Alex's brows lifted. "Did you?"

"Maybe."

"What is this?"

"A little something I put together. We've had so many incredible moments in places like this, but I wanted tonight to be special."

She looked around, the surprise in her expression softening into wonder.

"I thought we were just going for a walk," she said, laughter slipping into her words.

He shrugged, a boyish grin tugging at his mouth. "A walk... with a view, and maybe a little wine. You deserve it."

The thoughtfulness in his gesture pressed at her heart. She watched as he eased the cork from the bottle. He poured the wine with a care that made it feel ceremonial, and when he handed her a glass, their fingers brushed. Just a spark, but enough to remind her why she followed him across countries and cobblestone streets.

They clinked their glasses lightly. "To us," he said, voice low but steady.

"To us," she echoed, her lips curving into a smile.

For a long moment, they sat in silence, letting the scene do all the talking. The salt-tinged air, the wildflowers clinging to the rocks, the distant laughter of locals drifting up from the village below. He reached for a small lantern tucked beside the blanket and lit the candles inside.

Alex drew in a breath. She didn't need grand gestures. It was being seen and thought of that made her want to stay in this wandering life just a little longer. With every sip of the wine, they recounted their adventures and talked of future journeys to unexplored corners of the world. But beneath it all, there was a tangible energy that crackled between them. He swirled his glass and looked at her.

"If you could go anywhere in the world, no limits, no second thoughts... where would it be?"

There were so many places she still wanted to see, so many corners of the world left unexplored. But when she really thought about it, the answer bloomed in her mind like a flower.

"Paris."

He subtly lifted a single eyebrow. "Paris? Of all the places in the world?"

A faint smile touched Alex's lips as her fingers delicately traced the rim of her crystal wine glass. She could feel the heat of his curious gaze, but she kept watching the moonlight ripple over the dark water.

"It's not just about the place," she said wistfully. "It's the feeling."

Her response , filled with unspoken affection, melted the teasing smirk from his lips into a tender expression.

"What feeling?"

"Like I belong somewhere... even if just for a moment. Like I can breathe a little easier, like I don't have to rush to the next thing. Paris is..." She trailed off, a faraway look settling in her eyes. "It's home, in a way."

He could hear the longing in her voice. The desire for a place where she could slow down, where she didn't have to prove herself or chase the next thing. It wasn't about Paris itself. It was about what it represented.

"You've been before?" he asked.

"No. But I have a photo of the Eiffel Tower on my old vision board back home. I've probably stared at it a thousand times, imagining what it would be like to walk along the Seine or sit in some tiny cafe with a sketchbook in my lap." She bit her lip and shrugged. "I know it sounds silly, but I've always felt this pull to go there. Like I'm supposed to."

"It doesn't sound silly," he finally said sincerely. "It sounds like a place that's already part of you."

She hadn't expected him to take her words so seriously, but somehow, he did. "What about you? Where would you go?"

He had an almost mischievous grin as he pretended to consider the question. "Hmm..." he mused. "Honestly? Paris sounds perfect."

"Wait. You can't just steal my answer."

"Why not? You made it sound irresistible."

She shook her head with mock disapproval. "You're such a copycat."

Jamie leaned in slightly as if sharing a secret. "You just have good taste. I trust your judgment."

Her breath caught again. This time, it wasn't surprising, but the intensity in his gaze that made her heart pound.

"You know..." he said thoughtfully, "we could go there one day. If you wanted."

Her heart fluttered unexpectedly. She blinked at him. She was unsure if she'd heard him right.

"What?" she asked softly.

He smiled as though it was the simplest thing in the world. "Paris. We could go. Together."

The idea of seeing Paris had always felt so far away. It was just a dream she scribbled on her vision board, nothing more. But now, he was saying it so casually, as though the thought of bringing that dream to life was perfectly natural. And when she searched his face, she realized he meant it.

Her fingers curled lightly around the stem of her glass. She tried to hide her face from the sudden rush of emotion.

"You're serious?" she asked softly.

"Completely."

She couldn't breathe. And she knew it wasn't because of Paris. It was because of him. Because the man sitting across from her didn't just see her dream. He wanted to make it real. Just for her. She could picture it. The two of them holding hands and walking along the Seine. Sitting at a sunlit cafe with her sketchbook and his camera between them. Exploring Montmartre at dusk, with nothing but time and possibility ahead of them.

Her voice was barely above a whisper. "I'd like that."

# Chapter 29

Alex stared at the blank page in front of her. She'd woken up with an itch to create. It was a restless urge she hadn't experienced in a while, but now, sitting at the small sunlit table, she couldn't move. She hadn't even realized Jamie had come in until she heard the soft clink of a coffee cup being set on the table.

"For the tortured artist," he teased as he slid the cup toward her.

She looked at him and then let out a breathy laugh. "You startled me."

He flashed a smile as he pulled out the chair across from her. "You looked deep in thought. Didn't want to break your genius streak."

She tapped the pencil against the page. "Something like that. I keep having all these ideas, but when I try to put them down, they...don't come out right."

"What kind of ideas?"

"I've been thinking about everything we've seen so far and how it's changed the way I see the world. And...how it's changed me."

"Go on," Jamie encouraged.

"I want to capture it somehow. Not just the places, but the overall atmosphere. The colors, the energy, the way it wakes me up inside. But every time I try, the sheer scale of it feels overwhelming."

"That sounds like the start of something incredible. Why does it have to be perfect right away?"

"Because...I feel like I owe it to myself to get it right. Like if I mess this up, it'll mean I've wasted all this growth."

He set his mug down. "Alex, growth isn't about being perfect. It's about trying, learning, and letting yourself evolve. You don't have to capture everything in one sketch or one idea. Let it be messy. Let it take time."

She picked up her pencil and began to sketch. He watched her in silence for a few minutes before speaking again. "You know, I think you're onto something with this whole capturing the essence of a place. That's what I try to do with my photography. Not just depict the visual appearance of something, but its emotional impact."

"How do you do that? How do you decide what to focus on?"

"I don't decide. I let the moment tell me. Sometimes it's the light hitting a building exactly right, or the expression on someone's face. It's about being present and open to whatever speaks to you."

Jamie showed her shots from their travels.

"Look at this one," he said, sliding his phone across the table to her. It was a photo of her.

"I didn't even know you took this."

"You looked so...at peace. I couldn't help it."

She traced the edge of the photo on the screen with her finger. "It's strange, seeing myself like this. I almost don't recognize her."

"That's because you're still catching up to the person you're becoming," he said softly. "But she's been there all along."

After that, her sketches seemed to form more freely. She let her ideas flow freely without the usual self-doubt holding her back. By late afternoon, the once-blank page had transformed into a vibrant mix of colors and shapes, capturing fragments of the places they'd visited and the emotions they'd stirred in her.

Jamie returned from a walk just as she was adding the final changes. "Whoa," he leaned over her shoulder for a clearer view. "That's...incredible."

She blushed. "It's just a rough idea."

"It's more than that," he insisted. "You've got something here. Something powerful."

Alex looked at the sketch again. "You think so?"

"I know so. You've got a vision. And it's only going to get stronger the more you let yourself trust it."

She stared down at the sketchbook. The pages overflowed with rapid sketches, meticulously rendered drawings, and minuscule notes crammed into every margin. They were fragments of moments from their travels. Each seemed a memory frozen in time. They were pieces of herself she hadn't realized she'd been documenting all along. She ran a finger over the lines of her latest sketch of the iconic blue domes. She sketched it with a looseness she never would have allowed herself before. "It's strange," she admitted. "I've always been so focused on getting everything perfect. But this... this just seems right."

Jamie sat beside her. "Because it's honest. Art isn't about perfection. It's about connection. And this?" He tapped the sketch. "This connects."

"I think I want to do something with this. Not just for me, but...for others. To share these stories and feelings with the world."

A warm, welcoming smile spread across Jamie's face. "In my opinion, you ought to. What's your idea? An exhibit? A series?"

"Maybe both. But first, I need to keep creating. Keep exploring."

Jamie raised his glass to her. "To the artist finding her vision."

"And to the photographer who helped her see it."

That evening, she sat on the terrace looking at the stars. The act of sharing her desire to create something meaningful was like stepping into a latest version of herself. One she was embracing.

Jamie emerged from the kitchen, carefully carrying two

steaming mugs of tea. He handed one to her. "Still at it?"

Alex set her pencil down and sighed. "Kind of. I've been thinking more than drawing."

"About what?" He was inviting her to open.

"About what's next," she said. "If I really want to do this, turn my art into something bigger, then how do I even start? It seems…overwhelming."

"It's common to have that reaction. Big dreams always begin impossible. But you've already taken the first step by deciding you want it."

"I guess. But deciding something and doing it are two quite different things."

"You're not doing it alone. You've got me. And I know a thing or two about starting from scratch."

Alex looked at him. She like how his confidence in her was unwavering. It was something that she wasn't used to. "It's just… a lot. The idea of putting myself out there like that."

"Of course it is. Anything worth doing is. But you've already taken the hardest step. You've realized what you want. The rest? One day at a time."

"You make it sound possible."

"That's because it is."

She looked down and turned the pages slowly. She thought about all the moments that had led her here. The first time she picked up her pencil in Italy, the quiet mornings sketching in sunlit cafes, and especially the way he encouraged her to see the world differently.

"What kind of reactions do you want to inspire in those who see your work?" He asked after a moment.

"I want them to sense what I've experienced these past few weeks. That sense of wonder, of seeing the world and yourself in a new way. I want my art to remind people that there's beauty everywhere, even in the unexpected."

"That's an amazing 'why,' Alex."

Her cheeks flushed. "It's a start, I guess."

"Your art has that effect on me," he said.

Her eyes lifted to meet his. The quiet honesty startled her in his tone.

"What do you mean?" she asked.

He gestured toward her sketchbook, which lay open on the table beside them. "Every time I look at one of your drawings," he began, "I feel like I'm seeing the world through your eyes. It's... different. More vivid. More alive."

His gaze found hers again. "You make me want to slow down and actually see things. Not just capture them, but really notice them."

Alex felt her chest tighten. She hadn't expected that. She hadn't realized how much it would mean to hear someone see her art that way. She searched his face, trying to read between the lines for some deeper implication, but there was none. Just sincerity. Her throat tightened as emotion rose. She let out a soft, self-conscious laugh, brushing a strand of hair behind her ear in an attempt to ease the weight of the moment.

"Careful," she said lightly, "keep talking like that and I might start to believe you."

"I love how your artwork expresses your inner state."

He wanted to say more, but the words caught in his throat. He longed to share how she provided him stability and gave him a sense of belonging. Instead, he abruptly changed the subject to a lighter tone.

"Hard to believe we're flying home in a couple of days," he said.

Alex looked down at her sketchbook.

"Yeah," she murmured. "It went by fast."

"Too fast," he said, and when she glanced up at him, she caught the flicker of something in his expression. Something that made her heart squeeze.

"You're not going to miss dragging your camera gear through crowded streets?" she teased.

"I'll miss a lot of things. Mostly I'll miss this."

Her breath caught mid-inhale, her pulse tripping unexpectedly. This.

"This?" she asked.

"You. Us. This whole… thing we've been doing. Wandering through unfamiliar places. Watching the world come alive through your sketches. Laughing at my awful Italian and pretending we don't get hopelessly lost every time we go out without a map."

Her lips curved, a faint smile tugging at the corners despite the pressure building in her chest. She wanted to laugh, to say something playful and light. But the way he looked at her made it impossible to hide behind deflection.

Her eyes lingered on his face, memorizing the slope of his cheek, the way the light touched the edge of his jaw, the furrow in his brow like he was still trying to find the right words. Then, slowly, she lowered her gaze to the sketchbook in her hands.

"Yeah," she murmured. "I'll miss it too."

# Chapter 30

The airplane's engines droned a steady rhythm, creating a comforting vibration that filled the cabin. Alex rested her head against the window, watching the ground transform into streaks of color below. Beside her, Jamie shifted in his seat as he adjusted his seatbelt. He glanced over and said, "You've been quiet since we left the villa," his voice barely audible over the flight crew's announcements.

"Just thinking, I guess. About everything."

He gave her a knowing look. "Everything is a lot to think about."

She let out a short laugh. "No kidding."

As the plane took off, Alex felt an unfamiliar heaviness in her chest. Leaving Italy stirred a deep longing within her, like closing a beloved book that remains unfinished yet treasured. With her forehead resting against the cool windowpane, she looked down at the patchwork of vineyards and terracotta rooftops. The warm, golden tones of the countryside gradually dissolved into a soft haze, and soon they were soaring above a blanket of clouds.

A few hours into the flight, Jamie tapped her shoulder, holding up the in-flight menu. "Want anything? Pasta, chicken, or the mystery vegetarian option?"

"I'm good, thanks. Not really hungry."

"You know, you don't have to figure everything out right this second."

"I know. It's just hard. Being here, traveling, creating. It's like I finally felt like myself again. But now we're heading back to reality, and I don't know what that looks like anymore."

"Reality isn't some set thing. It's what you make of it.

You've changed. You're not the same person you were when we left. And that means your reality doesn't have to be the same either."

"It's easy to say that here, while we're thousands of feet in the air. But what happens when I'm back in my apartment, sitting at my desk, staring at the same walls?"

"You'll figure it out. And if you don't want to do it alone, you won't have to."

Alex was surprised. She didn't expect him to say that. She turned back to the window and watched as the clouds stretched below them. "You really think I can do it, don't you?"

"I don't just think it. I know it. I've watched you grow into someone who doesn't just dream but does. You took risks, you made mistakes, and you kept going. That's more than most people can say."

His confidence in her made her heart swell, yet she felt a persistent knot of uncertainty. "What about you?" she turned to face him. "What's next for you?"

"I'll probably go back to editing photos, putting together the pieces for my next project. But honestly? I don't have it all planned out either."

"That makes me feel a little better," she admitted. "At least I'm not the only one."

"You're definitely not. And for what it's worth, I'm glad you're going back with more than you left with."

The remainder of the flight blurred into a mix of restless sleep and quiet reflection. When the plane finally touched down, Alex felt the crushing burden of responsibility and regret. The airport buzzed with noise and activity, which was a stark contrast to the peaceful mornings and vibrant sunsets they had shared. As they waited for their luggage, Jamie nudged her shoulder. "You excited to be back?"

"Not really," she answered. "It's feels weird. I feel like I should be excited to be home, but I'm not."

"It's normal. You're coming back different. It'll take time to adjust."

Outside the terminal, a sharp breeze cut through the air, and she pulled her jacket tighter around her. He flagged down a cab, and they loaded their luggage into the trunk.

"Where to first?" the driver asked as they slid into the backseat.

He looked at Alex. "Do you want to drop you off first?"

Her apartment was only a short drive away, but the thought of stepping back into her old space felt suffocating. "Actually, would you mind if we went to your place first? Just for a little while?"

"Not at all."

Jamie gave her a reassured smile before turning back to the driver. "My place first, then."

As the car pulled away from the curb, she exhaled slowly, pressing her hands together in her lap. The city outside the window felt strangely unfamiliar, even though it had been her home for so long. The towering buildings, the flashing lights, and the constant hum of movement were all the same, yet something inside her had shifted. Jamie must have noticed her apprehension because he reached over and gave her hand a quick squeeze. "You okay?"

"Yeah. Just… adjusting, I guess."

"I get it," he said softly. "Re-entry can be weird."

They rode the rest of the way in silence. When they pulled up outside his building, he grabbed their bags from the trunk and led her inside.

The soft glow of the lamps, the lingering scent of his cologne, and the familiar warmth of the space helped her shoulders relax. The framed black-and-white photos on the wall, the stack of travel magazines spilling from the coffee table, and the worn leather jacket draped casually over the back of a chair all distinctly reminded her of him.

Jamie set down his bags and turned to her. "Welcome to my humble abode." He observed her as she took in the surroundings. "Would you like to sit?"

She slipped off her jacket, letting it fall onto the arm of

a chair, and sank into the couch, tucking her legs beneath her. Her eyes wandered over the images adorning the walls. "It's funny," she began. "After all our time traveling together, this is the first time I've been here." She turned to him, her gaze soft and almost wistful. "Yet it feels so comfortable."

Jamie leaned lightly against the door frame, watching her with quiet amusement.

"Well, that's a good sign," he teased softly. "Means I didn't screw up my interior design too badly."

She let out a breathy laugh, but her eyes were still on the photos.

"I've been to some of these places now. But seeing them through your lens... it's different."

Jamie sat down beside her. "That's the thing about photography. About art, really. Everyone sees the world a little differently. That's why your work is going to matter."

"I hope you're right."

He nudged her playfully. "You know I am."

Alex smiled, but it didn't quite reach her eyes. Her fingers traced an invisible pattern on the soft fabric of the couch, looping over and over again like she could smooth out the thoughts tangled in her head.

The past few weeks had cracked something open inside her that had long been buried beneath routines and responsibilities. There was a hunger now. For more. For art that wasn't confined to sketchbooks collecting dust. For days spent chasing color and light. For moments that made her feel alive. Traveling had given her a glimpse of the life she hadn't let herself imagine. Of who she could be if she stopped playing it so safe. But now that she was back, the edges of that dream blurred. Reality crept in like a cold draft. *What if it was just a phase? What if you can't keep this up in the real world? What if you go back to who you were before?*

She sighed, barely audible, still drawing circles on the cushion.

Jamie watched her for a moment, quiet and patient.

Then, gently, he reached out and held her hand with his own.

"Hey," he said softly, "whatever it is you're thinking, you don't have to figure it all out right now. Just promise me one thing."

She looked up, eyes meeting his.

"Don't let go of the version of you that came alive out there."

"I don't know how to be her here," she admitted. "That version of me... she belonged to wide-open skies and cobblestone alleys. Not job interviews and grocery lists."

"She *is* you, Alex. She didn't vanish the moment the plane landed."

"I just—" she hesitated, her voice catching. "It's hard not to fall back into old patterns. Into the version of me that never takes risks."

"Then remind yourself of what you did out there. You chased beauty. You took chances. You *felt* everything."

His gaze softened. "So why do you keep doubting yourself?"

"Because it's what I do," she admitted quietly. "I second-guess everything. I convince myself I'm going to screw it all up before I even let myself try."

Her chest tightened as the words slipped out. Too raw, too honest. Regret washed over her as she wished she could take back her words, but Jamie's scrutinizing gaze stopped her. He didn't look away.

In a soft voice, he murmured, "Hey. Look at me."

Reluctantly, she lifted her eyes to his. She was half afraid of what she might see. But his expression was steady and calm. No judgment. Just him.

"You're not going to mess it all up. You couldn't even if you tried."

"You don't know that."

"Yeah," he countered. "I do."

The certainty in his voice made something in her chest ache like an old wound pressed too hard. She swallowed against the lump rising in her throat, blinking quickly, but her eyes were filled with tears.

She turned her face away, pretending to study the framed photo on the wall, anything to avoid the intensity of his gaze. "I'm not used to someone believing in me like that," she said quietly.

"You should be," he said. "You're easy to believe in, Alex."

She closed her eyes, inhaling slowly. The air felt thick, like it was holding the weight of everything she didn't know how to say. That maybe she was terrified to hope. That maybe part of her still didn't think she deserved the life she'd glimpsed abroad or the way he looked at her like she could have it.

"Hey," he said gently. "You don't have to look away."

She turned back to him slowly.

"I want to believe that," she said. "I really do."

Jamie held her gaze. "Then start here," he said. "Start with me."

And in the stillness that followed, a quiet question lingered between them. *Could she let herself trust it? Could she trust herself? Because if she could... everything might finally change.*

"I'm just... scared," she admitted.

"Of what?" he asked.

"Of everything," she whispered. "Making a mistake like this. Losing myself again is a concern. As the one who—"

Her voice broke off, and she bit her bottom lip hard.

But Jamie didn't pull away. Instead, he reached up, his fingers brushing against her cheek, tilting her face toward him.

"Alex," he said. "You will not lose yourself. You're not who you were before. And whatever comes next? You're not facing it alone. You got me and now that we're back, you got Sarah."

"Promise?"

"I promise."

The next afternoon, Alex returned to her apartment, and Jamie offered to drive her. She didn't decline, partly because she was still tired from the long flight and mostly because she wasn't ready to confront the quiet solitude of her space alone.

The drive was quiet, broken only by the gentle hum of the tires on the highway. As they passed familiar streets, they felt smaller and more muted or perhaps it was just her perception.

Resting her elbow against the window, she lightly touched her lips with her fingers, lost in thought. Glancing at Jamie, she noticed his focus was on the road, though she caught the brief, almost imperceptible flickers of his eyes toward her. He hadn't spoken much since they left his place, giving her space, but his presence was enough.

The gravel crunched under his tires as he pulled into the small lot outside her building, and she took a deep breath. Jamie put the car in park but didn't shut off the engine. He turned toward her slightly.

"Want me to walk you up?"

For half a second, she considered saying no, telling him she was fine. She should have been fine. But when she met his eyes, she realized she didn't want him to leave just yet.

"Yeah," he said, offering a faint smile. "I'd like that."

He then shut off the engine. Without a word, he stepped out, walked around the car, and opened her door. She looked at him and her heart tightened at the small, familiar gesture.

They walked side by side toward her building. He was carrying her bags. When they reached her door, she slipped the key from her pocket and slid it into the lock. Her hand stayed on the knob for a moment. She could already feel the weight of the quiet waiting for her on the other side. The stillness that would press in around her the moment he left.

He must have sensed her hesitation because he stopped her stopped her from opening the door.

"Hey," he said softly. "You okay?"

She forced a small smile. "Yeah. I will be."

She turned the knob and pushed the door open. Sunlight pooled through the window, illuminating the quiet space. Everything was exactly as she had left it. The blanket still draped over the arm of the couch, the stack of magazines she'd been meaning to recycle, the half-finished sketch lying next to her open notebook on the coffee table. It was all so familiar. Yet, somehow, it felt like walking into a stranger's apartment.

With measured steps, she entered the room, the quiet creak of the hardwood floor the only sound. He followed and set her bag down near the entryway.She just stood there. She wrapped her arms loosely around herself as she looked around her space. She exhaled softly, unsure what to do with the sudden silence pressing in around her.

Carefully, he watched her. He remained silent, waiting. Then, quietly, he asked, "Want me to stick around for a bit?"

She turned to look at him. She could have said no. She could have told him she needed time alone. But she didn't.

"Yeah," she whispered. "I'd like that."

"Okay." Without another word, he walked over to the couch and sat down, stretching his legs out slightly. He glanced at her with an easy, familiar grin.

"Come here," he patted the cushion beside him.

She simply stared at him, unsure why the sight of him sitting there made her chest feel lighter. Slowly, she walked over and sat down next to him. She didn't lean into him right away, so he lifted his arm and gently draped it around her to pull her in.

She softly exhaled and laid her head on his chest. His hand slowly traced along her arm. She closed her eyes and listened to the steady rhythm of his heartbeat. Neither of them spoke. They simply sat there. After a while, he whispered.

"You're not alone, Alex. You never were."

# Chapter 31

The next morning, Alex sat on the edge of the couch, cradling a mug in her hands. Lost in thought, she watched the city wake up. Jamie's jacket still hung over the back of a chair; she hadn't moved it. The trace of his presence lingered in the space, and the feeling of his absence settled like a familiar weight. Her mind kept drifting back to the night before: the warmth of his arms around her, the steady rhythm of his breathing, the way he held her without expecting anything in return. It had been a long time since she had felt that safe.

But now, in the quiet morning light, uncertainty crept in. She had spent so much of her life running from the unknown and fearing the parts of herself she might never get right. Yet last night, sitting with him, she realized something: she didn't want to keep running. She was tired of keeping herself small.

She placed the half-empty mug on the coffee table and slowly rose to her feet. Her gaze drifted to the far corner of the room, where an easel stood untouched. Its once-familiar appearance now felt almost strange. The blank canvas seemed to wait for her return.

For a long moment, she simply stood there, staring at it. Then, before she could second-guess herself, she walked to the table, picked up the brush, and set it on the easel. Dipping the brush into a pot of deep blue paint, she made her first stroke.

At first, her hand moved slowly, the bristles gliding across the smooth surface. The color bled into the canvas, bold and certain, contrasting with the hesitation still lingering in her chest. She exhaled softly and allowed her body to relax into the movement.

Lost in the rhythm of her brushstrokes, she was just beginning to immerse herself in the process when her phone buzzed from the counter, pulling her from her thoughts. She stopped mid-stroke, sighed faintly, and walked over to the counter. Picking up the phone, she opened it and saw a text from Sarah.

*Lunch? You've been back for a day, and I
haven't seen you! Need all the travel gossip.
Sure. How about The Bistro at 1?
Perfect! Can't wait!*

Alex set her phone down and exhaled. She hadn't even had time to process being home yet, and already, reality was creeping back in. Her suitcase sat unpacked in the corner, with her sketchbook resting on top of it. She walked over and ran her fingers over the cover and the memories of the past few weeks flooding back. Could she hold on to that feeling, the freedom, the inspiration, now that she was back?

Without thinking, she returned to the easel and picked up the brush once more. Dipping it into the blue paint, she dragged the bristles across the canvas with newfound certainty. Then she reached for the yellow, streaking it through the blue, allowing the colors to blur and blend effortlessly.

As the soft scratch of the bristles against the canvas created a rhythm, she lost herself in the way the colors shifted beneath her hand. She didn't overthink it; she simply let herself feel. For a while, she forgot about her lunch plans, her unpacked suitcase, and the world waiting just outside her door. All that mattered were the colors spreading across the canvas and the faint memory of sunlit streets she was trying to hold onto.

When she finally stepped back, her breath slowed and her shoulders relaxed. The painting remained unfinished, but she didn't mind. It wasn't about the final result; it was about the feeling she had captured in those strokes. Just then, her phone buzzed from the counter, pulling her out of her thoughts. She wiped her hands on a paint-streaked rag and walked over to check it. Another message from Sarah awaited her.

*See you soon! Can't wait for all the details.*

Alex smiled, feeling a little lighter in her chest. She set down her phone and turned her attention back to the painting, allowing the colors to settle in her vision. It wasn't perfect. The lines weren't quite right, and the shadows refused to behave, but it was *hers*. A piece of something real. Uncertain if she could hold onto the emotions from her trip, she worried that the upcoming weeks might pull her back into the old, stifling routines. But one thing was clear now: she wouldn't let that happen again. *Not this time.*

The version of herself she had rediscovered while wandering through sun-drenched villages and sketching by the sea wasn't just a fleeting vacation illusion. That was her; free, bold, present. And maybe she didn't know exactly what came next, but for the first time in years, the uncertainty didn't feel like a threat. It felt like possibility.

She cleaned her brushes slowly, letting the water swirl with soft shades of blue and coral. Her phone buzzed once, and she glanced at the screen.

*Already here. Got us the good corner table.*

Alex smiled again, grabbed her bag, and slipped on her shoes. Stepping outside, the late afternoon sun warmed her skin, and the city around her buzzed with its usual rhythm. And yet, she felt different moving through it. More rooted. More alive. The café was just a few blocks away. She pushed open the door and found Sarah already seated.

"There you are!" she exclaimed and stood to give Alex a tight hug.

"You look different. Glowy, maybe? What is it? The Italian sun? The Caprian beaches? Or maybe..." she said, wiggling her eyebrows suggestively.

Alex laughed and slid into the seat across from her. "It's not that dramatic."

"It is! You look amazing. Now, spill everything. I want to hear all about Jamie, the food, the art, everything."

"It was incredible. Everything about it. But being back is weird. Like, nothing here feels the same."

"Weird how?"

"I don't know. It's like I've changed, but nothing else has. My apartment feels too small, the city feels too dull, and I feel like I left something behind out there."

"Okay, that's deep," Sarah said. "But it makes sense. You've been gone for what, a month? Traveling the world, seeing beautiful places, falling for a dreamy photographer. "

"You're impossible," she muttered.

A wicked gleam shone in Sarah's eyes, her smile hinting at a cruel delight.

"No, I'm just a concerned friend who needs details," she teased, her voice sing-song. She rested her chin in her hand and arched a playful brow. "Now, stop stalling. Spill. Did anything happen with Jamie? When are you going to introduce us?"

She shook her head, but she couldn't suppress the involuntary smile tugging at her lips.

"Sarah..." she warned lightly, but her voice had no genuine conviction.

Her friend's grin widened.

"Oh my God, something totally happened," she declared triumphantly. She pointed her fork at Alex like she had just cracked the case. "You're doing that thing where you pretend you're being evasive, but your face gives it all away."

Alex rolled her eyes and exhaled. She fiddled with the corner of her napkin again, trying to downplay the giddy warmth spreading in her chest.

"Okay, fine," she admitted. "Something... happened."

Sarah gasped like she'd just won the lottery. "I knew it! Oh my God, tell me everything. Start from the beginning. No skipping the good parts."

Alex laughed, pressing a hand to her face to hide the blush that had already risen to her cheeks. "You're ridiculous."

"And you *are* glowing," Sarah shot back, sitting up straighter like she was preparing to receive classified intel. "Don't even try to deny it. Spill, Greer."

Alex bit her lip, her eyes darting down to her coffee for a moment. She stirred it absentmindedly, watching the swirl of cream fade into the dark liquid. Then, slowly, she looked back up, her smile softer now. "It wasn't this big, dramatic moment or anything. It just... happened. We were in this tiny cabin during a storm, and the power went out. We talked for hours. About everything. And at some point, he looked at me, and I realized I wasn't afraid of what came next."

Sarah's expression melted into something gentler, her teasing put on hold for a rare beat. "Wow," she said, her voice lower now. "So... what does this mean?"

Alex let out a breath, her fingers still nervously twisting her napkin. "I don't know exactly. But it felt real. Like... for the first time in a long time, I was exactly where I was supposed to be."

Sarah reached across the table and gave her hand a quick squeeze. "Okay, I love all of that, but I'm gonna need at least three more details and preferably one kiss-related moment before I let you off the hook."

Alex threw her head back, laughing. "You are *incorrigible.*"

"Not denying it," Sarah said proudly, lifting her cappuccino in salute. "To art, adventure, and hot photographers who make my best friend glow like she just walked out of a Nicholas Sparks movie."

Alex clinked her cup against Sarah's. "To all of it."

"Okay, you toasted. Now I want more. What happened

after the storm? I need at least one heart-melting detail or I might combust."

Alex took a slow sip, trying to decide where to start. There were so many small moments: fleeting glances, shared silence, the soft cadence of his voice in the dark. But one stood out.

"There was this time," she said, her voice thoughtful. "We were on the balcony. I was sketching, and he was editing his photos. We didn't say much at first. But he kept glancing over at me like... like I was part of the view. Like I belonged there."

Sarah let out a dreamy sigh. "Ugh, that's disgustingly romantic. I'm obsessed. Go on."

Alex smiled into her cup, then set it down gently. "He told me I make the world feel alive. That when he looks at my drawings, he sees things he didn't notice before."

"Okay, wait. Now I'm combusting," Sarah said, dramatically fanning herself with her napkin. "That's not even fair. Does this man have a brother?"

"It wasn't just one thing," she admitted. She glanced up at Sarah, her eyes soft with the weight of the memories. "It was... everything. The way he looked at me. He made me feel safe and free at the same time. It was slow and steady and—" she hesitated, her voice catching slightly. "And real."

Sarah's teasing expression softened.

"Wow," she said. "You're serious about him, aren't you?"

Alex tucked a strand of hair behind her ear and looked down at the table.

"Yeah," she admitted. "I think I am."

"Well, damn," she said with a slow grin spreading across her face. "You really did it, huh? You went and fell for the dreamy photographer."

Alex laughed, despite herself, and rolled her eyes.

"Stop," she said, but her smile gave her away.

Sarah's expression turned smug.

"I'm not wrong, though." She propped her chin in her

hand again. "So? When do I get to meet him? Because if you're this head-over-heels, I should at least be allowed to interrogate him a little. For friendship purposes, of course."

"God, you're relentless."

"Relentless and right," Sarah countered, a smug smile playing on her lips as she leaned back in her chair. With a sly grin, she wiggled her brows suggestively. "So? *When*?"

"I... don't know," she admitted. She glanced at Sarah. "We didn't really talk about what comes next. Not yet."

"Well, that's okay. You've only been back for a day. You don't have to figure it all out right away.".

"Yeah... I just—" she hesitated, unsure how to put it into words. She met Sarah's eyes again, her voice barely above a whisper. "I don't want to lose it, you know? What we had there... I don't want it to fade just because I'm back."

"Hey," she offered her a reassured smile. "You will not lose it. That was real, Alex. He's real. And if it were supposed to stay in Italy, it wouldn't be with you now."

Sarah squeezed her hand then went back to teasing.

"Besides," she added with a mischievous glint in her eye, "there's no way a guy who looks at you the way he does is just going to let you walk away without a fight."

"You're ridiculous," she muttered, but she couldn't stop the smile tugging at her lips.

Sarah grinned smugly.

"Maybe. But I'm also right. And I'm going to need a formal introduction to the dreamy photographer. Preferably soon."

Alex shook her head with a soft laugh, brushing a stray curl behind her ear as she sipped her water. Across the café table, Sarah was still grinning, her words echoing louder than the background hum of clinking cups and quiet conversation.

*That was real, Alex. He's real.*

Despite the uncertainty swirling in her chest, the ache of returning to routine after weeks of sun-drenched mornings and cliff side conversations, she knew Sarah was right. Jamie had become part of her story. N just in the photos he took or the sketches she now treasured, but in the quiet way he saw her when she wasn't even looking.

He wasn't here now, not physically, but he was still with her. In every sun-drenched memory. In every lingering laugh. In every brave beat of her heart that dared to believe the magic hadn't ended just because the trip had. And no amount of distance or ordinary days could undo what they had shared.

# Chapter 32

Later that evening, Alex sat at her dining table with her sketchbook open. She stared at the blank page for a long time, with Sarah's words echoing in her mind. She picked up a pencil and began to draw. Not for a client, not for work, but for herself. As the lines took shape, she felt a flicker of the passion she'd thought she'd lost.

Her hand moved instinctively, as though the memories themselves were guiding the pencil. She added delicate shadows along the jagged cliffs, capturing the rugged beauty of the Amalfi Coast as the sun melted into the horizon. The sea beneath it rippled with faint strokes, brushed in soft, uneven lines, as though it were still breathing.

She barely noticed the faint smudge of graphite on her fingertips as she turned the page and started again. This time, she traced the winding streets of Positano, letting her hand follow the familiar curves and slants. She shaded in the narrow stairways and tiny balconies; the ones draped in vibrant flowers that spilled over their railings. She could almost smell the faint trace of sea salt in the air as she etched in the cobblestones.

Her hand slowed slightly when she started on Santorini. She closed her eyes briefly, calling back the lantern-lit pathways, the soft glow of golden light catching on the whitewashed walls. When she opened her eyes, she started sketching the warm glow of the lanterns against the cool stone. She added faint stars overhead in the dark sky.

Her breath evened out, her shoulders loosening as she moved from one memory to the next. She turned the page again; her strokes became gentler, slower, as she filled the next section with Capri. The beach came first, the smooth shoreline, the gentle waves lapping against the sand. Then the rocky outcrops that jutted into the sea, stark and dramatic. She drew the soft reflection of the shimmering moon on the water.

The chaos of the city faded away, leaving her enveloped in the serene stillness of the apartment. She was unaware of the sky transitioning from dusk to night or the soft glow of the lamp beside her, which cast a warm light over her sketchbook. Deeply engaged, she immersed herself in the lines, textures, and fragments of her journey.

With a sigh of relief, she leaned back, relaxing the muscles in her hand as she flexed it, a slow, steady breath escaping her lips. Charcoal smudged her fingertips, and a faint streak of graphite marked the side of her hand, but she paid it no mind.

She gazed at the open pages before her. They were quick, imperfect impressions of the places she had fallen in love with, yet they felt more beautiful than anything she had created in months.

Her eyes wandered over the drawings, her fingers tracing the edges. She could almost feel the warm breeze again, hear the distant sound of waves lapping against the cliffs, and taste the salt in the air. The memories lingered, alive in the lines and shadows.

Her gaze lingered on the page where she had drawn the beach at Capri where they had walked beneath the stars. Without thinking, she picked up her pencil again. Her hand moved softly, sketching the faint outline of two figures in the sand. She thought of the way their silhouettes leaned toward one another and the faint brush of their hands touching.

At the sight, her lips parted ever so slightly in surprise. She set the pencil down, suddenly feeling the weight of the moment catch in her chest. She reached out and traced the faint outline of the figures with her fingertips and instinctively she was smiling.

A soft knock at the door startled her from her thoughts. She looked at the clock on the wall. She hadn't even realized how late it had gotten. With a wipe of a rag to remove the graphite smudges, she rose from the table and walked to the door. When she opened the door, a gasp escaped her lips. A crooked smile stretched across Jamie's face as he stood on the other side, his hands shoved into his pockets.

"Hey," he said softly.

A hint of surprise flickered in her eyes as her brows lifted slightly.

"Jamie?" she asked with confusion. "What are you doing here?"

He looked down before meeting her eyes again.

"I was home editing some photos," he admitted quietly. "And then I realized I didn't want to spend the night thinking about you when I could just be here instead."

Her breath hitched softly, and she stared at him for a long moment, feeling the warmth in her chest spread. Without thinking, she reached for his hand and pulled him inside. They didn't say anything for a moment. They simply stood there in the entryway, close but not touching, their eyes locked.

Then Jamie's gaze flickered over her shoulder, drawn to the sketchbook still open on the dining table. His eyes softened slightly as he walked over to it. He set his camera bag down and leaned over the pages.

"You drew this today?"

Alex nodded, still stunned by his sudden appearance, her heart racing as if it hadn't quite caught up with reality. "Yeah... I couldn't stop thinking about the cliffs," she said softly. "So I tried to hold on to the feeling."

He turned to her again. "It's beautiful," he said. "You captured it better than my camera ever could."

The compliment made her blush, but she didn't look away. Not this time.

"You really came all this way just to see me?"

"I couldn't stop thinking about you," he said honestly.

"And not just about the places we went or the sunsets we chased... but *you*. The way you see the world. The way you made me start seeing it differently."

Emotion swelled in her chest. She hadn't expected this. Hadn't dared to.

"Jamie..." she breathed.

"I don't know what happens next," he admitted. "But I didn't want to wait across an ocean to find out."

He traced over the faint outline of the two figures she had sketched on the beach. His eyes lingered on it for a long moment before he looked at her.

"That's us, isn't it?" he asked.

She held his gaze, her throat tightening slightly.

"Yeah," she admitted. "It is."

A wave of tenderness washed over his features, his eyes softening with a quiet, reverent awe. He said nothing, his eyes fixed on the floor. Gently he took her hand and pulled her close. She leaned her head against his chest and closed her eyes. Standing there, she felt whole, like the pieces of herself she had been searching for were falling back into place.

He pressed a light kiss to the top of her head. "I missed this. I missed you."

She let out a soft breath, "I didn't know how much I needed this," she murmured. "Not just you showing up, but... everything. Letting someone in again."

# Chapter 33

The next morning, Alex awoke feeling lighter, a sense of peace enveloping her. She stretched and noticed her sketchbook on the table, its cover slightly askew. The sight of her drawing from the night before filled her with a satisfying sense of accomplishment.

After getting up, she poured herself a cup of coffee and stood by the window, gazing at the bustling city streets below. Life continued as usual: cars honked, people hurried by, and the world moved forward without pause. Yet for the first time, Alex felt as though she wasn't just being carried along with it. Her phone buzzed on the counter, and she walked over to see a message from Jamie.

*Morning! I just sent you something. Check your email.*

Curious, she opened her laptop and went to her inbox. Among the usual clutter of newsletters and promotional emails was one from Jamie with the subject line: **For Your Inspiration**. She clicked it open and found a series of photographs attached. Each one was a moment from their trip together. The sun setting over the canals in Venice, the vibrant colors of the markets in Capri, the rolling vineyards of Tuscany. But what stood out most were her candid shots.

There she was, sketching by the water in Venice, laughing as they wandered through the streets of Rome, her face lighting up with wonder as she explored a site in Sperlonga. Jamie's photo captions were straightforward but deeply touching.

*"**Venice:** Where you saw yourself again."*

*"**Tuscany:** You were fearless here."*
*"**Capri:** The moment you realized your art is powerful."*

His photographs didn't just capture the landscapes they'd wandered through or the vibrant streets they'd gotten lost in. They captured *her*. The quiet moments she hadn't realized anyone had noticed. The spark in her eyes as she sketched under the Tuscan sun. The soft curve of her smile while she leaned over a balcony, watching the world go by. The way she had come alive again.

It was like watching someone she used to know emerge from beneath the weight of years of self-doubt. She saw the transformation she hadn't been able to name but had felt deep in her bones. She was still herself... just more. More open. More curious. More *brave*.

Her phone buzzed. She glanced at the screen, expecting another email, maybe a reminder. Instead, it was a message from Jamie.

*Thought you could use a reminder of how amazing you are. You've already done the hard part, Alex. Now it's just about... showing up.*

Her fingers paused mid-scroll, the message sinking in like sunlight warming her skin. She stared at it, her breath caught somewhere between a laugh and a sigh. *How did he always know exactly what to say?*

She set the phone down, blinking fast to keep the sudden rush of emotion from spilling over. She didn't need validation, but hearing the right words at the right time made all the difference. And coming from him meant everything.

A few hours later, with a new sense of purpose and her laptop tucked under one arm, Alex stood outside Sarah's apartment. She took a breath, lifted her hand to knock, only for the door to swing open first.

Sarah stood there, iced tea in hand, one brow arched and a knowing smile creeping across her lips. "Okay," she said, eyeing the laptop. "This feels important."

Alex smiled back. "It is."

Sarah stepped aside, ushering her in. "Good. Because I made cookies and I want *all* the details."

Alex laughed as she stepped inside.

"You made cookies?" Alex teased, slipping off her shoes. "You never bake unless it's a bribe."

Sarah grinned and handed her a warm chocolate chip cookie from a plate on the counter. "Exactly. I want answers, and I want them now. When am i going to meet Jamie? Did he call you yet?"

Alex took a bite, savoring the gooey center, and gave a soft, satisfied hum. "Okay, fine. But you have to let me sit down first. I've been thinking nonstop since this morning."

They made their way to the kitchen, where the table was already set with two glasses of iced tea and a notepad covered in Sarah's unmistakable curly handwriting. Alex shook her head fondly. "You took notes?"

"Only of the questions I'm going to ask," Sarah said proudly, sliding into her seat. "I figured I'd give this the same energy I'd give to true crime or a reality dating show. Honestly, your life has become wildly more interesting since you started traveling."

Alex sat across from her and smiled softly. "It has," she admitted. "And not just because of him... though he's definitely part of it."

"So? Spill."

"He showed up. After I got back. Just... showed up at my door with that quiet, confident look of his and said he didn't want to spend the night thinking about me when he could just be there instead."

Sarah's hand flew to her chest in dramatic fashion. "Oh my God. That man is a walking romance novel."

"I know," Alex whispered, unable to stop the smile spreading across her face. "And I think... I think I'm finally ready to stop doubting what this could be."

Sarah raised her glass in salute. "To love. And to you finally living the main character moment you deserve."

They clinked glasses, and for a long while, only the sound of laughter and soft music filled the air as the afternoon sun shifted across the walls. Then Alex stood, brushed cookie crumbs from her hands, and walked over to her bag. "I need your opinion on something," she said, placing it on the kitchen counter.

Sarah raised an eyebrow, already intrigued. "Is this about Jamie? Because if it is, I fully support whatever it is you're about to do.

"No, it's not about him. Well, not entirely. It's about this." She opened her laptop and pulled up the photos Jamie had sent.

Curious, Sarah set her glass down on the counter and leaned in. Her eyes darted between Alex, whose brow was furrowed with concern, and the rapidly changing numbers on the laptop screen.

"Okay…" she drawled. "What am I looking at?"

Alex clicked on a vibrant picture of her sketching by the sea. The photo was a breathtaking landscape that held them speechless for a moment. A look of mild surprise flickered in Sarah's eyes.

"Wait…" she leaned in closer. "Is that… *you*?"

Alex smiled and watched her friend's expression change. Sarah's playful curiosity melted into something quieter, something reverent. Her eyes stayed locked on the screen, and her fingers unconsciously tightened around the iced tea glass in her hand.

The photo was striking. Bathed in the golden hue of late afternoon sun, Alex looked almost otherworldly. Her wind-tousled hair fell messily across her face as she sat cross-legged on the rocky ledge, completely unaware of the camera. The sea behind her stretched endlessly, its blue surface catching the light like scattered glass. But it wasn't just the background. It was *her*. Her posture, calm and grounded, her brow furrowed ever so slightly in focus, her pencil gliding across the page of her sketchbook.

There was a serenity in the image. A quiet strength. A version of herself she rarely saw but instantly recognized. Sarah slowly shook her head.

"Alex... this is stunning."

Alex swallowed the lump forming in her throat. "I didn't even know he took it."

"It doesn't look posed at all. It looks like..." Sarah paused, eyes flicking up to meet hers, "*you*. The real you. Like you belong there."

Alex looked down at the image again, the faintest ache blooming in her chest. She hadn't realized how much she needed to see herself this way. Not polished. Not performing. Just being.

Alex brushed her fingers against the edge of the screen.

"He sent me an entire set," she mumbled. "From the trip."

She clicked through the rest. The sunset over the Amalfi cliffs, the quiet street in Positano, and the starlit beach in Capri. Each one was vivid and full of life, but what struck Sarah the most were the photos of Alex herself. Jamie had captured her in unguarded moments. His photos showed how her face softened when lost in thought, the slight tilt of her head when working, and the glimmer in her eyes when she smiled unconsciously.

"Okay, hold on," Sarah pressed a hand to her chest dramatically. "I need a second. Because I feel like I just stepped into some kind of romantic travel magazine." She pointed at the screen. "These are gorgeous."

She laughed softly, but she could feel her heart racing.

"I know," she admitted. "But... that's not why I'm showing you."

"Oh?" she asked, the playful glimmer in her eyes returned. "Then why?"

Alex hesitated for half a beat, then turned the laptop toward her and clicked over to a new tab. It was a blank website template. A portfolio page she had added late last night.

"I've been thinking about using it," she said softly, "as the cover photo for the site. Or maybe the introduction page of the portfolio."

"You have to. That photo doesn't just show your art. *It* is your art. It tells a story, the same way your sketches do."

"He saw me before I even saw myself."

"And maybe now you're finally ready to see her too."

"I want to put my work out there. No more excuses."

"Wait, wait, wait," she said, holding up her hand. "Are you telling me that you, Alex-who-overthinks-everything, is about to make her art public?"

"Maybe," she admitted softly. "I mean, I'm still working on the site. But... yeah. I want to do it."

Sarah let out a noise that was somewhere between a squeal and a gasp.

"Oh, my God." She smacked the counter with both hands. "Yes! Finally!"

Alex burst into laughter, half-surprised by her friend's dramatic reaction.

"Sarah—"

"No, no, no, don't you dare talk yourself out of this!" Sarah cut in, pointing a finger at her. "This is happening. You've been holding yourself back for too long." She turned the laptop toward herself and clicked through the photos again, shaking her head in awe. "Alex, this is you. The woman who traveled the world and saw it through her own eyes. The woman who makes art that makes people feel things. It's about time everyone else got to see her, too."

Alex's throat tightened unexpectedly at the raw sincerity in her friend's voice. She blinked quickly, forcing back the sudden sting of emotion behind her eyes.

"Do you really think I can do this?" she asked.

Sarah turned to her, no trace of teasing in her expression now. She reached over and took Alex's hand, squeezing it firmly.

"I know you can." Her voice was steady, unwavering. "And so does Jamie. Hell, half of Italy probably does, too."

Alex let out a watery laugh, blinking again.

"God, why are you so good at pep talks?"

"I've been waiting for you to believe in yourself as much as I do," Sarah said, her eyes filled with warmth.

"Okay," she said quietly, her voice steady. She turned the laptop back toward herself and tapped on the website template. "I'm doing this."

Sarah's face split into a wide, triumphant grin.

"Damn right you are."

A smile touched her lips as she realized how much her art had grown and matured. With newfound confidence, she began adding them to her portfolio.

The first photo she uploaded was one of the shots of her sketching by the sea in Capri. It felt right to start with that one. She added a caption beneath it: *Finding Myself Again.*

Next came her sketches from the night before, the Amalfi Coast, Positano, Santorini, and Capri. Each one held pieces of her journey, moments she had brought back with her in ink and charcoal. She scanned the pages and added them, labeling the section *Memories in Motion.*

She sifted through her older pieces. The ones that she had always been too critical of and was too hesitant to share. There was the watercolor of a foggy pier she had painted on a rainy morning. The charcoal sketch of a woman sitting alone in a cafe with a wistful expression. The abstract painting she had once thought was too bold, too messy, but now she saw it differently. She saw freedom in the chaotic brushstrokes.

One by one, she uploaded them. With each image, the collection grew more complete. It symbolized her growth, both in her artistry and in her personal journey.

Sarah leaned over her shoulder and watched the portfolio come to life.

"God, these are so good."

Alex's hands slowed as she reached the last section. She

hesitated for a moment, then opened a folder containing the photos from Jamie's email that he had taken of her. Her fingers hovered over the trackpad. She looked at Sarah.

"Too much?"

"No. Not too much. Those belong here. You belong here."

She created a new section titled *Through His Lens*. One by one, she uploaded the candid moments he had captured when she wasn't looking. This time, she omitted captions. She let the images speak for themselves.

With a deep exhale, she leaned back, work complete, feeling utterly relaxed. Her portfolio was no longer just a scattered collection of work. It was a visual narrative of her journey. Memories, the growth, the rediscovery. It was hers.

Sarah squeezed her hand, gleaming with pride.

"Look at you," she stated. "Finally putting your art out into the world. I'm so proud of you."

Alex glanced at the screen, a smile spreading across her lips. Although a hint of nervousness remained, it was overshadowed by a powerful sense of pride. She clicked Save and released a steady breath. It was done.

Her portfolio was live, her art finally out in the world. It was part of something real. Tangible. *Hers*. She stared at the screen as the confirmation message posted in the corner. The nervous flutter in her chest didn't disappear entirely, but it no longer felt like fear. It felt like anticipation. Like possibility.

She reached for her tea and took a slow sip. Across the room, Sarah looked up from her phone.

"Is it up?" she asked.

"It's up."

Sarah let out a cheer, sliding across the hardwood in her socks to pull Alex into a tight hug. "You did it!"

"I did," Alex said, almost in disbelief. "I really did."

"Now, let's celebrate the fact that you're finally getting back to your art. Wine or Tea?"

"Tea. I've got work to do."

"Tea it is. But don't think you're off the hook for a proper celebration later."

As she got up to get a glass, she turned back to her laptop and scrolled through the photos. Each one told a story of colors and movement, of quiet moments and grand landscapes, of the way she had felt in those places.

# Chapter 34

The next morning, Alex was finishing her coffee when her phone buzzed with a message from Jamie.

*Busy today? Come by my studio. I
want to show you something.*

A spark of curiosity flickered inside her. She hadn't been to Jamie's studio before. Never even thought of asking where he worked when he wasn't traveling.

*Sure. Send me the address.
How soon can you get here?*

Her smile widened at the playfulness in his message. She glanced at the clock. She didn't have any firm plans for the day aside from maybe adding more pieces to her portfolio, but the sudden invitation was far more tempting.

*Give me twenty minutes.
I'll be waiting.*

Feeling a spark of excitement, she set her mug down, washed it, and headed to her bedroom. Dressed in a pair of jeans and a soft, charcoal-gray top, she rolled the sleeves up to her elbows. After brushing her hair into a loose ponytail, she left a few strands free to frame her face. A casual, comfortable glance at her reflection was all she gave herself in the mirror. She grabbed her bag and headed out the door.

Fifteen minutes later, she was pulling up in front of a low-rise brick building in a quiet corner of the city. The structure had an industrial feel: large, steel-framed windows, and a weathered metal door with a simple plaque that read:

*Jamie Rivers Photography.*

She walked up to the door and pressed the buzzer. A moment later, his voice came through the intercom.

"Hey, come on in."

With a click, the door opened, and she stepped inside. She looked around and was instantly awed. Photos hung from clips and wires, and soft white prints were drying on a long table by the windows. To her right, a series of large-format prints leaned against the wall: black-and-white portraits, dramatic landscapes, and candid street shots. To her left, a wide wooden worktable was covered with prints, film rolls, and scattered sketches. A few camera lenses sat next to a half-full cup of coffee. It was a creative mess, but it was *him*. Honest, open, alive.

"Hey."

She turned at the sound of his voice. At the back of the studio, he casually leaned against the door frame, a smile on his face as he crossed his arms. He wore worn jeans paired with a soft navy Henley shirt that hugged his frame.

"Wow. This is... incredible."

He walked toward her. "Yeah?" he asked. "Not too messy?"

She shook her head, her eyes still wandering over the wall of black-and-white portraits.

"No. It's perfect," she whispered. "It feels... like you."

He smiled. "Good. That's the goal."

She strolled to the wall of photos and stopped in front of a large print. It was a candid shot of a woman walking alone through a rain-soaked street, her face turned away, blurred by motion. The reflections of streetlights glimmered in the puddles around her that created a dreamlike quality.

"This is beautiful," she said.

He moved closer just behind her.

"That was in Paris," he explained. "She was rushing home in the rain, but she stopped under the streetlight for just a second. It was like she was waiting for something. Or maybe someone."

She turned back to the photo. She could feel the story in the image. The longing, the unspoken hope.

"Come on," he said softly. "There's something else I want to show you."

He led her toward the back of the studio, weaving through tall shelves filled with frames and canvases. He guided her into a smaller, more intimate room with softer lighting.

As they stepped inside, the atmosphere shifted. The photos were more personal. There were candid portraits, unguarded moments, snapshots of joy and stillness. The kind of images that didn't scream to be seen, but whispered to be felt.

Her gaze traveled slowly from one frame to the next: an elderly man laughing mid-sentence, a child asleep on his mother's shoulder, a woman sitting alone in a café, writing furiously into a worn journal. And then she stopped. Centered on the far wall, bathed in soft light, was a photograph she hadn't seen before.

*Her.*

Sitting cross-legged on a sun-warmed stone ledge, sketchbook open on her knees, her head tilted slightly as she drew. Her hair was windblown, the light golden on her skin, the sea stretching endlessly behind her. She didn't even remember him taking it.

"I was going to ask before I put it up," he said. "But I couldn't not include it. That day, you were... everything I try to capture. Presence. Stillness. Something real."

"I didn't know you saw me like that."

"I don't think I ever stopped," he said.

She turned toward him, their faces inches apart, emotion tightening her chest.

"Jamie..."

"I wasn't sure if it was too much," he said quickly, but without retreat. "I just wanted you to know.... what you gave me...what you helped me see again...that mattered."

Alex didn't say anything at first. Her eyes stayed on the photo. It was so unguarded, so honest. She barely recognized herself. But somehow, through his lens, she saw something she hadn't allowed herself to believe in for a long time.

"You make it look like I had everything figured out," she said quietly.

"You didn't," he said. "That's what made it so powerful. You were *becoming*."

"I didn't know you were watching me like that."

"I couldn't not watch you. You were waking up bit by bit. I was lucky enough to witness it."

"Show me the others?"

He walked to a large drawer beneath one of the tables. He slid it open and pulled out a portfolio of prints, each one encased in thin, protective plastic sleeves. Wordlessly, he handed her the stack.

She carried it over to a nearby table and flipped through them. There was one of her at the window, morning light soft against her skin as she sipped coffee. One of her barefoot on the balcony, sketchpad in her lap, hair tumbling down her back. Another of her laughing, head thrown back, sun catching in her eyes, while they sat on the stone steps of a sleepy piazza.

And more. More than she could have imagined. On the balcony of their rental. Her turning to smile over her shoulder as they wandered through a market. Her leaning against a sunlit wall, eyes closed, completely at peace.

She stared at the images, her chest tightening.

"I was going to make this into a collection," he admitted. "But the more I looked at them, the more I realized... they weren't for anyone else. They were just for me."

She turned to face him.

"You did all this... for me?"

"I wanted you to see yourself the way I see you. The way you are when you're lost in the moment. When you're creating. When you're free."

She didn't say a word at first. Her heart was thundering

too loudly, her emotions tangled somewhere between awe and certainty. Slowly, she reached up and cupped his face in both hands, her thumbs brushing the faint stubble along his jaw. Her eyes searched his, finding all the softness and sincerity she'd been too afraid to name until now.

And then, she closed the space between them and kissed him. He drew her in with a quiet urgency, his arms wrapping around her waist like he was afraid to let go. She melted into him, her fingers slipping into his hair, holding him close like he was something precious.

"I'm so proud of you," he whispered. "For putting yourself out there. For being brave."

"I wouldn't have done it without you," she replied.

"Yeah, you would have," he whispered. "You just needed to remember who you were."

Alex let out a soft, shaky laugh and leaned into him again. He tightened his arms around her and held her there for a moment longer. When they finally parted, her heart was still racing with the sweetness of it. She carried that feeling with her through the evening, through the ride back home.

When she was settled, she sat on the floor surrounded by sketchbooks, loose sheets of paper, and a cup of tea that had gone cold an hour ago. She was staring at the sketches scattered in front of her. Each one carried a memory of her travels. But now, those sketches pulsed with newfound energy and represented a future she couldn't ignore.

The idea had taken root after she'd seen her transformation through Jamie's lens. If he could capture and share moments globally, what was stopping her from doing the same? Her phone buzzed with a ring that pulled her from her thoughts. She saw Sarah's name on the screen.

"Hey."

"Hey, you! Are we still on for later?"

"Yeah. I have something I want to talk to you about."

"Oh? Is it about Jamie? Because if it is, I need a full update."

"No, it's not about him. Well, not directly. It's about my art."

"I'm intrigued. Tell me everything, leave nothing out when we meet."

"I'll see you there; I can't wait!"

Alex was waiting for her when she arrived.

"You look serious," Sarah said as she slid into the seat across from her. "What's going on?"

"I've been updating my portfolio," she answered.

"Yeah?" she prompted.

Alex glanced at her with a small flicker of nervous excitement in her eyes.

"And I was thinking… since I'm already doing that, why not show some pieces as an art exhibit?"

"Wait. Hold on. Are you serious?"

"Yeah. I mean, I've never done anything like this before," she admitted. "But… I don't know. It feels right."

"Alex, I am so proud right now. My best friend, the artist, is doing her first exhibit." She wiped an imaginary tear from her eye. "You're going to be so famous. I'm going to have to start charging people to name-drop you."

"Yeah, but… what if no one likes them?"

With a quick wave of her hand, Sarah dismissed the idea.

"Stop right there," she said firmly. "First, your art is incredible; the vibrant colors and bold strokes are breathtaking. I'm not just saying that because I'm your best friend. I'm saying it because it's true. Your work makes people feel something. That's rare."

She reached across the table and squeezed Alex's hand.

"And second," she added, "who cares what anyone thinks? This isn't about them. This is about you. About sharing what you've created. About taking a step toward your dreams."

"I know, but putting myself out there like this it's so far out of my comfort zone."

"That's exactly why you need to do it. You've spent years hiding your talent. It's time to let the world see what you're capable of."

"There's a local gallery hosting a community art night next month. I was thinking about submitting my work."

Sarah's face lit up with a wide grin.

"Hell yes," she said, raising her glass in a mock toast. "To The Art of Alex Greer. Coming soon to a gallery near you."

"You're getting way ahead of yourself."

"Am I? You just said you're doing this. That's huge! So, tell me.. what pieces are you going to submit and when is it?"

"I haven't decided yet. I mean, I literally just made this decision five minutes ago."

"Which is exactly why I'm here, to make sure you don't back out. We'll start looking at outfits this week."

"What if I'm not ready?"

Sarah gave her a pointed look. "Alex, you've been ready. You just needed to believe it."

"Okay," she said, more to herself than to Sarah. "Let's do it."

"Perfect. You've got plenty of time to prepare. And I'll be there every step of the way. Whatever you need, just say the word."

"Thanks, Sarah."

"You're going to crush this," Sarah said confidently. "Now, tell me about Jamie. Has he seen your sketches yet?"

"He has, actually. He's been really supportive."

"I bet he has," Sarah teased, wiggling her eyebrows.

Alex rolled her eyes, but she couldn't fight the smile tugging at her lips.

"It's not like that," she said, though the warmth rising in her cheeks betrayed her.

Sarah gave her a look. One that screamed you're not fooling me for a second.

"Please," she scoffed. "I've seen the way you talk about him. You get all dreamy-eyed and soft-voiced. It's adorable."

"I do not."

"Oh, you absolutely do," Sarah countered with a wicked

grin. "So, come on. Tell the truth. Are you two officially... you know?" She wiggled her eyebrows again.

"No," she said casually. "Not officially."

Sarah's eyes narrowed, the corners crinkling slightly as she focused intently.

"But...?"

"But... it feels different with him. It's not rushed or complicated. It's just... easy. Natural."

Sarah's teasing expression softened into something warmer. "Hey, that sounds pretty official to me."

Alex glanced down. She could still feel the way Jamie had held her earlier.

"Yeah," she admitted softly. "It does, in a way," she replied.

# Chapter 35

Over the next few weeks, Alex poured herself into preparing for the exhibit, her heart still tethered to the places she had wandered—and to the person who had helped awaken something deep inside her. The memories of sunlit piazzas, cliff side sunsets, and the sound of waves crashing beneath a Capri balcony were stitched into every sketch she refined, every charcoal line she breathed new life into.

Her apartment slowly transformed into a makeshift studio. The floors and walls were covered with drawings that captured not just landscapes, but moments—laughter shared in foreign cafes, quiet afternoons spent sketching under olive trees, stolen glances that meant far more than they let on. For the first time in years, she wasn't just creating art—she was reliving it.

Each morning she woke with a renewed sense of purpose. Gone was the fog of routine; in its place, a quiet drive that thrilled and terrified her in equal measure. Late into the night, she worked under pools of warm lamplight, music playing softly in the background as she pushed herself to explore new textures, even daring to add color to a few of her pieces. It was like capturing pieces of her journey all over again, only this time, with bolder strokes.

Then one evening, just as she was cleaning graphite smudges off her hands, there was a knock at the door. She opened it to find Jamie standing there, travel-worn and smiling, holding two steaming cups of coffee and a paper bag crinkled from the rain.

"I figured you could use a break," he said, his voice low

and familiar, like a song she hadn't realized she'd been missing.

Her heart stuttered, warmth rising in her chest as she stepped aside to let him in. "Thought you could use a break," as his saw the scattered sketches and half-finished paintings.

Alex groaned and rubbed her temples. "I think I've officially lost my mind."

He set the drinks down, pulled out a pastry from the bag, and handed it to her. "Or you're just in the zone. Either way, eat."

"Thanks."

Jamie picked up a piece. It was a charcoal sketch of a street musician. "This one's new."

"I was experimenting. Trying to capture the essence of the moment, not just the details."

He smiled. "You nailed it."

A wave of emotion washed over her as his encouragement tightened her chest with a mix of excitement and gratitude. "Are you ready for the exhibit?"

A wide grin stretched across Jamie's face. "I was about to ask you the same thing."

"I don't know if I'll ever feel ready. But I'm doing it anyway."

"That's what matters."

They spent the evening hunched over her sketches. He was animated as he offered insightful suggestions,laughter and anecdotes from his own career in the art world.

The night of the exhibit arrived faster than Alex had anticipated. As she stood just outside the gallery doors, the soft hum of conversation and occasional bursts of laughter floated into the night air. Warm light spilled from the windows, casting a golden glow on the sidewalk. A swirl of excitement and nerves pulsed through her, tightening in her chest.

Beside her, Sarah glanced over with a knowing smile.

"You ready?" she asked.

Alex took a deep breath. "As ready as I'll ever be."

Sarah bumped her shoulder gently. "You've got this."

Alex straightened her shoulders, and stepped inside. A gentle hum of conversation filled the gallery. A wave of surreal emotion washed over her as she saw her sketches framed and displayed with such professional care and attention to detail. People were in front of them, studying the lines and the emotions captured in each piece.

Jamie stood proudly near her largest watercolor, a breathtaking Amalfi Coast scene. Their eyes met, and an encouraging smile spread across his face, lifting her spirits.

A woman in a sleek black dress approached her and gestured toward a piece depicting a quiet Santorini street. "This one... there's something about it. It feels so personal."

Alex's breath caught softly in her throat. She glanced at the piece the woman was referring to—the curved white buildings, the deep shadows of dusk settling over the narrow street, and a single figure leaning against a stone wall, sketchbook in hand, head turned toward the distant sea.

"It is," Alex said, her voice quiet but steady. "That moment... I remember feeling completely still for the first time in a long time. Like the world finally let me catch my breath."

"It shows. There's this... intimacy to your work. It's like we're not just seeing a place. You're letting us feel what you felt when you were there."

Alex felt warmth rise in her chest. For so long, she had doubted whether her art could connect with others. Now, hearing those words, it felt like something inside her had clicked into place.

"Thank you. That means more than I can say."

The woman moved on, and Alex wandered slowly through the gallery, pausing in front of each frame, reliving the moments she had captured: sunsets in Capri, street corners in Rome, lazy afternoons in courtyards where the light played like a living thing. With each sketch, she felt the journey all over again, but this time, shared.

When she finally made her way to the watercolor Jamie

stood beside, he turned as she approached.

"They love your work," he said softly.

She looked up at the Amalfi piece. "I think I might finally believe it."

He stepped a little closer, eyes gleaming with pride. "You should. You brought your journey home, and now the rest of the world gets to see it."

Her smile deepened as she took in the room again. It gave her the sense that something beautiful had taken root here tonight. The sounds of the night lulled Alex into a state of calm; she felt relaxed more as the hours passed. Her art wasn't just being looked at; people felt a profound connection.

The gallery owner approached them, breaking the moment. "Alex, I just wanted to say congratulations. Your work has been a huge hit tonight. We've had several inquiries about purchasing some of your pieces."

Her eyes widened. "Seriously?"

"Really," the owner confirmed. "You've got a gift. Don't stop sharing it."

As the owner walked away, she turned to Jamie. "Did you hear that?"

"I did," he said. "And I'm not surprised at all."

A warmth spread through her as she allowed herself to fully embrace the joy and pride bubbling inside her. She had done it, and a sense of accomplishment filled her as she looked back on her work. Overcoming her fear and doubt, she'd bravely shared her art; the sweet taste of success was a reward far beyond what she'd imagined. And as she stood there, surrounded by people who believed in her, she realized she believed in herself too.

The evening air rushed in as the last few guests left the gallery. She stood by the large windows replaying every kind word, each smile, and the warmth of the connections she made at the exhibit.

"Behind her, Sarah appeared with two flutes of champagne. "Well, believe it, babe," she said, grinning. "You absolutely killed it tonight."

Alex turned as Sarah handed her a glass. She took it with both hands, still slightly dazed. "I'm still processing," she admitted. "People want to buy my sketches, Sarah. Like, actually pay money for them. What?"

Sarah raised her brows and gestured dramatically. "What do you mean, 'what'? You're amazing. You've always been amazing. Tonight just proved it. Everyone else finally caught up."

A surprised, bubbling laugh escaped Alex's lips as she took a sip

Jamie approached them from across the room. "There you are," he said, a smile playing on his lips as he looked at her. "I was starting to think you'd slipped out to avoid all the attention."

"Tempting," she said.

"Don't you dare," Sarah said. "Tonight is for celebrating. Speaking of which, what's the plan? Because I'm not letting you go home and hide under a blanket after this."

A low chuckle rumbled in his chest as he slipped his hand around Alex's waist, the easy familiarity of the gesture making Sarah's eyes widen just a fraction. A blush warmed her cheeks, but she didn't pull away. Instead, she turned slightly toward him, feeling the strength of his arm as she leaned into the comforting warmth of his embrace.

"Actually..." she stammered, her eyes darting nervously between them, a blush creeping up her neck. "There's someone I want you to meet."

Sarah's eyebrows shot up, her lips curving into a slow, knowing grin. "Someone, huh?" she said, her voice laced with barely contained delight.

Alex bit her bottom lip and gave Jamie a quick glance before turning back to her friend. "Sarah, this is Jamie Rivers. Jamie, meet Sarah. My best friend, partner-in-crime, and the one who's been not-so-patiently demanding this introduction."

Jamie extended his hand, his signature easy charm in full effect. "It's great to finally meet you. I've heard... a *lot*."

Sarah shook his hand, eyes narrowing just slightly as she sized him up, her playful skepticism on full display. "Likewise. You're the guy with the camera and the mysterious influence that's got her glowing like a woman in a perfume ad."

Jamie laughed, rubbing the back of his neck. "Guilty, I guess."

Alex groaned but couldn't stop the smile tugging at her lips. "She's never going to let this go."

Sarah stepped back and crossed her arms. "Not a chance. But," she added, softening, "if this—" she gestured between them, "is what's been inspiring all that gorgeous art and this new version of you... I'm here for it."

Jamie's hand tightened slightly at Alex's waist, and she felt her breath catch again. "I'm also the reason she hasn't been sleeping much. She's been working on her portfolio late into the night."

Sarah's eyes widened, her mouth forming a perfect 'O' of exaggerated scandal.

"Oh-ho! Is that what we're calling it now?" she teased.

He laughed, and Alex gave her friend a sharp nudge with her elbow, but her face was already flushing.

"Okay, that's enough out of you," she stated.

Jamie chuckled, clearly enjoying the back-and-forth. "Guilty as charged, but strictly in the artistic sense," he added, raising his hands in mock surrender.

Sarah grinned, utterly unrepentant. "Mm-hmm. Artistic. Got it." She sipped her champagne, then pointed her glass at Alex. "Look at you. Blushing. You've got it *bad*."

Alex rolled her eyes but couldn't stop smiling. "I swear, remind me why I invited you ?"

"Because I'm charming, loyal, and know all your secrets," Sarah quipped, winking. "Besides, someone's gotta make sure this dreamy photographer of yours knows what he's getting into."

Jamie replied playfully. "Trust me, I already know. And I'm not going anywhere."

She gasped again, her smile softening as their eyes met. Sarah watched the exchange with a slow, satisfied nod and raised her glass once more.

"To love, late nights, and whatever kind of 'art' you two keep making together."

Sarah's eyes twinkled with mischief as she took a deliberate sip of her drink, the corners of her mouth lifting into a smug grin.

"I like him," she declared, looking at Jamie with approval. "You can stay."

He shot Alex a mock-serious glance. "Good. I was really hoping for her blessing."

With a sly smile, Sarah dropped her voice, as if sharing a secret.

"Just so you know, if you hurt her, I'll ruin you. Creatively, of course. Nothing illegal."

He nodded solemnly. "Duly noted."

Alex shook her head, but she was smiling. She slipped her hand into his, giving his fingers a light squeeze. Sarah's expression softened slightly, and she placed her hand over Alex's.

"Seriously, though," she said. "I'm thrilled for you."

The familiar knot of gratitude tightened in Alex's chest, bringing with it a rush of happy memories and a sense of peace.

"Thanks," she whispered.

Sarah's eyes, sparkling with mischief, darted from Jamie to Alex.

"Now, about this celebration," she chirped, the words bubbling with excitement and a hint of playful mischief. "You both are joining me, aren't you? I refuse to let you go home and do the whole 'cozy couple' thing when we should be drinking and dancing."

With a mock-serious expression that didn't quite reach

his twinkling eyes, he glanced at Alex. "Do we have a choice, or is this a non-negotiable?"

Sarah grinned. "Oh, it's absolutely non-negotiable."

"Then I guess we're going out."

Alex rolled her eyes good-naturedly but didn't protest. She squeezed his hand a little tighter, feeling a sense of lightness settle in her chest. For once, she wasn't overthinking or holding back. She was just here with her best friend and the man who had quietly become so much more than she'd ever expected. And tonight, she was going to let herself celebrate it.

Alex laughed, the sound light and genuine, the last traces of tension from the evening melting away. She looked up at Jamie, her eyes dancing. "I mean... she did bring cookies last time I had a crisis. I think we owe her."

"Fine. But only if there's good music."

"Oh, there will be," Sarah said, already pulling out her phone and scrolling with purpose. "I've got a playlist. I've got a rooftop spot. And I've got a sudden craving for champagne and bad decisions."

Alex raised her eyebrows. "Define *bad decisions*."

"You'll find out when the third round of cocktails hits."

As they made their way toward the exit, Sarah already launching into a story about the rooftop DJ, Alex paused to glance over her shoulder one last time. Her sketches lined the walls. Her journey—messy, bold, and brave—on full display.

Jamie leaned down to murmur in her ear. "You did this."

She smiled. "We did."

They didn't dive into the center of the dance floor like Sarah, who had already pulled two strangers into an impromptu trio. Instead, he stayed close as they found a quiet rhythm at the edge of the crowd swaying in time with the music. Every so often, Jamie would lean down and murmur something into her ear and her laughter would bubble up. The way he looked at her in those moments, like she was the most captivating thing in the room, made her heart skip every time.

At one point, Sarah twirled back to them, breathless

and glowing with energy. She grabbed Alex's hand and spun her out onto the dance floor with a dramatic flair that made the surrounding strangers erupt into cheers. Alex couldn't remember the last time she'd felt this carefree.

She felt Jamie's hand slide into hers and he led her off the dance floor. The pulse of music faded behind them and was replaced by the cool night air that kissed her flushed cheeks. Up ahead, Sarah danced barefoot along the sidewalk. She spun in a wide circle, arms stretched out like she could embrace the whole city.

"I love this place!" she declared to the sky. Then she whirled around and threw her arms around Alex in an exaggerated hug. "And I *love* you."

Alex laughed and hugged her back tightly. "Love you too, you maniac."

Sarah pulled away and pointed a finger at him with mock sternness. "You better take care of her."

"Always," he said.

Sarah gave them both a knowing grin before heading off toward the line of waiting cabs. "Go be disgustingly adorable somewhere else," she called over her shoulder. "I'm going home."

Alex laughed softly as she watched the cab disappear into the night. When she turned back, she found Jamie watching her with that look that always seemed to weaken her defenses.

Without a word, he took her hand again and they started walking.

"So, how does it feel?"

"It feels... real," she admitted. "Like I finally stopped holding myself back."

"That's because you did."

She glanced at him. "I don't think I could have done it without you."

"You could have. You just needed a little push."

"More like several pushes, a lot of pep talks, and maybe a

tiny existential crisis or two."

"All part of the process."

Alex couldn't shake the memory of the evening; the excited chatter surrounding her artwork and the quiet confidence she felt standing in the bright gallery. She was proud of what she had created.

"You know," she began, "I used to think success meant having everything figured out. But tonight, I realized it's more about just showing up, doing the work, and letting yourself grow."

"Sounds like an artist to me."

"Yeah," she whispered. "I think I finally believe that."

When they reached her apartment, she paused and turned around. "Jamie, I—"

He didn't say anything, just stepped closer and leaned in for a kiss.

"Thank you," she whispered. "Not just for tonight, but for everything."

He brushed his thumb across her cheek. "Always."

She unlocked the door to her apartment and slipped inside, her heart still racing from the evening. The exhibit stayed on her mind. The laughter, the sparkling conversations, the way people's eyes softened with admiration when they looked at her work. Compliments replayed like echoes, but beneath them was a quiet disbelief: had all of that really happened?

She set her bag down and wandered into the kitchen, reaching for a glass of water to steady herself. The knock came softly, unexpected, and she froze.

When she opened the door, she was surprised. "Jamie?"

"Hey."

"I thought you were leaving," she said. "Is everything okay?"

"Yeah," he replied. "I just... I couldn't go home yet. Not without seeing you again."

Something inside her tugged loose at his words. She

stepped aside to let him in. When she closed the door, she felt the shift between them; closer, quieter, more electric.

Turning back, she found him watching her with a look that made her pulse stumble. "Tonight was incredible," he said softly. "*You* were incredible."

"It still doesn't feel real," she said softly.

"It *is* real. And you deserve every second of it."

She searched his face. "Why did you really come back?" she asked.

He didn't answer right away. Instead, he reached out and took her hand. "Because I didn't want the night to end," he admitted. "Not without telling you how proud I am of you. How much you inspire me. And..." His gaze dropped to their joined hands before meeting hers again. "Because I just wanted to be with you."

Something shifted inside her then, as if the ground itself had realigned beneath her feet. The weight of his words sank into her. She tightened her grip on his hand. "Then stay."

A look of surprise was on his face as if he hadn't expected her to give him that piece of herself. But slowly, his expression softened, and he smiled.

"Okay," he said.

And just like that, the night wasn't over yet.

# Chapter 36

Alex lay on her side, watching the rise and fall of Jamie's breathing. He was still asleep, a gentle snore escaping his lips. His face looked unguarded in a way she rarely saw when he was awake. A faint shadow of stubble traced his jaw, and a strand of hair had slipped across his forehead.

She resisted the urge to brush it back, choosing instead to simply take him in. In the stillness of the morning, with the city just beginning to stir outside the window, she let herself savor this; him, here, beside her. It felt like a secret too precious to name aloud, and yet it settled inside her with a quiet certainty.

Last night had been... unexpected. But not in a way she regretted. She'd braced herself for nerves, for doubt, maybe even for the weight of second thoughts. Instead, waking beside him felt startlingly natural. The quiet glow of morning light spilling through the curtains mixed with the gentle warmth of his body close by was the most peaceful start she could remember.

Careful not to disturb him, she eased out of bed, slipping into an oversized shirt that brushed against her thighs. Padding softly toward the kitchen, she let the hush of the apartment wrap around her.

She filled the coffeemaker with water and scooped in the rich, fragrant grounds. As she waited, she leaned against the counter and looked out the window. The sun had fully risen now.

"You're up early."

"I could say the same for you," he teased, his eyes tracing her with a look that made her pulse skip.

"Didn't want you sneaking off and leaving me to wake up alone."

She rolled her eyes, though the smile tugging at her lips betrayed her. "I was making coffee. Not running away."

"Good," he said as he stepped closer. "Because I would've found you."

She lifted a brow, handing him a mug as he reached the counter. "Oh really? And what would you have done? Tracked me across the city like some romantic detective?"

He accepted the coffee with a grin. "Exactly. Don't underestimate me. I've got a very particular set of skills."

Alex laughed. "You're quoting movies before caffeine? Brave choice."

"Or charming," he countered, taking a sip and pretending to consider. "Yeah... definitely charming."

She shook her head, leaning against the counter beside him. "You're impossible."

"Maybe," he said, bumping her shoulder with his. "But you like me this way."

He set his cup down on the counter and stepped closer, close enough that she felt the soft brush of his breath against her temple.

"So," he teased. "How are you feeling about last night?"

Her lips curved in a faint smile. "You mean the exhibit? Or... this?"

His grin turned mischievous. "Both."

"The exhibit... it still feels surreal. Like I'm waiting for someone to tell me it was all a dream."

"It wasn't," he said firmly. His eyes softened as he watched her with conviction. "You did that, Alex. And it was amazing."

"Thank you."

"Now," he tipped his head, "what about the other part?"

She let out a breathy laugh. She was very aware of how close he was, how the morning light caught in his hair made it look a shade lighter, and how the faint stubble along his jaw made him even more distractingly handsome.

"This," she echoed, stalling by taking another sip of her coffee. She set her mug down and traced the rim with her fingertip. "Well... this still feels a little surreal, too." She looked at him. "You know, the part where Jamie Rivers apparently has terrible taste in women."

His lips curved into a slow grin. "Terrible, huh?" He set his mug aside and took a slow step closer. He was so close that the heat of his body warmed the space between them. "I must've missed that part."

Her lips turned into a smirk. "Oh yeah. I'm a mess, remember? Self-doubt, emotional baggage, and—"

His hands slid around her waist, silencing her mid-sentence with a tender touch. "Stop," he said.

The sudden shift in his tone surprised her. She could feel his thumbs brush soft, reassuring circles against her lower back.

"I don't see a mess," he whispered. "I see someone brave enough to take risks. To put herself out there even when she's scared. And I see someone I—"

He stopped himself. His eyes searched hers, but she could see it and feel it. It was heavy and unspoken between them.

"Jamie..."

He lowered his forehead to hers. "You're not a mess, Alex," he whispered. "You're incredible."

Her chest tightened, and the ache behind her ribs was almost too much, too full, too real. Taking a deep breath, she closed her eyes, savoring the familiar smell of his skin. And then, without thinking, she pressed her lips softly to his.

"I'm still figuring all of this out," she confessed softly. "But I know I want this." She slipped her fingers into his, linking them together. "I want you."

"You've got me," he squeezed her hand. "For as long as you want."

"I think that might be a while," she whispered.

"Good," he murmured, sealing the word with another kiss. "So... does this mean I get breakfast?"

She laughed. "That depends. Do you cook?"

"Not well," he admitted. "But I make a mean cup of coffee."

She raised her eyebrow in a mock expression. "So, you're saying I have to cook?"

"Only if you want something edible."

She shook her head but turned toward the fridge, already gathering ingredients. "Fine. But you're helping."

He held up his hands in surrender. "Deal."

They fell into a simple rhythm as they cooked. Jamie chopped the vegetables while she whisked eggs. He reached around her to grab a plate, and his fingers brushed against her waist. The simple touch sent a shiver through her, and she glanced up at him. He was already looking at her.

"You keep looking at me like that," she said, "and breakfast is going to burn."

His lips curved into a mischievous grin. "Worth it," he whispered.

His hand lingered near her waist, and she could feel the warmth of his skin through the fabric of her shirt. The scent of frying eggs filled her nostrils so she forced herself to look away and focus on the task at hand.

"Don't forget to flip the bacon," she said casually, "or they'll be black as coal and smell awful."

But he didn't move. Instead, with a slow, deliberate movement, his hand brushed past hers again, sending a shiver down her spine. This time, he brushed his arm against hers as he grabbed the spatula. His touch was brief but lingering and the way his fingers grazed her skin sent a subtle shiver down her spine.

"See? Helping," he teased.

"Mm-hmm," she was unable to hide her smiled. "You're so helpful."

A crooked grin stretched across his face as he set the

spatula down with a clatter.

"Hey," he said softly.

She turned to face him fully with the whisk still in her hand.

"Yeah?"

He didn't say anything right away. He just reached out and tucked a loose strand of hair behind her ear. The gentleness of the gesture made her stomach flip.

"You're really beautiful when you're happy," he said.

Her breath caught, and for a moment, she forgot everything. The eggs, the stove, the faint sizzle of the bacon. She was only aware of his warm eyes and the slight rasp in his voice that made the space between them feel smaller.

"Jamie..." she started before he closed the distance between them, silencing her with a tender kiss.

His lips brushed against hers. The briefest of moments that felt like an eternity. But the second she leaned into him, her hand instinctively slid up to rest against his warm chest, feeling the steady beat of his heart. His fingers skimmed lightly over her waist and pulled her closer. She melted into the warmth of his embrace.

The faint scent of coffee lingered on his breath, and she could feel the faintest smile tug at his lips when she let out a quiet sigh. Somewhere behind them, the eggs sizzled a little too loudly and snapped Alex back to reality. With a shaky breath, she pulled back.

"The eggs," she murmured.

With heavy-lidded eyes half-closed, his fingers remained loosely curled around her waist. "Let 'em burn," he whispered.

She let out a breathless laugh, but she didn't pull away right away. She lingered for a heartbeat longer, her forehead brushing against his. Reluctantly, she slipped out of his arms and turned back to the stove. The eggs were on the verge of burning, so she quickly stirred them with a wooden spoon to save them.

"See what you did?" she teased over her shoulder. "Distracting me."

"Totally worth it," he said smugly.

Jamie grinned and stole a strip of bacon from the counter. "I knew it," he said around a mouthful, retreating to the table before she could swat at him with the spatula.

They settled into the easy rhythm that had become so familiar—coffee mugs clinking, the scent of buttered toast hanging in the air, sunlight pooling through the kitchen window like a warm blessing. Jamie leaned back in his chair and watched her as she sat across from him.

"This is nice," she said after a while.

"Yeah," he agreed. "Feels like a Sunday morning painting come to life."

"So," Jamie said. "What's next for you?"

Alex put her fork down, letting the question settle. She glanced out the window, where sunlight flickered through the leaves, and then back at him.

"I'm not sure," she admitted. "I don't have a set plan. But I know I want to keep going. Keep creating. Maybe even start working on a new series."

He grinned. "I was hoping you'd say that."

She raised a brow. "Oh?"

"I might have told a few people about your work last night. There's a gallery owner who's interested in seeing more."

"What?"

"Don't look so surprised," he said. "Your work speaks for itself."

She stared at him. "Jamie, I don't know what to say."

"Say you'll keep going. That you'll see where this takes you."

Alex felt the familiar tightness rise in her chest, but this time, it wasn't fear. It was possibility.

"I think I will."

# Chapter 37

The evening was unusually quiet in Jamie's studio. A warm amber light from the overhead lamp illuminated the scattered photographs and canvases on the walls. Alex sat on the couch by the window watching the gentle drizzle tap against the glass. Thoughts swirled in her mind that she wasn't ready to share.

Meanwhile, Jamie sat a few feet away at his worktable, arms crossed. The unspoken tension between them created a heavy atmosphere in the room.

"You've been quiet tonight," Alex broke the silence.

He looked at her. "Just thinking."

Alex arched an eyebrow. "About what?"

"I suppose there are many things. Us, mostly."

"Us?"

He walked towards the couch and sat beside her. "Yeah. Us."

"What's going on? You've been acting different since the other day. Distant."

"I know. I've been in my head a lot lately. It's not about you, well, not in a bad way. It's about me."

"What do you mean?"

Jamie took a deep breath. He knew how to describe it, but the words wouldn't come out. He looked in her eyes and finally responded. "I've never been good at this," he admitted. "At opening up, at being vulnerable. Commitment has always been hard for me."

She didn't know where this was coming from or where it was going. They had agreed to take things slow. At least, she thought they had. But something in Jamie's expression told a different story.

"Why?"

Jamie met her gaze. His eyes were steady, but behind them was something raw. Unprotected. A kind of vulnerability she hadn't seen in him before.

"I've lived with this constant, crippling fear of ruining everything," he said softly. "My parents... their relationship was never whole. They were always just missing each other. Long silences. Too many goodbyes. My dad was always away —physically, emotionally. And my mom, she just... stopped expecting anything different."

He exhaled slowly, his voice thick with memory.

"I used to think maybe some people just aren't meant to be happy together. That even love, when it's there, isn't always enough to hold two people in place."

His words hung in the air between them, heavy with truth. And she realized that it wasn't about rushing forward. It wasn't even about her. It was about fear. His fear of repeating the past. His fear of losing something before he even had the chance to believe in it.

Her heart ached at the admission. "Jamie."

"Let me finish."

She nodded and waited for him to continue.

"For a long time, I thought keeping people at arm's length was the safest option. My mom would always look sad when my dad was on assignments for months at a time. It used to hurt me that I would hear her cry on their anniversary because he chose work. He saw it as providing for us. She didn't get to do the couple things or travel like we did."

He paused, the silence stretching just long enough to make her heart ache before his voice returned. It was quieter now. More certain, more exposed.

"That got me thinking," he said, eyes fixed on a point somewhere between them. "If you don't let anyone get too close, they can't hurt you, right?"

A dry laugh escaped him, but it lacked any real

230

amusement. His shoulders dropped slightly, and when he looked at her again, his eyes shimmered with something deeper.

"But then you came along," he went on. "You didn't do anything dramatic. You didn't try to tear them down. You just... showed up. With your sketchbook and your cautious smile. And somehow, without even trying, you made it impossible for me to keep you at arm's length."

His words settled into the quiet like soft rain, soaking through the layers she'd carefully wrapped around her own heart.

Alex didn't move. She was afraid that if she did, the moment might vanish.

"I kept telling myself it was temporary," he admitted. "That I'd go back to traveling, and you'd go back to your life, and we'd both be fine. But somewhere between the late-night talks and you falling asleep on my shoulder on the ferry, I stopped believing it. Because... you got in."

"Jamie..." she started. "You're not your dad. When things get hard, you don't disappear. You're here. You stay. That's who you are."

The gentleness in her voice calmed him, and he closed his eyes, feeling a sense of peace wash over him. Her voice grew quieter.

"And you didn't just let me in. You wanted me there. You still do. And so do I."

His eyes searched hers as if he were trying to memorize every word. "Alex..."

Her name on his lips was both a plea and a promise, and for a moment, neither of them spoke. They simply sat there, eyes locked, the weight of everything unspoken heavy in the air. And then he continued.

"I've been trying to find the words for this. Trying to figure out how to tell you what you mean to me without screwing it up."

"You won't," she whispered.

"I've spent so much of my life keeping people at a distance," he admitted softly. "Telling myself that it was safer that way. That if I didn't let anyone get too close, they couldn't hurt me."

His voice was quiet, but there was a rawness in it that made her throat tighten. "I got so good at it that I didn't even realize how empty it made me feel. Like I was just... floating through places. Passing through people's lives without ever really being part of them."

His fingers lightly brushed her jaw, and his voice softened.

"But then you came along."

Her breath hitched slightly, but she didn't speak. She just let him continue.

"You didn't push or ask for anything. You just... showed up. With your curiosity and your kindness. With that look you get when you're lost in your sketchbook, completely in your own world. And you made it so damn easy to let you in."

He let out a slow breath, as if even now he couldn't quite believe it himself.

"I didn't know how much I needed that until you," he said, his thumb brushing gently along her cheekbone. "You made it feel safe to stay. To be somewhere with someone."

Alex blinked against the burn behind her eyes, the emotion catching her off guard. The tenderness in his words wrapped around her like a thread pulling her closer, loosening all the defenses she hadn't even realized she was still holding onto.

She reached up, her hand covering his, anchoring it to her skin. "Jamie..."

His name came out like a whisper, half breath, half prayer.

He gave her a small smile. "I think I've been falling for you since that day in Capri. You were barefoot on the rocks, sketching the sea like you were trying to memorize it and I remember thinking... I want to know how she sees the world. I wanted to see you. All of you."

Her lips parted in quiet surprise, her heart hammering against her ribs. But it wasn't fear this time. It was recognition. It was home.

"I've spent a long time hiding too," she admitted. "Behind my art. Behind what was safe. But with you... it's different. I don't want to hide anymore."

Jamie's hand was still on her cheek, his thumb brushing softly against her skin, but his gaze had dropped.

"I'm scared," she continued, her words trembling at the edges. "Not of you. Not of this. Just... of how much it matters. Of what it means if I let myself fall all the way."

His eyes flicked back up to hers. There was something vulnerable in them like a window left open in a storm.

"I get that," he murmured. "More than you know."

"Then what are we doing, Jamie? Are we just going to pretend like none of this is real? Like it doesn't scare the hell out of both of us?"

He took a half step back, rubbing a hand over the back of his neck as if he needed space just to think.

"I've been trying to keep this easy," he said finally. "To stay in the moment, to not look too far ahead because..."

He stopped himself.

"Because what?" she pressed gently.

His voice nearly broke. "Because if I let myself care about you the way I already do, then I'm opening myself up to the possibility of losing you. And I don't know if I'm strong enough to handle that."

"I get it," she said. "I've been scared too. After what happened with my ex, I didn't think I could trust anyone again. I didn't think I'd want to. But you've shown me that it's okay to hope for something better."

"You deserve better. Better than someone who's afraid to give you what you need."

"Maybe what I need is someone who's willing to try."

"You really think we can make this work?"

"We owe it to ourselves to try. No one's perfect. We're all a little messy. But if there's one thing I've learned these past few months, it's that the best things in life are worth taking a risk for."

"That sounds like some good advice. I wonder where you got it from."

She teased lightly, "Some wise photographer I met in a cafe. Talks a lot about bold steps and seeing the world differently."

His lips curved into a crooked smile. "Sounds like a pretty smart guy. You should probably listen to him."

"I think I will," she whispered.

"Oh, you're something else, you know that?"

"So, I've been told," she teased.

Jamie chuckled, his hand tightening around hers. "Okay. I'm done letting fear paralyze me; it's time to face my anxieties head-on. With you, I'm willing to take that chance and face any uncertainties together. Let's see where this adventure takes us."

Her heart swelled, a warmth spreading through her chest as his sincere words washed over her. With a confident smile, she said, "Then let's do it. No pressure, no expectations. Just us."

"Us. I like the sound of that."

The next morning, Alex sat at the kitchen counter nursing a steaming cup of coffee. She'd slept surprisingly well, despite the whirlwind of emotions from the night before. Across the counter, Jamie was making breakfast.

"I thought you said you don't cook breakfast," she joked.

"I think I said not that well, but you can be a judge," he said as he pretended to concentrate hard.

She arched a playful brow, taking a slow sip of her coffee as she watched him. "Oh, so now you're a chef," she teased.

Jamie shot her a look. "Hey, don't judge until you've tried it," he countered, flashing her a crooked grin. "I can whip up a mean breakfast," he said.

It felt so natural to be here with him, watching him move around his kitchen like he belonged there. Like she belonged there. He brought the plates over and set one in front of her before settling onto the stool across from her. She glanced down at the eggs and toast, then back at him with a raised brow.

"So, am I going to regret this?" she asked, her eyes gleaming with teasing skepticism.

"Only one way to find out," he challenged playfully.

She narrowed her eyes in mock suspicion before picking up her fork. With a smirk, she speared a bite of eggs, holding his gaze as she brought it to her mouth. She dragged out the moment, chewing slowly and deliberately.

"Well?" he prompted, feigning impatience.

She tilted her head and with a deadpan expression said, "Honestly? Not terrible."

His mouth dropped open in mock offense, a playful. "Not terrible?" He repeated, clutching his chest dramatically. "That's what I get? After all my hard work? My culinary creation, a dish I poured my heart and soul into, received the lukewarm compliment of 'not terrible.'"

She took another bite, and exaggerated her chewing. "Maybe above not terrible," she teased.

"You're the worst," he muttered playfully. He grabbed a perfectly golden-brown slice of toast and took a dramatic bite to prove his cooking skills.

"Mm, yes," she quipped. "You really missed your calling. Clearly, you should have been a chef. All that photography talent? Wasted."

He let out a soft laugh, his eyes crinkling at the corners. "Alright, alright. Don't ask me to make you breakfast ever again," he teased, pointing his fork at her in mock warning. But the warmth in his eyes gave him away. The way they lingered on her a little too long, the way he softened when she smiled.

"So," he began with a playful smirk tugging at his lips.

"Was last night what you expected?"

Alex raised an eyebrow, her lips twitching into a smile. "You mean the part where you confessed you're afraid of feelings but still want to date me? Totally saw that coming."

"Fair point. I have a flair for dramatics."

"But no, it wasn't what I expected," she admitted. "It was better."

"Better, huh? I'll take that as a win," he winked.

"Truly, I mean it. I didn't think we'd have that kind of conversation so soon. But it felt honest. Real."

"It did. I needed that. To say it aloud, you know? It's one thing to keep all those fears bottled up but saying them to you it made them feel smaller. Less scary."

"That's because you're not facing them alone anymore."

"Thank you. For not running when I started rambling about my baggage."

"I have my own baggage," she replied with a shrug. "We all do. But if I've learned anything on this crazy journey, it's that the best things in life are worth working for."

His lips curved into a warm smile. "You're really something else, you know that?"

"That's something you've said before, but I'm happy to hear it again," she said playfully.

They ate in silence for a while, the sounds of forks scraping plates and the occasional bird chirping outside filling the room. But Alex could feel a question bubbling up inside her that she wasn't sure how to ask. Finally, she set down her fork and looked at Jamie.

"So, what now?"

He paused mid-bite. "What do you mean?"

"I mean us," she clarified. "We said we're going to try this, but what does that look like? Are we going back to normal life and just seeing where it goes? Or...,"

"Or are we doing something crazy, like booking another flight and running off into the unknown?" he finished for her mischievously.

"I wasn't planning on mentioning that, but since you brought it up."

"I get it. You're looking for clarity, right? Some kind of plan?"

"Something like that," she admitted.

"Here's what I think: we take it one day at a time. No rushing, no overthinking. We keep doing what we've been doing, being honest with each other, supporting each other. And if we want to jump on another plane at some point, we'll do it."

"Okay," she said. "That works for me."

"Besides, I don't think we need to plan every little detail. Sometimes the best moments happen when you least expect them."

"You would say that" she said. "Mr. Spontaneity."

"And you love it," he shot back.

As they finished their breakfast and cleaned up the kitchen, Jamie turned to her with an idea.

"Hey, I know it's not the same as hopping on a plane, but there's this little art gallery downtown that I think you'd love," he said. "They're doing a showcase on mixed media this week. Want to check it out with me?"

Alex smiled at the simple suggestion. "I'd love that."

"Perfect," he said. "Let's get dressed and make it a day to remember. Or we can just stay here, but I can't guarantee that I'll be able to control myself."

"Oh, is that right?" she challenged, arching a playful brow. "So, you're saying if we stay in, you might lose control?"

His lips formed a wicked grin, and his eyes darkened with unmistakable intent.

"I'm just saying," he answered, "the odds wouldn't be in my favor."

She seriously considered forgetting the gallery altogether. It would be so easy to stay wrapped up in him, lost in the warmth of his arms and the safety of his presence.

But then he brushed his knuckles lightly along her jaw.

His touch was electric. "Come on," he teased. "Let me take you somewhere."

She tried to steady her racing heart. With a soft smile, she set her coffee mug down. "Alright," she replied. "You win."

"Smart choice," he whispered playfully. "But just so you know…" he added, "this conversation is far from over."

"Noted."

She slipped off the stool and went toward the bedroom. "I'll be quick," she called over her shoulder.

He leaned against the counter and watched her with a smile. "Take your time," he called back. "We've got all day."

# Chapter 38

Alex was in Jamie's studio flipping through one of his portfolios. Each shot told a story that was fleeting moments of beauty from across the world. He perched on the edge of his desk meticulously tinkering with the old camera. He looked at her with a smile. "You know, if you keep flipping through that portfolio any slower, we'll still be here by morning."

Alex looked up with a mock glare. "Excuse me for appreciating your genius. These are incredible."

"They're just photos," he said with a shrug.

"Stop that." She closed the portfolio and set it aside. "You're always downplaying your talent. These aren't just photos. They're windows. Into other worlds. Other lives."

His gaze, hesitant at first, finally rose to meet hers. He didn't respond. A moment of quietude stretched between them, allowing her words to sink in. The sincerity in her voice disarmed him in a way he hadn't expected.

He let out a soft snicker. "Windows, huh?" he said. His lips curved into a lopsided smile. "That's a pretty poetic way to describe a few snapshots."

You don't just take pictures. You *see* people. Places. Moments that most of us miss."

Jamie rubbed the back of his neck, his smile faltering just slightly as if unsure whether to let the praise in. "I don't know... maybe I just get lucky sometimes."

"It's more than getting lucky. This one," she said as she pointed to a black-and-white shot of a street vendor in Morocco. His face, partially obscured by the swirling, fragrant steam rising from the food cart, revealed only his intensely detailed eyes.

"I don't know his story," she continued, "but when I look at this, I feel like I do."

"And this one..." she turned the page to reveal a portrait of an elderly woman sitting in the doorway of a weathered home in India. She clasped her hands tightly in her lap.

"The way you captured her," she whispered, "it's like you caught the entire weight of her life in a single glance."

She wasn't just complimenting his work. She was seeing him. Seeing the heart, he poured into every frame. He shook his head. "You give me too much credit."

"Remind me again why you're not the one up on gallery walls?" he asked, teasing but sincere.

She nudged him with her shoulder, a blush touching her cheeks. "Maybe one day," she said quietly. "But for now, I'm happy reminding you just how extraordinary you are."

Jamie exhaled, the tension in his shoulders loosening. "You always know what to say, don't you?"

"Only when it matters," she replied.

The tenderness in her voice caught him off guard, and for a moment, he could only stare at her. There was no trace of doubt or hesitation in her voice. He placed the old camera down on the desk. "Alex..." he started.

"Why do you do that?"

He blinked, confused. "Do what?"

Her thumb brushed over the back of his hand. "Downplay everything you are," she whispered. "You're one of the most talented people I've ever known, but you act like you're just... making it up as you go along."

"Because half the time, I am making it up as I go along."

"Well, you're doing a pretty damn good job of it."

Then, slowly, he lifted her hand to his lips and pressed a light kiss against her knuckles. His eyes held hers.

"You're kind of impossible, you know that?" he said softly.

Her lips curved into a small smile. "So are you."

"Stay a little longer?"

Her eyes softened, and she squeezed his hand lightly. "I'm not going anywhere," she whispered.

Without thinking, he slipped his arms around her waist and pulled her closer. She melted against him. For a long moment, they simply stood there holding each other in the quiet warmth of his studio. And just before he lowered his lips to hers, he whispered. "You're my favorite view."

The words sent a shiver down her spine, and then his mouth was on hers. The warmth of his kiss melted into her, making her fingers tighten lightly against the fabric of his shirt. She sighed against his lips and leaned into him.

"You're impossible," she said.

He smiled. "Only for you," he teased.

She let out a soft laugh. "Do you always say things that make it hard to be mad at you?"

"Hmm. Only when I'm trying to impress a ridiculously talented artist," he said with a smirk.

"Oh? Is that what I am now?"

"You've always been that."

His sincere tone unexpectedly made her heart tighten. The warmth in her cheeks burned prompting her to lower her eyes for a moment to compose herself. To ease the sudden tenderness swirling between them, she smirked and gave him a playful nudge. "Alright, fine. Since we're apparently being honest..." she said, "I'll admit your photos are actually pretty good."

He let out an exaggerated gasp and clutched his chest dramatically. "'Pretty good?'" he repeated. "That's all I get? Pretty good?"

"Yeah. I mean... they're all right. I guess," she teased.

"Wow. Brutal. Here I was thinking you were my biggest fan."

She shrugged. "Hey, I just call it like I see it."

"Okay, fine. I'll admit they're not terrible. But you're not exactly a slouch yourself, you know," he added. His eyes held hers steadily. "Your sketches," he said, "especially the ones from Santorini? They're stunning."

"Thanks. I'm still getting used to the idea of people actually liking my work."

"Well, you better start getting used to it," he nudged her shoulder. "Because you've got something special, Alex."

She let her gaze wander over the walls that were covered with his work. It was a creative chaos. Like the kind of space where ideas seemed to come alive.

"You know," she said, "What if we combined our talents?"

"What do you mean?"

"I mean, think about it," she turned to face him. "Your photography and my sketches. We've spent so much time traveling, capturing these amazing moments. What if we created something together? Like a collaborative project."

"Go on." He could see where she was going.

"We could create a collection. A mix of your photos and my sketches, side by side. We could tell the story of our journey, what we've seen, what we've felt. It could be a book, or an exhibit, or even something digital. Something that inspires people to explore the world and find their own creative sparks."

His eyes shined with excitement as a vivid picture formed. "A multimedia project. Photos, sketches, maybe even some written pieces. Like a travel diary, but on steroids."

"Exactly!" Alex said with excitement. "And it wouldn't just be about the places we've been. It would be about the connection between art and experience. How travel changes you and opens you up to new perspectives."

"I love it. And you know what? Let's include a section that shows how different perspectives capture the same moment. My photographs versus your sketches.

"Yes!" she clapped her hands together. "That's perfect. It would show people that there's no right or wrong way to create. Just different ways of seeing."

"We could also include some behind-the-scenes stuff, like the stories behind the shots and sketches. The misadventures, the people we've met along the way."

"You mean like the time you nearly fell off that cliff trying to get the perfect shot?"

"Hey, that was a calculated risk. And it was worth it. That shot was amazing."

"Sure, Mr. Daredevil. But you're right. The behind-the-scenes stories would add so much personality to the project."

His eyes sparkled with excitement. "We could start small," he suggested with quiet confidence. "Maybe test the waters with a pop-up exhibit here in the city. See how people respond. And if it goes well, we could expand. Take it on the road. Maybe even launch it online to reach a bigger audience."

The possibility sent a thrill through her. "On the road?" she asked with a disbelieving smile. "You mean, like... city to city?"

"Yeah. Why not?" he said with a casual shrug. "Your work deserves to be seen. And not just by a handful of people in one place. Imagine a traveling exhibit. You'd be displaying your art to people all over. And with an online launch, you could reach even more. We could make it something special."

Her heart fluttered at the word *we*. The idea itself was exhilarating, but the thought of doing it with him made it even more so. Still, doubt flickered at the edges of her mind.

"Do you think we could pull it off?" she asked, as if afraid to hope.

"I know we can," he said without hesitation. "You've got the talent. I've got the resources. And most importantly..." he paused, "we've got the passion. That's all we need."

She stared at him for a moment. Her chest ached with a strange mix of emotions. The part of her that still clung to caution wanted to question the logistics and to overthink every detail. But the part of her that had spent the last few months falling in love with the unknown and who had left her apartment and crossed oceans, wanted to believe him. "Okay. Let's do it."

His face lit up, and without a word, he held out his hand.

She looked at it, then back at him. She reached out and slipped her hand into his. "Deal," he said.

Her fingers lingered in his longer than necessary. "Deal," she echoed.

For the next few hours, they brainstormed ideas, sketching rough concepts and jotting down notes on scraps of paper. The studio buzzed with energy as they exchanged ideas, their excitement fueling their creativity. During one point, Jamie leaned back in his chair at Alex as she wrote in her sketchbook. "You know, this is what I've always wanted."

"What do you mean?"

"This," he gestured between them. "Working with someone who gets it. Who sees the world the way I do. I've always thought of photography as a solo thing, but this feels different. It feels right."

"It does, doesn't it?"

"We're going to create something amazing, Alex. I can feel it."

# Chapter 39

The next morning, Alex walked into her apartment with her arms full of supplies for their new project. Soft sable brushes, thick spiral-bound sketchbooks, and stacks of creamy, ivory-colored paper she had everything she needed to create. She dropped them on her dining table and stood there for a moment, looking around her space, which suddenly felt smaller compared to the vast horizons they had been dreaming of.

"Can I really do this?" she said to herself as she ran her fingers over one of the sketches.

Her phone buzzed on the table, interrupting her thoughts. She picked it up and noticed Sarah's name flashing on the screen.

"Hey, you," she answered, sounding full of energy.

"You sound suspiciously cheerful," Sarah teased, "like someone who's overthinking everything, and humming a little tune to themselves."

"How do you always know?"

"Because I know you. And because you've been texting me about this project every five minutes since yesterday," Sarah said with a laugh. "So, spill. What's going on in that overactive brain of yours?"

"It's just a lot, you know? We have these tremendous ideas for this project, and I'm so excited, but part of me keeps thinking, what if it doesn't work? What if people don't care about what we're creating?"

"Alex, do you remember when you used to talk about art like it was just a hobby? Since then, your progress has been truly remarkable. You're no longer passively doodling in the margins of your life; you are actively creating a masterpiece. And more importantly, you're taking yourself seriously. Not only that but your aspirations, your goals, and your dreams.

"It's just scary, you know? Putting yourself out there like this. What if it's not enough?"

"First," Sarah said firmly, "you are more than enough. And second, who cares if it doesn't go perfectly? The point is that you're doing it. You're taking a risk, and that's huge. Besides, you've got Jamie, right? He believes in you."

"Yeah, he does."

"And I do too," she added with certainty. "You're going to knock this out of the park, bestie. I just know it."

"Thanks for the pep talk. I don't know what I'd do without you."

"Oh, you'd probably implode," she deadpanned, "or dramatically flee the country again. You know, in true tortured-artist fashion."

"Yeah, that sounds about right."

"But seriously," Sarah continued. "You've got this. You're stronger than you think. And no matter what happens, I'm right here."

As the tension eased, a comforting warmth spread through Alex, chasing away the tightness in her chest. "Right back at you."

"Now, go work on your art. And don't forget to breathe, okay?"

She let out a playful sigh, feigning exasperation. "Okay, Mom," she teased.

"Damn right."

"Talk to you later?"

"Of course," Sarah said, before hanging up. "And remember … breathe."

Alex set her phone down and stared at the blank canvas she had propped against the wall. It stood there untouched, daring her to make the first move. With hesitant steps, she moved closer, her fingers tracing the polished surface, feeling its coolness. For a moment, she stood there with swirling thoughts in her head.

Jamie's words played in the back of her mind, calming her racing thoughts. *You've got the passion. That's all we need.*

Her chest tightened at the memory of his unwavering faith in her. She closed her eyes and pictured the way he had looked at her. The quiet certainty in his eyes and the warmth in his voice. It gave her the courage she needed.

A deep breath steadied her hand as the soft graphite of the pencil glided across the paper. Her initial attempts were timid, but as her focus sharpened, her lines gained strength and precision. She began by sketching a scene from Venice, capturing the way light danced on the water as they glided through the canals. Then she added a tiny figure sitting at the edge of a gondola, staring into the distance. It wasn't until she was halfway through that she realized the figure was Jamie. She smiled to herself. "*Of course.*"

A knock at the door interrupted her thoughts. She set the pencil down and crossed the room to answer it. Jamie was there holding two cups of coffee and grinning.

"I come bearing caffeine and moral support," he held out one cup.

She laughed and stepped aside to let him in. "You have perfect timing."

"I like to think so," he said as he set the cups on the table and looked at the sketch she had started. "Is this Venice?"

"Yeah," she suddenly felt self-conscious. "It's still rough."

As he stepped closer, his eyes scanned the lines with the focus she'd only ever seen him give his photography. "It's incredible," he said softly. "The detail and the movement you've captured it perfectly."

She blushed. "Thanks."

He turned to her with a serious expression. "You really need to stop doubting yourself. This," he pointed to the sketch, "is why I wanted to work with you. You see the world in a way that's completely unique."

She looked down at her hands. "I'm trying," she whispered. "It's just hard sometimes."

"Of course it's hard," he said. "That's how you know it matters. But you're going to do great. I believe in you."

Her heart fluttered at the intensity in his eyes. She didn't know how he did it, how he always seemed to see the version of her she struggled to believe in. A breeze drifted in from the open window, lifting a corner of the sketchbook. She tucked it back down, suddenly aware of how his presence made the room feel full and steady.

"You always know what to say," she murmured.

"Not always. But when it comes to you, I try to get it right."

"So, what's on the agenda for today?" he asked, trying to change the mood.

She looked at the mess of supplies scattered across the table, charcoal pencils, brushes still stained with dried paint, and her sketchbook lying open beside the canvas she'd just completed. "I was thinking of working on a few more sketches," she said. "Maybe start piecing together some ideas for our project."

His lips curved into a playful grin as he grabbed a nearby stool and plopped down. "Mind if I stick around?" he asked. He was already making himself comfortable. "I can work on editing some of my photos while you sketch. That way, we can bounce ideas off each other."

Her heart gave an involuntary flutter at the thought of spending the afternoon with him. "I'd like that."

For the next few hours, they worked side by side, enveloped in a comfortable silence that was occasionally interrupted by brief conversations. The gentle scratch of her pencil on paper blended with the soft clicks of his laptop as he sifted through his images. Every so often, they would steal a glance at each other's work, exchanging quiet compliments or asking for feedback.

Eventually, Jamie turned his laptop toward her. "What do you think of this one?" he asked.

It was a photo from the narrow alleyways of Positano washed in golden light. "God," she whispered. "It's stunning."

He smiled at her praise, but then, with a playful grin, he turned the screen back toward himself. "Good. Because I was thinking it might make a perfect centerpiece for the exhibit," he said with a mischievous grin. "You know, right next to your masterpiece."

"Oh, so now it's a competition?" she teased.

"Absolutely," he deadpanned. "And for the record, I'm winning."

She laughed and returned to her sketch. But a few moments later, she felt his eyes on her. When she looked up, she found him watching her with a soft expression.

"What?" she asked, suddenly self-conscious.

"Nothing," he answered. "Just... you. You look really happy right now."

She held his gaze for a moment, then looked back at her sketch. "I am," she admitted.

# Chapter 40

The sudden chime of the doorbell broke Alex's quiet thoughts, pulling her from the pages of her sketchbook. She had spent the morning leafing through it, pausing now and then to run her fingers over familiar lines, tracing the journey of her own transformation. The evolution in her work was unmistakable; bolder strokes, deeper contrasts, and a confidence that hadn't been there before. Even her reflection in the mirror told a different story now: sleeker lines in her clothes, a self-assured glint in her eyes.

And now, the person she most wanted to share it all with was finally here. She opened the door to find Sarah beaming like a proud stage mom. She was holding a bottle of wine in one hand and a bag of aggressively crunchy snacks in the other.

"Ta-da!" Sarah announced, stepping in like she owned the place. "I come bearing carbs and judgment. Show me the art!"

"Wine and chips?" Alex asked, raising an eyebrow with a grin.

"Don't knock on my pairing skills. I know you've been working nonstop on your project, and I thought it was time for some much-needed girl talk and celebration."

"Celebration? What are we celebrating?"

Sarah spun around dramatically and set the wine on the counter. "You, obviously! Look at you, Miss fearless artist extraordinaire, jetsetter, and soon-to-be exhibit star. You've come so far, and I think that's worth toasting to."

"I wouldn't call myself fearless just yet."

"Don't sell yourself short. I remember when you were stuck in that soul-sucking job, doubting every little thing about yourself. And now look at you, creating art, collaborating with Jamie, and putting yourself out there. It's inspiring."

Alex felt her throat tighten. She hadn't realized how much she needed to hear those words. "It hasn't been easy," she admitted. "There are still days when I feel like I'm faking it or like I'm one wrong step away from messing everything up."

Sarah reached out and squeezed her hand. "That's normal. But you're not faking it. You're doing the work, and it shows. Do you have any idea how proud I am of you?"

She blinked back tears and gave a small laugh. "You always know exactly what to say."

"That's because I know you," Sarah said with a wink. She grabbed the bottle of wine and began twisting off the cap. "Now, where are the glasses? Let's toast to your awesomeness before you start crying on me."

Alex laughed and pulled two glasses from the cabinet. As Sarah poured, she felt some tension in her chest ease. They settled on the couch, with the bag of chips between them and their glasses in hand. Sarah raised hers. "To Alex Greer, who is brave, talented, and finally realizing how amazing she truly is."

She blushed but clinked her glass against Sarah's. "To Sarah Matthews, the bestest friend anyone could ask for."

"So," Sarah said, setting her glass down and turning to Alex with a conspiratorial grin. "Tell me everything. How's the project going? How's Jamie?"

She rolled her eyes but couldn't help the smile that crept onto her face. "This project is excitingly challenging. We have been working non-stop, and it's coming together. It's exciting but also terrifying. And Jamie ..." She hesitated, her cheeks flushing.

"Oh, don't you dare stop there. Spill it!"

"Fine! He's amazing. He offers unwavering support, patience, and a belief in my capabilities. It's scary how much I care about him."

"You deserve someone like that. After everything you

went through with what's-his-name, it's about time you found someone who sees you for who you are."

"It's just fresh territory for me. Being with someone who encourages me instead of holding me back, it's overwhelming in the best way."

"That's how it should be," Sarah said. "You push each other to grow. Based on what you've shared, he sounds like the type of person who would appreciate that.

"He is. He's already taught me so much, about seeing the world differently, about taking risks. I just hope I can keep up."

"He's lucky to have you. And honestly, anyone who sees your art at this exhibit will be captivated by its raw emotion and feel a profound connection."

"You say that like I haven't had at least five meltdowns and two very questionable crying sessions in front of my sketchbook."

"And yet here you are," Sarah said, reaching for another chip. "Thriving. Flourishing. Rebranding into your confident artist era."

"My what?"

"You heard me. This is your soft-launch as an international art darling."

Alex laughed. "I love how your version of encouragement sounds like an Instagram caption."

"Listen, I contain multitudes," Sarah said, feigning offense. "And also, have you looked at your portfolio lately? It's like someone bottled sunshine and lined it in charcoal."

"I really do feel different. Like something shifted on that trip."

"You found yourself again, Alex. It shows. In your work, in your voice, in the way you don't second-guess every little thing."

Alex swirled the wine in her glass. "I just don't want to lose that."

"Then don't. Put it in the art. All of it. Even the messy bits. Especially the messy bits."

"I've been thinking about that. Letting it be more personal. Not just pretty scenes, but... what they meant to me."

"Now that," Sarah said, pointing at her with a chip, "is the good stuff. Vulnerable art? We love to see it."

"You're ridiculous."

"Accurate," Sarah agreed, taking a dainty sip of wine with an exaggerated flourish. Then she leaned forward with excitement. "So," she said, cradling her wine glass with both hands. "What's the plan for the exhibit? Do you have a theme? A centerpiece?"

Alex's eyes brightened with excitement. She set her glass down and grabbed her sketchbook from the coffee table.

"Actually, I do," she said, flipping it open. "I've been working on this series inspired by the places we visited. Each piece holds a moment etched in my mind; I can still feel the emotions and hear the sounds."

She turned the sketchbook toward Sarah to reveal a two-page spread of a bustling Venetian canal. The pencil strokes were delicate yet vivid, and the water rippled beneath the gondolas with a sense of motion. She flipped to the next sketch. It was Tuscany at sunset. It depicted the rolling hills bathed in amber light and a lone farmhouse nestled in the distance.

Sarah's jaw dropped as she leaned in and studied each one.

"Holy crap," she whispered in awe. "These are incredible. You've captured so much emotion in these. They're more than just landscapes. They tell a story."

Alex's cheeks flushed faintly. She felt both proud and vulnerable.

"That's what I was hoping for," she admitted. "I want people to feel like they're experiencing the journey with me."

A sketch of a Positano cafe, with lanterns caught Sarah's eye as she flipped through the pages. The details were striking. Alex seemed to capture the weathered cobblestones and the delicate folds of a tablecloth caught in the evening breeze. She let out a slow breath.

"They will," Sarah said with conviction. "These are going to blow people away."

"I hope so," she said. "I really do."

Sarah's expression softened, and she reached over and squeezed Alex's knee.

"They will. And when they do, we're going to celebrate with an even bigger bottle of wine than this one."

Alex let out a soft laugh, warmth flooding her chest. She grabbed her own glass and clinked it against Sarah's, the faint chime ringing softly through the room.

"To good art," Sarah toasted.

"To good friends," Alex replied, smiling.

"And to Italian cafes that apparently inspire award-winning talent," Sarah added, wiggling her eyebrows.

"I think it was less about the café and more about the company I had there."

"Ooh, is that a reference to Jamie?"

"Maybe."

"Just saying, you sketch better when you're in love," Sarah said with a wink.

"Okay, now you're pushing it."

Sarah smirked and reached for another chip. "Fine, fine. But when you're giving your acceptance speech at some fancy international art show, don't forget to thank me. And wine. And Italy."

Alex leaned back against the couch cushions, her heart full. "Deal."

# Chapter 41

Alex stood in front of the gallery, staring up at the sleek black awning with their names printed in elegant white letters.

**Alex Greer & Jamie Rivers: A Journey in Art & Photography.**

Her name. His. Side by side.

It felt like a dream she hadn't dared to say out loud finally unfolding before her. All the nights spent sketching until her fingers cramped, all the mornings they chased the perfect light, all the quiet moments of doubt and discovery had all led to this.

Jamie stepped beside her. "You ready?" he asked.

She let out a breath she hadn't realized she'd been holding. "As I'll ever be."

"Good. Because people are already showing up."

Alex turned to see a small crowd gathering near the gallery doors, some leaning in to peek through the glass at the displays inside. Her stomach fluttered with nerves. *What if her work didn't hold up next to Jamie's stunning photographs? What if she didn't belong here at all?*

Sensing the shift in her mood, he whispered in her ear. "Breathe, Greer. You've got this. Your work's breathtaking. And tonight, they're going to see what I've seen all along."

She looked up at him and saw the smile that made her believe in herself. The butterflies in her chest didn't go away, but they softened. With a deep breath, she reached for the gallery door and pushed it open.

The moment they stepped inside, she was met with a

wave of warmth. Laughter and conversation filled the space. The walls told their story. *Her* sketches. His photographs. The places they'd seen. The moments they'd captured. The way they'd seen the world together.

Jamie touched her hand lightly. "This is just the beginning."

She smiled. "I know."

Her sketches hung alongside his photographs, each pairing telling a story. A sketch of a bustling Venetian market next to his photo of the same spot. A delicate charcoal rendering of a vineyard paired with an ethereal sunrise photograph capturing the same place. She spotted Sarah near the refreshments table, sipping champagne and beaming with pride.

"Would you look at this? People are obsessed with your work."

"You're exaggerating."

Sarah grabbed her arm and tugged her toward a group of attendees. "Is that so? Because these people just couldn't stop talking about how amazing your sketches were."

Alex let out a small laugh, but before she could protest, Sarah was already pulling her toward the group. Unsure of how to handle the sudden attention, she found the warmth in her best friend's eyes.

With a playful grin, Sarah announced, "Everyone, meet the artist. The woman behind all the magic."

The group turned toward Alex, and their faces lit up with genuine admiration. A tall man with salt-and-pepper hair extended his hand first.

"Alex Greer, right? Your work is breathtaking. The Amalfi Coast piece…. It's like you captured the light itself. I could almost feel the salt in the air just looking at it."

The compliment caused her to blush as she shook his hand. "Wow, thank you. That means a lot."

A sharply dressed woman, in black, quickly interrupted her, gesturing towards the nearby wall of sketches before she could recover. "I'm crazy about the Positano piece," she declared enthusiastically. "The way you layered the charcoal and shading, it's so evocative. Like the entire street is alive."

Alex looked at the sketch in question and she felt an unexpected wave of pride swell in her chest. She had spent hours refining the shadows and highlights, trying to capture the way the late afternoon sun cast warm streaks along the pastel buildings. Seeing someone connected with it made her throat tighten.

She said "Thank you. I'm so glad it spoke to you."

Sarah gave her a playful nudge. "Told you."

More attendees filtered in. She found herself in conversations that surprised and delighted her, filled with laughter, and shared insights. She discussed her creative process, shared the stories behind each sketch, and absorbed the genuine awe in their voices.

A man with glasses and wearing a navy blazer pointed to her Santorini series. "You have such a distinctive style." He reflected, "It has an honest quality. It doesn't feel manufactured or polished for the sake of being perfect. It feels… real."

"Honestly? That's the best compliment I could ask for."

With a smirk, Sarah, the ever-proud best friend, clinked her champagne glass against Alex's. "See? Obsessed," she teased and raised her eyebrows.

Alex let out a soft laugh, but this time she didn't deflect. She allowed herself to soak in the validation, the joy, and the pride. She caught Jamie's eye from across the room. He was standing by the window watching her with a proud smile. Their eyes locked and the weight of his gaze sent warmth coursing through her.

Sarah leaned in. "You did this," she said with emotion. "You're not dreaming. This is real."

Alex tightened her fingers around her champagne glass as she looked around the gallery. The room buzzed with quiet appreciation. She turned back to Sarah. "Yeah," she said with a mixture of disbelief and wonder. "It is."

An older woman in a stylish pair of glasses and a flowing blue dress stood before her.

"You're the artist?"

"Uh, yes," she forced herself to stand taller.

"Your sketches have so much soul. I can feel the emotion in every line. They make me want to visit these places."

"Thank you so much. That really means a lot."

As the evening progressed, Alex let herself enjoy the moment. Every time someone complimented her work, her confidence grew a little more. She found Jamie near a large canvas print of one of his favorite shots. It was of her standing on a balcony in Tuscany with her sketchpad in hand.

"You put this in the show?" she asked with a mixture of embarrassment and admiration in her voice.

He had a playful glint in his eyes. "It's one of my best pieces."

She rolled her eyes. "You're impossible."

"Maybe," he said, stroking his chin, "But I'm also right."

A middle-aged couple approached them. The man gesturing toward the artwork. "Excuse me, are you both the artists?"

"We are," Jamie said.

The woman smiled. "We were just talking about how beautifully your work complements each other. It's like each piece has a companion."

Their eyes met, a silent understanding passing between them as the world seemed to fall into perfect harmony.

"Thank you," she said, a smile gracing her lips. "That was the goal."

As the night ended, Jamie pulled her aside. "I have something for you."

She raised an eyebrow. "Another surprise?"

He grabbed a bag from under a table and handed it to her. She pulled out a personalized leather sketchbook. "For your next sketches. Wherever we go next."

Alex's heart skipped. His words and efforts left no doubt in her mind that their journey of creation would continue. She ran her fingers over the soft cover. "Where are we going next?"

"Wherever we want."

The night had been a success. It was more than she had ever dared to hope. Being dramatic, Sarah plopped onto the worn velvet chair and kicked off her heels. "If I have to smile at one more art critic, I swear I'm going to..." She paused and grinned. "Okay, fine, this was amazing. You killed it. Again."

She laughed. "Thanks for being my personal hype woman."

"Always. But seriously, how do you feel?"

"In all honesty? Like all the pieces of a puzzle finally fit together, I feel a sense of purpose and fulfillment."

"About damn time."

Across the room, Jamie was talking to his guests. Their eyes met. A spark ignited between them, and he excused himself.

"You realize we just pulled off our first exhibit together?"

"I know. It's surreal."

Jamie reached for the bottle of champagne on the table and topped off both their glasses. "I think this calls for a toast."

"Ooh, I love a good toast."

He lifted his glass, the ice clinking against the crystal. "To Alex, who finally took a chance on herself and is officially an artist."

Her cheeks flushed. "Oh, come on. I've always been an artist."

"Yeah. But now the entire world knows it."

Sarah raised her glass high, the celebratory champagne bubbling over the rim and sparkling under the lights. "To Alex, for being brave enough to share her magic with the world. And for absolutely crushing it."

She smiled as she felt the warmth of their words settle deep in her chest. She clinked her glass against theirs. "To taking chances," she added.

They all took a sip of their drinks, and Sarah nudged Alex with a teasing grin. "So, what's next? A European tour? A private showing in Paris? Maybe a collaboration with some fancy designer?"

"Oh, slow down. I just survived my first exhibit. Let me savor these next five minutes of peace before we unleash our plans for global domination."

"Fair," Sarah smirked. "But just so you know, I'm totally your agent if you become famous. I want my ten percent."

Jamie laughed as his eyes remained on Alex. She caught the look, the unmistakable pride and admiration flickering in his gaze. It made her stomach flutter.

"Hey. I'm really proud of you," he said softly. "I mean it."

Her breath caught for a second. His words left her breathless. "Thank you," she replied.

Sarah, acting oblivious to the tender moment, clapped her hands together.

"Okay, enough of this sentimental stuff. Let's get some food before the champagne goes to my head. I saw a taco truck parked around the corner. Who's in?"

Alex turned toward her with a playful eye roll. "Tacos? You're so classy."

"Don't judge! Nothing says, 'successful art exhibit' like cheap street tacos and questionable salsa."

Jamie grinned. "She's got a point."

Alex looked around the gallery once more. The room still buzzed with conversation and laughter. It all felt surreal, but she let herself believe it. She let herself feel it, the pride, the joy, and the steady hum of hope thrumming in her chest.

"Okay," she said. "Tacos it is."

# Chapter 42

Alex hadn't felt this nervous in a long time. Standing in front of her parents' house, she twisted the hem of her sweater and glanced at Jamie beside her. He appeared completely relaxed. His hands were casually tucked into the pockets of his dark jeans, and his camera bag hung over one shoulder.

"You don't have to look so calm," she said as she gave him a side-eye.

He smirked. "Would you rather I be freaking out?"

"Yes. A little. At least pretend this is nerve-wracking for you."

Jamie chuckled but softened when he saw the tension in her face. He reached over and squeezed her hand. "Greer, it's just dinner."

She let out a sharp breath. "Just dinner? My mom has been dying to meet you ever since I mentioned your name, and my dad is probably going to give you the 'what are your intentions with my daughter' speech. "

"Should I have brought a ring to get ahead of that conversation?"

She smacked his arm. "Not funny."

He grinned but didn't let go of her hand. "It'll be fine. I want to meet them. I know they're important to you."

That made her smile. "Okay. Let's do this."

She rang the doorbell, and within seconds, the door swung open to reveal her mother, Lisa Greer. A petite woman with warm brown eyes, Lisa shared the same auburn hair as Alex.

"Finally! You're here!" She beamed before pulling her into a quick hug. Then she turned her attention to Jamie.

He smiled and extended a hand. "It's great to meet you, Mrs. Greer. Alex has told me so much about you."

She took his hand but tugged him forward surprising him with a hug. "Oh, we're huggers in this house."

He returned the embrace. "Good to know."

Her father, Daniel Greer, appeared next. His expression was more reserved. He was a tall man with broad-shouldered with graying hair. He held the kind of quiet presence that could intimidate if you weren't prepared.

"So, you're the photographer," Daniel said, arms crossed.

"Yes, sir. Jamie Rivers. It's great to meet you."

Daniel studied him for a moment before shaking his hand. "Come on in." He shot Alex a quick look that said so far, so good, before following her inside.

Dinner was not a disaster. But it also wasn't as smooth as Jamie had hoped. Lisa was thrilled. She asked him a million questions about his travels and how they met. Sarah had given her a rundown, but she still wanted to hear everything from his perspective.

"So, what made you take my daughter under your wing?" she asked as she sipped her wine.

"She sort of invited herself into my life."

Alex gasped. "That is not what happened."

A slow smirk stretched across his lips. "I was minding my own business in a coffee shop, and this woman just starts grilling me about my camera."

Lisa let out a joyous laugh. "That sounds like her."

"I was curious."

Jamie leaned toward her mom. "She acted like she didn't care about photography, but I could tell she wanted to ask a thousand more questions."

"So, Jamie, what's your plan?", Daniel asked to change the subject.

Jamie pushed his plate away. "My plan?"

"You've traveled the world, taken incredible photographs, but what's next? Are you planning to settle down?"

Alex knew her father well enough to recognize this was his way of asking, 'Are you serious about my daughter?'

Jamie, for the first time that evening, didn't say anything. He hadn't let himself think about the idea of settling down. He'd always thrived on movement, on capturing fleeting moments rather than planting roots. But as he looked at Alex, sitting beside him with those determined eyes, he realized something. The image of a future with her brought a smile to his face. It was something that he knew he wanted.

"Well," he began slowly but firm, "I've spent most of my life chasing what's just out of reach, new places, new experiences. I've never really considered staying in one place for too long." He looked at Alex. "Until now."

She was unsure if she'd heard him correctly. But the slight upward curve of his lips told her she had. Jamie shifted slightly in his chair. The soft touch of his fingers against hers, under the table, made her heart flutter. It was a silent reassurance.

"This year, traveling with your daughter, I realized it's not about the place. It's about who you're with. And if I have her, I don't need to keep running. Being with her makes me want to build something that lasts. So, yes, I guess you could say I'm thinking more about permanence."

A brief silence fell over the table. Alex felt a rush of emotions swelling in her chest. She squeezed his hand gently beneath the table.

Lisa let out a soft, "Oh. That's a beautiful answer."

Daniel gave a small nod, as though silently approving of the answer. "Building something that lasts," Daniel repeated thoughtfully. "That's not always easy."

"I know," he said simply. "But I'm willing to put in the work."

He picked up his glass and gave a slight tilt toward Jamie.

"Well," he said, almost gruffly, "here's to that."

Jamie blinked in mild surprise but quickly recovered and

lifted his glass to meet Daniel's. Alex exhaled, realizing she had been holding her breath. She looked at her father, searching for any trace of disapproval, but instead saw a glimmer of cautious respect.

Lisa clapped her hands. "Alright, enough serious talk. Who wants dessert?"

Later, after they said their goodbyes and stepped out into the cool night air, Alex turned to Jamie. "That was something."

"Your dad is intense."

She laughed. "Yeah, but he liked you. I could tell."

Jamie arched a skeptical brow. "That was liking me?"

"Trust me. If he didn't, he would've made you squirm."

"Good to know."

"What you said at dinner …"

Jamie glanced at her. "Yeah?"

"Did you mean it?"

"Every word."

She took his face in her hands and pulled him into a slow kiss. When they broke apart, she whispered, "I don't want you to run anymore either."

"I won't. Not from this."

They took a walk around the corner to enjoy the night air. The dinner with her parents had gone better than she expected. With a firm squeeze, Alex redirected his attention. "You really did great back there."

"Are you sure? Because your dad looked like he was deciding whether or not to throw me out."

"Trust me, if he didn't approve, he would've 'accidentally' mentioned his gun collection."

"Good to know I dodged that."

They reached his car, but neither of them made a move to get inside. Jamie leaned against the passenger door, slipping his hands into his pockets as he turned to face her.

"So… did I pass the final round of the Greer family trials?" he teased.

She rolled her eyes with a grin. "You more than passed. You charmed my mom, impressed my dad, and you didn't run for the hills." She stepped closer, her arms loosely wrapping around his waist. "I think that makes you officially part of the inner circle."

His grin widened as he brushed a strand of hair away from her face. "Does that come with any perks?"

"Hmm. Let me think..." She trailed her fingers slowly down the front of his jacket. "You get exclusive access to my art exhibit previews, first dibs on my new sketch series..." A mischievous glint shone in her eyes as she leaned in. "And maybe, you'll get to hear all the embarrassing stories Sarah likes to talk about me."

"Oh, I'm definitely in it for the stories," he teased. But then his expression softened. "But mostly, I'm just in it for you."

Her heart stuttered at his words, and for a moment, she forgot to breathe. "You really mean that?"

He brushed his lips lightly against her forehead. "Yeah, I do."

She pulled back just enough to meet his eyes. "Good," she whispered.

Then, without another word, she closed the remaining distance between them and kissed him. Her hands slid around his neck, and he responded instantly. His arms wrapped securely around her waist, anchoring her to him. "Jamie?"

"Yeah?"

"You're kind of stuck with me now."

A slow grin spread across his face, and he tightened his hold on her. "Good," he whispered. "Because I'm not going anywhere."

Eventually, Jamie pulled back just enough to look at her. His eyes were soft, but there was a glimmer of uncertainty beneath the tenderness. He slowly exhaled. "Alex... can I be honest with you about something?"

Her brows knitted slightly. "Of course."

"I meant what I said earlier about not running anymore. But I also know we've built this whole life around movement. We travel, we create, we don't stay still. And now, we're back here, in reality."

"I think .. Reality is whatever we decide to make it. We don't have to go back to the way things were before we met. Let's build something new, something strong and beautiful, something that will bring us together."

"And what does that look like to you?"

"I want to keep creating. I want to keep exploring. But I also want to have a place that feels like home. Somewhere we can return to after every adventure. A space that's ours."

He studied her carefully, noting the way her hair fell around her shoulders and the subtle curve of her lips. "You're not saying we should settle down, are you?"

"Not in the traditional sense. I don't think we're the type to buy a house with a white picket fence and stay put forever. But I think we can have both. A life of movement and a place to ground ourselves when we need it."

He believed that staying in one place would stifle him. But with her, everything felt different. The idea of having a home with her, not as an anchor, but as a foundation, felt right.

"I like that idea."

She reached for his hand. "Maybe we start small," she offered. "Take a weekend trip, just us. Something easy. No airports. No rush. Just time."

He gave it a soft squeeze. "We don't have to chase the world every weekend," he murmured. "There's a cabin a couple hours north. No WiFi, no tourists. Just trees, a lake, and the sound of nothing."

Her eyes lit up. "That sounds... perfect."

"I thought maybe we could make breakfast together. Sketch on the porch. I'll build a fire. You can roll your eyes at how bad I am at it."

"Only if you promise not to complain when I bring three sketchbooks and hog the best view."

"I'll even carry your pencils," he said. "Let's go. Just you and me. No distractions."

Her breath caught in her throat at the simplicity of it all. At how right it felt.

"Okay," she whispered, her voice thick with emotion. "Let's go."

# Chapter 43

Even though they were heading toward a quiet lakeside cabin, it felt like a different challenge to Alex. As much as she loved the thrill of traveling, she wondered: *What would their relationship look like without the backdrop of an adventure?*

Jamie seemed at ease. One hand rested on the steering wheel, the other reached out to interlace his fingers with hers.

"You're quiet," he remarked. "Any doubts?"

"No second thoughts. Just adjusting."

"Adjusting to what?"

She stared out at the passing trees. "To the stillness. When we're traveling, every unfamiliar sight, sound, and smell is thrilling and unexpected. But now, it's just us. Uninterrupted attention. No outside chaos."

Jamie squeezed her hand. "And that scares you, does it?"

"Perhaps just a tad."

"I get it. We built this thing in motion. It's easy to wonder if it holds up when we slow down."

She looked at him, noticing the way the sunlight caught his hair. "And do you think it does?"

"Guess we'll find out."

Reaching the cabin, Alex took a deep breath, inhaling the sights of the cozy home and the smell of woodsmoke and damp earth. The small wooden house sat perched on the edge of a lake. The water appeared calm and shimmered under the late afternoon sun. Two kayaks were secured to a sturdy dock extending over the clear blue water.

He cut the engine and turned to her. "Welcome to our weekend escape," he said.

She stepped out and inhaled the fresh air. The scent of

pine filled her lungs and invigorated her senses. "It's peaceful," she admitted.

He grabbed their bags from the trunk. "Come on. Let's get settled in."

Inside, the space was cozy. It had wooden walls, a stone fireplace, and large windows overlooking the lake. There was no TV, no distractions. Just them.

Jamie set their bags down and stretched. "Alright. We've got two whole days. No work, no city noise, just nature. What's the plan?"

"You're asking me to decide? That's a first."

"Fair point. But I figured we could mix things up. How do you feel about kayaking?"

She looked at the lake, then back at him. "I've never done it before."

"Perfect. I *love* watching you try new things."

"Oh, so you just want to watch me flail around in the water, huh?"

He walked over and wrapped his arms around her waist. "Absolutely," he teased. "It'll be adorable."

She poked him in the ribs to make him flinch. "You're terrible."

"Hey, you knew what you were signing up for," he shot back.

"Alright," she said with mock exasperation. "I'll try kayaking. But if I capsize, I'm holding you personally responsible."

"Understood." He pressed a quick kiss to her lips. "But you're going to love it. Trust me."

They spent the next hour unpacking and settling in. She pulled a knit sweater from her bag and draped it over her shoulders, while he stoked the fire by adding another log until the flames crackled and danced higher.

After changing into more comfortable clothes, they grabbed a couple of blankets and made their way to the dock.

"Come on."

He led her to the weathered wooden dock, where the kayaks bobbed gently in the water. As she settled into one, she felt a slight wobble and tightened her grip on the sides to regain her balance.

"Steady," he soothed with encouragement. "You've got this."

She shot him a wary glance. "If I fall in, I'm making you fish me out."

He was already easing into his own kayak with practiced ease. "I'm sure you'll be a natural."

Once they were both settled, they pushed off from the dock. The water rippled beneath them as they paddled into the lake. At first, their rhythm was slow. Alex struggled to maintain even strokes while Jamie kept pace beside her.

"Relax your grip a little," he advised. "Let the paddle do the work."

With a subtle shift of her hands, her movements became smoother. As she glided across the water, her tension eased.

Jamie glanced over at her. "See? You're a natural."

She gave him a mock glare. "You're just saying that, so I don't quit halfway through."

"Nah. I'm saying it because it's true."

A comfortable silence settled over them as they paddled; the rhythmic splash of paddles, the whispering wind in the reeds, and a bird's distant call were the only sounds. Jamie slowed down to let her kayak drift closer.L "Hey," he said softly.

She turned to face him.

"This is nice," he said. "Just us. No distractions."

A gentle smile touched her lips at his kind words. "Yeah. It really is."

They stayed on the water until the sun went down. When they paddled back to the dock, her arms were sore, but her heart was light. As they made their way back toward the cabin, he reached for her hand to hold them. The simple gesture made her stomach flip. "So... kayaking tomorrow morning, too?"

The sound of her laughter filled the air as her shoulder bumped against his in a playful gesture. "Let's see how sore I am first."

He laughed. "Fair enough."

They made their way back to the cabin, but instead of going inside, Jamie veered toward the fire pit near the dock. With the ease of familiarity, he gathered some kindling and struck a match, bringing the flames to life.

Alex stood nearby watching him work the flames. When he looked at her, he saw her teeth chattering and her body trembling from the cold.

"Cold?" he asked as he put the last log in place.

"A little," she admitted.

Without hesitation, he grabbed the thick blanket they'd left on one of the chairs, draped it around her shoulders, and pulled her close. She let herself melt into him as he pressed a lingering kiss to the top of her head.

He tugged her hand reassuringly. "Come on."

They wandered to the edge of the dock and sat down with their feet dangling above the water.

The wooden planks beneath them were smooth and warm from the day's sun, and the faint crackle of the firepit behind them sent comforting waves of heat over their backs. Alex laid her head on his shoulder. He slipped his arm around her waist, drawing her closer with a quiet kind of certainty.

"I was worried," she said softly .

Jamie glanced down at her. "About what?"

She took a breath. "That without the thrill of airports and new cities... without the movement, the chaos... we'd lose *us*. That maybe we only work when everything around us is in motion."

He didn't respond right away. Instead, he took her hand to reassure her.

"We were never just about the places," he said finally. "We were the constant in all of it. And maybe that's the real adventure. Not the cities or the planes or the new views. Just...

being with you. Wherever that is."

She turned toward him. "I don't want to lose this," she whispered.

"You won't," he said.

He took her hand in his. "Alex, adventure isn't what makes us work. We make us work." He turned, tilting her chin so she met his gaze. "No matter where we are, or what we're doing, it's always gonna be you and me."

"I didn't expect this," she whispered.

"You mean tonight?"

"Or us. The way it feels now... it's different. Deeper. I thought maybe when we stopped moving, the spark would go out."

"I think this is the spark, Alex. The quiet. The space to finally feel everything."

She shifted closer, tucking herself beneath his arm as the firelight flickered behind them. "It's scary," she admitted.

"I know." He pressed a kiss to the top of her head. "You and me, we're used to chasing beauty and capturing moments. But this, what we're building, it's not meant to vanish. It's meant to stay."

Her smile bloomed. "Don't you see? It's always been you. It's us. I'd follow you anywhere. Even if it's just to a cabin tucked in the quiet of nowhere."

He tipped her chin gently so she'd meet his gaze. "Then you don't have to be afraid. I'm not going anywhere. Not tomorrow, not the day after. You have me for as long as you'll have me."

Something in her chest eased, the knot of fear unraveling thread by thread. She let out a soft breath and whispered, "That's all I needed to hear."

He kissed her temple. "Still cold?"

"A little," she admitted, curling deeper into his side.

"Good thing I happen to be excellent at keeping you warm," he winked.

She swatted at him, but he caught her wrist, pressing a

kiss to her knuckles before tugging her onto his lap.

"Jamie," she laughed.

"What?" he asked innocently with his hands at her waist. "I'm just trying to help. You said you were cold."

"You're ridiculous."

"Maybe," he replied , "but you love it."

And with the fire crackling low and his laughter mingling with hers, Alex realized she did. She loved every bit of it.

# Chapter 44

A month has passed since their cabin trip, which exceeded Alex's expectations. Now, she wants to discuss their future plans following their joint exhibit. It should be an exciting topic and a natural next step in their journey. However, the conversation has taken an unexpected turn, with their dreams and expectations clashing in a way neither of them anticipated.

"I know this isn't what you want to hear," he said gently, "but the time has come for our next journey. I can feel it in my bones."

"Can't we just take a breather? We finished our first project together only a couple of months ago, and the cabin trip was just last month."

His eyes lit with that restless spark she knew so well. "With a universe brimming with untold stories, there's no time for rest."

Her arms crossed, though part of her ached at the distance already forming between them. "So you just want to pick up and leave again?"

Jamie exhaled sharply. "This was always the plan. Travel. Capture the world. That's what we do."

She set her mug down with a little too much force. "No. that's what you do. I never said I wanted to live out of a suitcase indefinitely."

He frowned. "You love traveling. You were the one who said you never wanted to be trapped in that suffocating, hopeless feeling again."

"I don't," she admitted, "But that doesn't mean I want to

spend my life constantly moving from one unfamiliar place to another, never having anywhere to truly belong."

"I thought I was giving you freedom," he said quietly. "I didn't realize it might feel like I was taking something away."

"You gave me freedom," she whispered. "But maybe what I want now is a place to land, too."

"So what? You want to stay here? Settle down? Get comfortable?"

"Why do you say that like it's a bad thing?"

"Because that's exactly what you were running from before!" His voice rose, edged with disbelief. "You hated feeling trapped. You were miserable."

"That was different."

"How?"

She didn't know how to say it. He wasn't entirely wrong. She *had* felt suffocated in her old life. Back then, she had been pursuing someone else's dream. But this was different. She had a choice. And that choice was far more complex than he seemed to understand.

"I don't want to go back to being the person I was before," she admitted. "But I also don't want to lose everything we've built just because I can't keep up with your pace."

He stared at her. "You think I'd just leave you behind?"

"I don't know. Would you?"

"This is the only life I know. I don't know how to stop moving."

The admission caught her off guard. She'd expected more fire, another defense, maybe even anger. But what she heard instead was fear. Fear of standing still, of losing momentum, of losing himself.

Her heart softened. "Jamie," she whispered. "I'm not asking you to stop being who you are. I love that you see the world as something worth chasing. But not every part of life has to be a chase. Sometimes… it's okay to just be."

He looked at her with a conflicted expression. "So what do you want from me? To change who I am?"

"I'm not asking you to stop. I'm asking you to meet me in the middle."

"And what does the middle look like?"

She searched for the right words. "It looks like a home base somewhere we can return to, somewhere that's ours. It doesn't mean we stop traveling, but it means we have something to come back to."

He was silent as his eyes locked onto hers.

She reached for his hand. "I love this life we've created. But I also want stability. I want to grow, to build something real. I don't want to feel like I'm constantly chasing the next destination just because we're afraid to stand still."

Jamie looked down at their hands. "I don't know if I can do that."

"Can't or won't?"

"I don't know. I've never stayed in one place long enough to even picture it. The idea of settling somewhere... it scares me."

"I'm not asking you to give up everything. I'm asking you to build something with me. Something that's ours."

"And what if I can't?"

The words stung more than she wanted to admit. She squeezed his hand before letting go. "Then I guess we have a real problem."

Jamie stood motionless, his hand still tingling from where Alex had held it. He didn't know what to say, and that scared him. He had always been good at moving forward and avoiding attachments that might tie him down. But she wasn't just someone. She was his home, even if he had never let himself say it aloud.

Alex turned away first and walked to the window. She wrapped her arms around herself as she stared at the city skyline.

"Jamie, I don't want to fight," she said finally.

"Neither do I."

"Then what are we doing?"

He chose his words carefully. "I just.. I don't know how to do this. I don't know how to be in one place."

She turned to face him. "I'm not asking you to stop being who you are. I love that you're always searching for something new. But I need something steady. I don't want to wake up one day and realize I've spent my life running just because I was afraid to stop."

"And what if stopping makes me lose myself?"

"If it doesn't, then what? What if staying in one place sometimes doesn't mean you're stuck? What if it just means you finally have something worth holding onto?"

Jamie looked at her and wondered. He had always been so sure of himself, his choices, and his path. But she had a way of making him question everything and making him want things he never thought he needed. "I don't want to lose you."

Her breath caught at the vulnerability in his voice. "Then don't."

"It's not that simple."

"It never is."

They stood there wanting the same thing but afraid of what it might cost. "I don't have all the answers," he admitted. "But I don't want to figure them out without you."

"That's all I need to hear."

His eyes closed for the briefest moment, as though he were memorizing the feeling. When he opened them, there was no hesitation left. He brought their joined hands to his lips and kissed them.

"I've spent so much of my life moving. Running if I'm being honest. From place to place, moment to moment. Never staying long enough to let anything stick. But you... you're the first thing I've wanted to hold on to."

"Then hold on."

"You make me want more," he whispered. "More than just special moments or surface-level connections. You made me want something real. And that scares the hell out of me."

"It scares me too," she admitted. "But I would rather be

scared with you than safe without you. All I'm asking for is a compromise. Meet me halfway."

"It's not as easy as that. You're asking me to change who I am. Who I was when we first met."

"I never told you to abandon your true self. I fell in love with you, your laughter echoing in my mind, your smile unforgettable. You've helped me to stop doubting myself and pursue my passion. But we've also agreed that we would have somewhere to come home to between adventures. Are you saying that now you're changing your mind, and you don't want to build with me?"

Jamie's breath caught at her words. He felt the sharp tug in his chest. The raw vulnerability in her voice made it impossible to avert his gaze.

"You know that's not what I'm saying." He pleaded. "I'm not changing my mind about you. I'm still figuring out how to do this. How to be someone who stays."

A flicker of fear darted across her eyes and she took a hesitant step back. It wasn't a great distance, but the space separating them felt charged with the weight of their unspoken feelings.

"Jamie." Her voice was steady, but he could see the hurt in her eyes. "We talked about this. About building something together. About having a home base, our base, between the adventures. That was something we both wanted." She shook her head slightly, disbelief flashing across her face. "Unless... was I the only one who meant it?"

"No," he said quickly, taking a step toward her. "You weren't."

"Then why does it feel like you're pulling away?"

He hated the doubt in her eyes and the way she suddenly seemed so unsure of him.

"Because I'm terrified," he admitted hoarsely. "The thought of losing you terrifies me. It reminds me of how my dad lost my mom, and the devastating emptiness that followed. I watched her spend years waiting for him to come home, and when he finally did, they barely knew each other. I don't want to keep you waiting. While I'm off on my next adventure, I don't want you to feel alone in building this."

She reached for his hands.. "I'm not asking you to give up everything you are. Your passion, freedom, and unique perspective on the world are what made me fall in love with you. I don't want you to lose that. I never did. But I also want to know that after the adventure, after we develop the photos and share the stories with laughter and tears, we will have a home together. A place we come back to. Somewhere we belong."

Jamie's throat tightened. He stared at her, her hands still clasped in his, and felt his chest constrict with the weight of it all. The love, the fear, the longing.

"Alex..." His voice broke slightly. "That's what I want, too. I swear I do. This is a first for me. I've never built a home with someone."

Her lips curved into the faintest smile, her eyes soft with understanding. "You won't be building it alone."

# Chapter 45

The next morning, Jamie woke before the sun had fully risen, slipping out of bed carefully so as not to wake Alex. He needed space to think, to breathe, to make sense of everything. But no matter where he walked, her words followed him. *Meet me in the middle.*

He shoved his hands into his pockets as he wandered through the still-sleeping streets. Coffee shops were only just stirring awake. Normally, mornings like this filled him with restless energy. The thrill of a new place was urging him to move, to capture, and to keep going. But today, each step felt heavy.

Her voice wouldn't leave him. The thought of a home base was like asking a tide not to rise. Yet when she spoke, he'd seen the hope in her eyes. He saw  a vision of belonging that wasn't about being trapped but about being anchored. And the truth was, part of him wanted that too. It scared him more than he could say.

He should have felt alive. Instead, he felt torn between the life he knew and the life she was asking him to imagine.

Eventually, he found himself at Mark's place. He hadn't planned to come here, but it made sense. He knocked softly, almost hoping there wouldn't be an answer, but within moments the door opened.

"Jamie?" Mark's brows lifted in mild surprised.

"Sorry. It's early," he stammered . "I just… didn't know where else to go."

"Come in."

When he stepped in n, he could already smell the coffee brewing. Jamie went straight to a chair in the kitchen while

Mark busied himself giving him space to gather his thoughts.

When Mark finally slid a steaming cup in front of him and sat across the table, Jamie just started talking. The words tumbled out before he could stop them: the fight with Alex, his fears about stopping, the gnawing weight of uncertainty pressing down on him.

Mark had listened patiently as his friend unloaded. When Jamie finally ran out of words, he took his chance.

"You know, for someone who spends his life capturing the beauty in the world, you sure have a hard time seeing what's right in front of you."

He rubbed his hands together. "Yeah? And what's that?"

"Love," Mark said simply.

"It's not that I don't see it. It's just love always comes with expectations. With roots. And I don't know if I can be the kind of person Alex needs me to be."

"You ever think maybe she doesn't need you to be anything other than who you already are?"

"That's easy to say, but what if I can't give her the life she wants?"

"And what life do you think she wants, exactly?"

"Stability. A place to call home. Something more than just the next adventure."

Mark nodded. "Alright, sure. But do you ever think that maybe home isn't just a place? That maybe it's a person?"

Jamie looked down, rubbing the back of his neck. "Yeah, well... what if I'm not enough to be that for her?"

Mark let out a short laugh. "You're such an idiot."

"Excuse me?"

"You really don't get it, do you?" He shook his head, almost in disbelief. "You keep thinking that you have to measure up to some perfect version of yourself, like you must give her some picture-perfect life. But man... she didn't fall in love with some perfect guy. She fell for *you*. You made her feel safe by taking her hand in a new city. You're the guy who can make her laugh even when she's terrified. The guy who—"

Mark gestured vaguely at him. "—wants nothing more than to freeze moments in time because he's afraid they'll slip away."

Jamie stared at him, momentarily speechless.

"You're already her home, man. You just have to stop running long enough to see it."

The words hit Jamie in a way he hadn't expected, cutting through the cloud of doubt and uncertainty that had been clinging to him.

Mark sighed. "Look, kid. You've spent your whole life moving. Always looking for the next thing, the next moment to capture. But love? Love's not about standing still. It's about choosing someone repeatedly, no matter where you are."

"And what if I screw it up?"

"You will. That's the deal. But if you love her, and I mean really love her, you won't let that stop you."

Jamie knew that his mentor was right. Love might not be a choice between roots and freedom. It was about finding someone who made the journey worth it.

Mark crossed the room to a shelf and pulled down an old photo album. He flipped through the pages slowly, as though sifting through time, before pausing and turning the book toward Jamie. The image showed a younger Mark, arm around a woman with kind eyes and a radiant smile. They stood in some far-off country, the two of them bathed in golden light.

"You've never asked me why I settled down," he said.

Jamie answered. "I thought maybe you were just exhausted from all the constant moving."

"Not even close. I fought it for years. I convinced myself that being in one place would kill my passion, that love would make me lose myself." His smile faded a little. "And then I lost her because I was too afraid to choose."

"You got her back, though."

"I did. But only because I realized something too late. I wasn't afraid of losing myself. I was afraid of changing. Of being vulnerable. But Jamie, the right person, doesn't take away who you are. They add to it. They help you see things in a way you never could alone."

"I just don't want to wake up one day and feel like I made the wrong choice."

"You've spent your whole life chasing something. Perhaps it's time to stop and ask yourself if you're running toward something or away from it."

Jamie let those words sink in. He thought of Alex and the way her eyes lit up when she sketched, the way she challenged him, and how she grounded him. He thought of the fight and remembered the pain in her voice when she said she needed something steady. And then it hit him. He wasn't afraid of staying. He was afraid of losing her.

The realization propelled him to his feet. "I need to go."

Mark laughed. "Go get your girl, kid."

He left with a clarity he hadn't felt in days. Every step carried him closer to her, though a knot of dread tightened in his chest. He didn't know what he'd say when he saw her, but he knew he couldn't let the silence between them stretch any longer.

Alex sat curled up on her couch with her sketchbook in her lap. She had opened it, although she hadn't drawn a single line in the past hour. She had been staring at the blank page. Waves of sadness, anger, and fear crashed over her in a tumultuous storm of emotions.

She loved Jamie. That much was undeniable. But love alone wasn't always enough. It needed trust, compromise, and something steady to hold on to. A sudden knock at the door startled her. Slowly, she rose, each step carrying a swell of hope she tried to temper. She took a breath and opened the door. He was standing there.

"Hey," he said softly.

Her fingers tightened around the edge of the door. "Hey."

Her voice was calm, but she didn't know what to expect. If he were here to say goodbye or to fight for her. She was terrified to find out.

Jamie was clearly nervous. His throat bobbed slightly,

but his eyes never left hers. "I, uh… I wasn't sure you'd open the door."

"I wasn't sure I would either."

"Understandable. Can I come in?"

She stepped aside. He walked in, rubbing the back of his neck as he turned to face her.

"I talked to Mark," he admitted.

That caught her off guard. "You did?"

Jamie nodded. "Yeah. He made me realize something." He drew in a deep breath, steadying himself. "I've been so scared of changing, of settling down, that I never stopped to think about what I'd be losing if I didn't."

"And what's that?"

Jamie's gaze held hers, steady now, filled with a raw honesty that left no room for doubt. "You."

A lump formed in her throat. "Jamie…" she started.

"I know I've hurt you. I know I made you feel like you were asking for too much, but you weren't. You never were." He swallowed hard, his eyes filled with guilt and longing. "You were asking for something I should've been willing to give from the start. You. Me. A life we build together. And I want that. I want you."

The tears she had been holding back started spilling freely down her cheeks. "But what about everything you said? About not being able to stay in one place?"

"I was scared," he admitted. "Scared that if I stayed, I'd lose the part of myself that's always been searching for more. But what I didn't realize until I was away from you… is that you are the more I've been searching for. You're the best thing I've ever found."

A quiet sob escaped her lips, and she pressed a trembling hand to her mouth.

He took another step forward and gently pried her hand away so he could see her face. His thumbs brushed over her damp cheeks. "I'm done running. I don't care if we stay here or travel or build a treehouse in the middle of nowhere. As long as you're with me, that's enough. You're enough."

She had spent so long preparing herself for the possibility that he would walk away and convinced herself she'd be okay if he did. That she would be fine. But now, faced with the reality of him choosing her, all that resolve melted away. Alex let out a shaky laugh. "You're terrible at this whole grand romantic speech thing."

He let out a soft, breathless laugh. "Yeah? Well, you're stuck with me, so you better get used to it."

"You know," she said, "for someone who's been running his whole life, you're surprisingly stubborn about staying put right now."

"I guess you make it worth it."

"Oh, yeah?" he teased. "Maybe you're just a tough audience."

She arched a playful brow. "Or maybe you just need more practice."

His grin widened slightly, and he kissed her. When he pulled back, his voice dropped to a low, raspy tone that sent a shiver through her. "I'm happy to keep practicing. As much as you want."

She whispered softly, "Don't stop."

"I won't."

# Chapter 46

Alex had spent the entire morning flipping through her sketchbook. Page after page carried her back through the whirlwind of the past year. Each drawing held a memory, a fragment of a life that had changed her in ways she was only beginning to understand.

She traced the lines of one sketch with her fingertip, remembering how Jamie had coaxed her into capturing a vineyard at dusk. What began as a taking a leap had turned into a journal of their journey together.

Closing the book, she leaned back against the couch,smiling. Change had always scared her, but now she wondered if maybe the beauty of their story wasn't in holding on tightly to one path, but in learning how to walk it side by side. A sudden knock at the door startled her.

"Coming!" she called as she made her way to the door.

When she opened it, Jamie stood there. He had his hands behind his back and a playful smile on his face.

"Hey, stranger," he greeted.

She smirked. "You just saw me yesterday."

"Yeah, but today's special."

"Oh? And why is that?"

Jamie pulled a small envelope from behind his back and held it up between his fingers. "Because of what's inside of this."

She took it out of his hands. "What's this?"

He grinned. "Open it and find out."

She hesitated for a second before carefully tearing it open. Her fingers slid the paper free, and her eyes landed on the bold black letters. A plane ticket. She shrieked when she read the destination printed on the paper. *Paris.*

Paris? Are you serious?"

Jamie leaned against the door frame, looking far too pleased with himself. "Last I checked, the ticket looked pretty real."

She laughed, shaking her head in disbelief. "You don't just casually show up at someone's door with a plane ticket to Paris."

"Sure you do," he said with a shrug. "It's called spontaneity. I thought you liked that."

"I like coffee. I like sketching in quiet parks. Paris is... that's huge."

"Exactly," he teased. "Big city, big art, big croissants. What's not to love?"

She pressed the ticket against his chest, narrowing her eyes though her smile betrayed her. "You can't just bribe me with pastries."

"Bribe?" He clutched his heart dramatically. "This isn't a bribe, Alex. This is me being a hopeless romantic."

Her heart pounded. "But why?"

"Because I remember that night when you told me Paris was your dream destination. And I also remember the hesitation in your voice, like you weren't sure you'd ever actually go. I wanted to change that."

She felt a lump rise in her throat. "You .... you did this for me?"

"I know how much this means to you, and I wanted to be the one to make it happen." He took a step closer. "I want you to know that this isn't just about travel. It's about us. I'm all in. This shouldn't be a temporary adventure; I want it to last. I want to keep exploring the world with you. But more than that. I want to build something real with you, no matter where we are."

She couldn't speak. She'd never doubted their connection but hearing him say it aloud like this made it feel even more real. She looked back at the ticket. "I don't even know what to say."

He cupped her cheek gently. "Then just say yes."

A slow smile spread across her face as tears formed in her eyes. "Yes."

He grinned before he pulled her into his arms and held her close. She melted into his embrace. This wasn't just a ticket. It was a promise. A promise of adventure. A promise of love. A promise of forever.

When he finally let her go, Alex sank onto the couch, the ticket still clutched tightly in her hand. She stared down at it, trying to process the weight of it all. Paris. The one place she had always dreamed of visiting but had never truly believed she'd see. At least, not so soon. Not like this.

He sat beside her, clearly amused. "You're still staring at it like you think it might disappear."

She let out a shaky laugh. "Because I still can't believe it's real."

"Well, believe it. We're going to Paris."

Her stomach fluttered at the word *We.*

"Of course, we. Did you really think I'd send you off on an adventure alone?"

She smirked. "I don't know. You are a fan of pushing me outside my comfort zone."

"True," he admitted. "But that was before I realized how much fun it is to be outside of it with you."

Her lips curved into a teasing smile. "Oh, so now you're saying you prefer stability over spontaneity?"

"Let's not get carried away. But I am saying I prefer you."

Her heart fluttered at the words, and she stared at him for a moment, still struggling to fully grasp the reality of it. They were going to Paris. Together. She glanced back at the ticket. The words were still right there, black, and white proof that it wasn't a dream. Round-trip ticket. Departure: next Friday.

She shook her head with a breathless laugh. "Paris. I mean, I know we talked about doing a bigger trip one day, but... this is—"

"Exactly what we need," Jamie finished for her. His tone was certain, steady. "You've spent the last year pouring yourself into your art. You've built something incredible. But now it's time for you to live it to be inspired again."

Her eyes softened. She knew what he meant. As much as she had grown to love Lakehaven, the life she was building with him, the stability, it wasn't her entire world. Her art was born from movement, from exploration, from seeing unknown places through fresh eyes. And the thought of exploring Paris, the city of light, of romance, of infinite inspiration, alongside him made her pulse quicken with anticipation.

"You know, you're kind of amazing," she murmured.

"Oh, I know."

She laughed softly and swatted his leg, but the warmth in her chest lingered.

He brushed his lips against her temple. "So... are you ready?" he asked quietly. "For another adventure?"

Her smile widened, and she lifted her head to meet his gaze. "With you? Always."

His lips curved into a slow, contented grin. "Good." He shifted slightly, brushing his knuckles over her cheek. "Because I want to see your face the first time you set foot in the city. I want to hear you gush about the art, the architecture, the food. I want to experience all of it with you."

She exclaimed. "This is actually happening."

"It is. And not just the trip."

"What do you mean?"

"It's not just about traveling together. It never was. I love what we're building. I love how we push each other, how we grow together. And I don't want that to end."

Her heart pounded. "Jamie"

"I know we're still figuring things out, but I don't want to go back to living separate lives, waiting for the next trip to bring us back together. I want to build something real with you, no matter where we are."

Tears pricked her eyes. She had been searching for something for so long; purpose, direction, belonging. And here it was, right in front of her, in the form of the man who had challenged her to embrace life fully.

"I want that too."

"Good. Because I have already started making a list of all the places I want to take you. Cafes, gardens, art galleries..." His eyes glimmered mischievously. "And I may or may not have something special planned for you."

She stared at him in mock disbelief. "You've already made plans?"

"Oh, I'm just getting started."

A playful grin tugged at her lips. "So, this is happening? You're officially turning into a full-blown romantic?"

His eyes gleamed with mock seriousness. "Don't tell anyone. I have a reputation to protect."

She let out a soft, breathless laugh before leaning in to kiss him. The moment their lips met, she felt it all; the excitement, the anticipation, the promise of what was to come. When she pulled back, she smiled softly against his mouth. "Paris doesn't stand a chance."

# Chapter 47

The flight passed in a dreamlike blur—city lights fading into darkness, then a sunrise spilling pink and gold across the horizon as the plane descended into France. By the time they stepped out of the airport, Alex drew in a breath and stilled. The air was cool and crisp, laced with the scent of fresh bread and espresso. It wrapped around her like a promise, like the first note of a song she'd been waiting her whole life to hear.

Jamie hailed a cab, and soon they were weaving through the streets of Paris. Alex pressed her forehead lightly against the cool glass, her eyes wide as she drank it all in— the wrought-iron balconies draped with flowers, the narrow, winding streets alive with bicycles and chatter, the cafes spilling with laughter and the aroma of fresh pastry. It was everything she had imagined... and somehow more.

When they arrived at their hotel, a charming boutique tucked along a quiet cobblestone street in the Marais, Alex reached for the door, eager to see inside. But before she could step through, Jamie caught her hand. The warmth of his fingers wrapped around hers, halting her in place with a look that promised something more than just check-in and luggage.

"Come on," he said.

"Now?" she laughed. "We just got here."

"There's no way I'm letting you waste even a second of our first night in Paris stuck inside," he said as he pulled her down the street.

They walked hand in hand along the cobblestone streets as the cool evening air brushed softly against their skin. Paris seemed to hum around them with a quiet kind of magic. The low murmur of conversation spilling from bistros, the flicker of candlelight glowing through café windows, and the faint notes of an accordion drifting from somewhere nearby.

He looked at her with excitement. "You're way too calm for someone who's in Paris for the first time."

She let out a breathless laugh as she let her gaze sweep over the surrounding scene. "I think I'm still trying to convince myself this is real." She slowed her steps to take in the golden glow of the streetlamps and the soft murmur of French floating through the air. "It's even more beautiful than I imagined."

He gave her hand a light squeeze. "Just wait. You have seen nothing yet."

They wandered aimlessly by letting the city guide them. Alex couldn't stop staring at everything. The quaint boulangeries with their delicate pastries displayed in the windows, the weathered doorways draped in ivy, the laughter of strangers clinking glasses at tiny sidewalk tables. It felt like stepping into a painting she'd once admired in a gallery, a place too lovely to be real. And yet here she was, walking through it, living it.

After a few blocks, Jamie tugged her toward a side street that was narrower and less crowded. "Where are we going?" she curiously asked.

He cast her a mischievous glance over his shoulder. "You'll see."

After a few more turns, they stepped into a quiet, hidden square tucked away from the busier streets. Only a few people lingered on benches, speaking in hushed tones or simply enjoying the stillness. The square was enchanting. It was surrounded by centuries-old buildings with weathered shutters and delicate wrought-iron balconies. At its heart stood a stone fountain, its gentle trickle lit by the warm glow of a nearby lantern, casting soft reflections across the cobblestones.

Alex stopped. "Jamie..."

He smiled at her expression and tugged her gently

toward the fountain. "I found this place the last time I was here," he said softly. "It's a little off the tourist track. I figured it could be our spot."

Her chest tightened with emotion. She stared at the fountain for a moment and then turned back to him. "It's perfect."

He pulled her into his arms and wrapped his arms around her waist. For a while, they just stood there, holding each other beneath the quiet spell of the city.

"You know," Jamie kissed her temple, "I was going to wait until tomorrow for this, but I'm not that patient."

Alex pulled back slightly, staring in confusion. "Wait for what?"

His hand slipped into his coat pocket, and when he pulled it out, he was holding a small box.

She stared at the box, then back at him, her eyes wide. "Jamie..."

"Before you freak out, it's not what you think." He smiled. He opened the box to reveal a delicate silver necklace with a small pendant in the shape of a compass.

Her eyes softened as she stared at it. She could already feel the sting of emotion at the back of her throat.

He brushed his thumb over the pendant. "I saw it a few weeks ago and thought of you. You're always my compass, Alex. No matter where we are."

Her eyes shimmered with tears. She reached out for the tiny charm. "It's beautiful."

He stepped behind her and gently clasped the necklace around her neck. When he came back around, his eyes met hers. "I wanted you to have something that reminded you that no matter where we are in the world, you'll always be my home."

Her heart squeezed painfully in her chest. She cupped his face in her hands. "Jamie..."

He leaned in, brushing his lips softly over hers. The kiss was slow and reverent and full of unspoken promises.

"You realize you just completely ruined me for romantic gestures, right?"

He smirked. "Good. That was the goal."

They stood there a little while longer, arms wrapped around each other, the gentle bubbling of the fountain filling the quiet space between them. Eventually, he pulled back just enough to meet her eyes, a playful smile tugging at his lips.

"Alright," he said, sliding his fingers through hers. "You ready to keep going, or should we just make out by this fountain until sunrise?"

A soft laugh escaped her, easing the last of the emotion lingering in her chest. Her eyes were sparkling with joy.

"I think I can handle a little more exploring," she said, squeezing his hand gently.

He kissed her forehead before they began walking again.

"Good answer," he said before he led her back into the winding streets of Paris.

They walked in unhurried steps as they strolled along the riverbank. The Seine glimmered beneath the city lights. Across the water, the faint outline of Notre-Dame Cathedral stood like a guardian over the night.

Jamie gave her hand a light squeeze. "You know, for someone who claims she's terrible with directions, you somehow led us right to the most beautiful spot in the city."

"Oh, please. I've just been following you the whole time."

He glanced down at her with amusement. "So, you're saying I'm the one who got us lost in that alleyway for fifteen minutes?"

She held back a laugh. "Technically, yes. But you looked so confident the whole time, I didn't have the heart to tell you."

He pressed a hand to his chest in mock offense. "Unbelievable. You let me wander around like a clueless tourist while you knew exactly where we were going?"

"Hey," she teased, "sometimes it's fun to get lost."

Jamie stopped walking to make her turn toward him. The lights from the river glowed softly against her skin.

His expression softened, the playful glimmer giving way to something far more tender. "Yeah," he said. "It is."

Her breath caught slightly at the quiet intensity in his voice. Without a word, he pulled her close into an embrace. For a moment, neither of them spoke. He gave her light kisses on her temple before he trailed down to the corner of her mouth.

The only thing she could feel was him. The warmth of his mouth, the subtle pressure of his hands as they slid up her back, the gentle sigh he released against her lips. When they finally pulled apart, her eyes remained closed for a lingering second, as if trying to hold on to the moment.

"God," Jamie whispered. "I could get lost in you forever."

Her eyes fluttered open. "Then don't find your way back," she murmured.

"Deal."

They continued walking along the river as if time itself had softened around them. The city shimmered under the streetlights. The scent of rain still lingered faintly in the air, and the cobblestones beneath their feet glistened with the remnants of the evening drizzle.

As they reached a quiet stretch of the riverbank, they stopped beside the stone railing. The water below moved lazily, catching the reflections of distant lights like a living painting. Alex leaned on the cool stone as she looked out over the water. Jamie stepped up behind her and wrapped his arms around her waist. She sank into him without hesitation.

His chin dipped to her shoulder, and he pressed a kiss to the curve of her neck.

She closed her eyes at the contact, her breath catching softly. "You know," she murmured, her voice barely above a whisper, "this might be my favorite version of us."

"Mine too."

They stood that way for a long moment. No rush, no noise, just the gentle ripple of the river and the quiet kind of magic that only came when two hearts were perfectly in sync.

"Tell me something," she said.

"Anything," he replied.

She opened her eyes and stared out at the water. "When you think about home… where do you picture it?"

His arms tightened slightly around her, but he didn't answer right away. For a long time, he just held her and watched the river with her. "Right here," he said simply. "Wherever you are."

She turned slightly in his arms. "I still can't believe we're here."

"I can. You were always meant to be here."

"That sounds an awful lot like something you planned all along."

"Maybe I did."

Alex rolled her eyes but couldn't help the smile tugging at her lips. "And what exactly made you so sure I'd be ready for this?"

"Because I've watched you grow into the person who was always waiting to step into this life. You just needed the push to see it."

"I was terrified at first," she admitted. "Every step of this journey, I kept wondering if I was making a mistake. Leaving my job, taking this leap … and falling for you."

"And now?"

"Now, I can't imagine my life any other way."

He cupped her cheek. "Me neither."

The next morning, sunlight streamed through the sheer white curtains of their cozy Parisian apartment. Alex stretched lazily in bed as the scent of fresh coffee drifted through the air. She rolled over, expecting to see Jamie beside her, but his side of the bed was empty. The sound of soft movement from the other room caught her attention. Curious, she slipped out from under the covers, padding barefoot across the wooden floor.

She found him seated by the large window with a sketchbook in his hand. He was deep in thought as he captured something on the page. She leaned against the doorway. "Since when you sketch?"

He looked up. "Since I started dating an artist." He turned the sketchbook around and revealed a rough but surprisingly good drawing of her, still asleep, peaceful, and with the early morning light hitting her face.

She blinked. "That's beautiful."

He shrugged, a bit sheepishly. "I wanted to see if I could capture the way you looked this morning. Content. Like you belong here."

She moved closer to sit beside him. "I think, for the first time in my life, I felt like I belong."

He set the sketchbook aside and took her hands in his. "That's what I wanted for you all along. For you to see what I see."

"And what do you see?"

He studied her for a moment before speaking. "I see a woman who took a leap of faith and found herself. Who creates beauty with every stroke of a pencil, every piece of art she touches. Who inspires me every day."

Emotions swirled inside her. "I never imagined my life would look like this."

"Neither did I. But I wouldn't change a thing."

She exhaled, glancing at the sketchbook again. "I want to start a travel art series. The places we visit and the people we meet will be sketched by me. I want to show the world what I see through my lens."

"That sounds incredible. And I can photograph the process, capture you capturing the world."

She couldn't believe that he agreed to the thought of them truly merging their passions. "We could even turn it into an exhibit one day."

"Absolutely. This is just the beginning."

From the open window, they could hear all the sounds of the city. A distant bell, the soft hum of voices from a nearby cafe, and the occasional whir of a passing scooter. But none of it existed for them. They were in their own little world, enjoying each other.

She looked at his sketch again. It wasn't perfect. Her hair was a little messier and the shading a little uneven, but that only made it more beautiful. It was raw, real, and created with love.

"Jamie," she turned back to him. "I mean it. This is beautiful. You're talented, whether or not you admit it."

"I'm more of a stick-figure kind of guy, but I'll take the compliment," he joked.

"I'm serious. You've been quietly sketching without telling me? What other hidden talents are you keeping from me?"

He pretended to think. "Well, I can make a mean cup of instant ramen. Does that count?"

She laughed. "Impressive. Truly. I think I might just marry you for that."

"Careful," he replied. "You say things like that, and I might actually start making plans."

She loved the banter between them and how he could just make her feel the way she'd always wanted to feel. And yet he looks so content.

"You're dangerous, you know that?" she whispered.

"Only for you."

"Speaking of hidden talents, what were you working on before you got distracted by my questionable sketching skills?"

She stood up to get her sketchbook on the table. As she walked back, she flipped to the page of her latest sketch. It was a few loose pencil strokes of a cafe she had started the night before. The faint outline of tables and chairs lined the edges, but it was unfinished. She ran her fingertips lightly over the page as she imagined the colors that would soon fill the blank spaces.

"I was thinking about doing a whole series," she said with excitement. "Not just Paris. Everywhere we go. Sketching the places, the people, the little moments that most people miss. I want to share my unique perspective with the world, revealing the beauty and wonder I see in every corner."

His expression softened as he listened. "You already do," he said. "Every time you pick up a pencil, you show people the world through your eyes."

She stared at him, taking in the sincerity on his face. The man who had always seemed so free, so unbound, now looked at her as if she were the anchor he'd been searching for his whole life.

"What if we combined it?" she asked animatedly. "My sketches... your photographs. We could create a series together. Or another joint exhibit. It could be a visual story of our travels. The world through both of our eyes."

"That is the second-best idea you've ever had. The first being traveling with me."

A giddy laugh bubbled from her throat, and she grabbed his hands. "We could also turn it into a book. Your photos and my sketches side by side. A visual travel journal. The places we've been, the people we've met. Everything."

His eyes widened slightly, and she could see the wheels turning in his mind. The idea was taking root and blooming right in front of her. He had the familiar spark of inspiration igniting behind his eyes.

"Alex..." he started. "That's brilliant."

She grabbed his sketchbook and held it up. "We could even include little bits of our own personal glimpses. The behind-the-scenes moments. Like... you sketching me in the morning light."

He wrapped his arms around her waist and pulled her onto his lap. "You really want the world to see my amateur doodles?"

She cupped his face in her hands. "Absolutely. The world deserves to see the way you see me."

He pulled her into a kiss. "This is it, isn't it?" he whispered. "Our next adventure."

"Yeah," she replied. "And I can't wait to get lost in it with you."

# Chapter 48

Jamie had been quieter than usual throughout dinner. He watched her intently every time she spoke, and his fingers traced absent patterns on the tablecloth. Alex had noticed but hadn't questioned it. She thought maybe he was soaking in their last few days in Paris before they went back home. Now, as they walked hand in hand along the cobblestone path, she stated. "This trip has been perfect."

Jamie smiled. "Has it?"

She squeezed his hand. "Each part of it is special to me. Paris has been like a dream."

He pulled her to a stop near a small, secluded spot by the water that was away from the bustling tourists. A street musician played a soft melody on a violin, the sound weaving into the night air like magic.

"You know," he rubbed the back of his neck, "I didn't bring you here just because it's beautiful."

She arched a brow. "Oh?"

He took a deep breath, suddenly looking more serious and more vulnerable than she had ever seen him.

"From the moment I met you in that cafe, you were different. I knew it even before I understood why. You were searching for something, but what I didn't realize was that I was, too." His voice was steady, but there was emotion beneath it. Alex felt her heart tighten. He reached into his pocket and pulled out a small velvet box. He held it between them as he locked his eyes onto hers.

"I don't want this journey to end. I don't want to go on another adventure without knowing you'll be beside me wherever we go next."

Her breath caught as he opened the box, revealing a delicate gold ring with a small, deep-blue sapphire at its center.

Her eyes widened, the world narrowing down to the soft glint of the sapphire and the unguarded emotion in his gaze. The distant sounds of the city faded into a gentle blur. All she could hear was the steady rhythm of her heart, loud and wild in her chest.

He stepped closer. "This isn't about doing things the traditional way. It's not about settling down or following a script. It's about choosing someone, choosing *you*, over and over again, no matter where we go or what changes."

Alex felt her emotions clogged her throat as her fingers hovered just above the box. She looked from the ring to his face, to the place in his eyes where she saw every moment they had shared: every sunset, every sketch, every quiet conversation that had slowly unraveled their walls.

"I don't need a map or a plan," he added. "I just need you. So… what do you say? Will you keep traveling the world with me?"

A thousand moments flashed through her mind. The late-night conversations, the stolen kisses in foreign cities, the way he always knew how to bring her back to herself when she felt lost. Every adventure, every challenge, every dream they had faced together. And now, he was asking her to choose him. To choose *them*.

Tears shimmered in her eyes, but her smile was radiant, breaking through like sunlight after rain. "Yes," she whispered, her voice catching. "Yes, yes. A thousand times yes."

Jamie exhaled a breath of relief, laughing softly as he slipped the ring onto her finger. The sapphire glinted in the low lamplight, as if it had been waiting all along to find its place there. She wrapped her arms around his neck, and he pulled her into him, holding her like a promise. The violinist's song swelled, perfectly timed, as they kissed beneath the stars. Two souls who had once been lost, now standing at the edge of something entirely new, together.

Jamie slipped his fingers between hers, giving her hand a gentle squeeze as they strolled back. The city felt different now, warmer somehow, even as the night breeze brushed against their skin. The world around them seemed softer, blurred at the edges, as if they were walking through their own private dream.

He glanced down at her every few steps, watching the way she kept turning her hand ever so slightly to admire the ring. The small, delighted smile tugging at the corner of her lips made his chest tighten with affection.

"You keep looking at it like it might disappear," he said, a teasing lilt in his voice.

Alex shot him a mock-glare, but her eyes sparkled. "I'm just… making sure it's real."

"It is," he said, his thumb brushing over her knuckles. "*You're* real. *We're* real."

She looked up at him then, her heart aching in the best way. The city lights reflected in her eyes, but it was the love in his gaze that made her feel like she was glowing from the inside out.

"You know," she murmured, "when I first met you, I thought I was running away."

"And now?"

"Now I think I was running toward something," she said softly. "Toward this. Toward you."

Jamie stopped walking, gently tugging her closer. "Good," he said, leaning in until his forehead rested against hers. "Because I don't want to miss a single part of this life with you."

"I keep thinking I'm going to wake up and this will have all been a beautiful, fleeting illusion," she sighed.

He took her left hand in both of his and held it with deliberate tenderness. With a mock-serious expression, he brought her hand to his lips and pressed a lingering kiss to the sapphire.

"Nope. Still there," he said. He kissed it again. "And just

so you know, I'm never taking it back. Ever."

She let out a breathless laugh; the sound laced with pure joy. "Good," she teased. "Because I wasn't planning on giving it back."

"That's my girl," he winked. "You know Sarah's going to lose her damn mind when you tell her."

Alex's eyes widened in realization. "Oh my God," she pulled her phone from her coat pocket. "I need to call her right now."

"I should probably stand back for this. She might break my eardrum with that scream she's about to let out."

She shot him a playful glare but didn't bother arguing. Her fingers trembled slightly with excitement as she hit the call button. It only rang twice before Sarah's voice crackled through the speaker.

"Hey, babe! Oh my God, how's Paris? Are you guys having the time of your—"

"WE'RE ENGAGED!" Alex practically yelled, cutting her off mid-sentence.

There was a pause. A beat of pure silence. And then, a shriek so loud and high-pitched that Jamie winced and took an exaggerated step back and pretended to shield his ears.

"WHAT?!" Sarah screeched so sharply that Alex had to pull the phone slightly away from her ear. "Oh my God, are you serious?!"

"Completely serious. He proposed by the Seine. It was perfect, Sarah. Absolutely perfect."

Jamie smiled as he watched Alex gesture animatedly while she recounted the moment in breathless detail. Her voice was giddy, almost trembling with happiness.

Sarah let out a delighted squeal. "Wait, what does the ring look like?! Is it gorgeous?!"

Alex held out her hand toward him. "It's beautiful," she admired it all over again. "A sapphire. It's perfect."

"Oh my God, that's so classic, but still so you. God, I'm going to cry. Bestie, this is huge! You're going to be a freaking wife!"

Alex's breath caught at the word. A wife. His wife. She turned to him and mouthed the word softly. *Wife.*

He smiled back, as if he could read her thoughts. His warm, tender eyes, shining with so much love, made her chest ache with a feeling of overwhelming affection.

Sarah's voice jolted her back to the conversation. "You guys better not elope over there. I need a front-row seat for this wedding. Preferably with an open bar and a hot groomsman seated next to me."

He let out a low chuckle. "Don't worry. You'll get the VIP treatment. Front row, signature cocktail in hand."

"Damn right," she said dramatically. Then her voice softened. "But seriously, Alex... I'm so happy for you. You deserve this, babe. You really do."

Alex's throat tightened at the sincerity in her best friend's voice. She glanced at Jamie, her heart swelling with emotion.

"Thanks, bestie," she blinked back the sting of tears. "I love you."

"Love you too," Sarah said. Then she quickly added, "Now go make out with your *fiancé* or something. I'll scream into a pillow and cry happy tears from here."

Alex laughed, shaking her head as she ended the call. She slipped her phone back into her pocket and turned to Jamie, who was watching her with an amused smile.

"Fiancé, huh?" he came closer and looped his arms around her waist.

"Yeah. I kind of like the sound of that."

He grinned and leaned down. "Good. Because you're stuck with me now."

"Oh, I was stuck with you a long time ago," she whispered playfully.

With a low laugh, he kissed her again. With the soft glow of Parisian lights painting the night, and the gentle sounds of the city in the background, she realized this was more than travel. She was building a life with the person she loved most. And this was only the beginning.

They strolled through the Parisian streets, the night alive with the hum of the city. Cafes still bustled with laughter and conversation, the scent of fresh pastries and espresso wafting into the cool air.

"So, tell me, "He said. "Were you expecting it at all?"

"Not exactly, but..." She looked up at him. "You've been acting a little weird all day."

He feigned innocence. "Weird? Me?"

She nudged him playfully. "Yes, you. Fidgeting, looking at me like you were keeping a secret. It was very suspicious behavior."

"Ah, so I wasn't as smooth as I thought."

"Nope, but it was still perfect."

They reached a cozy little cafe on the corner with outdoor seating.

He tugged her gently toward a small table. "One more toast before we call it a night?"

"Absolutely."

They settled into their seats, and he ordered a bottle of champagne.

"To us," Jamie said as he poured the bubbly into two delicate glasses.

"To us."

# Chapter 49

The hum of the airplane engines filled the cabin with a steady, low vibration. Alex sat by the window with her head on Jamie's shoulder. Paris was now behind them, but its magic lingered in her chest. The scent of freshly baked croissants from the cafes, the golden shimmer of the Seine at night, and the sound of his voice when he asked her to be his forever. She glanced down at the sapphire ring on her finger, turning it slightly so it caught the light. It still didn't feel real.

Jamie's thumb brushed over her knuckles. "You've been quiet," he said softly. "What's going on in that beautiful head of yours?"

She turned her hand over to lace her fingers through his. "Just... thinking about everything." She looked at him. "Paris almost feels like a dream now. Like I'm going to wake up and it'll all be gone."

He squeezed her hand lightly. "I promise it's not a dream." He brought her hand to his lips and pressed a gentle kiss to the back of it. "You're still wearing the ring, and you're still stuck with me. That's pretty real."

Her lips curved into a tender smile as she nestled closer, feeling the steady rise and fall of his breathing. She closed her eyes briefly, letting herself sink into the moment.

When she opened her eyes again, she caught the flight attendant passing by with a coffee cart. He caught her gaze. "You want one?" he asked.

She shook her head. "No, I'm good."

"I figured you'd be half-asleep by now. You barely got any rest last night."

"Whose fault is that?" she arched a playful brow.

Jamie grinned. "Hey, don't blame me," he said with a mischievous glint in his eye. "You were the one who wanted to watch the sunrise over the Eiffel Tower."

She gave his hand a gentle squeeze. "I didn't want it to end."

A wave of tenderness washed over his features, softening his gaze. "It doesn't have to. Paris was just the beginning."

Her heart skipped slightly at the promise in his voice. She turned back to the window, watching the sun climb higher over the endless stretch of clouds. She caught a glimpse of the ring's sparkle in her reflection. *Fiancée*. The word still made her stomach flutter.

He shifted slightly in his seat to adjust his long legs, but he kept his hand firmly wrapped around hers.

"You know, I think you're going to have to prepare yourself for how insufferable Sarah is going to be when we get back," he said with a lopsided grin. "She's probably already planned three engagement parties in her head."

Alex let out a soft laugh. "Oh, absolutely. And she's going to demand at least two outfit changes for each one."

"Think she'll offer to officiate the wedding too?"

"Are you kidding? She's probably already googling 'how to become a certified officiant.'"

"You know, we could just run away and elope," he whispered playfully. "Save ourselves from all the chaos."

She tilted her head, feigning contemplation. "Hmm... tempting," she teased. "But no way. You're not getting out of a proper celebration. It's important to have Sarah and Mark there. I want all the people we love watching us promise forever."

He smiled and closed his eyes briefly. "Forever," he repeated.

They sat in silence as the plane departed. Alex's eyes grew heavy at the rhythmic sound of the engines and the warmth of Jamie's arms around her. She let her eyes close while her hand was still curled in his.

The wheels of the plane touched down on the runway, jolting Alex from her slumber. She looked at Jamie, who stretched in his seat as he smiled sleepily.

"We're home," he squeezed her hand.

Home. The word felt different now. It wasn't just a place. It was a feeling. And as much as she had loved the whirlwind romance of Paris, the quiet vineyards of Tuscany, and the endless discoveries of Sperlonga, she was ready for this next chapter.

As they exited the airport, the cool air of Lakehaven wrapped around them. The familiarity of the streets, the skyline, and the hum of everyday life made her heart swell. It was strange how much had changed since she'd last stepped foot here. A part of her had feared coming back, worried that she would feel trapped again. But as he laced his fingers with hers, all she felt was excitement.

"Back to reality." he slung an arm around her shoulders as they walked toward a cab.

"I don't know. Reality looks rather good these days."

Alex set her bag down by the door, glancing around as if seeing it for the first time. The framed photos on the shelves, the half-finished sketches on the coffee table, Jamie's worn leather jacket draped over the back of the couch. It was all theirs, a collection of moments and memories they had built together.

Jamie kicked off his shoes and stretched. "Never thought I'd say this, but I missed this place."

"See? You're getting soft."

He wrapped his arms around her from behind and laid his chin on her shoulder. "Not soft. Just happy."

She traced her fingers over the sapphire ring, now nestled perfectly on her hand. "Me too," she said.

"Wow. I can't believe we were gone for a month."

"I know. Part of me feels like we never left, but the other

part feels like we've been gone for years."

"Everything's the same, but we're different."

He flopped onto the couch. "It's weird, isn't it? Settling back in?"

"You? Settling? That's a first."

"Hey, even I can admit it feels good to have a place to land." His gaze softened. "Especially with you."

Alex felt warmth spread through her chest as she sat beside him and leaned her head against his shoulder. "So... where do we start?"

"Unpacking? Grocery shopping? Or figuring out how we're going to merge our brilliant artistic talents into a business empire?"

She laughed. "Maybe all the above?"

He shifted to face her. "Are you ready for this? I mean, the engagement, the career shift, working together? It's a lot."

"I've never been more ready for anything in my life."

The following week was a blur of activity. They spent their days transforming Jamie's photography studio into a shared creative space. Alex set up a corner for her sketching and digital work, while he organized his darkroom and editing station.

The late afternoon light poured through the studio windows, casting golden streaks across the floor. The scent of fresh paint still lingered faintly in the air as Alex stood in her corner, wiping her hands on a rag. Her old drafting table sat beneath the window, bathed in natural light. It was the perfect spot for sketching. Her new digital tablet rested nearby, propped on a sleek stand Jamie had insisted on buying for her. A corkboard covered in pinned sketches, color swatches, and clippings of inspiration filled the wall behind her.

She took a step back, surveying the space they had created over the past week. It still felt surreal. Their space. A shared hub of creativity. Her chest tightened with a strange mix of excitement and disbelief. From across the room, the gentle tap-tap-tap of Jamie's fingers on the ornate wooden worktable accompanied the quiet rustle of the photos as he adjusted their positions. He glanced over his shoulder, catching her thoughtful expression.

"Don't tell me you're already second-guessing the layout," he teased, walking over and sliding his arms around her waist from behind. "I will not move that table again, Greer. My back barely survived the first time."

"No, it's perfect. I was just… taking it all in. I can't believe we pulled this off."

He kissed to the side of her neck. "Believe it. You're officially a partner in crime. There's no going back now."

Her lips curved into a smile as she glanced at the far corner where he had meticulously organized his darkroom. The shelves were neatly stocked with developing chemicals, and his photos hung from wire clips, still drying. A sleek new monitor shone brightly beside his editing station, accompanied by the quiet whir of the laptop and the subtle blinking lights of the external hard drives.

Jamie followed her gaze and smirked. "I'm pretty sure my computer's jealous of your fancy new tablet setup."

"Hey, you're the one who insisted I needed the best of the best."

"Of course I did. I take my investment in your genius seriously."

She turned in his arms. "Is that right?"

"Mm-hmm." He brushed his nose lightly against hers. "You're the future of this operation, Greer. I'm just riding your coattails."

She rolled her eyes but smiled. "You're ridiculous."

"Maybe."

"You know what I've been thinking?"

"That I'm devastatingly handsome and your life would be meaningless without me?"

She swatted his chest. "No. I've been thinking that this… what we've built here … it could be more than just a studio. What if we made it into a gallery space, too? Not just for us, but for other artists. Local creatives who are just starting out and looking for a place to showcase their work."

His brows lifted slightly, surprise flickering in his eyes. "You mean... kind of like an open studio concept? With rotating exhibits?"

"Exactly." Her eyes brightened. "We could host monthly showcases. Invite emerging artists to collaborate, offer them a platform. We could even hold workshops, combine photography, painting, and mixed media. Make it a creative hub. Not just for us, but for the community."

Jamie's lips slowly curved into a grin. "You really want to turn our creative space into an empire, huh?"

"I mean... you said you were ready to build one with me."

"God, I love you."

Her heart fluttered at the easy, unguarded way he said it. No hesitation. Just truth.

Before she could respond, he stepped back slightly. "You know... we could make it happen. The gallery idea. I've still got contacts from my travel photography days. Some of them would probably jump at the chance to partner with us. And your art? You've already made a name for yourself. People are going to want to see what you do next."

She shook her head slightly, her eyes shining with disbelief. "Are we really doing this? Building something from the ground up?"

"Hell yes, we are."

"Okay, then. Let's do it."

He pulled her into his arms again. "You know, we're going to need a name for this entire empire of ours."

"Hmm... any brilliant suggestions, Mr. Rivers?"

He pretended to think. "How about... Jamie & Alex's Totally Rad Art Palace?"

She snorted and smacked his chest playfully. "God, no."

"Okay, okay. Something more... refined." He paused, then arched a brow. "Studio Verve."

Her eyes narrowed slightly. "Verve?"

"Yeah." He rubbed his thumb over the back of her hand. "It means energy, spirit, or enthusiasm. It fits us."

"Studio Verve." She tried the name out, liking the way it sounded. Bold. Strong. Full of life. Full of them.

Jamie leaned down, brushing his lips over hers again. "Perfect," he whispered. "Just like us."

She pressed her forehead against his, feeling the steady, reassured beat of his heart against her chest. Their creative empire. It was just the beginning, and she knew in her bones that this was going to be the most beautiful chapter of their story yet.

# Chapter 50

That weekend, Sarah insisted on throwing them a welcome-home-slash-engagement party. Alex had barely finished unpacking before she bombarded her with plans: venue options, guest lists, and an overenthusiastic list of potential decorations.

"It's just a small get-together," she had protested over the phone.

"No, it's a celebration! You two have been gallivanting around the world, falling in love, and now you're engaged! This deserves more than just 'small.'"

Jamie had been listening from the couch. "Just let her have this," he whispered. "Less work for us."

Alex rolled her eyes but relented. And now she stood near the patio table, refilling her glass of wine. She scanned the backyard and shook her head with a bemused smile. *Small get-together, my ass.*

Sarah had truly outdone herself. Lanterns hung from the trees, creating a soft, flickering canopy of light. White tablecloths adorned the tables, which were decorated with vases of wildflowers and scattered candles. Platters of food lined a buffet table, while a bartender mixed cocktails near the corner. It was elegant but casual, exactly the kind of celebration she hadn't known she needed.

Jamie wandered over with an amused expression. "Having fun at your *small* get-together?"

She shot him a mock glare. "You're enjoying this way too much."

He grinned and took a sip of his drink. "I tried to warn you. Your friend doesn't do small."

"Of course not. She practically threw together a wedding reception without the wedding."

"Well... if you're ever in the mood for a spontaneous wedding, I'm game. We can save her the trouble of planning the big one."

Her eyes widened slightly, but his playful smirk told her he was only half-serious. She arched a brow. "Tempting... but I think we should at least wait until I've picked out a dress."

Just then, Sarah appeared at their side. "Okay, okay, tell me I was right."

"Fine," she hugged her friend. "It's amazing. Thank you."

"Don't thank me yet. I still have a surprise planned."

"Should I be worried?"

She just winked before leaving to greet more guests. Mark even showed up, giving Jamie a knowing look as he clapped him on the back.

"So, you finally stopped running, huh?" Mark teased.

"Yeah, well, took me long enough, right?"

Mark smiled with a mix of affection and smug satisfaction. "Nah. You got there when it mattered." He clapped Jamie on the back again. "And you picked a good one."

Jamie's eyes drifted toward Alex, who was laughing with Sarah near the buffet table. Her cheeks flushed with happiness, and the light caught her ring every time she moved. His chest tightened with quiet awe.

"Yeah," he said to himself. "I did."

"You know, I was thinking you'd never get there," he said honestly. "You've always been chasing the next big thing. Another country, another project, another horizon. I figured maybe you were just one of those people who would never stay."

He was still watching Alex. "I used to think that, too."

"And now?"

Jamie finally turned to look at him. "Now, I get it." He smiled. "All those places I was chasing. I was looking for something that felt like home. I just didn't know it then."

"Look at you getting all sentimental on me."

"Don't get used to it."

But Mark shook his head. "You should hold on to that. Don't worry, you're not losing yourself. You're finally finding something worth standing still for."

Jamie glanced back at Alex just as she caught his eye across the yard. She smiled softly, as if she could feel him watching her. And in that moment, everything clicked into place. Without another word, he clapped Mark on the shoulder and crossed the lawn toward her.

When he reached her, he put his hands around her waist. "Having fun?" he asked.

"I actually am," Alex admitted. "You?"

"Yeah. It's nice seeing everyone again. But mostly, I'm just happy to be here with you."

"You're getting smooth, sir."

"It's the engagement effect," he teased as he held up his hand as if showing off an invisible ring.

Before she could respond, Sarah clinked a spoon against her glass, calling for attention. "Alright, everyone! Time for the moment for which you've all been waiting. The toasts!"

Alex groaned. "Oh, no."

"Oh yes," Sarah said, grinning mischievously as she took center stage. "As you all know, Alex is one of my best friends in the entire world. And she has been many things over the years. Ambitious, talented, stubborn as hell—" laughter rippled through the crowd, "but never, in all the time I've known her, have I seen her light up the way she does when she's with Jamie."

He squeezed her hand, and her heart fluttered.

"Now, when she first told me she was traveling with some charming photographer, I did what any good friend would do. I immediately stalked him online to see if he was a serial killer."

The crowd erupted in laughter.

"And when I met him, I realized two things: one, he's

actually not a serial killer, big plus, and two, he was exactly what she didn't know she needed."

Alex swallowed the lump in her throat as she turned toward them. "You two have built something beautiful together, and I couldn't be happier for you. To Alex and Jamie!"

"To Alex and Jamie!" the guests echoed, raising their glasses.

Jamie lifted his drink toward her. "That was perfect, Sarah. Thank you."

"I know," she said smugly, before waving a hand. "Now, someone else say something before I cry and ruin my mascara."

To her surprise, Mark stepped up next. "Alright, my turn," he said, clearing his throat. "I've known Jamie for years. I've seen him in every phase, broke artist, semi-successful artist, guy who takes too many pictures of strangers in cafes —" Jamie laughed, "but when I saw the way he looked at Alex, I knew this was different."

He turned to him. "Man, I've never seen you look at anything the way you look at her. Not even that Leica camera you refuse to replace."

"It's vintage," he defended, making everyone chuckle.

"But seriously, I'm proud of you both. You didn't just find each other, you grew together. And that's rare. To Jamie and Alex!"

Another round of cheers, loud and boisterous, filled the air, and Alex, overwhelmed with emotion and tears in her eyes, turned to Jamie. "You really love that camera more than me," she said, her voice laced with playful jealousy.

He laughed. "It's a close call."

As the party continued, Alex found herself pulled from one conversation to the next: old coworkers, childhood friends, even distant cousins she hadn't seen in years. It was a whirlwind of hugs, congratulations, and endless stories about her travels.

At one point, she found a quiet moment on the patio,

sipping her drink as she looked out at the glowing backyard. She felt... content. And that was new.

Jamie found her moments later. "Hiding?"

"Just taking it all in," she turned toward him. "This is the first time since we got back that it's really hit me. We're home. This is real."

"Yeah. It is."

They stood there for a moment as the sounds of the party faded into the background.

"I was just thinking. What's next for us?" she asked softly.

"Since we're already working on our next exhibit, why don't we take it on the road? Bring it to the world. This way it keeps us traveling when we want but also gives us a foundation here."

Her eyes lit up. "Like a traveling gallery?"

Jamie's lips curved into a grin, his eyes glimmering with excitement. "Exactly. Think about it. We could highlight your sketches and my photographs in different cities. Pop-up galleries, unique venues, maybe even collaborate with local artists. It'll let us keep exploring, but we'll always have a home base here."

The idea was thrilling. It was a perfect blend of their passions, their love for travel, and the life they were building together. "I love it," she answered. "It's everything we've talked about. Creating, traveling, but still having something that's ours. Something lasting."

"That's what I want. For us to build something real. To keep creating fresh stories together, no matter where we are."

She stared at him, overwhelmed by how deeply he understood her. It was the life she hadn't dared to dream of, a perfect balance of freedom and stability, of passion and permanence. She could see it now. They had woven their work and journey into something tangible to share.

"Let's do it."

"You sure?"

"Good. Because I've got one more surprise for you."

Alex raised an eyebrow. "If Sarah's involved, I swear—"

"This one's just me," he promised. "Come with me."

He led her toward the backyard, where someone had set up a small projection screen. The crowd quieted as he pressed play.

The screen flickered to life, showing clips of their travels. Venice's many canals, the cliffs of Santorini, the vineyard where they had their first real heart-to-heart. Jamie had turned their journey into a short film, capturing not just the places they had been, but the way they had looked at each other along the way.

Alex felt tears prick her eyes as the last frame lingered. It was a candid shot of her, sketchbook in hand, laughing at something he had said off-camera. As the film faded black, she turned to him, speechless.

Jamie rubbed the back of his neck. "I know we don't have everything figured out yet. But no matter where we go next, I wanted you to know that this is only the beginning."

Alex stared at him with tears building up. For a moment, she couldn't speak. Her throat tightened with emotion, and her fingers trembled slightly as she reached for his hand.

"Jamie..." she breathed. "I—"

But the words got caught somewhere between her heart and her lips. She didn't need to say them, though. The look in her eyes, the awe, the gratitude, the depth of her love, said everything.

Jamie gave her hand a gentle squeeze. "Hey," he whispered. "You okay?"

She gave him a thumbs up. "I'm so much better than okay."

The surrounding crowd clapped, a few whistles and cheers breaking the spell of the moment. Sarah wiped at her eyes with a dramatic sniffle, earning a playful nudge from Mark, who was grinning like he had seen the entire thing coming. But they were barely aware of it. They were absorbed in their own little world.

"Where did you even find the time to do this?" she asked, her voice still thick with emotion.

"Late nights. Lots of coffee. And some help from my very nosy but extremely talented fiancée, who just happens to be a brilliant artist and didn't even notice me stealing clips from her portfolio."

She parted her lips slightly in mock outrage, but she was too moved to scold him. Instead, she let out a laugh. "You're impossible."

"You love me for it," he teased.

"I do," she whispered. "I love you so much."

"Good," he replied huskily. "Because I'm not going anywhere."

And then he kissed her like he had all the time in the world. The crowd whooped and cheered in the background, but they barely heard it. In that moment, it was just the two of them wrapped in their own unshakable, unbreakable bond.

Their embrace ended, and a breathless laugh escaped Alex's lips. "You know this is completely unfair, right?" she teased. "Now you've set the bar so high, I'm going to have to spend the rest of my life trying to top this."

Jamie grinned wickedly. "Oh, I'm counting on it."

"You meant what you said…about this being only the beginning?"

"Every word," he promised. "There's so much more ahead of us, Alex. More adventures, more late nights, more morning sketch sessions over coffee. More of everything. Together."

"Together," she echoed.

# Epilogue

Alex stood near the entrance of the studio as she took in the scene before her. It had been six months in the making, but they were finally ready for their first travel gallery. The "*Through Our Eyes*" art and photography exhibit's opening drew an enormous crowd.

She turned to Jamie, who stood beside her. "Can you believe this?" she whispered, watching a group of people study one of their pieces; a side-by-side composition of one of his photographs and her corresponding sketch. The image was of a street musician in Paris, lost in his music, captured in both sharp details through Jamie's lens and soft pencil strokes from Alex's hand.

Jamie glanced over at the piece, then back at her, his expression full of quiet awe. "Believe it?" he murmured, his hand brushing against hers. "I watched you bring it to life."

Alex's heart fluttered at the warmth in his voice, but her eyes remained fixed on the crowd moving through the studio, stopping, pointing, smiling. The soft hum of conversation surrounded them, but it felt distant by the significance of the moment.

"That one," Jamie nodded toward the Paris piece, "has always been one of my favorites. You didn't just sketch what he looked like. You caught the way the music felt."

Alex swallowed hard, a mixture of pride and disbelief rising in her chest. "It's surreal seeing people connect with it. With all of it."

"They're not just connecting," he said, stepping closer. "They're feeling it. That's the whole point, right? Letting people see the world the way we felt it."

That was the initial aim. Their art wasn't just about displaying beautiful places. It was about capturing the emotions, the stories, and the transformation that came with stepping outside of one's comfort zone. Their journey had led them here, and now they were inspiring others to embark on their adventures, whatever those might be.

An older woman approached them. "You two have created something truly special," she said. "This isn't just an art exhibit. It's a movement."

Alex felt her heart swell. "Thank you. That means everything to us."

The woman nodded. "I used to dream about traveling the world, but life got in the way. Seeing this …it reminds me that it's never too late."

Jamie leaned in. "It's not. Where would you go first?"

The woman paused, then chuckled softly. "Italy. I've always wanted to see Tuscany."

Alex and Jamie exchanged a knowing glance. "You should go," Alex said. "Even if it's just for a quick trip. Do it for yourself."

The woman's smile deepened. "Maybe I will."

As she walked away, Alex exhaled, feeling the impact of the moment. It wasn't just about travel. It was about inspiring people to choose adventure, to step into the unknown, whether that meant visiting a new country or pursuing a passion they had long set aside.

A few minutes later, Sarah found them beaming with pride. "You two have built something amazing. I mean, look around. Your work has moved people."

"It still feels surreal," she admitted, her voice barely audible over the quiet buzz of the exhibit.

Sarah nudged her with a knowing smile. "Believe it. This is your legacy."

Alex's gaze swept the space, taking in the details she'd obsessed over for months. Each sketch hung with intention, each photograph positioned to tell a story. People lingered longer than she'd expected, absorbed in the quiet pairing of her lines and Jamie's lens. A man in a navy scarf stood in front of the Venice canal series, head tilted, murmuring something to his partner. A young girl pointed at the Paris street scene with wide eyes, tugging her mother's hand excitedly.

."I used to think I'd be lucky just to show my art in a coffee shop."

"And now you've got a gallery full of people drinking in your work like it's the best thing they've seen all week," Sarah said, waving her hand at the crowd. "Correction: all year."

"I was terrified to do this."

"And you did it anyway," Sarah replied, her voice softening. "You turned your fear into something beautiful. Into this."

"I can't believe it. It worked."

"Of course it did," Sarah said. "You two would never fail. This..." she gestured around the room, "was meant to be."

"Alex!"

A wide grin spread across Mark's face as Alex spotted him making his way through the crowd, effortlessly maneuvering between guests with the ease of someone who'd done this a hundred times before. When he reached them, he clapped Jamie on the back in greeting and pulled her into a quick, familiar hug.

"Wow," he said, glancing around the gallery with open admiration. "You two really outdid yourselves."

He pointed toward a nearby display with a mischievous glint in his eye. "Also, heads up. I just bought one of your pieces. Figured I should tell you before you saw the 'sold' sticker and had a minor panic attack."

Alex's eyes went wide. "You did?"

Mark smirked. "Of course. I need to own at least one original from the great Alex Greer before your work ends up in the Louvre."

She felt a wave of gratitude wash over her.

As the evening went on, more visitors arrived, their

laughter and chatter filling the air as they spoke with them. Some who'd never journeyed beyond their hometown, felt a newfound inspiration, while others, who'd once chased creative dreams only to abandon them, felt the familiar pull to reignite their passions. The air crackled with a renewed sense of purpose. Their journey had started with a simple leap of faith, and now it was sparking something in others.

A middle-aged couple wandered over, their eyes still shining from the art they'd just taken in. The woman, with silver-streaked hair pulled into a loose twist and soft crow's feet framing her kind eyes, stepped forward and offered her hand to Alex.

"Hi," she said, her voice gentle and genuine. "I just wanted to tell you how much I loved your sketches. There's so much emotion in them—it felt like I was right there with you, feeling everything you felt."

Alex smiled, her heart catching a little. "Thank you. That means more than I can say."

The man, tall with a weathered face and deep laugh lines, turned to Jamie with an appreciative nod. "And your photographs? Incredible. The way you caught the light in that Tuscany vineyard piece? Just... stunning."

Jamie's grin was immediate, touched with pride. "Thank you. That vineyard was one of my favorite stops. The light there felt like magic."

The couple exchanged another warm smile before moving on to the next display, but their words lingered, wrapping around Alex like a soft blanket. She glanced at Jamie, and he was already looking at her. No words passed between them, but none were needed—their shared smile said everything.

Jamie squeezed her hand. "See? People love it. They're connecting with the stories we've told."

Her eyes roamed over the crowd again, seeing people laughing, discussing the pieces, and even taking photos of the displays. She spotted Sarah showing off one of Jamie's photographs with exaggerated enthusiasm, which made the group around her laugh.

"You know," she mused. "When I was sitting in my apartment, staring at that blank canvas all those months ago, I never imagined this would be my life."

Jamie turned to her with tender eyes. "I did. I knew this was meant for you. For more than just hiding your art away. I saw it from the moment you showed me your first sketchbook."

"Tell me, what else do you know since you know me so well?"

"You are the love of my life, and I can't imagine a future without you beside me."

She blinked, caught off guard by the quiet intensity in his voice. Her heart skipped a beat as she turned to face him fully, her breath catching at the look in his eyes.

"Jamie..." she whispered above the soft music still playing in the background of the empty gallery.

"I mean it," he said softly. "I've spent my whole life chasing moments through a lens, but nothing's ever grounded me the way you do."

"You always have the right words."

"No," he said, his voice thick with emotion. "I just finally found someone who makes me want to say them."

Her hand found his, fingers slipping between his with instinctive ease. She glanced around the gallery—*their* gallery—walls lined with the story of their journey. Then she looked back at him.

"I don't want a future without you either," she said quietly. "Not anymore. Wherever we go next, I want us to go together."

"Good," he murmured, leaning in until their foreheads touched. "Because I'm not going anywhere."

www.ingramcontent.com/pod-product-compliance
Lightning Source LLC
Chambersburg PA
CBHW070914260626
47162CB00007B/2669